AM I CAPABLE OF MURDER?

My hands. My hands were covered in red. Not a bright stop-sign red or an orangey clown red. It was the terrible brown red of blood. The whorls of my fingerprints stood bold against the deep crimson. I'd fallen out of bed before, lots of times, but *this*? This was new. *What's going on?*

I looked over at Maya's bed, but she wasn't in it. Instead, she was sprawled, unmoving, on the floor on the other side of the room. The same red smudged and streaked the floor between us.

I stared down at my red hands.

No. I couldn't have. I crawled toward her, trying to make out the rise and fall of her chest. Daring myself to touch her foot. To wake her up. But I couldn't make myself.

I forced out a breath I didn't know I was holding. *I don't know what I've done, but not that. Never that.*

Maya pushed herself up on one arm. "What the hell? Is this some kind of hazing?"

She pushed the bushy hennaed hair out of her eyes. Her fingers left a smear of red across her face, and I saw, with a strange sense of relief, that Maya's hands were also stained with red.

"I woke up on the floor too. I don't know what happened." It was true, I didn't know. But I also didn't mention that the window was open a crack. Which was impossible, since they'd nailed it shut yesterday.

Something happened to us last night. Something bad. I didn't know if it was the drugs or this creepy school, but somehow, without either of us remembering, we'd gotten out of our sealed room. Or someone else had gotten in.

OTHER BOOKS YOU MAY ENJOY

HARBINGER

HARBINGER

Sara Wilson Etienne

speak
An Imprint of Penguin Group (USA) Inc.

HARBINGER

SPEAK

Published by the Penguin Group

Penguin Group (USA) Inc., 345 Hudson Street, New York, New York 10014, U.S.A.

Penguin Group (Canada), 90 Eglinton Avenue East, Suite 700, Toronto, Ontario, Canada M4P 2Y3
(a division of Pearson Penguin Canada Inc.)

Penguin Books Ltd, 80 Strand, London WC2R 0RL, England

Penguin Ireland, 25 St Stephen's Green, Dublin 2, Ireland (a division of Penguin Books Ltd)

Penguin Group (Australia), 707 Collins St., Melbourne, Victoria 3008, Australia
(a division of Pearson Australia Group Pty Ltd)

Penguin Books India Pvt Ltd, 11 Community Centre, Panchsheel Park, New Delhi–110 017, India

Penguin Group (NZ), 67 Apollo Drive, Rosedale, Auckland 0632, New Zealand
(a division of Pearson New Zealand Ltd)

Penguin Books, Rosebank Office Park, 181 Jan Smuts Avenue, Parktown North 2193, South Africa

Penguin China, B7 Jaiming Center, 27 East Third Ring Road North,
Chaoyang District, Beijing 100020, China

Penguin Books Ltd, Registered Offices: 80 Strand, London WC2R 0RL, England

First published in the United States of America by G. P. Putnam's Sons,
a division of Penguin Young Readers Group, 2012
Published by Speak, an imprint of Penguin Group (USA) Inc., 2013

1 3 5 7 9 10 8 6 4 2

Copyright © Sara Wilson Etienne, 2012
All rights reserved.

THE LIBRARY OF CONGRESS HAS CATALOGED THE G. P. PUTNAM'S SONS EDITION AS FOLLOWS:
Etienne, Sara Wilson. Harbinger / Sara Wilson Etienne. p. cm.
Summary: In a near future in which the diminishing oil supply has led to mass rioting, sixteen-year-old
Faye is sent to an educational facility for "delinquents and crazies," where she is tormented by strange
visions of a being sent to destroy the earth in order to save it.
ISBN: 978-0-399-25668-4 (hc)
[1. Supernatural—Fiction. 2. Nature—Effect of humans beings on—Fiction.]
I. Title. PZ7.E8525Har 2012 [Fic]—dc23 2011013309

Speak ISBN: 978-0-14-242393-6

Printed in the United States of America

Text set in Adobe Garamond

for tony.
because you are my sky.
my earth.
my infinite sea.

Sculpture Garden

Free Time Area

Knowledge Annex

Meditation Center

HOLBROOK

Welcome Ga

Holbrook Academy
"Where we walk the path, together."

Holbrook Beach

Compass Rose

Student Dormitory

HARBINGER

"Nay, are there not moods which shall find no expression unless there be men who dare to mix heaven, hell, purgatory, and faeryland together, or even to set the heads of beasts to the bodies of men, or to thrust the souls of men into the heart of rocks? Let us go forth, the tellers of tales, and seize whatever prey the heart long for, and have no fear. Everything exists, everything is true, and the earth is only a little dust under our feet."

—from *The Celtic Twilight,* by William Butler Yeats

1

MY NOSE PRICKLED with the stench of dead flowers and mildew. *I wish I had allergies. Or asthma. Or the Black Plague. Anything to get me out of here.*

"Faye, I want you to think of Holbrook Academy not as a facility, but as a refuge." Dr. Mordoch beamed at me from across her antique wooden desk. Her gray-blond ponytail swung in emphasis with her fervent words. "I built this school for teenagers like you, struggling to cope with reality. Sheep without a shepherd."

I'm a sheep? I glanced at Dad, wondering if he'd heard enough, but he looked dazzled by her little speech. My stomach flip-flopped.

When he turned, his eyes had that glow they got whenever he came back from one of the Cooperative's motivational sing-alongs. "I know this past year's been hard on you . . ."

I nodded at him, playing along. *Baaaaaaa.* I'd met my end of the bargain. I'd come here and "looked around." Now I wanted to go home.

Outside the lace-curtained window, the last of the light reflected off the silver generator buoys, collecting energy as they bobbed on the dark waves. A throng of oil rigs glowed against the gray horizon.

Their great flames competed with the first few stars to shine through the smog.

It must be, what? Seven? Seven thirty? I tried to sneak a look at Dad's watch. The ferry left for the mainland at nine o'clock tonight, and I was going to be on it.

"The turmoil in our world manifests itself in so many ways. Delusions, rebelliousness, suicidal behavior." Dr. Mordoch looked pointedly at me, and I made the mistake of meeting her eyes. Though her face was calm, almost expressionless, her eyes were filled with . . . *what?*

I held Dr. Mordoch's gaze, and her agitated emotions swarmed into my head. They were desperate and fierce, stinging at me until they crystallized into a single, sharp thought: *"At last."*

A thousand bristling secrets hid behind Dr. Mordoch's thought. *What did she mean? "At last" what?*

Then she pulled her eyes away from mine, like someone yanking their hand off a hot stove. But in the moment before she looked away, I saw her eyes go wide with shock. It was so quick, no one else would've even noticed.

But I did.

Because that's how it always happened. When I walked down the hallway at school, one by one, kids turned to face their lockers or their friends. Teachers shuddered when they called on me in class. Even the school counselor kept her eyes glued to her notebook during our sessions. As if people could feel their secrets leaking out to me.

So usually I tried to be invisible. I'd keep my eyes down and exist in a universe of one. I'd learned early on that secrets were insidious things. And I had my own. Maybe the only reason people avoided my eyes was because they saw the wrongness inside me.

Now, covering her own discomfort, Dr. Mordoch unlocked the polished wooden filing cabinet behind her. She caressed the folders as she pulled the drawer open, the file tabs making a *flick-flick-flick* sound against her hand. "See, Faye! These are all children I've been able to help here. What I've devoted my entire life to . . ."

Dr. Mordoch rubbed her forehead, pausing for a moment. Then she was back in motion, moving to the last drawer. "Ah, here you are, Faye. I've kept this one a long time."

She spread the folder open on her enormous oak desk and took a seat in the equally massive chair. Her angular frame was so slight, she should've looked like a little kid playing office, but somehow she pulled it off. A queen ruling from her throne.

"I only wish we'd had more time to work together when you were a child. You were such a special patient to me. Of course things were simpler then. Just me, in that tiny office." She laughed—a tight, little huff from her nose that pulled her mouth down. "But now, at Holbrook, I have the facilities to really help you, Faye. We have a chance to pick up where we left off."

Dr. Mordoch might have fond memories of me, but I didn't remember her at all. Before last week, I hadn't even known we'd lived in Maine. My parents told me we'd moved away when I was six, but there were no pictures of me collecting shells or playing in tide pools. Nothing from our life before Pittsburgh.

She smoothed the file flat and sifted through the stack of pages. "Here we are." She slid a single sheet across the desk. "Your schedule."

I shouldn't have a schedule. I'm not even registered here. Dad smiled at me. Was it a "let's humor her" smile or a "just take one more step into that infinite pit of doom" one?

The schedule started at 6:30 a.m. and went till 10:00 p.m., each hour neatly color-coded and labeled. The yellow blocks were classes.

My eyes went straight to Art and Life. What would they study at an "academy" full of delinquents and crazies? The fine art of finger painting?

There was also Coastal Biology and English Literature. At least this place was making an effort to sound like a real school.

The blue blocks were a little more revealing. Each of them was marked "Mandatory," and they had names like Socialization, Private Guidance, and Free Time. How do you make free time mandatory?

Say something. My jaw tightened, and my tongue felt clumsy in my mouth. *Tell her.* I took an uneven breath and managed to squeeze the words out.

"Thanks, but we're just here to look around."

Dr. Mordoch came over and sat right next to me, her breath smelling like stale coffee and licorice.

"Buddha once said, 'No one saves us but ourselves. No one can and no one may. We ourselves must walk the path.'" She leaned in close, like we were at a sleepover, whispering in her singsong voice. "Won't you walk the path with me, Faye?"

I shook my head, looking to my dad. Trying to figure out what was going on. But he wouldn't meet my eyes either.

"You're staying with us," Dr. Mordoch said bluntly, reaching out to pat my hand.

I pulled away, my fingers rasping against her sandpaper skin. Even though the room was sweltering, I broke out in a cold sweat.

Shivering, I waited for Dad to correct her. But he didn't.

A drop of water fell from the ceiling, making a wet splotch on my schedule. Then another drop fell. And another. *This is how it always started.* I pretended I didn't see anything, keeping my eyes glued on Dad's down-turned face.

"Your father's brought you here because he cares about you. He wants you to get better. To be better. Don't you want to be better, Faye?"

Better than what, Dad?

Finally he looked up, but not at me. His eyes locked on the headmistress, and she nodded at him encouragingly. "Dr. Mordoch thinks she can help you . . ."

The steady *drip-drip-drip* of water made it hard to concentrate on his words. I closed my eyes, hoping it would go away. *No, no, not now.*

". . . we've tried everything, honey. The Cooperative's worried . . ." He cleared his throat and started again. "We're *all* worried about your antisocial behavior. Not to mention the nightmares and insomnia . . . You have no idea what your mom and I have been going through trying to help you."

What they've been going through? Water flooded in under Dr. Mordoch's closed door.

Dad went for my hand this time, but I didn't want his pity. "And after your episode on the school roof, well . . ."

My episode. "Panic attacks," my school counselor called them. I don't know what she thought happened to me during one of my "attacks," but not this. Who would even believe me if I told them? This wasn't panic, this was madness.

But right now, I needed to act as normal as possible, and I was willing to try anything. What was that mantra the counselor taught me? *Fear is an illusion. I'm in control of . . . of my own reality. Fear is an illusion. I'm in control—*

My boots squished in the icy blue waves foaming across the floor. I tucked my legs up under me.

I'm in control—

I could smell the tang of the ocean as it gushed in around the edges of the office windows. Tangled ropes of emerald seaweed coiled around my knees.

I'm in control of—

Did he think I liked being the freak who started screaming when she fell asleep in class? The girl no one would even look at? The windows smashed open and the ocean burst through in a silver tide of foam and froth. The sea came just for me.

As the water rose up around my neck, all I could say was "Don't leave me here."

Dad cleared his throat and looked away, fumbling in his pockets like he was searching for his keys.

Water crept over my lips. It trickled into my ears. My schedule floated past me on a swelling wave. I tipped back my head to gulp the last sliver of air above the surface.

Dad's jaw moved up and down in a string of muffled words.

Then Dr. Mordoch's. Then Dad's. But all I could hear was the steady *whoosh, whoosh, whoosh* of the blood pulsing in my ears. Clutching at my smooth leather chair, I tried to tether myself to reality. My lungs burned, and my hair billowed in a cloud around my head.

They both peered down at me.

What if I just floated up and let the water carry me away? I loosened one hand from the chair. My body felt lighter, almost free.

Dad leaned over me, worry creasing his forehead.

I let go and the cobalt waves buoyed me up. Taking me away from my dad, Dr. Mordoch, and, most of all, Holbrook.

2

"NO!" I FOUGHT AGAINST the hands crushing me into the floorboards. The office came back into focus bit by bit. After the saturated blue of the waves, it was like flicking through old black-and-white snapshots. A drab wall of ancient filing cabinets. Faded diplomas hung in elaborate frames. An overturned gray, leather armchair. And Dr. Mordoch's blanched face hovering over me.

"You're going to hurt yourself. Stop it this instant!" Dr. Mordoch's singsong voice was gone now, her tidy ponytail falling apart. She had me pinned to the floor with her full weight.

"Talk to me, honey." Dad knelt next to me, his forehead wrinkled. His scared eyes focused on where his hand touched my shoulder, practiced at avoiding mine. Even now. "I'm right here."

Dr. Mordoch had her knee planted on my chest. Despite her small size, I had a hard time pushing out the words. "What happened?"

I remembered the water coming for me. And then, nothing.

I'd never blacked out before. Dread squeezed my throat, making it hard to catch my breath. The hallucinations were getting worse. I had to find a way to control them, or at least hide them, or people really would think I was crazy. Then again, what could they do to me? Send me to Holbrook?

I struggled to sit up, but Dr. Mordoch tightened her grip on my arms.

"That's enough." Dad's voice had that edge to it and I obeyed, letting the tension go out of my body. But his anger was directed at Dr. Mordoch. A tiny flare of hope caught in my chest.

"Of course." Dr. Mordoch released me with a concerned smile. She offered me a hand up, but I ignored it, letting Dad help me back into my chair. I ran my finger along a rip in the leather that hadn't been there before, trying to think of the exact right thing to say. Maybe there was still a chance to change his mind.

Dr. Mordoch must have thought so too, because she tucked her hair back into place and smoothed out her suit. Transforming back into the competent professional. "The biggest danger at times like this is the patient hurting themselves. You were right to bring her here. Faye needs someone to protect her from herself."

I didn't want to be protected. As scary as the visions and nightmares were, they were mine. There was a vividness to that relentless ocean that was different from the dull roar of kids surging through my school. From the teachers blabbing on about vectors and tangents like everything was normal. Without my "episodes," I was afraid I'd get lost in all the noise. Fade into the Formica and steel.

"And the doctor says there are no physical reasons for Faye's attacks?" Dr. Mordoch was talking about me like I wasn't there. I stared at Dad, begging him not to listen to her. Begging him not to leave me.

But he ignored me. "No, he assures us that she's perfectly healthy."

"Emotional pain reveals itself through dangerous, deviant patterns. It doesn't matter whether it's drug use or fighting or suicide attempts . . . They're all cries for help. My school is here to answer those cries with open arms. This isn't the same world you and I grew up in, Mr. Robson. It's violent and ugly. Faye needs a sanctuary from all of that. She needs a trained staff around her twenty-four hours a day. She needs the compassion of other kids who are struggling to adjust. She *needs* Holbrook Academy."

Finally, Dad turned to me and I saw the question in his eyes. Like he was hunting for a reason to bring me back home. Remembering all those ordinary fathers and daughters I'd seen around the Cooperative, I tried to project a version of myself that he might want. A Faye my dad would tell dumb jokes to or have lunch with or at least want to look at. Someone he wouldn't abandon here.

"Okay." He stood up, not finding whatever it was he was searching for. "Do what you have to do."

Down by the car, Dad pulled out a suitcase I'd never seen before. Betrayal finally cut through the numbness. This whole trip was a lie. My parents had always planned on leaving me at Holbrook.

The huge fortress of a house rose up in front of me. A tumble of red stone and shingles growing out of the rocky ground. Towers and turrets climbed high into the humid night.

Blinking, I grabbed the suitcase handle, already sticky with sweat. Dad's face went blurry as I pushed back hot tears. The floodlights glinting behind him. Escaping into an old game, I thought about how I'd draw the colossal house.

But there was something wrong with the building. It was off-center. Instead of facing the driveway like it should have, the house twisted away from us, its back corner sticking out over the ocean. I imagined my brush pen sweeping across the page of my sketchbook. Mentally, I squared off the awkward angle. Now, the intricately carved columns marched straight up to the great arched doorway engraved with the words *Compass Rose*. Then I straightened out the front path, so that it no longer had to twist around an enormous tree.

"You'll be all right?" Dad's voice dragged me back. He sounded desperate for me to absolve him.

Now I understood why Mom hadn't come along on the trip. She'd explained that they'd only been able to bargain for enough gas to get Dad and me to the school, without her added weight. But that wasn't it. She hadn't been sure that she could stab me in the back and walk away. So she'd stuck my father with the job. *Sucker.*

Well, he could leave me here, but he couldn't make me stay. *No one could.*

"I think Faye and I can go it alone from here," Dr. Mordoch said, giving my dad a way out. Her voice was sweet again. "We have a lot to catch up on, and it'll be easier with just us girls."

My dad shuffled toward me with outstretched arms. I stepped back, holding the suitcase like a shield between us. Unsure, he turned the hug into an awkward sort of hang-in-there-champ arm pat and headed to the car.

Well, Mom had certainly picked the right man for the job. The engine roared into life and he pulled away. What was going through his mind as he wound his way down the endless driveway back to the road? Was he glad to be alone now, driving by himself through the night? I pictured him fiddling with the radio, bobbing his head to the music. Had he rolled down the window to savor that extra rush of freedom?

As his taillights glimmered through the trees, a small breeze lifted the oppressive heat of the night. The wild sharpness of pine trees clashed with the salty breath of the ocean, and I was sucked back ten years. I felt awkward and alone, like I was six again. Old memories fluttered in their cages and then vanished again as the air stilled. Then the taillights blinked out into nothing, leaving me in the dark with her.

"Let's get you settled." Dr. Mordoch took my arm and led me

uphill, into the dark forest. It seemed impossible that there were this many trees left anywhere, let alone in one spot. The woods closed ranks, hiding the driveway and the off-kilter Compass Rose behind us. My throat tightened, and I lost my bearings as the path wound through a dense tunnel of leaves.

Which way is the driveway? How will I get back to the main road later?

I'd only been in a forest once before, and I remembered the same disorienting panic. My fifth-grade class had taken a field trip to Raccoon Creek State Park. It was only a year or so after the oil had peaked out, and people were still trying to act like nothing had changed. Before the Peak War. Way before the rangers started carrying guns.

We were there to "commune with nature." But it wasn't lovely and pristine, like our teacher had said. I remembered how I'd felt out there under all those trees, all those tangled, twisted branches reaching for me. The wind crashing through them, howling at me. I couldn't breathe.

It was the same way now.

The woods blotted out the sky and I hunched low, wishing I could reach up and smash through the overhanging branches. Finally, the trees broke open and we stood looking up at the dorms. The graphite-colored stone and slate roofs squared off in a practical, U-shaped building.

"These dormitories are more than eighty years old. In fact, the buildings on campus are the oldest structures left on the island. The locals tore down the last of the old houses for firewood last winter. We're lucky that Holbrook Estate is an official historic landmark . . . and that the Compass Rose and dormitories are made of stone." Dr. Mordoch winked at me like she'd made a joke.

But it didn't add up. No official designation would protect all these trees in January when people were freezing to death. *What's Dr. Mordoch leaving out of her history lesson?*

As we followed the path into the courtyard, Dr. Mordoch gestured at the dorms, the wings of the building stretching out on either side of us. "This is part of an old monastery built after the Holbrooks lived here. Of course, we had to make a few improvements."

I didn't think she was talking about flowered curtains or rainbow wallpaper. No, the monks might have called their rooms cells, but I didn't think they were the ones who put bars on the windows.

With a jangle of keys, Dr. Mordoch unlocked three sets of bolts on the front door. *I guess I won't be leaving that way.* Fluorescent lights flickered on, and I blinked. It wasn't the dank, barren hallway I'd expected from the outside, but a living room with pasty-green linoleum and bright plastic chairs bolted to the floor.

"Most of the other students will be here by tomorrow morning. There're a few other early birds, like you, who came up with their parents. The student nurse is down the hall, so don't feel too lonely."

Translation: We're keeping an eye on you.

Up the stairs. Third door on the left. The bedroom had the same sterile decorating theme as the living room. It felt like a hospital, except the furniture was all secured to the floor or walls and there was a definite lack of balloons.

"I'm so glad to have you back with us, Faye. You were too young when we had our sessions together. We never had time to dig deep enough."

Dr. Mordoch walked to the tiny connecting bathroom. I heard the faucet running, and she came back out with a cup of water and a blue pill.

"You need a good night's sleep." She smiled sweetly and held it out to me.

Like that would even be possible in this place. I shook my head.

"Standard procedure for the beginning of the semester. It's always hard to adjust to a new place. And we want things to go smoothly."

Go smoothly for who? Her smile tightened, and I remembered how she'd pinned me on the floor earlier. But I wasn't just going to roll over and play dead. I took the pill and a gulp of water and swallowed.

"Show me your mouth."

My stomach clenched and I opened up just a little.

"Wider. Under your tongue."

I moved my tongue to the side, trying to sweep the hidden pill along with it, but the traitorous blue must have peeked out.

"I know all the tricks. You can play this game, Faye. But know this now: you'll lose. So you might as well swallow the pill and go to bed."

Defeated, I maneuvered the pill to the top of my tongue. Bitterness spread through my mouth, twisting it with distaste. I swallowed for real this time and opened wide again as ordered.

"Sweet dreams." She smiled and shut the door. The lock snapped into place.

3

I DIDN'T WRESTLE with the knob or slam my fist against the door. It wasn't going to open that way, and I couldn't afford the extra attention. Not if I was going to find a way out.

They'll feed me pills and propaganda until I'm all fixed. Until I have nothing but empty, fluff-filled dreams.

No. I dreaded the visions and nightmares, but I craved them too. The landscape of my life was painted in browns and grays, but the visions brought a rush of intensity that hinted there was something more. No matter how much I hated being shunned and ignored, I wasn't willing to sacrifice the only part of my life that felt important.

How long did I have till the drugs kicked in? Five minutes? Fifteen? A half hour?

I scanned the dimly lit room. A bathroom, two beds, two desks, a girl in front of the window—

"Shit!" I almost fell down in shock. A sallow girl stood facing me, her black eyes glaring out from behind dingy, dark hair.

It was just my reflection. The world fell into place again, bringing cold reality with it. Even I was afraid of the girl mirrored in the window. Did she really see secrets in people's minds? Did waves really come for her? It was terrifying to think it was all a delusion. But even scarier to believe that it wasn't.

I should smash her into a million shards.

I took a deep breath and walked toward the window, blurring the reflection. They'd left that girl behind. But I wouldn't. I wasn't going to let her stay here.

I'd been wrong about the windows. There were only bars on the first floor, not the second. But the window wouldn't budge. There was no knob or bolt or lock. It just wouldn't open.

I yanked hard on the handle at the bottom of the frame, jarring my whole body with the force. Nothing happened. Resting against the wall, I noticed the sheen of the paint continued seamlessly from sill to window. It was painted shut. I banged on the frame, and small cracks formed in the seal. *Will the nurse hear me?*

I didn't care anymore. The room was too hot and musty. I couldn't breathe. Raking my fingernails along the edge, I clawed at the congealed paint. Years flaked away in a flurry of paint chips. Cream. Mint green. Lavender. The colors blurred together, and I could feel the pill dragging at me. I had to get out of here while I still could.

I pulled on the window again. It groaned and muttered.

I was suffocating. Panic pumped through my veins. *Whoosh. Whoosh. Whoosh.* Pushing my forehead into the wooden frame, the smell of cedar caught at me, and underneath it, a hint of the salty night air. I breathed in the tantalizing scent and it anchored me, focusing my mind. I needed to get out of this stifling room. To get out of here.

I grabbed the handle with both hands, my whole body concentrating on that one thought, that smell, and pulled with everything I had. The window let out a tiny sigh and flew open. Fresh air hit my face, and I laughed as my head cleared a little.

A metal ladder glinted in the faint glow of the dorms. Probably an old fire escape. It was a few rooms away, near the corner of the building. A narrow, decorative ledge ran right beneath the windows, between me and the ladder.

I crawled out and stepped onto the tightrope of stone just as the lights in the whole building went out, like someone had thrown a switch. The dorms were plunged into darkness. I couldn't see the window, the ledge, or the ground beneath me. I fought to keep my balance.

What am I doing here? The drugs were definitely kicking in. My thoughts inched their way through my brain, trying to come to some sort of conclusion. I clutched at the rim of the window, letting the solid stone steady me.

You have to get off this ledge.

Yeah. I know that.

How?

My eyes adjusted to the night, and with it came a little clarity. By the lopsided moon and the spotlights lining the courtyard, I could make out the ladder again.

Yes. That's right.

Very carefully, I pulled off my boots, knotted the shoelaces together, and hung them around my neck. My bare feet gripped the warm stone and my mind cleared a little more. I turned and hugged the wall, inching toward the ladder. Not looking down. Not thinking about how stupid it would be to die like this.

Then my fingertips touched the rough grit of metal and I grabbed on, swinging myself onto the ladder. The iron rails smelled like monkey bars, and a kid's thrill of danger tingled through me.

My feet gonged softly on the rungs as I climbed down. I just needed to make it to the ground and head for the road. From there

I could walk to the dock. Or maybe hitch a ride. If there were any cars still running on this island.

The stench of cigarettes interrupted my thoughts. I froze. A dull glow floated in the dark, about sixty feet away, near the ground. A man, cigarette in one hand, leaned against the front door of the dorms, puffing smoke into the air. He clicked on a flashlight and scanned the courtyard and the surrounding woods. *Security.*

I knew I needed to worry about him. To be careful. But my fear was remote. Like watching a horror movie and yelling, "Don't open that door!"

I tried to focus my thick mind on the guard as he puffed another big cloud of smoke into the air. Willing my feet to be silent, I went back up the ladder. My damp palms slid on the rungs as I climbed all the way up.

He couldn't stay there all night. I'd wait. Avoiding the gutters, I pulled myself up onto the roof and my breath caught in my throat.

I'd never seen anything like it. Standing there, at the edge of the roof, the world opened up to me. Trees . . . No, a forest, a real forest, swarmed across the hills. The ocean curved in around the coast, embracing the cliffs. Welcoming me. Out on the horizon, the mob of oil rigs blazed in the hot night. Pinhole stars peeked through the hazy air, glittering against the inky sea. Like broken glass on asphalt.

It was beautiful.

Below, the lights of the castlelike Compass Rose shone from a hollow at the bottom of the hill. Far across the grounds, another light flickered in the dark. Smoke reached my nose, and my throat cinched tight as I remembered last summer's riots down in Pittsburgh. When the whole city lit up the sky, and armed helicopters buzzed back and forth over the South Hills Cooperative.

Calm down. That fire had stunk of burnt tires and charred flesh. This was different.

The air was filled with the earthy smell of singed leaves and tree sap. Maybe the woods weren't as protected as Dr. Mordoch thought.

I climbed to the crest of the roof to get a better view, my feet feeling their way up the smooth slate tile. Standing on the flat ridge that ran along the peak, I saw that it wasn't a forest fire either. A bonfire burned on a cliff on the other side of the Compass Rose. Flames jumped into the sky, licking at the stars. Tall shadows stood black against the firelight.

There's other people out here.

Then the music started. It was soft, just a sigh in the muggy night. Then it grew into a groan. The sound was mellow and rich. Not a flute, but something like it. The strange instrument seemed familiar, like something I'd listened to a long time ago on one of my parents' worn-out, wobbly tapes.

A drum joined in. Then a second and a third. They matched the rhythm of the ocean, echoing the insistent waves. The music drifted across the valley, from the people around the bonfire. I counted them. Seven dark figures ringing the fire. Were they more security guards? Other students? Locals? But the night was hot; why would anyone waste the wood?

Who, then?

The smell of burnt pine needles stung my nose, and I fought against its overwhelming scent. Against the smoke and questions filling my head. Then one of the shadows stepped closer to the bonfire. A figure stark against the orange brilliance. Eclipsing the flames.

Fear pricked my temples and I dropped behind the ridge of the roof. *They're too far away to see me.* But I couldn't shake the feeling that I was being watched.

Creeping back over the peak, I eased myself down the other side of the roof to get a closer look. A tile broke away under my feet, skittering, *skritch-scratch* down the slope. My feet slipped out from under me, following the tile down, slamming my chin against the slate. I caught at the slick roof, trying to stop myself as I slid down it, but I just gained momentum. Any second I would fly off the edge. I squeezed my eyes shut just as my feet hit the copper gutters and stopped my fall.

Under the music, under my breathing, the tile smashed on the ground. A thousand pieces on the concrete.

Lying there, heart pounding, I tried to make the world stop spinning. Below me, on the ground, footsteps rounded the building. The guard.

I pressed myself flat. The beam of his flashlight skidded along the gutters. *Can he see me?*

I held still, the sharp taste of blood filling my mouth. I held my breath as my heart pounded out the rhythm of the drums. I held my thoughts steady while the light made woozy circles along the rooftop.

Then I heard the flick of a lighter. I craned my neck to see what was going on. The guard sucked in on a new cigarette, kicked the broken tile and his cigarette butt into the bushes, then disappeared back into the dark. A ways off, I heard a door slam.

I crawled, panting, back up to the ridge. My legs wobbled under me as I stood again. The bonfire and the blazing silhouette were still there. The drums still pulsed with the hungry tide.

The ring of black shapes seemed to leap and fall in the flickering firelight. The silhouetted figure threw up its arms and a wailing song split the night. The voice sliced at me. Digging at my mind.

I tried to shut my thoughts to the song's steady beat, but my feet obeyed anyway. I danced the sea's rhythm out across the slippery ridge. The music throbbed in my bones. *Now you,* the drums chanted. *It's time. For you.*

The wind rose. Flaring up the flames and rushing at me.

I leaned into the wind, letting it hold me up. Its warm arms wrapping tight.

The trees around me came alive, their dark leaves quaking. Their branches waving in time. I gave in to the music, stomping my feet. I gave in to the drugs, thrusting my hands in to the sky. Even the stars cried out as they blazed their fierce arcs of light.

My arms spread wide, and I spun too. Tracking their orbit. The drums raced and my body crescendoed into delicious, dizzying circles. Like a roman candle waiting to blaze.

The music soared and I soared up with it. I towered over the insatiable ocean. Feral shadows danced far beneath me. The moon was just a chunk of ice at my feet.

Then the song died. Hovering at the edge of the roof, the sea splayed below, I whimpered in the empty silence. A sliver of memory cut its way out of the fog. A rushing wave of froth and ice ripped through my mind. Screaming, I was dragged down into the darkness.

4

"WHERE DO YOU want this one? Zach Watson." A man's faraway, gravelly voice filtered into my sleep.

Everything hurt. The side of my face throbbed, and my shoulder felt like someone had tried to wrench it out of my body. The air tasted thick and sticky, with a twinge of rotting fish. My right arm came into focus, dangling off the edge of the roof. The rest of me was just inches away from joining it in midair. *Not good.* I eased my aching body away from the edge, trying not to throw up.

It was barely light, but the shadowy courtyard was already in motion. Hulking guards strode in and out of the yard. Some of them hauled sagging teenagers across the lawn, jerking them around a little harder than necessary. Others just circled around the sidewalks, their hands hovering right above their belt holsters. As if they were eternally ready for a shoot-out. *Tell me they don't use guns against a few messed-up kids.*

At home, there were security teams to protect the food and gas rations from scroungers, but they were never this twitchy. And there were never this many of them.

The gravelly voice spoke again, coming from right below me.

"Come on, Nurse. I'm effing tired. I need a shower bad and a beer worse."

A woman with a clipboard frowned up at an enormous guy with a face like mashed-up hamburger. Or the guy from that old horror movie. Freddy Krueger. While one hand shoved a cigarette in and out of his scarred, pockmarked face, the guy's other hand rested intimidatingly on the neck of a short, pudgy teenager. A cringing boy in handcuffs versus a six-and-a-half-foot-tall bouncer. *Yeah, that's a fair fight.*

"I've been up for thirty hours watching this one." Freddy Krueger shook the guy, Zach, making his neck snap forward. Zach seemed to fold into himself, his shoulders slumping, his face going slack. Like he was vacating his body.

The woman, Nurse, fired back with a sharp, nasally voice. "Watson . . . Watson. Here we are. Take him to Room Twenty-one. And I'd better not see any bruises from those handcuffs. We don't need another cell phone picture fiasco like last year," Nurse shouted after him as he pushed the boy toward the dorms. "I'm still hearing about how many Cooperatives pulled their kids after that one. Mordoch wants these brats under control, but she doesn't want to know about it."

I sat up fast. *Dr. Mordoch. The drugs. The fire.* Nausea churned through me again and I closed my eyes, steadying myself. The night before was just a blur of darkness and drugged sensations. A shrouded memory, tinged with screams, nudged at my mind. I pushed it away. From what I saw going on in the courtyard, I didn't want to stick around to remember what it was.

I wasn't going to get far with bare feet. My boots were lying, still tied together, near the peak of the roof. I studied the hazy campus while I put them on.

In the dawn light, it was easier to get my bearings. It was mostly woods with clumps of solar panels sticking out here and there. In the middle of the sea of trees, the Compass Rose sat on an island of grass. It hung precariously out over the ocean at the bottom of the hill.

I remembered how the water had looked last night. Glittering and dangerous.

A little farther into the woods, another large house poked through the trees. Despite its size, the other building looked plain and shrunken next to the stone towers of the Compass Rose.

The dense trees made it easy to see the boundary of the school grounds. Brutally straight lines sliced off the forest, marking the end of Holbrook's "refuge" and the beginning of a clear-cut, littered with old stumps. A single road ran through the wasteland, leading to town. The closest edge of the woods was only 100 yards away, on the other side of the dorms. I just had to get past the guards.

A car squealed in the distance, and shouting erupted from the woods leading up to the dorms.

Nurse yelled, "Caretakers report to the incident!"

She and her "caretakers" ran off toward the chaos. A few perimeter guards stayed put, but they were chomping at the bit. They paced, squinting through the trees in the growing light, ready to jump into the fray. This was my chance. I half crawled, half skidded down the roof to the ladder.

Balanced at the top, I remembered my sketchbook back in the dorm room. There were six months' worth of drawings and notes in there. Six months of me. For a second, I thought about trying to sneak back in through my window. But I'd never make it out again without being spotted. I had to leave it.

Scurrying down, fear rang in my ears. Adrenaline must have dulled the pain, because my bruised body moved quickly down the rungs. But ten feet off the ground, I ran out of steps. There was another section of ladder, which was supposed to slide down, but it was secured with a heavy padlock. Clearly, fire safety was not Holbrook's main concern.

The noises from the woods were close now. A shrill girl's voice yelled obscenities with the rhythm and enthusiasm of a cheerleader. Angry shouts followed in its wake.

"Stop!"

"This is your final warning!"

I hurried, sliding my hands down the sides of the ladder, lowering myself until I was dangling from the last step. Suddenly, I was terrified. The fall from last night was still fresh in my mind. My sweaty fingers slipped on the rung as I was bombarded by memories.

The music calling. The frigid waves surging toward me. Drowning in the never-ending darkness. And then, the screaming.

I slammed against the ground. Clinging to the grass in the courtyard, my whole body shook with fear. *I have to get out.*

That one thought shouted itself over and over in my mind. *Out! Out! Out!* Pushing myself up, I dove into the woods just as a girl with bright turquoise hair burst into the far side of the courtyard.

"*Viva la revolución!* You'll never catch me, bastards!" The girl's blue hair was spiked into a Mohawk that defied gravity, and she pumped her arm high in the steamy morning air. She flashed a devious smile my direction, and I pulled farther back into the protection of the trees. Then she turned her attention back to the guards. The meat-faced guy, the one I now thought of as Freddy, barreled after her, dripping sweat. On his heels was a ropey, muscular woman, with dragon tattoos on both arms, and an onslaught of guards.

Freddy reached out to grab the girl and missed. Somehow she managed to stay a millisecond ahead, jogging along the sidewalk that circled the courtyard. I wasn't sure if she was crazy or fearless or just stupid.

"It's been a tough race, but Nami Fujita's coming up on the final lap. She's the long shot, but it looks like she just might make it. Dah-daaah-daah-dah dum-dum." She was singing "Chariots of Fire." "Dah-daaah-daah-dah-dum."

Dragon-tattoo guard put on a spurt of speed, closing in on the girl, who I guessed was Nami, and grabbed her arm. The woman yanked hard enough to cause whiplash. Freddy was right behind them and swung back like he was going to backhand the girl.

"Uh-uh-uh." Nami shook her finger at the guy, grinning. "No breaking the merchandise." Her flared skirt swayed as she wiggled her hips.

Wow. I want to be her when I grow up.

Dragon flexed her arm and in a single, blurry movement, Nami was flat on the ground. Then the guard slammed her weight onto Nami, pinning her facedown on the wet grass. Finally, Nurse caught up to them.

"Enough!" Nurse shooed Dragon away and reached down to pull the girl up.

Finally, someone to help. Nurse said something I couldn't hear, and Nami, her Mohawk crooked, crossed her arms defiantly. Fighting to paste her cocky smile back on. Then Nurse calmly pulled something from her holster and sprayed Nami directly in the face with it. Nami gasped in shock and thrashed on the ground, clawing at her eyes and screaming.

Time to go.

I bolted into the woods, adrenaline flaring through my body. Trees walled me in on every side, all looking exactly the same. My sense of direction abandoned me. The same tree trunk sprang up in front of me again and again. The same pine needles stung my skin. As I barreled downhill, all I knew was that each step was taking me farther from that repulsive scene.

Branches grabbed my already damp T-shirt. Roots shot up, out of the ground, to trip my feet. Trying to keep me at Holbrook. Then I slammed into a chain-link fence.

Tall trees had hidden it from the roof, but now nine feet of fencing knocked the breath out of me, absorbing my momentum in a thunder of wire. The fence ran as far as I could see in both directions, cutting off a rocky, tar-covered beach from the rest of the campus. The smell of the sea made me hungry. A deep-down, in-my-bones kind of hunger to be closer to it. I wanted to feel the water swirling around my legs. The waves gently tugging me away from here. Away from this.

I threaded my fingers through the chain-link, wishing I could get past it. So that's why there were still trees on Dr. Mordoch's "historic" estate. Barbed wire was coiled along the top of the fence, making it impossible to get in or out. Somewhere in the distance I heard the rumble of a car.

The road.

I swung around and took off back the way I had come. If I skirted around the dorms, if I managed to keep my sense of direction, I'd eventually hit the road. If not, maybe I'd at least cross the long driveway leading to it.

My legs pounded up and down. My body dodged through brambling bushes and green-painted solar towers and low-hanging branches. Dust coated my mouth with chalky film.

The trees thinned slightly, and I made out the charcoal smudge of the driveway. I smiled as I turned onto it, my feet hitting the gravel. The crunch, crunch, crunch underfoot and the strip of faded gray sky made me feel stronger. In control again.

An engine roared behind me, and I ducked back into the woods just as a white, unmarked van zoomed by. It was getting lighter, and soon I'd be easy to spot among these wide-legged evergreens and shrubby saplings. I put on a burst of speed, picturing myself reaching the twisty island road. Following it away from this place. Following it anywhere. No plan was still better than staying at Holbrook.

Razor wire glimmered up ahead of me. The driveway that had been unblocked last night, welcoming us with open arms, was now shut off by a tall gate. Severing the school from the outside world.

"No!"

I grabbed the chain link and pulled, trying to slide the gate open. It didn't budge. And there wasn't just one gate. There were two, with an intercom and car-length space in between, making it impossible to just slip out. There was no way to get over the sharp slices of metal that curved off the top in all directions.

"No." Even though I was used to fences at home, this one was different. The fence around South Hills made me feel safe. Keeping scroungers out, instead of me in.

The growl of another van hit my ears, and I jumped back into the trees, breathing hard.

Freddy rolled down his window and buzzed the intercom.

"Quittin' time." He saluted a camera sitting on top of the fence.

A camera. That I'd been standing right in front of.

The intercom staticked into life, and I didn't stick around to hear what it said. I heard the van door slam behind me.

"Faye! Faye Robson. There's no use running." He was close, his gruff voice booming through the gray dawn.

I dove behind a decaying log, terrorizing an emaciated squirrel who'd been gnawing on a bone, and flattened myself against the dirt. Trying not to make a sound. Trying not to breathe in the stench of damp, rotting leaves.

But Freddy's brutal arms bulldozed through the trees toward me.

A small smirk twitched on his face as his eyes scanned the forest. Terror pushed into my temples, and I thought about Nami's look of panic right before she was pepper sprayed.

Without thinking, I picked up the bone the squirrel had dropped. It was part of a fibula, maybe from a feral cat or a raccoon. My fingers rubbed the smooth surface of the bleached bone and a calm fell over me. The world went quiet.

I'd collected bones for most of my life. When the oil supplies peaked out and the country's reserves ran low, Pittsburgh became very dangerous, very fast. So our suburb was one of the first to transform into a Cooperative. Then the Peak War started overseas, bringing more energy restrictions and all kinds of rationing.

Fences went up around South Hills. Guards were hired and cars stopped working. I felt more and more trapped. All those people, all that fear screaming in my brain and I couldn't get away.

Then I found the river. It wasn't that far from my house, but no one went there. The water was covered with a greenish sheen, and I held my nose, trying to block the putrid stench of chemicals and sewage mixed with rotting animals. Dead fish and squirrels and who knows what else were scattered everywhere, washed up on the banks. Most of the corpses still buzzed with flies, but one delicate skeleton was just bright white bones. Glaring in the sun.

I gently picked up what used to be a bird and was suddenly wrapped in total, blissful hush. It was such a relief from the pressure of all those people crammed together in the Cooperative, worried about having enough gas, enough money, enough food. Enough.

I took the bird home with me and hid it away in the crawl space in my room. Soon I added others. As the energy shortage went on, the bones were easier to find. The best place was around food storage sheds where they put out poison. They were mostly mice and raccoons, but once I found an owl, which like so many wild animals now was practically extinct.

But I was picky. Only perfect vertebrae. Curved ribs. Fragile wing bones. I cradled them in my hands, meticulously drawing them in my notebook, and then hid them away with the others.

One day in junior high, I came home from school and heard voices coming from my room. I crept upstairs, listening. Mom and Dad were talking in the same careful tones they'd used when my grandfather had died. My throat ratcheted so tight, I couldn't breathe. I forced myself to turn the corner and I saw my parents sitting on the floor surrounded by hundreds and hundreds of skulls and femurs and tiny skeletons. A gleaming sea of white.

When Mom saw me standing in the doorway, she was startled into looking at me. She stared right into my eyes and shuddered. I didn't imagine it. She actually shuddered, and her obvious disgust shivered through me too.

Before that moment, I'd only ever sensed strong emotions emanating from people. But that day my mother's repulsion was so strong that for the first time, a clear word emerged from the murky surface of her thoughts: *"Abomination."*

That word rang out again and again inside my head. It was the last time I looked my mom in the eye. In fact, I was careful with everyone after that. Afraid I'd see her verdict confirmed. A couple of weeks later, the first of the Holbrook Academy brochures had shown up.

I dropped the bone. *I have to get out of here.* From behind the log, my eyes scoured the fence for any way out. A tree branch that reached over the barbed wire. A tiny hole in the chain link. Anything. *Even if I have to tunnel out with a cafeteria spoon.*

But the fence was immaculate. The trees had been cut away from this side of the barrier, and there was nothing but stumps on the other side. Layers of sparkling razor wire vined through the wire mesh. There was no going up or over this thing.

"Fa-aye!" Freddy paused, muscles braced for the slightest sound, like we were playing a sick game of hide-and-seek. He was so close, I could see the trickle of sweat running down his thick neck now. The shadow of stubble on his chin.

Cicadas shrieked, their pulsing song filling the woods. *The other way. Please, go the other way.*

Freddy shrugged and swung away from me, moving back toward the drive.

I forced myself to take a deep breath, the humid air heavy in my lungs. Pulling myself up, my mind buzzed, searching for a way to get out of here. I kept low, tiptoeing over fallen branches until I couldn't stand it anymore and made a run for it.

"Come out, come out, wherever you are!" Freddy's voice came from right ahead of me now, sounding relaxed, almost playful. *Did I get turned around or did he double back?*

Changing directions again, I sprinted up a hill. I gained speed, ignoring the cramp squeezing at my lungs. Then, suddenly, I hit the end of the forest. The end of the fence. The end of everything. I slid to a stop just before the ground dropped away, forty feet down, to a nasty finish of sharp rocks and rabid waves.

And beyond those frothing teeth were more waves. And more. All the way out to the smoggy, puce horizon. The hypnotic eternity of ocean was broken by squalling seagulls, generator buoys, a few lumps of islands, and the barrage of tankers teeming around the oil rigs.

Of course, Freddy was relaxed. He didn't have to race after me. I had nowhere to go.

I looked down into the waves, that hunger growing in me again. Pulling me to it.

No. I thought of Nami and backed away from the roaring ocean and the bare, lichen-covered cliff. She'd run, not because she thought she could escape, but because she didn't want to make it easy for them. *Well, me either.*

I pushed deeper into the trees where it was darker. My dread of getting lost among these monsters warred with my dread of getting caught. The forest grew denser and I ran blindly, trying to keep myself from sprawling on the ground.

I almost crashed straight into her. She'd blended right into the trees. The girl, frozen in mid-scream, panic engraved into her metal face.

Her weathered bronze hands were thrown up in front of her. Her eyes hysterical and huge. The girl reminded me of those statues cast from the ruins of Pompeii. People stuck, for all of eternity, watching everything they loved be consumed by the fires of hell.

Her pain was too much. Too private. I looked away and saw another statue. And another. And another. Black shapes stark on the hill. All that was missing was the bonfire.

Six statues stood in a circle, their mouths stretched in horror. One was turning to run. Another was howling up at the early-morning sky. Each of them in silent agony, trapped in some never-ending nightmare. And I was trapped with them.

5

I LOOKED FOR SIGNS of the fire, but there weren't any. There was no burned patch on the ground. No charcoal. No ash.

Was it the drugs, then? Did I imagine it? The flames? The music? My chest squeezed as I realized something else.

I counted again. Last night there'd been seven figures around the fire. Now there were only six.

"Sometimes, I think I can hear them screaming." A soft voice came from right over my shoulder.

I spun around, ready to run. A girl, a real one this time, stared past me at the statues. She wore a white sundress, and her hair was pulled into a long, blond braid running down her back. I guessed that she was my age, maybe a little older. Another student trapped at Holbrook.

"What are they?" I kept my voice quiet, thinking of Freddy still in the woods somewhere.

"The Screamers. Can you hear them too?" Then her gaze shifted toward me, and I saw there was something a little off about her. Even though she was facing me, the girl's eyes were wild and unfocused.

I just shook my head, afraid to startle this odd girl. On the other side of the clearing, tree branches smashed and Freddy's swearing traveled through the woods. But the girl just stood there, her expression far away, as if she didn't hear any of it. It was unnerving.

And yet, with guards crawling all over Holbrook, here she was. Wandering around free. This girl might be in her own little crazy-world, but maybe she could help me. The barest shadow of hope traced itself in my mind. "Do you know how to get out of here?"

Her face pulled tight across her cheekbones, her forehead wrinkling in thought. As she looked out over the sea, the early-morning light etched lines across her almost transparent skin and circles under her eyes. "The path is here. Only I can't seem to find it . . ."

Her words faded to barely a whisper. "I'm lost myself."

Freddy was getting closer now. "Fa-aye, Faye!"

His shouting finally caught her attention and the girl glanced in my direction. She didn't shy away from my gaze, but the eyes that met mine were vacant and clouded. She smiled and held out her hand. "Are you Faye, then? I'm Rita. How nice to meet you."

Yep. Crazy. I almost laughed at the absurdity of the situation. Some thug was after me and she was making proper introductions? But what did I expect, I was at Holbrook after all.

Then Rita's face creased again in concern. "Be careful. The path is hard to follow."

There was a crash and I whipped around to see Freddy break through the trees. A terrifying grin on his face.

"Please! What path?" I turned back to her, begging. But she was gone.

"Got her, up here by the sculpture garden," Freddy bragged into his earpiece. "I'm handling it."

I just stood there petrified. Like one of the blackened, bronze statues.

He paused, listening to the response in his ear. Anger twisting his mouth.

"Uh-huh."

His face went from medium rare to bloody.

"Uh-huh."

Not a man of many words.

"Said I'm handling it." And he started for me.

Freddy clutched his pepper spray and edged closer. His eyes were everywhere, checking out the area around us, evaluating my movements. Then he looked straight at me, and I saw a flicker of fear in his eyes before he looked away. Like I was an escaped tiger who might attack at any second. I had the urge to do just that. To rave and scream and claw. But my sense of defeat overwhelmed everything else.

Sweat slipped down my forehead, stinging my eyes. I touched my back pocket, wishing my sketchbook were there. I'd draw myself into someplace safe. Without possessed statues or sadistic schools. I'd make my life make sense again.

Freddy was feet from me, inches now. This wasn't gonna be pretty. I'd seen what they'd done to Nami. His fat hand twitched, eagerly, and I braced myself.

Then his radio beeped again. He paused, listening to his earpiece.

"Crap. Another one." Freddy's watery eyes filled with regret. "I don't have time to teach you a lesson right now. But I promise, I'll get to it soon enough. And I'm a man of my word."

Freddy grabbed my sore arm and dragged me back into the trees. The branches bent low, tangling in my hair. Ripping it out as Freddy pulled me along.

I wished I were back out under the open sky of the clearing, even if it meant being near those creepy statues. Or listening to Rita.

Be careful. The path is hard to follow. There'd been something in her voice, an urgency, that made it hard for me to just shrug her off.

But Rita and her path vanished from my thoughts as soon as I saw Dr. Mordoch waiting outside the Compass Rose with her satisfied little smile.

"Thank you, Caretaker. I assume she wasn't too much trouble."

"Oh no, Dr. Mordoch. We can handle the students. Firmness and restraint. Just like it says in the handbook." Behind Freddy's smile was a glint of spitefulness, but Dr. Mordoch didn't react. She sent Freddy off toward the next "incident" and turned to me.

"I'm glad this happened before we officially started our semester." Dr. Mordoch motioned for me to follow her back up the hill, in the opposite direction from the dorms. A breeze swatted uselessly at the stagnant air. We skirted around the other house I'd seen from the roof that morning. Its wooden porch sagged and the paint was faded and chipped. A brass plaque gleamed incongruously on the weathered door, reading *Knowledge Annex*. Next to the house was a wide, empty corral, big enough for cows or horses. *Some sort of barnyard therapy?*

"It allows me to be lenient. I'll give you this chance before we begin our term to decide whether you're going to allow Holbrook to help you. Perhaps, if I give you some time to think it over, you'll come around." She beamed at me as she led me up a dirt trail through the oppressive woods. "Meditation can work wonders."

We came to a small skinny building that looked a little like an old rest-stop bathroom. Only a row of metal ventilation pipes on the roof kept the place from blending into the trees completely. Five doors evenly divided the wooden building, each with a stick-on silver number labeling them one through five.

"The monks used this building for contemplation." Dr. Mordoch unlocked the fence that circled the building. No razor wire here. "The Meditation Center serves the same purpose for us at the Academy.

At every turn, I've tried to incorporate the values of self-reflection and discipline when designing this school. The outside world can be such a distraction from . . ."

I stopped listening to her lecture. Dust clogged the air as we crossed the barren yard. Hundreds of resistant feet had obviously beat any grass into submission. My translator finally kicked in as she unlocked door number three. Meditation Center = solitary confinement.

Dr. Mordoch guided me into the closet of a room. It was sweltering and reeked of sweat. My chest squeezed tight with anxiety. I wanted to bolt, but I already knew there was no place to go. Plus, Dr. Mordoch was blocking the only exit.

I took it in quickly. Six feet wide and eight feet long. Cement floor. A wooden platform stuck a couple of feet out of the back wall. A large metal ring was mounted near the floor. *I don't even want to know.*

"Swami Sivananda once said, 'Meditation is painful in the beginning but it bestows immortal Bliss and supreme joy in the end.' Faye, sometimes pain is the only way." She gave me a benign smile and shut the door.

Then I was alone in the blackness. I tried to push down the panic. But the adrenaline rush from this morning had gone clean through my body, making me feel washed out and weak. There was no inside doorknob, but I shoved my shoulder into the door anyway. Hoping.

The lock held and fire ripped down my already bruised arm. A low animal moan escaped my throat.

"Fear is an illusion. I'm in control of my own reality." My words sounded muffled in the walled-off space, making me feel even smaller.

How did I end up here? It'd just started out as bad dreams. Night terrors, the doctor had called them. Always the blue waves rushing at me. Pulling me down. But the nightmares of drowning were less terrifying than the kids who cried just because I looked at them. Or the teachers who called me a liar and a bully.

Doctors checked my eyes, my ears, my brain, searching for a reason for my strangeness. They tested me for ADHD and dyslexia. By junior high I'd been poked and prodded and screened for everything in the book, and they still had nothing to blame it on. But by then I'd figured out how to hide it. At night, I took refuge in the empty streets of the Cooperative. Out under the dark sky, there were no lies to tiptoe around. No eyes to avoid. There was no one to hear my screams.

But, last year, the nightmares had found their way into the daylight and everything had fallen apart. My parents realized I would never be like everybody else. And I realized I didn't want to be.

So here I was. Locked away in a place where I couldn't pretend even if I wanted to.

Pacing, my boots thumped out a steady rhythm on the cement floor. Blood pounded in my ears, keeping time. *Whoosh. Whoosh. Whoosh.* My shins hit the platform at the end of the room. *Whoosh. Whoosh. Whoosh.* I ran into the door.

The drumbeat from last night came back to me. *It's time.* The song pulsed in my veins. *For you.* It throbbed through my head until it hurt to move. I leaned against the door, letting it hold me up.

Fresh air wisped through the spaces between the close-fitting boards. As I breathed in the sweet smell of pine sap, something stirred inside me.

Under the insistent drumbeat and the whooshing in my head, I could hear the creaking of the branches. I imagined swaying in the breeze. The sound of the wind rustling through leaves.

I clung to that sensation of being outside. I pressed my hand into the wood, trying to share its solidness as the music hammered at me. My feet rooted to the floor, even as my head spun.

I didn't want to lose myself here in the dark. "Please."

Something shattered inside me when I heard my feeble voice pleading with a locked door. Throwing my head back, I screamed. I screamed at my father, who'd left me here. At my mother, who was too big a coward to even come. At Dr. Mordoch, who thought she had some special right to drug and imprison me.

I threw my body into the door and pain thrilled through me. I used it, adding it to the rage. I kicked the door, slamming my sole into the wood. Striking that rhythm again and again.

I slammed my palms against the boards, pushing back against the drumbeat, against everything. "No! Fear is an illusion!"

Splinters cut my hands. But I couldn't stop. Couldn't control the deep, welling rage, even if it was about to swallow me up.

The boards gave a little. I was stronger than all of them. Stronger than the door. The flats of my hands pummeled the wood harder. And with a crack, a board loosened, letting in a tiny rift of light. I stood blinking in the yellow beam and shouted, "I'm in control of my own reality!"

A scraping sound came from the other side of the door and it swung open. A figure was silhouetted by blinding sunlight. She stepped inside and I saw it was Dr. Mordoch. Relief flooded through me. She would help me. She would save me from myself.

"Faye, you need to try harder. How can we help you if you fight us like this?" Dr. Mordoch touched the crack I'd made in the boards, testing it. But the wood held solid now.

I blinked, my eyes straining to adjust to the sunlight. As Dr. Mordoch ran her hand over the crack again, lines pulled down her mouth and crinkled her forehead, her face a mix of surprise and worry.

"I w-want to come out." My voice was weak.

"I know you do, but we can't always have everything we want. Until you can settle down, until you can be quiet and show us that you're ready to accept our help, I can't let you out. It would hurt your recovery." Dr. Mordoch grabbed my hand, her rough fingers closing around mine. For the first time she really looked at me. "Faye, I don't want to hurt you."

I couldn't answer, because the world was dissolving around me. The sunlight faded into darkness and the tiny room had been replaced by icy waves. Dr. Mordoch and I were the only things still the same.

We were standing in the ocean, the full moon shone a deep crimson, and the stars burned bright without smog. Dr. Mordoch still gripped my hand, but somehow everything had gotten flipped around backward. I was seeing from inside Dr. Mordoch. One of her muddy hands was fighting against the oncoming tide, the other holding on to my own tiny hand. The hand of a half-drowned six-year-old Faye, standing in the tumbling waves.

"Faye, I don't want to hurt you." I felt myself saying the words, but they were Dr. Mordoch's words. Dr. Mordoch's voice.

Six-year-old Faye pulled against my hand, trying to wade deeper into the waves. Her hand slipped out of mine just as a tall wave crashed over us.

"Faye!" I screamed at her in Dr. Mordoch's voice. But it was like she didn't hear me. Spitting out salt water, she tilted her head back and started singing. It was the same eerie melody that'd been haunting me since last night. And for a second I just stood there, stunned, rooted to the spot as she moved farther and farther away from me.

Another wave rushed toward her, and unflinching, she let it engulf her. Her song cut out and I shook off my terror, springing into action. I dove into the water and raced after Faye. Groping for her in the dark waves. Pushing my way through ropes of seaweed and clouds of sand, till my hands found her tiny body. I clutched her to me, our wet clothes dragging as I fought my way back to the beach.

Footsteps pounded across the sand and my parents, disheveled and dirty, ran toward us, shouting. Faye struggled in my grip and cried for her mom and dad. She yanked her hand out of mine.

And the connection was severed. I was me and not Dr. Mordoch. The sea disappeared and the harsh morning sun returned. I was back in the room, staring up at Dr. Mordoch, yanking my own hand out of hers. *What was that?*

Dr. Mordoch also looked shocked, and for a second, I thought she'd seen the vision too.

But she just looked down at her empty hand and repeated to herself, "I don't want to hurt you."

Then she turned and walked out.

"No!" I started toward her. But I slammed into the closing door.

With the darkness, the vision came back and with it, the blue-black sea. Swirling around me, tugging at my feet.

"Help!" My fingernails scraped against the crack in the door, trying again to claw my way out. "Somebody! Please."

"It's time," the waves whispered. They dashed against me, pulling me under. Pounding at me like drums.

I wanted out of this place. Out of this room. Out of the fences. Out of my mind.

But the rhythm rang out louder and louder, eddying around me in that same insistent song. Until I was chanting along.

"Now you. It's time. For you."

One last thought surfaced through the panic. *Maybe they're right to leave me here.* Maybe I needed to be locked up in a place like this, surrounded by barbed wire and security guards and rooms with bolts on the outside.

Maybe I am crazy.

6

KNOCK, KNOCK.

The noise sifted down through my terror, cutting across my whimpering.

Knock, knock.

Who's there? So crazy. So crazy who? So crazy. So crazy who? So crazy So crazy So crazy.

Knock, knock. There it was again. Someone knocking on the wall.

Blinking in the thick darkness, the ocean waves threatened to crash over me again. I tried to sit up, but my body seemed locked in its position, curled tightly against the wall. A terrible animal sound came from somewhere, and I realized it was me.

I reached out my hand to answer back, then stopped. It could be a trick. Some test to see if I was behaving. But if it was, it was a stupid one. I knocked back.

My knock was returned, this time a little ways down the wall from me. I succeeded in sitting up, ungluing my sweaty legs from each other. A sharp twinge from my stiff knees cleared the fog from my mind. I followed the noise and knocked back. The next time was a few feet farther, moving away from the door.

It was a pointless game. But, the Marco-Polo back and forth was slowly returning me to myself. I followed the knocking down the wall, finally army-crawling under the platform at the end of the tiny room. The solid cement floor pressing against my skin made me calmer somehow, and some of my fear evaporated.

I knocked again, right near the floor, and my knuckles grazed a rough spot. It was too dark to see, but I traced the area with my fingers. There was a small knothole in the wood.

"Mayday. Mayday." A muffled voice drifted through the hole. A guy's voice. "Can anyone hear me?"

It was like someone turning on a night-light. Just to hear another voice in the crushing darkness. I nodded, then remembered that whoever he was couldn't see me, and tried out my voice.

"Yeah?" The darkness weighed heavy against me while I waited for an answer.

"You okay? Are you hurt in there?"

My face flamed, thinking about the horrible mewing sound I'd been making.

"No." My throat was raw from shouting or singing or whatever that'd been.

"No you're not okay or no you're not hurt?" There was real concern in the muted words, and I closed my eyes, grabbing on to it. *I am not alone.*

"No, I'm not hurt." *Okay is another matter entirely.*

"Oh. Good . . ."

Then the room fell quiet again and I could hear him breathing through the knothole. Even with the wall, the physical closeness was comforting in a way I wasn't used to. My breath fell into rhythm with his and I laid my cheek against the cool floor. The warm scent of ginger on his breath mixed with the chalky concrete.

"I feel like a dog in a cage. In hell." His low whisper was raw, and tinged with panic. "And there's no way out . . . The walls, the door, everything's solid. Just this friggin' hole. God, it's way too hot for September."

I belly-crawled, inching closer to the hole, craving this new connection that kept away the dark and the waves. His voice sounded a little clearer.

"By the way, I'm Kel."

My name jammed in my throat like an insidious glob of peanut butter. I swallowed, easing my sore throat. "Faye."

"What're you in for?" Kel's tone was forced, trying to make a joke.

At Holbrook? In Solitary? I didn't even know where to start. Silence welled up around us, pressing in with the darkness.

"Sorry. Too personal. I'm just a little flipped." He sounded as overwhelmed as I felt. "Yesterday, everything was normal. Then two guys bust into my room in the middle of the night and order me out of bed. I was about to scream bloody murder when my stepmom popped her head in and told me to brush my teeth. 'Cause, of course, dental hygiene is super-important when you're being kidnapped."

A smile tugged at my lips, but then it fell off when I remembered that my own mom hadn't even been home when Dad and I left for Holbrook. No hug. No kiss. Not even a wave good-bye.

"And you know what my dad said?" The humor disappeared from his voice, and I could almost taste the bitterness in his words. I shook my head, forgetting again that he couldn't see me. But it didn't matter, Kel kept talking, his voice dropping into a gruff imitation. "He said, 'Son, we're only doing this because we love you so much.' Bullshit. I mean, love may come in many forms, but kidnapping isn't one of them."

Lying isn't one either. I thought about my dad pulling that suitcase out of the trunk, and it stung all over again.

We sat there, both lost in our own betrayals. Kel's story was totally different from mine, but it was like looking at a blurry reflection of my own life. I rested my hand against the wall between us. The wood seemed to vibrate under my fingers.

The boards creaked slightly as Kel shifted around on the other side of the wall, humming to himself. Was he waiting for me to say something? I wanted to. But I didn't trust my voice. Or myself. As it was, it was hard enough to breathe in all this blackness.

Kel's hum died out. "You still there?"

"Yeah?" My answer came out like a question.

"Mind if I keep talking? This sounds crazy, but I feel like the dark is strangling me."

Sucking out all the air.

"It's like this at night sometimes. With all that smog blanking out the stars. But talking helps."

Then keep talking.

"Though I guess you could be some sort of spy over there, waiting for me to spill my guts. You're probably infiltrating the student ranks, a tiny tape recorder in one hand and fake psychosis in the other. But I'm too tired to care."

Pause.

He cleared his throat. "The thing is, last night? I wasn't really surprised when it happened."

I was. But I should've seen it coming. My parents had turned their backs on me years ago, I just never realized it.

"I mean, some of the other kids in the van were. You could hear them yelling as the guards dragged them out of their houses. And some of them looked stunned, tears streaming down their faces while they got handcuffed to the van seats. But I just kept thinking, 'Of course.'

"It's just that Dad and I *never* got along. Even when I was little, before the war, we always moved around for his job and he was never home . . ."

I let Kel's stream of words anchor me. My whole life, people had glanced at me and turned away. Whatever they saw in my eyes was enough to frighten them off. But with the wall, everything was different. Every word Kel spoke seemed to cinch us closer and closer together.

"I guess he never really got me, you know? I'm not sure anyone did, except Mom. And then . . . well . . ." Kel's voice went quiet. "She died. Cancer."

I pressed my hand into the wall. "I'm sorry."

Kel's faint humming filled the dark again, a melancholy song that wrapped around me like a blanket. I breathed it in along with Kel's spicy scent.

Kel stopped mid-hum, as if embarrassed about a bad habit, and picked up the conversation again.

"Thanks. It's okay. Well, it's not. But that's what we're supposed to say, right?" His words tumbled out in a rush. "After Mom died, the whole world went to shit. Then I got sick too, and, well, maybe Dad just couldn't do any more hospitals or doctors."

Then Kel's voice went hard and scary. "Like I could?" And a sudden blow struck the wall between us.

I jerked in alarm, crashing my head into the platform I was lying under.

"Shit!" Our voices chorused in the darkness. A bark of laughter came from the other side. Or was it anger?

"Sorry," we both said. And he laughed again. A real one, this time.

"Wow." The anger was gone from Kel's voice. "That really hurt my hand. What's that they say about an irresistible force meeting an immovable object?"

I rubbed the sore spot on my head. "Maybe you're not as irresistible as you thought."

"Ouch, that stings worse than my fist."

It was like learning a new language, this back and forth. Kel's voice was sad and rough and funny all at the same time, and it made me want to tell him things. Things that had been chasing their tails around and around inside of me for as long as I could remember. But it wasn't something I'd ever done before. I wasn't even sure I knew how.

The scrape and shush of Kel settling on the other side of the wall filled the quiet, and I held my breath. Waiting for him to speak.

But instead he started humming to himself again. The closeness was intoxicating, even with the wall. Or rather, because of it. I knew only too well what would happen if it wasn't there. He'd stay away like everyone else.

Still, I ached for it to be real. So I took a deep breath and started talking.

"My dad told me we were just looking around." I blurted it out and rolled right into the next sentence, afraid to stop now that I'd started. "Then he dumped me here. And my mom didn't even bother coming to say good-bye."

"Did they say why?" The question hovered between us. Kel was looking for his own answers. But I could only give him mine.

"I'm different."

"Everyone is," he interrupted.

He thought I meant cheerleader versus art nerd kind of different. Not letter jacket versus straitjacket.

"No, I'm—" I'd never tried to explain before. Not to my parents, not to counselors, definitely not to other kids.

This must be what confession is like.

"I see things sometimes. Stuff other people don't see."

A heavy silence filled the tiny room, choking me. *I should've kept my mouth shut.*

"Like you imagine things?" he asked warily.

"No. Not imagining."

How can I expect him to understand when I don't?

But he was still listening, and that in itself was something. "One day at school, last spring, I was standing by my locker. Everyone was laughing and shouting and elbowing each other. They were swarming through the hallway like rats, and suddenly, I couldn't stand it anymore. I had to get out of there."

I felt the same anxiety now, just talking about that day. The same need to breathe fresh air. To see the sky. That morning, I'd bolted for the nearest stairway, my sandals smacking up the steps all the way to the roof, the door slamming shut behind me.

It'd just rained, purging nearby Pittsburgh of its perpetual film of smoke and soot. Leaving us with one of those shimmering days that had been getting rarer and rarer.

"Up on the roof, the sky was so clear that I could pick out the glare of beat-up solar arrays on the other side of the Monongahela River. The river was all yellow foam and mud, but all I wanted to do was follow it somewhere else."

Kel started singing the same tune he'd been humming, the words carrying softly through the wall. "I wish I had a river . . . I could skate away on. I wish I had a river so long . . ."

The song tremored through me and I was lost in my memory. The dying river. The dirty city laid out in front of me. It wasn't just that I'd wanted to get away from there. I'd searched the blue horizon, looking for something. Hungry for something I didn't even understand.

"What happened?" His voice came through the hole and latched on to me again. Tethering me to the now.

"It was the first warm day we'd had, and I splashed through puddles up on the roof. I remember thinking how good the water felt on my toes."

I also remembered thinking that it smelled like the ocean, even though I wasn't sure how I could know what the ocean smelled like. And I heard the steady rhythm of the waves.

"Then, somehow, there was water everywhere, pouring in around me. I screamed and—"

The fear of that first vision was still with me. I hadn't slept in days. All week I'd been avoiding the dreams, but up there on the roof, I could feel them waiting for me. I still didn't know what the trigger was—the airless hallways or splashing through that puddle or how tired I was—but the indigo waves came, vivid and dangerous. Pulling me into a waking nightmare.

Just like today, I'd gasped for breath, drowning under the weight of all that water. Then a hand had grabbed my arm. The water disappeared and a fireman hauled me over his shoulder and lugged me down a ladder. The whole school was out there by then, along with the fire trucks and flashing lights, catching it all with their cell phones. I instantly went from being an invisible freak to a celebrity freak. And it wasn't a good change.

"After the fire truck showed up and they'd dragged me down, people just kept asking me, over and over, 'Why do you want to kill yourself?' And over and over, I told them that I'd just wanted to find somewhere quiet, where I could hear myself. But no one would listen."

Another Holbrook Academy brochure had showed up that same

day. I remembered staring at it in a stack of mail on the counter, mixed in with the phone bill and our ration receipts, while Mom and Dad asked the same questions again and again. My parents latched on to that brochure like it was a godsend. I should've known then that my refusal wasn't going to stop them.

"A couple of years ago, Dad and I stopped talking and I took off for a while." Kel's words had an edge to them, and I guessed there was a lot more to the story than he was telling.

Where does someone go when they "take off"?

"There was this old building I camped out in. At sunset, I'd climb up to the roof. And I'd stand right at the edge, looking at all those desperate people down in the filthy streets. Kids huddled around smoky fires. Scroungers knifing each other over trash."

I had my answer. No one went to the cities anymore, unless they had no place else to go.

It'd been years since my family went to Pittsburgh even though it was only twenty miles away. The closest I got was clips on the news about riots or raids on the hospitals. Now I thought past Kel's voice whispering to me through the darkness. *Who is this guy?*

Then I pictured him again, up on the roof, like me. He stood alone at the brink. Looking down into his own hell. And for the first time, I wanted this wall between us to disappear. I wanted to tear it down myself.

Kel went on, his voice sharpening into a kind of savageness. "All those people scurrying around. Did they really think there was any-where better to go? I'd look at them down there and tell myself, *Just one more step.*"

Then Kel's voice broke and the air resonated with his song again. "I wish I had a river so long. I would teach my feet to fly."

Kel held on to the last note, his rough voice easing off of it. Letting it fade into the darkness.

Then Kel laughed. A solid, normal sound. "Please tell me they blew up one of those giant cushion thingies for you to jump on."

It took me a second to figure out he was talking about me, up on the school roof. Shaking off the misery I'd heard in his voice, I played along. "Sorry to disappoint. No cushion thingy. But I did ride in an ambulance."

Kel laughed again, low and soft. "You make me feel like I should throw a car chase or something into my story. Though I did have a little excitement. I was a little, um . . . irritated when I got here this afternoon. I think I might have punched one of the . . . what do they call them? Caretakers?"

"I think just 'Takers' might be more appropriate."

"Takers. I like that."

Then something else Kel had said caught up with me. "Afternoon?"

"What?"

"You said you were angry when you got here this afternoon."

"Yeah. What about it?"

My mind raced. If the sun had come up around six, that meant Dr. Mordoch would've put me in here around seven this morning, eight tops. But I couldn't have been in Solitary for more than a couple hours.

"What time is it?"

"I don't know. They took my cell phone. Maybe four o'clock?"

Nine hours. I'd been in here for nine hours. The blackness and heat closed back in on me. I braced myself on the wall.

It's time. A prickly shiver spider-walked its way up my spine. I could feel the waves coming back for me. The drumbeats in my head.

"Faye?" Kel's voice was distant now. "You still there? Talk to me."

I could hear his voice, but I couldn't answer. I was doing battle with the darkness. Kel knocked again and the joke came back to me. *So crazy So crazy So crazy.*

No. I wasn't going to do this.

There was the scraping sound of a key in the lock. I sat up, hitting my head on the platform again in a bright flash of pain. I scrambled out and across the floor, pressing myself against the wall as the door swung open. Not wanting to give Kel away.

I blinked into the sudden light, welcoming the ache. Dr. Mordoch came into focus. "Have you reflected on your situation? Faye, do you want Holbrook to help you?"

I nodded. *I've got to get out. I've already lost a day in this place.*

"I need to hear that you are willing to try, Faye, before I can trust you again. Do you want to try?"

"Yes." My voice came out strong. My throat ached as I thought about Kel, alone on the other side of the wall. But me staying here wasn't going to help him. And what if they came for him too? *Then I'd lose him anyway.*

"Yes, what?"

"Yes, I want to."

"I believe you, Faye." Dr. Mordoch sounded pleased. "Let's go to dinner, then. I'll let you sit with the rest of your Holbrook Family Unit."

"Thank you."

She'd locked me in the dark and I said thank you.

7

THE STINK OF CAFETERIA FOOD assaulted my nose as I entered the long, thin room that must've once been a ballroom. Rather than risk me exploding, Dr. Mordoch had been generous enough to let me use the facilities before dinner. So the dining room was already packed with misfits. Too fat. Too scrawny. Too angry. The kind that usually populate the neglected corners of lunchrooms.

But unlike a normal school cafeteria, there was no talking. No food on the tables. Nothing but me, weaving my way through the hushed room, looking for my seat. Well, nothing but me and a hundred other students watching and waiting. Even the dim light of the old-fashioned chandeliers did nothing to shield me. I kept my eyes glued to the round, wooden tables. After everything else that'd happened today, I had no desire to see other people's secrets.

Finally, I found my assigned table and the rest of "Family Five." I recognized the pudgy kid (Zach, I think) that I'd seen from the roof that morning. He was wearing a T-shirt, with a backward Superman emblem on it, that was big even for him. Like he was hoping to get lost in it.

There was an empty chair on either side of him. To his left, a girl with hennaed hair and plaster-white skin had her feet kicked up on one of them. She made no effort to move. In fact, she ignored me with a studied "fuck-you" attitude. I had the urge to yank it out from under her feet, but with the entire room staring at me, I thought better of it.

I pulled out the other chair, wincing as it grated against the polished floor. Thunder in the oppressive silence. Zach winced too, glancing up at me. He was definitely zoned out on something, the puffy skin under his eyes mimicking the same bruised blue of his glassy irises. I recognized the self-loathing in his eyes before they darted away from mine.

Zach hurried to scoot over, as if sparing me the unpleasantness of being close to him. But his chair rammed into the one next to him, causing a loud thud and knocking the girl's feet off of it. She glared and Zach flinched, shutting off his whole face.

"Welcome to Holbrook Academy." Dr. Mordoch's voice boomed across the room as soon as I sat down. Her podium and the teachers' tables sat on a short platform at the other end of the hall. I recognized Nurse, her pinched face matching her voice, sitting at one of the tables behind Dr. Mordoch. "Whether you know it or not, each one of you is at a critical turning point. If you are willing, there is still time to turn back from the terminal paths you have chosen. But Holbrook is your last chance. In the peace of these woods, we can lead you back to society, show you how to assimilate, nurture appropriate behavior. But if you turn your back on this final opportunity, the rest of the world will not be so kind."

I wasn't sure who she was talking to. The tense faces around the room knew better than to expect kindness. I stole a glance at the rest of my table.

I wasn't the only one looking. The henna-haired girl couldn't keep her eyes off the guy next to her. He definitely had the tortured, angry thing going for him. His skin was the color of raw sienna, and against his black hoodie, black fingerless gloves, and black hair, it practically glowed. Making him beautiful and fierce at the same time.

The guy on my right wasn't bad to look at either. But where the hoodie guy was stretched thin and taut, this guy was all shoulders and chest and arms. His tan T-shirt tucked into camo pants made me think Marines. Without really looking, he gave me a subtle nod. The gesture was restrained, just like the rest of him. Hands resting flat on the table. Body perfectly straight and still in his chair. Even his hair was buzzed into submission. Like sketched charcoal against the burnt umber of his face.

"The people at your table will be your Family for the next semester. You're all newcomers here, and your Family will be your support as you find your way. They will be your peers, your disciplinarians, and your counselors."

How could these four strangers be my family? There was still an empty chair at the table, and I wondered what'd happened to the missing person. Were they locked up in Solitary? Was Kel still there too? Alone in the dark? I scanned the faces around the room, wondering if I'd somehow know him if I saw him.

"Tomorrow you'll meet each other, but tonight you will sit quietly and eat. In order to focus our minds and learn discipline, meals are to be completely silent. As Buddha said, 'Do not dwell in the past, do not dream of the future, concentrate the mind on the present moment.' To that end, here at Holbrook, you will not be distracted by what to wear, what music to listen to, or how to spend your time. There will be no communication with your families or friends outside this school. No phone calls. No letters. No e-mails."

"Eff that." The henna-haired girl dug her chin into her sternum as she muttered to herself. Anger made her pale face even paler. Her heavy eyeliner popped bold against her skin, but did nothing to hide her radiating insecurity. As the girl continued her inaudible tirade, she kept tugging on the sleeve of her homemade T-shirt, which declared in dripping, red letters, MEAT IS MURDER!

All around my table and the rest of the cafeteria, it was clear that other students were also stunned by this declaration. Chairs creaked, feet shuffled, and a low murmur rippled through the room.

"That will be the only time I am interrupted, or there will be no dinner. Am I clear?" Dr. Mordoch looked around as if daring us to try her.

Only one person in my "family" hadn't reacted. Across from me, the guy in the black hoodie and leather gloves was an island unto himself. He just sat staring at the table, arms tight across his chest, shaggy hair shadowing his eyes, hands balled into fists. He must have been roasting in his baggy sweatshirt, but he didn't seem to notice.

I checked out the rest of the room, trying to spot Rita, but I didn't see her long braid anywhere. Soft clinks and thumps interrupted the silence as the Takers arrived with plates of soggy, canned corn and steaming meat loaf. It was clear that Dr. Mordoch liked to put on a show. Pricey meat. Zen quotations. But like the open fences from last night, I bet we'd be in for more rude awakenings.

Next to me, Zach picked up his fork. Out of nowhere, the guy in the hoodie shot out his long arm and grabbed Zach's fist, crushing Zach's pudgy hand inside his gloved one.

What the hell?

Zach froze, panic making his eyes way too big in his pasty face. He tried to pull away, but the guy in the hoodie just squeezed tighter, his long brown fingers smashing the plastic prongs of the fork into Zach's pale ones.

Everyone in the "family" watched the drama, following Hoodie

Guy's gaze across the room to where two Takers were closing in on a girl. She was eating quickly, shoveling food into her mouth. One of the Takers laid a hand on the girl's shoulder while the other took away her still-full plate.

"Hey! I was—" Her words were cut off as they yanked her from her seat and dragged her from the room. Zach, eyes still wide, nodded gratefully to Hoodie Guy. His gloved hand released its grip and then he crossed his arms again. As if nothing had happened.

The whole table seemed to let go of the breath we'd been collectively holding. For a minute, we'd all been on the same side. Hating the Takers. Relieved it hadn't happened to us. Then the moment was over and everyone was lost in their own heads again. But it'd happened.

Zach stared red-faced at the table, looking like he was trying to keep a grip on himself. Meat-Is-Murder Girl glowered at her plate. Only the Marine guy next to me was still looking around the table. He studied Hoodie Guy, as if calculating a detailed risk assessment.

The Marine was huge, a solid wall of muscle, but in a fight, I'd put my odds on the guy in the hoodie. A kind of feralness was drawn into the angles of his clenched jaw. It was quietly traced into his tight fists. It was the line that pulled his whole body together.

Dr. Mordoch's voice cut across my thoughts. "Look carefully around your tables. Each of you is projecting an image of who you are to the world. A cool kid. A rebel. A dropout." She pointed at different kids as she talked. "By tomorrow, this facade will be stripped away. If you are open, if you are strong, if you can pull together as a Family, you will thrive and make different choices. If not . . . well, it'll be a difficult year."

Dr. Mordoch finally gave the order to begin eating and the sound of chewing mouths filled the room. I took one bite and gagged. Not as pricey as I'd thought. But I forced down more of the salty meat-mush anyway, trying to fill my empty stomach. Next to me, the Marine did the same. Zach, appearing to have lost his appetite, smashed corn kernels into oblivion. The guy wearing the hoodie and gloves jabbed his fork dangerously at the meat loaf, like he was daring it to start something. But Meat-Is-Murder Girl didn't even pretend to eat. She raised her hand high in the air.

Either no one saw her or, more likely, she was being ignored. This was not the unquestioning discipline Dr. Mordoch had asked for, so it simply wasn't happening. But the girl kept her hand up anyway, a stony look on her face. After a few minutes, she spoke up. She started quietly.

"Excuse me."

Forks stopped mid-bite, and mouths mid-chew.

Dr. Mordoch got up slowly from her table and went to the microphone, motioning for the Takers to hold their positions along the wall.

"I believe I made myself clear about our no-talking policy." Dr. Mordoch gave a plastic smile, then turned back to her seat.

"I don't eat meat." The girl was speaking louder now, her voice carrying across the dining room.

Dr. Mordoch swiveled back to the microphone. "You will eat what you are given, when you are given it. End of discussion."

Evidently not.

Meat-Is-Murder Girl was yelling now. "I won't! Do you know how much more energy it takes to raise a cow than soybeans? I do! All that cattle feed. All those fields that could be used to grow crops. Gallons of water. Gasoline. And the feds just turn a blind eye so that rich kids can have their meat loaf. While we're tucking in our napkins and licking our lips, people are starving. Packed into cities, living off garbage and pathetic federal 'supplements.' I won't eat corrupt, murdered flesh."

"Then you will not eat. It makes no difference to me." Dr. Mordoch nodded at Freddy and he sprang into action, heading for the girl.

The girl dropped her head again. I thought she was giving up, but instead she grabbed her plate and hurled it to the floor. The heavy plastic clattered loudly, food flying everywhere.

Five or six other Takers followed Freddy now, moving in on our table. They moved slowly, almost casually, basking in the anxiety that saturated the room. The girl narrowed her eyes at them and then, tensing her too-skinny body, jumped onto her chair and up onto the table.

"The government is subsidizing the rich while the voiceless get trampled. While animals are getting slaughtered. Well, I have a voice! Meat is murder! Meat is murder!" she chanted, stomping her feet in time.

The room watched the girl silently as the distance closed between her and the Takers. Most people had probably already witnessed Holbrook's own unique brand of discipline or experienced it first-hand. They weren't about to miss the drama.

"Family Five may be excused," Dr. Mordoch said calmly into the microphone.

No one at my table moved. No one even knew what was going on.

"These are the Consequences. Caretakers, please escort them back to their rooms. From this point forward, Family members stay together."

I gazed longingly at my meat loaf jiggling with the rhythm of Meat-Is-Murder Girl's stamping feet. It was far from appetizing, but I hadn't eaten since yesterday. More Takers pulled away from their ranks along the wall and headed for us. With a slow, twisted smile, Hoodie Guy flexed his hands and stood up, stomping his feet in time.

Amid the chaos, the Marine went back to emptying his plate.

One efficient forkful at a time. But Zach glanced nervously at the Takers flocking toward us. Then, he looked up at Hoodie Guy with a kind of reverence. The possibility of a fight had loosened up Hoodie Guy, who'd uncrossed his arms and uncurled his fists. But it did the opposite to Zach. Zach's bulky body went rigid and he nodded to himself as he physically pushed himself up out of his chair. Despite his obvious terror, Zach shifted back and forth in his own lock-kneed version of stomping. I was impressed.

"Don't you see you're devouring the Earth?" Meat-Is-Murder Girl pointed to a guy at the table next to us with gravy dribbling down his chin. "We've squeezed our planet dry. Stomped the hell out of it with our carbon footprint. Sent cow shit and pesticides sludging through our rivers and drinking water."

The girl kicked over her cup for emphasis, spraying the table next to us.

Dragon and her tattooed arms were ten feet and closing now, so I figured I might as well go on my own terms. I stood up, slamming my feet in time with the others. Only the Marine stayed planted in his seat, counting the number of incoming Takers under his breath.

The thumping of our feet egging her on, the girl screamed, "Don't any of you get it? Our world is melting, frying, starving, and suffocating, and you just keep right on chewing. Meat is murder! Meat is murder!"

The Takers tried to wrestle the girl down from the table. Freddy yanked her arm hard and she lost her balance. The Marine jumped out of his chair, cursing, and threw himself toward her flailing body. But he couldn't get around the table fast enough, and she slammed into the stone floor.

A stunned silence fell over the room as we all watched Meat-Is-Murder Girl lying, completely still, on the floor. Then a groan as she struggled to sit up. She looked around her and slowly, amazingly, got to her feet. She replaced the look of shock with a smile and turned to face Dr. Mordoch up at the podium. Gingerly she raised one foot and then the other, stomping out her defiance.

I hesitated for a second, but after all I'd been through that day, her pounding feet made my heart thud with rebellion. I stomped as the Takers grabbed us. The others joined in as we were shoved and herded into a line. The Marine and Meat-Is-Murder Girl in front. Then me and Zach and Hoodie Guy behind him. They marched us out of the room, our shouts competing with the Takers' commands.

"Meat is murder! Meat is murder!"

I'd been lied to, threatened with pepper spray, and locked in the dark. What more could they do to me?

8

NEVER, NEVER, NEVER ask that question.

As soon as the Takers maneuvered our line out of the cafeteria, Meat-Is-Murder Girl let out a wailing scream. I didn't know what'd happened. Only that the girl was on her knees. Then I saw the Taser.

"Get up." Freddy stood leering over her.

So the Takers weren't carrying guns, just Tasers and pepper spray. *How humane.* The girl didn't move, and he shocked her again. She shrieked and curled up in a ball.

"Stop!" I shouted.

Another, lower voice crisscrossed my own. "Stop! You're hurting her!"

Kel. It was Kel's voice coming from right behind me.

I spun around, looking for him, just as a jolt of electricity hit me square in the shoulder. The Taser filled my world with pain and I dropped slo-mo. My body was still turning as my knees gave way. I saw Kel, one piece at a time, as I fell. Dark hair tumbling across his face. Hands hidden in gloves. Thin shoulders beneath a black hoodie. And his eyes.

Deep brown eyes, spiderwebbed with green. I cringed as they met mine, ready to see the usual flicker of revulsion and fear. But his eyes held on to me, like his voice had in Solitary.

I wish I had a river so long. I would teach my feet to fly.

His hand reached out for me, trying to catch me. But he'd been tased too. Our fingertips brushed against each other as we fell, and a sharp ache filled my hand where he'd touched me. My knuckles suddenly stiff and swollen. My skin stinging. Then the pain was eclipsed as my whole body smashed into the floor. Nothing but deadweight.

My muscles, my brain, my mouth . . . Nothing would work. Kel hit the floor an arm's length away. Deep lines of pain cut across his frozen face. The flecks of green in his eyes flared with the same strange agony I'd felt when he'd touched me.

Then his eyes cleared. Immobilized on the floor, we stared at each other and the questions flew out of my mind. It was more intoxicating than I'd ever imagined to have someone look at me like that. To let me see into them without flinching.

All the things Kel had told me in Solitary—his father, the kidnapping, standing on the roof—were embodied in front of me. How had I not recognized him earlier, sitting at the table? The same sardonic edge in his voice was mapped into his angular face. Rage barely hidden in his eyes. His mouth turned up a little at one corner, fully aware of the irony of our situation.

It was like we were right back in Solitary. We were lying on the floor, inches apart. But still separated.

Sensations started returning in strange bursts. The musty smell of the stone floor. Distant shouts. Scuffed boots coming closer. The world sped up again, and we were yanked to our feet. I was pulled to the front of the line and Kel to the back. But my eyes stayed glued to him, still fitting the voice from the dark with the person in front of me.

Kel's stark face was framed by coal-black hair that made me think of ravens. His lips were pale against his brown skin, and his nose was a little crooked, like it'd been broken in a fight. But it was his dark hazel eyes that I couldn't look away from.

I wasn't used to people meeting my eyes. And Kel didn't just look at me. He looked *into* me, like he could see every thought in my head. And whatever he saw there now, he must have liked. He gave me a slow smile that made me blush.

Then the line pushed forward, and I tripped over my own feet. The Marine reached out to steady me, and I pulled my attention back, nodding my thanks. We moved forward as a group again. *Well, we're pulling together as a "family," just not quite the way Dr. Mordoch imagined.* Half stumbling, half dragged, I led our perverse parade down the path to the dorms.

Back in my room, a pair of fluorescent orange jumpsuits greeted me, laid out neatly on the two beds. Other than the hideous outfits, the room was empty.

"They took it," I mumbled, feeling numb to any more surprises. And I'd thought there was nothing left for them to take.

With my last ounce of energy, I searched the room. Under the bed, in the desk, in the bathroom, everywhere. But I already knew my sketchbook was gone.

Something inside of me shattered. I crawled onto the bed, letting the tears that had been building for the last twenty-four hours burn down my cheeks. *Fine. They win.*

The lock clicked and the door opened. Meat-Is-Murder Girl, holding an ice pack on her arm, was "helped" into the room by Nurse.

"Get changed," she ordered. Nurse was the same height as

Meat-Is-Murder Girl but her cropped hair and rigid stance made her much more intimidating. "Both of you."

"Where's my sketchbook?" I didn't bother to wipe the tears off my cheeks.

Nurse stone-faced me, not meeting my eyes. "I'm not here to answer your questions. Now both of you, get changed and hand me your clothes."

"The hell I will." This girl wouldn't give up that easy. But after Solitary, after getting tased, after Kel's look had split me open, I didn't have anything left to fight with.

"If you don't start changing in the next thirty seconds, I'll come over there and help you." I could see the Taser peeking out of her pocket. Meat-Is-Murder Girl scowled and grabbed a jumpsuit, heading for the bathroom.

"No," Nurse said. "Change out here where I can make sure you don't hide anything from your pockets."

The girl, who thirty seconds earlier had been gearing up for battle, now skulked into a corner. Facing the wall, she went through an elaborate maneuver of changing into the jumpsuit while keeping her other clothes on as long as possible.

Her humiliation was palpable, and I turned around to give her privacy while I stripped to my underwear. The woman could've just as easily checked our pockets, but the goal was obviously to degrade us. To leave us with nothing. And there wasn't anything we could do about it.

The jumpsuit chafed as I pulled it on. The cheap fabric was stiff, and the huge zipper running up the front scratched my skin.

"Now take this." Nurse handed us each a pill.

I swallowed it without a word. It would almost be a relief to get away from this place and these people. But there was no escape yet.

Nurse pulled my jaw open and squeezed my cheeks, "checking for compliance."

"Lights out in five," she snapped, grabbing our bundles of clothes. With a loud click the door shut and locked behind her.

"I'm getting out of this Nazi camp tomorrow." Meat-Is-Murder Girl had also swallowed the pill, but her hard eyes hadn't lost their defiance. It was only a matter of minutes.

"I all— I all—" My throat clamped shut in frustration. I started again. "I already tried."

"Yeah?"

"Yeah. Razor wire and cameras." I glanced over at the window I'd climbed out of the night before. Four shiny new nails had been hammered into the frame so it wouldn't open anymore. We were stuck.

The lights flicked off and back on again. There weren't any light switches or small lamps in our room. Just the main fluorescent light in the middle of the ceiling, with no way to control it.

Meat-Is-Murder Girl yanked the covers off the bed and dumped them on the floor. Even though it was dark outside, it hadn't cooled off. She sprawled on the mattress, her frizzy, reddish hair spread in an arc around her head.

"I'm Maya."

"Faye."

"Why'd you do that?" She stared up at the ceiling, glaring at it.

"What?" I looked around, trying to figure out what I was being accused of.

"You and that freak with the gloves. You got yourselves tased." Maya propped herself up on her elbow, waiting for my answer. She aimed her glare in my direction, and all her grief, all her outrage at the unfairness of life, hit me in the gut. And as I read it in her eyes, the pain was fresh to her as well. Shuddering, Maya dropped her gaze to the faded sheets.

I sat down on the bed, trying to clear the flood of emotions from my head. Trying to figure out how to answer her. A mosquito bit me, and I swatted and missed. My head still throbbed from the jolt of electricity. I pictured Kel, his eyes holding me even as I fell.

Why did we try to stop the guards? Maya was right. We didn't know her, didn't owe her anything. But she'd had no one else. How could I explain my sense that we were already tied together in this place? Finally, I turned toward Maya and shrugged.

She shrugged back, like this made as much sense as anything else at Holbrook. "What's wrong with you?"

I wasn't used to people my age asking questions or even talking to me. I pretended to be busy arranging my sheets. Was it so obvious that I was broken? Well, I guess we'd all been sent here for some reason. Judging by Maya's fit tonight, she most likely had "problems with authority." I was probably going to have this conversation over and over again at Holbrook, and I was already tired of it. What could I say? *My parents think I'm crazy?*

"I get these panic attacks."

"No, stupid. Why are you wearing dead cow on your feet? You know there used to be National Forests in this country? National Parks too. After the Peak War started, they cleared them all. Some they strip-mined for coal. Some they cut down for wood. But some they clear-cut for cattle, to replace the meat and leather they couldn't import anymore. God forbid we stop killing animals. Or that you have to go without."

I looked down at my hiking boots, the only clothes of mine I still had, besides my underwear. *We've just been tased and she's worried about my shoes? Unbelievable.*

"Why do you even care?"

"Because someone has to." Maya's voice was quiet, and she stared down at her empty hand like she was looking for something she'd lost. Then her face went stony again and her words came out in a long tirade.

"Because no one else is even thinking about how screwed we are. You think cellophane-wrapped meat just magically appears in your fridge? You think ninety-degree weather in September is normal for Maine? You think it's okay for people to wipe their asses with thousand-year-old trees. No!" Maya shouted the last part, sitting straight up in bed.

I hadn't ever heard anyone talk like this before. I mean, I'd heard about rumors of sabotage from Greenpeace extremists, but they never showed that stuff on TV. Everyone at the Cooperative, my parents, teachers, kids at school, acted like this was all just a temporary glitch. For now we'd throw up some windmills and combine our food resources, but soon we'd win the war and there'd be plenty of oil again.

My dad still talked about going back to the city to work at his PR firm. My mom insisted that once the Cooperatives turned back into suburbs, the housing market would be the first thing to rebound. She'd look around the neighborhood and say, "They'll be clamoring for realtors once this is all over, and I'll be back in business! Some people just hate staying put."

But nothing ever got better. When oil peaked out and China started hoarding barrels, the news channels said it was just a phase. When war broke out, the President said it was a strategic strike. Now, four years later, the Peak War was still going strong and everything that could be used for energy in this country had been drilled and mined and slashed. Maya's rhetoric sounded a little crazy, but maybe it was saner than everything else.

"The Earth's been raped and the Cooperatives are pretending it's business as usual. A water quota here, a food ration there. Just bribe enough people and keep quiet and hope it won't affect you. But it will. Because no matter how much money you have, no matter how deep you bury the problem, it'll never go away. You know what it took to raise that cow?"

She jabbed her finger at my leather boots and started rattling off facts. "Too much! Enough water to float a destroyer. Not to mention twenty-five hundred pounds of corn, three hundred and fifty pounds of soybeans, and a ton of black market gasoline to haul all that crap around. And after all that, let's not forget they murdered the innocent animal. All so you could strut around covered in skin while people in the cities starve."

Strut around? Maybe. Maya's rhetoric was getting muddled in my drugged-out brain. Murdered animals, government bribes, starving people, the screwed-up environment. I wasn't sure I got what she was saying, but what kept sticking in my mind were the news reports I'd seen of Pittsburgh. It was like a war zone there. Scared kids, gaunt faces, and all that anger. "They don't have to stay there."

Disgust registered on Maya's face. "Right. 'Cause I'm sure your Cooperative is throwing open its doors, offering to share its wealth. Just because there aren't any fences keeping people in the cities doesn't mean they have a choice."

Kel's words echoed in my head: *Did they really think there was anywhere better to go?*

I couldn't process all this. My whole body ached from the day. Every inch of me was sticky from the heat. My muscles burned, bruises throbbed. I rubbed my hand.

Was I imagining it? Or was it still sore from where Kel had touched me? A woozy feeling swept over me as I untied my boots. I shut my eyes and all I could see was Kel. The ache of his eyes cutting into me. The drugs were really kicking in now.

I shoved the offending boots under my bed and searched my blurry mind for anything I could say to shut Maya up.

"Um . . . sorry" was all that came out.

"Save it for the cow."

I can't take this. Not after today.

I crawled into bed, and turned my face to the wall just as the room went dark.

9

THE FLOOR WAS GRITTY and hard under my body. Despite the stifling heat of the room, my teeth chattered. I wasn't in bed, and my jumpsuit was soaked with sweat. I must've had one hell of a nightmare.

The overhead lamp buzzed on and I covered my eyes, blocking out the gloomy fluorescent light. There was a steady *shunk-shunk* noise of bolts being unlocked, and a loudspeaker crackled on.

"You girls have ten minutes to be in the shower room at the end of the hall," Nurse's pinched voice squawked through the intercom. "Anyone who's late will be scrubbing out toilets during Free Time. Understood?"

My hands. My hands were covered in red. Not a bright stop-sign red or an orangey clown red. It was the terrible brown red of blood. The whorls of my fingerprints stood bold against the deep crimson. I'd fallen out of bed before, lots of times, but *this? This* was new. *What's going on?*

I looked over at Maya's bed, but she wasn't in it. Instead, she was sprawled, unmoving, on the floor on the other side of the room. The same red smudged and streaked the floor between us.

I stared down at my red hands.

No. I couldn't have. I crawled toward her, trying to make out the rise and fall of her chest. Daring myself to touch her foot. To wake her up. But I couldn't make myself.

"Tell me you're not sitting there watching me sleep."

I choked back a yelp. Maya's voice was muffled by her arm, but she was very much alive. "I'm going to count to sixty, and when I open my eyes, you'd better be gone."

I forced out a breath I didn't know I was holding. *I don't know what I've done, but not that. Never that.*

Maya pushed herself up on one arm. "What the hell? Is this some kind of hazing?"

She pushed the bushy hennaed hair out of her eyes. Her fingers left a smear of red across her face, and I saw, with a strange sense of relief, that Maya's hands were also stained with red.

"I woke up on the floor too. I don't know what happened." It was true, I didn't know. But I also didn't mention that the window was open a crack. Which was impossible, since they'd nailed it shut yesterday.

Something happened to us last night. Something bad. I didn't know if it was the drugs or this creepy school, but somehow, without either of us remembering, we'd gotten out of our sealed room. Or someone else had gotten in.

Maya scrutinized me. But when I met her eyes, I saw that she was scared too. She twitched and dropped her gaze to the linoleum. Then, just as quickly, she stood up and circled around the red blotches on the floor. Her voice quivered just the tiniest bit. "What *is* it?"

I'd thought they were just random smears, but there, in a sea of smudged red handprints, was a rough design. My lungs cinched tight as I asked myself the same question.

The picture reminded me of something, but I couldn't quite place it. The music I'd heard up on the roof drifted into my head.

"Is it a bird, maybe?" Maya squinted down at the design and I saw what she meant.

From this direction, it looked a little like the way kids draw birds flying through the air. A V-shaped body with two lines for wings coming out on either side.

Tilting my head, I looked at it the other way around. "Maybe a mountain?"

Or some sort of symbol? A chill of recognition gripped me. I tried to focus on the shape, but as I reached for it, the memory disintegrated. Like scraps of a nightmare in the morning sunshine.

Footsteps smacked down the hallway. Girls running to the showers.

"Whatever it is, we'd better clean it up. I don't think they'd believe anything we said, even if we *had* an excuse to give them." Maya stomped into the bathroom and turned on the sink.

I hurried over to the window to shut it. A red handprint smeared the frame, and I laid my hand on top of it. A perfect match.

Somehow I opened the window. Did I draw that symbol too? A hot breeze pushed its way through the narrow opening, carrying the smell of salt and dead fish. A silvery trickle of water spilled over the windowsill.

No. No. No.

For a second I stood frozen, watching the puddle growing on the floor. Shimmering against the pale linoleum. *It's all in your mind. Fear is just an illusion.*

Then I noticed a rusty nail lying on the floor. I spotted three more nearby, bent and tarnished. Nails that were no longer holding the window shut.

Are the nails real? Is the handprint? How can I tell?

That was the scariest part. Knowing that I wasn't sure anymore.

A freezing wave gushed through the window and into the room. I snatched the nails off the floor right before they got swept up in the ice-blue current.

I squeezed my hand tight, feeling the heads of the nails pressing into my skin. They were real. I was real. But I had to find a way to control the water. Before I passed out again. Before Maya decided I was too messed up and reported me. Before I got pulled under.

"I'm in control." Blood rushed through my ears. *Whoosh. Whoosh. Whoosh.* I gripped the nails tighter, the points jabbing my palm. Even though the metal was corroded, I still felt its strength.

"Fear is an illusion."

"Did you say something?" Maya called from the bathroom. Her voice was muted by the spit and splash of water frothing over the windowsill. Churning around my bare feet.

I shivered and focused on the feel of the nails against my fingers. I stood taller, letting the cool steel anchor me to the here and now. "I'm in control."

Outside the window, a wave hovered on the horizon. The color of thunderclouds.

My legs grew steady under me as I conjured images of massive bridges and impenetrable tanks. Hammers rang out against anvils, filling my head with their terrible noise. A strange exhilaration gripped me, and my skin burned. The taste of iron filled my mouth.

"Fear is an illusion," I whispered to myself, hurling the handful of nails out the window. Four shiny flecks of metal caught in the sunlight. A shower of silver tumbling to the ground.

I'm in control. I closed my eyes and slammed the window shut.

"Here." Maya's voice startled me. She stood there with a strange look on her face, holding out a damp clump of toilet paper. The water was gone. No more waves. No puddles. Only the red hand-print broadcasting my guilt.

I snatched the toilet paper from her and turned the print into a red smudge before Maya could make the same connection I had.

While Maya worked on the floor, I went into the bathroom and turned on the faucet as hot as it would go. Dirty, bloodshot water spilled over my hands and swirled pink and gray down the drain. I longed for privacy. A bathroom with a door. A few minutes to pull myself together. But I didn't have any of that. All I had was the minute or two left before we had to be in the showers.

Hurrying, I scoured my already ragged cuticles and scraped at the red grit pushed deep under my fingernails. I scrubbed at my palms with the scalding water. But I could still see the stain.

This isn't going away.

Maya squeezed around me in the tiny bathroom and flushed a clump of pink-tinged toilet paper. "I'm going. Don't want to give them a reason to come in here."

I nodded, brushing dirt off the bottoms of my feet and raking my fingers through my tangled hair. Then I followed her down the hall.

We made it to the showers with only seconds to spare. One other girl slipped in behind us, and I recognized her from the courtyard yesterday morning. Mohawk Girl. Nami, I think that was her name. She looked like she hadn't gotten much sleep, and her blue spiky hair was smushed over to one side.

The rest of the girls from the floor were already lined up outside the shower room. Dragon was there, gripping a stopwatch in her hand. Standing flush against the wall, I hoped to hide my stained hands and dirty feet. I was grateful there was only one dim hallway light.

"We do this seven girls at a time. When it's your turn, strip, put your dirty clothes in this basket, grab a toothbrush set, and go stand under a showerhead." The Taker's bark ricocheted down the narrow hallway. "Your morning routine has been designed by Dr. Mordoch as an exercise in efficiency. You will have exactly two minutes of water for showering and brushing your teeth. Use the soap dispensers on the walls for washing your hair and body. The plastic toothbrushes already have toothbrush powder on them."

I guessed that the timed showers had less to do with us learning efficiency and more to do with water rationing and the high price of heating it. Dragon clicked the stopwatch on and off, in rhythm with her staccato words.

"At the end of the two minutes, you will have three minutes to towel off, put on new underwear and jumpsuits from the cabinet, and exit the room. At the end of the five-minute cycle, the showers will begin again with a new set of girls. The system is on a timer. There will be no exceptions or complaints. Any problem students will be assigned bathroom duty for the rest of the week. Is that clear?"

I counted down the line. I was number nineteen of twenty. While the groups of girls filed in and out of the shower room, my thoughts went back to my fingerprints on the window.

It seemed impossible. First of all, nails don't just rust overnight. Second, no one could've gotten to the nails from outside the window. But then again, how could I have pulled them out? Not to mention balancing across that ledge, climbing down the ladder, and going *wherever* without remembering any of it.

And what about Maya? Had she followed me?

A shiver of fear played down my neck when I thought about the Takers all over Holbrook. *What if we'd gotten caught? What if we did get caught and something happened?* I looked down at my red hands again. Well, if something had happened to one of the guards last night, I was sure to hear about it soon enough.

"I said, next group!" Dragon shoved me, and Maya and I stumbled into the shower room. I pulled off my clothes, plunging them as far down into the dirty-clothes basket as they would go so no one would see the mud on the cuffs. The smell of bleach and mildew made my empty stomach turn. I grabbed a toothbrush packet and splashed over the moist, salmon-colored tile to one of the spigots jetting out of the walls.

Some of the other girls were embarrassed, their arms wrapped across their chests, shielding themselves. But standing next to me, Maya's discomfort went deeper. Shame dragged at her thin body, her hands falling limp at her side. Like she didn't even have enough strength to try to cover herself up.

When the showers finally sputtered on, the tepid water was practically icy on my too-hot skin. The sudden temperature change made me giddy, and when I turned my head into the coolness, water rushed up my nose. Choking, I soaked my hair as fast as possible and pushed the lever of the metal dispenser on the wall. Horrible pink powder spewed out and instantly clumped on my damp hand. My long hair knotted as I tried to work the harsh soap through it.

Across the room, Nami was singing her head off, her voice a sultry hybrid between a growl and a purr. Blue dye splashed against the walls as she flung her hair around to the beat. *Does anything faze that girl?*

"Four minutes left!"

I yanked my fingers through my tangled hair and a twig washed free, riding a current across the floor. It circled around and around the floor drain. Soap stung my eyes, but I ripped the plastic off the toothbrush and shoved it in my mouth. Maya muttered as her toothbrush slipped out of her hand and landed in a pool of congealed soap and hair. Over the sound of the water, I could only make out the words *disposable fuck.*

"Three minutes!" Dragon shouted from the doorway.

The showers trickled off again, leaving me with a mouthful of awful mint powder.

I spit out the gritty paste and surveyed the carnage. There was soap in girls' eyes, in their hair, globbed in gummy piles on the floor. A shrill whistle blasted in our ears.

"Hustle, girls! Get dressed and get out."

We mobbed the basket of tiny, scratchy towels, trying desperately to mop off the crusty soap. I didn't have time to be grossed out by the communal underwear cabinet. I just grabbed a dull gray pair out of the medium section, a pair of socks, and a stretchy exercise-looking bra, throwing them on with a fresh jumpsuit.

"One minute and counting."

I raked a comb through my hair and stole a glance in the mirror. My skin was red from the abrasive soap, and dark half-moons hung under my eyes. *Keep it together, Faye. You haven't even made it to breakfast yet.*

Clumpy oatmeal and gritty orange drink didn't improve anything either. At least there was no bacon, so Maya didn't have to give a repeat performance of last night. Kel, Zach, and the Marine were already sitting at the table, decked out in lime-green jumpsuits. But Kel was still wearing fingerless gloves and the same hoodie pulled over his uniform.

I took the seat I'd had at dinner the night before, between the Marine and Zach. Nami sat down on the other side of Zach. That solved the mystery of the empty chair. Despite her performance in the shower, Nami didn't look so good. Her skin had a sallow tinge to it, and her strip of aquamarine hair was limp and clumped.

No one else looked much better. Whatever Zach had been on yesterday had obviously worn off. Unfortunately, the zoned-out look was replaced by a kind of frenetic energy, his jittering hands and knees vibrating the whole table.

The Marine was missing some of his composure too. Although his body held the same stillness, the calm had evaporated. His eyes roamed around the room as he gulped down aspartame-flavored "juice."

But Kel was the worst. There were purple smudges under his eyes like thumbprints, and the pain I'd felt last night was there in his eyes.

He was the only person in the entire cafeteria wearing any of his own clothes. The lone aberration in the herd of identical jumpsuits. Did he have some kind of pull with Dr. Mordoch? What could he have traded to be able to keep these vestiges of his life?

I flushed, thinking about the things I'd confessed to him in Solitary, the closeness I'd felt. *He wouldn't have—*

But then why the sweatshirt?

Why gloves? They looked like something a guy with a motorcycle would wear, but I couldn't picture that either. Just the tips of his fingers, his red-stained fingernails, were sticking out.

Red-stained fingernails.

Kel had the same red tinge to his fingertips as I did. I caught his gaze from across the table. He was exhausted, but the green in his eyes was still blazing. And the message in them was clear: "*Look!*"

Then slowly, deliberately, he looked around the table.

I watched as the others ate their oatmeal in silence. Picked up their glasses. Wiped their mouths. Maya, Zach, the Marine, and even Nami had the same pink tinge to their hands. And the same half circle of red under their nails. I glanced at the nearby tables, but everyone else's hands were clean. Goose bumps shivered up my neck.

Then, as if there'd been a secret signal, my whole family looked up from their breakfast. Each of them met my eyes, and this time they didn't look away. I saw the usual flicker of fear, and it tremored through me too.

What the hell happened to us?

10

"**WELCOME TO SOCIALIZATION.** Please make a circle on the floor." The teacher's black, curly hair flounced as she unfolded her chair and motioned for us to sit around her.

After breakfast, we'd been marched out to the Knowledge Annex, near the Meditation Center, for our first class of the term. But the only sign that this was a classroom was a chalkboard shoved into one corner.

The teacher smiled with faux warmth as she pulled out a clipboard and a yellow Nerf ball. "We're going to play a little get-to-know-you game."

Everyone arranged themselves neatly in a circle, in the same order as our cafeteria table. Even though we'd known each other for less than twenty-four hours, we were already functioning as a group. Bonded not just by Tasers or forced medication. But by something to hide.

Zach sat on one side of the teacher, so I planted myself cross-legged on the other side of her as she started speaking.

"I'll be your Family's Aunt while you're here at Holbrook Academy. And this is the Speaking Sphere."

I smirked at the pretentious title, for her and for the ball. An almost inaudible snort of laughter echoed my amusement. Kel's eyebrow was arched, a sardonic gleam in his eyes as he met mine. My face threatened to break out into a grin, and I dropped my gaze.

Kel's eyes still weighed on me from two spots away and I could barely listen to what "Aunt" was saying. I concentrated on staring at the faded blue carpet, but my eyes kept being pulled to his hand tapping out a steady rhythm on his knees.

I imagined drawing his fingers, long and graceful, hidden under black leather. His gloves were a little uneven, like he'd cut them off himself, exposing just the very tips stained with red. I shivered as I wondered again what had happened to us the night before.

"Faye, please show me the respect of looking at me." The Aunt's voice jerked me back to reality.

Her scolding tone made my face burn and sent me straight back to elementary school. Teachers were always sending me to the corner for not paying attention. My eyes flitted up to Kel's face. *Or for paying attention to the wrong things.*

I shifted around on the carpet, my jumpsuit already clinging to me in the hot room, and craned my neck to look up at the Aunt and her canary-colored Nerf ball. Our eyes met for a second before she looked away, just long enough for me to be stung by the spitefulness glittering in her black pupils. I definitely didn't want to be related to this woman. Not even in an imaginary, crazy-school way.

"Thank you. When we're in a circle like this, you must be holding the Sphere if you want to talk. Our first exercise goes like this. Each of you will hold the Sphere and say your name, where you're from, and how you're feeling this morning. Like this: I'm Aunt and I'm from New Mexico. I feel excited to be part of a brand-new Family today." As she spoke, she looked around the circle, pausing on each face. When she got to mine, her eyes flickered for an instant, then rushed on.

"That's all there is to it. Easy-peasy. See how I made eye contact with you all as I spoke? Now you try, Zach." Her snub nose crinkled, and she handed him the ball.

"I'm Zach." He gazed around the circle, not quite daring to look in anyone's eyes. He focused just below them, like he had a secret fetish for noses. "And I'm . . . I'm from Indiana . . . Broad Ripple Cooperative."

He squeezed the ball so that it pumped in and out with the same manic energy that ran through his body. "I don't know what else to say. I feel unnerved. No. Discombobulated . . . Yes. That's it."

He shrugged awkwardly and turned to Nami to rescue him.

"I'm Nami and—"

Aunt cut her off. "I'm sorry, dear, but you spoke before you had the Sphere."

Zach looked stricken and shoved the ball into Nami's short fingers.

"Please go to the back of the room and face the wall." Aunt spoke in a friendly voice, the same tone someone uses to say, "Have a nice day."

"Really?" A twitch of amusement streaked across Nami's face. "But don't you wanna hear *all* about me first?"

Aunt examined Nami like she was a bug she'd caught, as if she were deciding how to display this blue-haired specimen in her collection. Finally, Aunt's face resolved into a sympathetic smile.

"I'm sorry, but rules are rules." Like it was completely out of her hands. If I hadn't hated her before, I did now.

"But . . ." Zach's voice cracked. "It was me. I was the one who forgot to give her the ball."

"You can join her, Zach, since you've spoken without the Sphere as well."

Zach's whole body deflated as he looked at the Nerf ball he'd just given Nami, then back at his own empty hands. Nami's half smile turned to ice as she watched Zach crumble. With the same look I'd seen on her face yesterday morning, she let the ball fall out of her hands.

"Oops!" Nami watched the Speaking Sphere roll across the floor, her eyes huge. *The girl's got balls.*

"Pick up the Sphere and bring it here. Then go to the back of the room, before I call a Caretaker to remove you." Aunt never lost her smile as she gave instructions in her even, pleasant tone. "You will both stand facing the wall, spread-eagle. Damion, you look like a military man. Maybe you can show them what I mean."

Aunt looked meaningfully at the Marine. Even I knew what *spread-eagle* meant, but clearly she was fishing for an ally. The guy, Damion, looked uncomfortable being singled out. He stood up anyway, tall and straight, like someone used to taking orders. Not the Holbrook type at all. *What's this guy's story?*

Aunt pointed toward the back of the room. Damion's face looked conflicted, but he obeyed. Striding back there alongside Nami and Zach. She had her first recruit.

Aunt nodded as Damion helped the offenders into the standard pat-down position. Making sure they made a perfect X against the back wall.

"Toes, knees, and nose touching the wall, please," she corrected in a cheery voice.

Damion adjusted Zach's thick limbs until he was awkwardly close to the wall.

"I want you all to understand," Aunt went on, "this is not a punishment. It's a learning tool. Now you'll remember the rules and we can avoid future unpleasantness."

Damion hesitated before putting his hand on Nami's arm. I saw him mouth *"Sorry"* to her as he maneuvered her curvy body into the correct position. Her lips moved in a whisper near Damion's ear and his eyes went wide. He grinned, but the smile fell right off, like he couldn't remember what to do with it. And I was surprised by what was left behind, a raw grief that pulled at every line of his face.

Blinking hard, Damion refocused on his task, bending Nami's knees so they touched the wall. Then a flash of anger passed across his face as he looked at Nami standing there in that uncomfortable pose, nose smashed against the plaster. I didn't want to watch either. It was humiliating.

"Thank you, Damion, that's perfect," Aunt cooed, and he came back to the circle, shooting a worried glance back at Nami. "Let's try again, shall we?"

Aunt handed the Sphere to Maya. Maya held the ball for a second, her fierce eyes suspicious. It was the look she'd given me the night before when she'd asked why Kel and I had gotten tased for her. Remembering our conversation, I answered her look with the same shrug.

She shrugged back at me and in an irritated tone said, "I'm Maya, I'm from Rockport Cooperative, Massachusetts, and I feel like this is bullshit."

An ugly grin passed across Aunt's face so fast I wasn't sure I'd seen it. By the time she'd grabbed the ball from Maya, she was back to her cookie-cutter smile. "Inappropriate language will not be tolerated. You may join Zach and Nami."

Maya thrust her chin out at me and headed to the back of the room. I guessed this was as close as she was going to come to saying thank you for our show of solidarity at dinner the night before.

"You must all learn that here at Holbrook, Consequences are cumulative. Thanks to Maya's misbehavior, those in the back will now be squatting on the floor. Hands clasped behind their backs."

Maya took her place next to the other two as they all rearranged. They hunkered down, weight on their ankles, like someone trying to keep his butt from getting wet on the grass. As Zach put his hands behind his back, he wobbled, fighting to keep his balance. It looked painful.

"I can teach class just as well whether you're all squatting in the back or sitting in a circle." Aunt smiled broadly and sat back in her seat. She was enjoying this, showing us who was in charge.

Not so fast. It was down to Kel, Damion, and me. Kel looked at me, raising his eyebrow in a challenge, and I realized I had something new to lose. My universe of one had expanded, whether I'd wanted it to or not. Kel and I and the rest of this family were stuck together at Holbrook, and after whatever had happened the night before, drawing attention to ourselves was the worst move we could make.

But when I looked back at Kel's sparking eyes, all I wanted to do was join him in rebellion. I wanted to make Holbrook eat it, and with that thought, a little thrill of power shot through me.

The ball was in our court. Literally.

Kel didn't even bother taking the Sphere from Aunt.

"I'm Kel." He made a show of looking me and Damion in the eye while he spoke. "I'm from all over the place, and I feel like squatting."

He walked over to the wall and carefully lowered himself into position. But Aunt had already changed strategies. She knew she had one more shot at stopping the mutiny. With utter solemnity, she offered Damion the ball. As if entrusting him with our future.

He took it, looking uncertain. He stared at the ball as he tossed it up in the air and caught it again. Toss. Toss. Toss. As if it had the right answer.

"Damion?" Aunt pinned him with her eyes.

"I'm Damion." He looked over his shoulder at Nami. His studious frown morphed into a grin as he tossed the ball to me. "I'm from Otis Air Force Base in Cape Cod, Massachusetts," he said, getting up. "And I don't feel like playing ball today."

Aunt looked down at me from her chair. Gone was her amiability. Gone was her nose crinkle. Instead, her taut face had the cruel curl of a smile.

"Think carefully, Faye," she warned me. "Right now, people are just uncomfortable. Sure, they'll have to finish the Consequence that their actions invoked. But when class is over, you can all go to lunch, enjoy the rest of your day, and we can try again next time. On the other hand, if you don't behave, you'll all be staying right here until I'm convinced you understand the lesson."

I just wanted this to be over. To be out of this airless room. Away from this woman.

Gripping the ball, I watched Maya balance awkwardly, shifting her weight from heel to heel. Even though she hadn't understood why Kel and I'd stuck our necks out for her the night before, she'd returned the favor in full. Kel, Nami, and Damion kept their backs straight as they faced the wall. Zach's legs trembled, but he also seemed determined to hold the torturous pose.

"If you disobey, this will become a matter for Dr. Mordoch to settle. Is that what you want?"

No. That is definitely not what I want.

"I'm Faye," I said, and Aunt smiled at me with approval.

I looked around the circle like I was supposed to, but there was no one left to make eye contact with. I dropped the ball and headed over to join my Family.

11

"EVERYBODY ON YOUR FEET." Even facing the wall, I recognized Freddy's growl.

Though I wasn't overjoyed to hear his voice, I was thankful that he'd interrupted Aunt's endless string of words. For the last half hour or so, while our leg muscles turned to jelly and our arms stiffened into agony, Aunt had subjected us to some sort of Holbrook manifesto on how to become a good citizen.

Aunt let out an irritated hiss. "Nobody move a muscle. We're not finished here."

But I couldn't take it anymore. I unclasped my hands and fire shot through my arms. I craned my neck toward the classroom door, wanting to savor the showdown between these two bastards.

"I have orders to collect them," Freddy insisted.

"Well, now you have different orders. Come back in an hour."

We all stayed crouched, but like me, the others flexed their fingers and silently stretched their arms. Only Damion stayed exactly where he was supposed to be.

"Mordoch says to bring all the kids for lunch, and that's what I'm gonna to do."

"Outside." Aunt bit off the word and spat it at Freddy. Her feet clacked across the floor. Then to us she said, "Anybody try anything and you'll be spending class like this for a week."

The door shut, though we could still make out her shrill voice. "How dare you question my authority in front of these children."

Kel let out a groan as he slumped against the wall. He just sat there, staring at the floor, forehead creased, like that threadbare carpet was the most important thing in the world.

My legs trembled and I followed suit, collapsing to the floor in a heap. If we'd get punished together anyway, I might as well be comfortable. Kel's face was gray, and sweat beaded on his upper lip. Everything in me wanted to go over to him, to make sure he was okay, but my body wouldn't seem to move.

Maya was on her feet, grumbling and wincing. "Haven't they ever heard of the Geneva Convention?"

Nami reached out for Maya to help her up. But Maya ignored the gesture, pacing along the back of the room. I wasn't sure if she was clueless or just wasn't quite ready to be a joiner.

Nami got up on her own. With exaggerated care, she brushed dust off the legs of her jumpsuit and patted her hair. Then in a faux-haughty voice she said, "Yeah. I'm definitely not giving this place five stars. And next time, I'm trying out the waterboard facial instead."

Zach snorted, sinking onto the floor with a thump. "Maybe a nice Sodium Pentothal injection? They're supposed to be very soothing."

Nami grinned at him. "I knew that whole deer-in-the-headlights thing was just a ruse."

Zach blushed, then winced as he stretched out his legs, his face going pale. "What do you think they're gonna do to us?"

Maya rounded on him. "Nothing. If they try anything, I'll—"

"You'll what?" Damion, who'd been silent and holding his

position, was suddenly on his feet, right in Maya's face. "You'll throw a fit like last night? Get us all in trouble again?"

Maya involuntarily backed up a step, arms wrapping around herself. There was real fear in her eyes. "What's your problem? I just—"

"You just nothing. Maybe you can all afford to dick around in here, but I can't. From now on we're gonna make nice and do what they tell us. Until—" Damion held out his hands, showing us the red that spiderwebbed across the creases of his palms and stained his dark fingers. "Until we find out exactly what's going on."

His eyes went to the shut classroom door, and for a minute, we all listened to Aunt's shrill outrage battle Freddy's guttural growl.

When Damion spoke again, it was almost in monotone, his voice completely calm. "Last night I fell asleep in bed, locked in our dorm room. This morning I was on the floor, my hands like this. Zach was the same way, sprawled on the linoleum. Like he was dead . . ." Damion's words faded out and his hands shook. He stared at the floor, like he could still see Zach's body. I saw a glimpse of the sadness again as his face froze in a horrified grimace. Like he was trapped in his own nightmare.

Nami stepped between Maya and him. Her arm brushing against Damion's. Somehow, she managed to make the action look both natural and accidental. He came back to himself, and for a moment, they looked at each other. A grateful smile hovering on Damion's lips.

Then his face went serious and he took a very deliberate step away from Nami. "Someone is fucking with us, and until we know what kind of game we're playing, we're going to fall in line. Now, everyone tell me exactly what happened to them last night." He scowled down at Kel. "You start, Hoodie Boy. And you mind telling us why you're the only one here with a stylish wardrobe?"

"Leave it." Kel's eyes blazed with the same buried rage I'd seen in him at dinner the night before.

"Trading favors with Dr. Mordoch? She's a little old for you, but she's probably all you could get."

"I said, leave it." Kel's words were rigid. The same tension filled his body as he sat up straighter, but he didn't move from his spot on the floor.

Damion stayed perfectly still too, but his body practically hummed with adrenaline. Gearing up for a fight.

"Now, now, boys. Play nice." Nami interrupted the standoff. Kel shook his head, slouching against the wall again. Damion relaxed too. As if Nami's voice had pulled them both back from the brink. "I woke up on the floor too, right next to the window. And it was open."

"Ours too." Zach tried to sound nonchalant, but a tremor in his voice betrayed him.

We were all trying hard not to make too big a deal about the night before. I mean, what if it *was* just some sort of hazing?

"Thing is," Nami went on, and now an edge of fear sneaked into her voice too, "I tried to open my window last night, as soon as they moved me from Solitary. The thing was stuck. Painted shut and not even budging. My roommate tried it too. No one could've got that thing open."

I did.

But I kept that to myself. I wasn't about to put myself at the center of this.

Then Maya did it for me. "Anyone else have a creepy drawing on the floor?"

The others looked blank or shook their heads. *Just us, then. Great.*

"What kind of drawing?" Kel's deep hazel eyes were alert, the green sparking in interest.

I thought about the blood-red symbol that'd seemed so familiar. But before I figured out what to say, the door opened.

Damion dropped back into the crouch, whispering, "If any of you did anything to me . . . If I find out it's any of you, I will end you."

Aunt clacked back into the room. "Back into your positions."

Maya took in a sharp breath to say something, but Damion cleared his throat and she closed her mouth.

It really was torture to force our bodies back into that squat. But we sat there while the other students tromped down the hallways to lunch. We sat as the building went silent. We sat there, all our minds wondering about last night. And about what other punishments we'd be facing if someone found out.

Aunt kept on reading Holbrook propaganda. Until our knees were on fire. Our muscles shaking. Until finally the door opened again and I heard Freddy's boots stomp in.

"Hurry up and get in line!" Freddy ordered. "Provided that's okay with Auntie here."

Even facing away from him, I could hear Freddy's sneer when he said "Auntie."

"Of course. I've done all I can for them. They're in Dr. Mordoch's hands now."

Aunt smiled at us as we forced our stiff bodies to stand up. Her joyous expression made me wonder what else we were in for.

"I said, get up." Freddy's big boots made a step toward our Family and I saw the focus of his wrath.

Kel was still on the floor. He'd managed to get out of the crouch, but sat with his back braced against the wall, breathing slowly. Hair fell across his eyes, but it didn't hide the torment contorting his face.

Do it.

Before I lost my nerve, I crossed in front of Freddy and held out my hand to Kel. My fingers slid over his, interlacing with his gloved ones. And again, in the instant when I touched him, something happened. Not pain this time, but overwhelming. Like being drawn into Kel.

My head filled with the buzzing of a thousand bees. Angry and treacherous, Kel's thoughts swarmed around me. Poised to sting.

I'd never picked up thoughts at this kind of intensity before, and in my mind's eye, I kept very still. They began landing, one by one, covering all that was me. My whole being vibrating and pulsing with their anthem.

Then, as quickly as it came, the deafening hum died. I was back in the classroom. Kel standing in front of me now. His face dangerously close to my own. His breath on my cheek. The peppery scent of ginger humming through me, making me dizzy.

Kel's gloved hand wrapped mine tighter. Holding me up. His dark eyes held the same question I had.

What was that?

"Get in line!" Freddy jerked Kel away from me and shuttled us all out of the classroom. And only one thought consumed me as Freddy corralled us out of the old house.

Come back.

Because when Kel touched me, I was terrified. Terrified and so very alive.

We marched past the empty fenced-in yard and I craned my neck to look back at Kel. His whole body seemed to be shaking as we walked down the path to the Compass Rose. Freddy paused to talk to a Taker at the front door.

I forced myself not to look at Kel again. Desperate for distraction, I focused on the porch column in front of me. Tracing the pattern carved into it with my eyes. Lines and twists and—

The flying bird. The same winged-V from this morning was carved into the stone column, part of a complicated design weaving its way up the granite.

"They're ready for you. Move it," Freddy ordered.

The same unnerving sense of recognition immobilized me. It was like I was standing in the dorm room again, staring down at the crimson-streaked floor. I reached out and traced the symbol with my finger. The rumble of drums reverberated through my mind. Rising into a fevered pulse that crescendoed in a wave of memory.

Hands clawed at the red earth. Blood dripping down the fingers.

Kel's cough brought me out of the vision. His eyes were looking at Freddy. The Taker was fingering his Taser like an Old West gunslinger. I shut the bloody image out of my mind, turned away from the column, and hurried into the Compass Rose.

I'll come back for you.

I didn't let myself glance at Maya. Maybe she hadn't noticed the symbol. Instead, I paid attention as Freddy led us to the cafeteria. A left turn. Then a right. Another left.

The bizarre layout of the Compass Rose gave it a lopsided feeling, like the entryway was just pasted onto the side of the house. I needed to learn my way through the maze of hallways connecting the front room to the rest of the building.

Like ants, we marched one after the other, down the dark, stuffy passageways. A right. A long hallway. Then a left. One more left, and we were at the cafeteria.

A hundred hungry faces glared at us as Freddy marched us toward Dr. Mordoch and her podium.

"The student body is whole again." Dr. Mordoch started clapping, and all the Takers, Aunts, and Uncles lining the walls joined in.

Dread sat heavy in my stomach. What would the Consequences be? Was Dr. Mordoch going to lecture us in front of the whole school? Or would we get locked in Solitary again? Worry tightened across my chest, making me struggle for air.

"Now, I know you're all hungry for lunch. But as I said earlier, these students need our help." As Dr. Mordoch continued her performance, Freddy lined us up facing the students. Like prisoners facing a firing squad. On my right, Zach practically vibrated with anxiety. Every muscle in his soft body was pulled taut, like it physically hurt to be standing up in front of all these people. On my other side, Damion's mouth stretched into a straight, grim line as he stared out at the students. The tables of day-glo green and orange jumpsuits looked absurdly festive against the mass of resentful faces.

"While all of you were engaged in Socialization this morning, learning how to communicate"—Dr. Mordoch's voice projected out over the tables of students—"this Family was disrespecting the rules of Holbrook. And disrespecting you. At Holbrook Academy, as in life, one person's behavior affects everyone else. While you were sitting here patiently, they were facing the first part of their Consequences."

The other students didn't look patient. The clock on the far wall said it was 12:41. Which meant they'd been sitting here, in silence, for more than an hour, watching their mac-and-cheese congeal into an orange, plasticky glob. They looked hungry and hot. And mad.

"Now we must wait a little longer as we all participate in the second phase of Family Five's Consequences. As these students"—Dr. Mordoch stepped off her platform, microphone still in hand, and gestured to our Family with a dramatic sweep of her arm—"are learning to respect discipline, they must also learn to respect you, their peers. There is only one way to come through this journey, and that is together."

Dr. Mordoch was getting her audience warmed up. Her voice grew louder as she strode back and forth in front of us. Her tone had an edge to it. And after an hour of doing nothing, people were ready for some excitement.

"Buddha says, 'There is nothing more dreadful than the habit of doubt. Doubt separates people. It is a poison that disintegrates friendships and breaks up pleasant relations. It is a thorn that irritates and hurts; it is a sword that kills.'"

A few heads were nodding now. They might not know what she was talking about, but they could smell blood.

"This Family has wounded you all with the seeds of doubt they've planted. Can you trust them? Can you trust the people sharing the table with you? Can they trust you?" Dr. Mordoch paused dramatically.

Students were looking around their tables, examining their Family members. Dr. Mordoch had them right where she wanted them.

"We must heal that wound through open, honest dialogue. This Family needs to hear how their disrespect made you all feel." She turned to us. "I will start."

"I feel like you were selfish to disobey your Aunt." Dr. Mordoch looked at me, but I refused to meet her eyes. I had no interest in seeing what lurked inside that woman's mind. "I feel like you were selfish to feed your own egos while the rest of the students were hungry and waiting.

"Now it is your turn to repeat what I've said. I must know that you've heard my feelings. I must know you are engaged in the healing process. You will answer my statement with 'We were selfish.'"

Is she kidding? I felt Dr. Mordoch's eyes on me again. Daring me to speak. To protest. To struggle against the humiliation. The silence stretched on until two of the Takers stepped toward us, Tasers at the ready. Then Damion's booming voice shook me.

"We were selfish." Damion was standing at attention. He frowned at the rest of us, and I remembered what he had said about falling in line.

Reluctantly taking his cue, I mumbled along with the others, "We were selfish."

"Now who will stand up and go next?" Dr. Mordoch's face was calm and reverent. Her arms opened wide, entreating the room full of silent students. But they weren't quite ready to turn on us.

"Only when we understand one another can we be a community. And only then can we sit down and eat together."

That was the final push they needed. Hearing the word *eat*, a skinny guy sitting in the back stood up. Dr. Mordoch was throwing us to the wolves.

12

"**PLEASE COME TO THE FRONT** and share with the Family."

The volunteer didn't look like he enjoyed the eyes of the whole school on him as he walked through the tables. But once he was standing in front of us, face-to-face, he seemed more confident.

"You think you're better than us."

I knew he was probably just hungry. I knew he didn't know me personally, but I still felt like I'd just been smacked. Dr. Mordoch turned to my Family, cueing us with the right response.

"We think we're better than you," we mumbled, repeating the words.

"Louder!" Dr. Mordoch shouted.

"We think we're better than you." My thin voice was amplified by the group, so our words filled the cafeteria. Giving them the weight of truth.

Dr. Mordoch smiled and turned back to the lanky guy. "Thank you. That was very brave of you to go first. You have earned the right to reclaim one of your confiscated possessions."

That got the room's attention. Four more people stood up, and standing next to me, even Damion seemed unnerved. He glanced at me, and in his eyes I saw the wall that he had built there. A wall that Holbrook was destroying, brick by brick. *What happens when it falls?*

As students moved to the front, I studied the new volunteers. They still looked nervous. But I could see an eagerness in their faces as they tried to think up good enough complaints to earn back their treasures.

A geeky boy spoke softly, focusing in on me. I could smell the sour sweat on him. "You're on a power trip. You just love us sitting here, waiting for all of you."

"We're on a power trip," we echoed.

Dr. Mordoch nodded her approval at him and the volunteers got gutsier.

"You think you're such a rebel." A mousy girl with a long nose jabbed her finger at Nami's hair. Then she turned on Kel. "And you in those stupid gloves. Looking so goddamned smug."

The next person interrupted, not waiting for us to repeat. And the next. And the next. All those years of being outcasts, of being bullied by kids, yelled at by teachers, analyzed by counselors and parents, had prepared these students perfectly for this moment. Those endless taunts and accusations had become ammunition they spewed at us.

"You screwed up your life!" a guy yelled at Zach, his twisted face glowing in the suffocating heat. "But you're not gonna screw up mine."

People murmured and nodded in agreement. The whole room stank of malice. And they kept coming. Finally, they had someone to blame for being abandoned here.

Our whole line backed away from the horde, but we only gained a few inches before the backs of our legs hit up against the platform that held the teachers' tables. Damion managed to keep his face blank, but red patches darkened across Kel's cheekbones. Anger drawing his whole face tight. He pulled on the neck of his hoodie, like he was trying to loosen it. Maya and Zach both turned inward. Zach's body hunched, trying to present a smaller target. Maya folded her bony arms tight across her chest, like literal body armor. Nami shielded herself with a permanent smirk that only seemed to be making people madder.

"You hate us. You don't even care what happens to us." They were building momentum.

"You hate everything about your stupid little life." Building on each other's words.

"I'm not gonna take your shit anymore!"

It was an intoxicating chorus. Dr. Mordoch's eyes sparkled as she called on them, one after another. But she kept the smile off her face. Giving credibility to this mob scene.

"You're nothing!" a girl screamed at me.

And then a wad of bread hit me in the face.

There was an almost imperceptible pause while the whole room absorbed what'd happened. Dr. Mordoch just stood off to the side, a peaceful look on her face. *Is this the compassion from other troubled kids that she told my dad about?*

Then all hell broke lose. A volley of limp green beans pelted us. Blobs of artificial cheese flew through the air. Streaking my jumpsuit. Salty on my lips. Someone shoved Damion and I heard him mutter, "Stand down," to himself, even as his whole body leaned forward. Straining against his urge to fight back.

"Enough!" Dr. Mordoch's voice rang out from the sidelines. The whole room froze as her words echoed off the walls.

"I understand your anger. You are here trying to get better. But these students"—she waved in our direction—"are standing in your way."

Dr. Mordoch's words seemed to sap the energy from the near riot. A disappointed-looking girl dropped her handful of squooshed vegetables. A squat guy in mid-swing looked up at Damion's bulk and backed away. One by one, they returned to their seats.

"We must not give in to violence. But, I believe your honesty today has helped these students. Perhaps they will decide, as you have, to seize this opportunity to choose a new path. Let us solidify our new openness by sharing a meal."

All I wanted was a cool shower to wash off the slime. But now we had to endure lunch. None of us looked around as we threaded our way through the tables to our seats.

Dr. Mordoch's eyes stayed on me, so I forced myself to take a bite. Bile launched itself up my throat and I fought to swallow. The rest of the Family didn't even bother to pick at their food. We gazed around the table at each other. Where there had been fear this morning, now there was only anger. It's never good to know you can be traded in for cold macaroni-and-cheese.

The rest of the day was a sort of fog. The food stains on our jumpsuits were like the bandages on a leper. The other students avoided us, moving as far away as possible as my Family trudged to English class, back to the cafeteria, and finally to our rooms.

The linoleum was clean, without a trace of the disturbing events of the morning, and I hoped it would stay that way. Neither Maya nor I talked as we crawled into our beds, the nightly drugs seeping into our systems. But this time, it was exhaustion that kept us silent. We were on the same side now.

13

I FELT LIKE I'd been run over by a truck. At least that would be something I could explain. As it was, I was on the floor under the window, my mouth tasting like clay and pennies. Grit crunched between my teeth, and my hands were stained blood-red again. Maya, eyes closed, was sprawled across from me in the same condition, and between us was another picture on the floor. Or more accurately, there was more of the same picture.

In the light of early morning, I could make out a thick, crudely drawn person on the linoleum. Like something out of a cave painting. One solid line outlined stubby arms and legs. But no face.

Instead of a mouth or eyes, there was the exact same symbol from the first morning in the exact same spot on the floor. The V with wings.

Plunk.

A fat drop of water splashed to the floor. The first of a hundred tiny wet circles.

Plunk. Plunk. Plunk.

I turned my palms over, catching the rain seeping from the ceiling. Letting it wash away the red grime from my hands. The water was so cold that it burned my skin. The ice froze my thoughts. It seeped into my chest.

Fear is an illusion.

I forced myself to take a deep breath. But more water surged under the door, its blue foamy fingers reaching for me. Clawing at my feet. Drenching the legs of my jumpsuit.

The waves swirled around the picture on the floor, leaving the drawing untouched. I waded over to the island of dry linoleum in the center of the turquoise water. I'd seen this shape before. I knew I had, but I couldn't remember where.

Beneath the roar of the incoming waves, I heard the eerie music again. I traced the person and the symbol with my finger, and there was familiarity in the movement. This picture was in my style. These were my lines. *I'm in control.*

An edge of excitement gilded my fear. I'd lived so long with these nightmares and visions. And now, for the first time, I dared to think there might be a reason. *I'm in control.*

The music rumbled through my bones and my heart pounded with it. *Fear is an illusion.*

When I looked back down, the water was gone. My jumpsuit was dry. I was kneeling bloody handed on the floor, but now the arcane symbols were a puzzle to be solved.

"Another one?" Maya was awake now, looking at me.

How does she know about the visions? Did she see the water too?

She pointed at the floor. "But this one's different."

Maya was talking about the drawing. Of course she didn't see the water—it was a hallucination. My excitement drained away. Maybe the symbols were nothing more than my next stop on the crazy-train.

Keeping the disappointment off of my face, I nodded at Maya and she crawled over, inspecting the figure and symbol drawn on the linoleum. In the dawn half-light, Maya was a study in shadows, darkening her eyes, outlining her jutting collarbones, hiding her face behind her hair.

"You know what it means. Don't you?" She stared at me, her look tinged with suspicion. By now, I recognized her distrust for what it was. The haze through which she viewed the entire world.

I went to the bathroom, grabbing a wad of the scratchy toilet paper. Buying time. Scrubbing at the floor with the flimsy square sheets. But Maya waited for me to answer.

Finally, I forced myself to meet her gaze and she looked back. Her pain infested me, and for the first time, it wasn't just emotions. Or words. Vague shapes played out scene after scene, like hideous shadow puppets cast against the wall of my subconscious.

A man pinning Maya's hands behind her, his fingers crushing her wrists.

A boy who promised to protect her, but lied.

Maya hiding under her bed, a skinny cat clutched in her arms.

Suddenly, our first conversation replayed in my head.

"Why do you even care?" I'd asked her.

"Because someone has to."

But who had cared about Maya? As the twisted shadows acted out the nightmare of her childhood, we both shuddered. I kept my eyes on Maya, even though I didn't want to, witnessing her torment. Because someone had to.

Finally, the memories cleared, and on the other side of all that violence was the same steely-eyed Maya. It seemed unbelievable that she was unfazed by the shared vision. Was it possible that those scenes were always unfolding in her mind? That because she lived in that eternal hell, she hadn't noticed that, this time, I'd seen it too? Or maybe it hadn't happened at all.

Either way, Maya sat there looking at me. Still waiting for my answer.

What could I tell her about the drawings on the floor or our red hands? *I keep having these hallucinations, but it's no big deal?*

Oh, don't worry. I'm sure I didn't kill anyone?

"Come on, Faye. I saw you looking at that column yesterday with the same mark on it. What's going on?"

A warm breeze trickled in through the open window, whispering of ancient forests and murky seas. I felt the contradictions of this place. This patch of forest surrounded by wasteland. A Family bound together but without trust. And I made a decision.

"Maya, I really don't know what's going on." Nausea rolled in my belly and I was still dizzy from the torrent of Maya's shadow scenes. Her pain had been so vivid, like the terror I'd felt through Dr. Mordoch in Solitary. But that vision of the beach had been my memory too. Only it'd felt like I was remembering something backward. Or maybe inside out.

With Maya, each memory had been ripe with new horror. That'd never happened before. And I hoped it never happened again. I pushed the images away, filling the space with a stream of words. "I didn't want to say anything yesterday, 'cause Damion was kinda . . . intense about what'd happened to us. But I think that flying-bird-V-thing is some kind of symbol. It's like something from a dream. But I have no idea what it means. If I did, I would tell you."

She squinted at me, crossing her arms. Years of betrayal binding them across her chest.

"I promise." I willed her to believe me.

The overhead light flicked on and Maya made a decision too. She nodded at me and went to get more toilet paper.

As Nurse's voice screeched through the speakers, I closed the window for the second morning in a row. A flicker of green streaked across the rooftop of the other wing of the dorm. Then it was gone.

And like with everything else that'd happened since I came to Holbrook, I was left with one more question.

Kel wasn't at breakfast. Damion and Zach just shrugged when I looked pointedly at the empty seat. A cold knot of fear formed in my belly as I remembered how gray Kel had gone yesterday in Socialization.

Today there were grits and greasy sausages on our plates, the first meat we'd had since the meat loaf, and I saw the outrage on Maya's face. Damion must have seen it too, because he shot her a threatening look, showing her his red-stained hands. Reminding her why we couldn't risk getting into any more trouble. A war waged across Maya's face as she stared from the sausages to her own hands. Trying to decide where her loyalties lay.

Nami ended the stalemate. She unfolded her paper napkin and, keeping her hands low, placed her sausages at the center. Then she removed the offending sausages from Maya's plate too, and handed the napkin to Zach. He glanced quickly around the room, hesitating. But Nami gave him a nudge and he followed suit.

I added my sausages to the collection, but when I offered the oily napkin to Damion, he wouldn't take it. He and Maya locked eyes, a silent standoff. This time, Maya showed Damion *her* red-stained hands, and gave him a bitter smile. Turning the warning back on him. Nami added a little eyelash batting to the mix and Damion shoved his sausages into the napkin. Crisis averted.

I glanced around the room. Had anyone else noticed our little drama? But the other tables were busy with their own power struggles. Here and there, scattered around the cafeteria, were tiny marks of individuality. A pair of earrings. A baseball cap. Pink lip gloss. All the students with accessories had two things in common. Each of them had a smug smile and an aptitude for berating us at lunch yesterday.

A big guy, with a gold chain around his neck, grabbed the last sausage off a runty kid's plate and stuffed it in his mouth. There was no protest, no reprisal. A new hierarchy was emerging at Holbrook, and I guess I had my answer about Kel's hoodie and gloves. And a hundred more questions. Was he spying on our group? On me? Was this why he wasn't at breakfast? *What secrets is Kel trading for his freedom?*

I pushed away the suspicion. Instead, as the Takers led us out of the cafeteria toward class, I focused on the winding hallways of the Compass Rose, searching for another flying-bird symbol anywhere. But there was nothing.

We didn't go back to the Knowledge Annex for classes. Instead an "Uncle" with a trim beard and a paunch met us outside the Compass Rose.

"Welcome to Art and Life. The essential lesson you must learn is that art is first and foremost about truth. Before you call yourself an artist, you must be able to accurately perceive reality and reproduce it faithfully. Only then can we see the truth of ourselves within this reality." Art Uncle counted us and frowned, looking as if he didn't like the reality that he saw in front of him.

There was still no sign of Kel when Dragon showed up with a note and a nasty look on her face. And I regretted the ugly assumptions I'd had about Kel at breakfast.

Worry settled in, nesting in my mind. It whispered nagging thoughts to me. *Maybe he's sick. Maybe he's locked up again. Maybe he's been sent away.*

Art Uncle read the note and started down a trail. "Okay, let's go, then."

Damion, always the good soldier, was right on his heels. Nami sidled into line in front of me, giving me a wink and a little eyebrow waggle in Damion's direction.

Art Uncle led us into the woods, and as the trees closed in around me, I could feel their branches reaching down for me. Their roots snaking up through the earth toward my feet. As I climbed up the hill on the far side of campus, the wind picked up. It hissed through the branches like it was calling to me.

I tried to shake off the sensation, but my legs were stiff and my brain was sluggish. A blur of white caught the corner of my eye. Rita, her blond braid glowing in the sun, wandered through the trees, heading toward the ocean. With everything that'd happened in the last two days, I'd forgotten about her. But here she was again, free and alone, without any Takers.

As she disappeared into the woods, I longed to run after her. To beg her to show me how to get out of here. But I remembered Damion's warning to us. Fall in line.

So I did just that. Forcing my feet to march one in front of the other on the well-worn path, I watched the mix of boot and sneaker treads imprinted in the dirt. And then I noticed the footprints.

I stopped dead. Zach ran into my back and Maya into him.

"What is it?" Maya demanded in a harsh whisper.

Hoping to stop her questions, I said, "Tell you later."

Then I hurried to catch back up with Nami and the rest of the line. Now that I was watching, there were footprints everywhere. Toe and heel marks where bare feet had walked this path. Recently.

Art Uncle stopped at the top of the hill near a stack of easels. But the path went on, toward the Screamers. The bronze statues lurked in the distance, almost hidden by the trees. I shivered, thinking about their terrorized faces.

"Everybody gets one." Art Uncle handed me a set of watercolor paints and my mind went blank. All I could see were twelve bright circles of color nestled in the plastic box.

It reminded me of my first watercolor set I'd gotten right before I started elementary school. It must have been just after we moved to Pennsylvania, but before oil levels had peaked and fallen. My mom had taken me grocery shopping. Thinking back now, it seemed impossible that there were ever shelves and shelves of food. A whole aisle of cereal. Twenty different kinds of toilet paper. Now, even with mandatory paper recycling, there was still just the government-issued kind.

But back then, the grocery store had everything. They'd set up a little back-to-school display with markers, boxes of waxy-smelling crayons, and paints. I'd flipped open the lid of the plastic box, and suddenly, nothing else mattered. I wanted those colors so badly.

"We don't have time for your wandering." Mom grabbed the paints out of my hands, shoving the box onto a shelf with crayons and colored pencils. "The Samsons are expecting me at their house in twenty minutes."

She'd loved being a realtor back then, when there was still plenty of money to be made in the housing market. When people didn't have to go through a whole application process to be accepted into a Cooperative.

In the checkout line, Mom chatted with the cashier, practicing her client smile while she rummaged for her wallet. I could see the back-to-school display from there, the pristine, white box of paints sitting crookedly in the wrong part of the display. My mom was focusing too hard on being charming to notice me.

So I ran over. When I reached out my hand, I swear I was only going to return the paints to their right place. But as soon as I touched them, I knew they belonged to me. I knew I needed them.

"Faye!" Mom called over her shoulder in her realtor voice. "Get your patootie over here."

In the car, I was terrified. I shoved the paints down into the crack in the seat and sat on the edge that was sticking out. I didn't dare touch them while Mom gave her tour of the house. Or while she pumped more gas into our SUV. I didn't let myself open the box until I'd sneaked them up to my room and locked the door.

And there they were. Those bright colors were all mine. Standing on this hillside now, years later, I ran my finger along the stubby paintbrush, and the same greedy need growled in the pit of my stomach.

"Grab an easel, a board, and a dish of water. Then set up looking at something you want to paint." Art Uncle pointed to a stack of splattered particleboard and the banged-up aluminum easels. Damion, standing closest, reached for one, but Nami snatched it first.

"Thanks." Nami tossed the word over her shoulder.

Damion's eyes followed Nami as she sauntered off toward the cliff. His feet stayed put, but his body leaned forward ever so slightly, as if trying to stay closer to her. Nami planted her stolen easel so it looked out over the water toward three small, barren islands sticking up into the smoggy sky. Tankers sounded their low horns as they crossed the oily, rainbowed water, eternally questing to make up for the lack of foreign oil.

Damion frowned at Nami and shook his head, but then set up his easel right next to her anyway. He went through the motions of pretending to be interested in the same ocean vista. And Nami let him keep his facade.

Maya took an easel and walked to the edge of the clearing, facing the distant Screamers. Zach hung back, finally choosing to paint the dense forest behind us.

"Pick just one thing and try to portray it accurately," Art Uncle admonished us. "A single tree . . . a pinecone . . ."

"A scenic oil rig . . . a trash-covered beach . . . ," Maya sniped. "A clear-cut viewed through razor wire—"

"That's enough." Art Uncle shot her a warning glance, then went on. "The goal isn't to make it scenic or pretty, but to make it authentic."

Picking up my supplies, I ran my finger across the paper already taped to the board. It was thin and cheap, but I didn't care. I was just glad to get a chance to paint again. Tasting the anticipation in my mouth, I looked over the cliff. It was always a delicious moment, trying to choose just what part of the world to paint. And I already felt stronger with the watercolors in my hand.

Far below us, Rita reemerged on the fenced-off beach. Clearly she did know a few secrets about how to get around Holbrook. What had she said that first morning? "The path is hard to follow"?

Is that the path she was talking about?

Down on the beach, waves shimmered white and blue as they crawled over the generator buoys and up onto the exposed shore. I placed my easel a little ways off from Damion's and Nami's. Where I could keep an eye on Rita.

It was low tide, and seagulls swarmed the wide beach, sorting through remnants of plastic lids, shreds of fishing nets, and thick ropes of seaweed. It was disgusting, but also glorious. Sun flashed off the underwings of scavenging birds. Waves crawled up the stony beach again and again, fighting the moon's pull.

A sudden attachment to this barren landscape ambushed me. Forgetting about Rita, I angled my easel so I had a better view of the trashed shoreline. I felt the tenuous current of vitality under the grime. Yes. This was the right place.

I dipped my brush into the water and started with blue. The first streak was pale and watery. I remembered how disappointing it'd been for me, using that first set of paints. All those rich circles of red, orange, blue, and brown were so bold and solid in their box, but on paper they were only ghosts of themselves. Inadequate to portray the scenes in my imagination. I'd experimented, using the barest drop of water or pushing just the edge of the brush against the paper. Finally, the colors had popped off the page, like they did inside my mind.

Now, my brush danced across the page in a staccato of blue, leaving room for cresting waves. Anxiety jittered through me as I remembered the water from this morning. The same music drifted through my mind, but this time, the steady beat soothed me. My chest loosened, letting my breath flow in and out easily. It was just me and the colors and the beach below.

The blue water morphed into a black sky, crowded with stars. The beach lay silvery and pristine. And there were people there. Two dark figures standing knee-deep in the water. The smaller one singing up at a blood-red moon. The larger one reaching out her arms.

Even though the figures were vague shapes, I knew it was Dr. Mordoch and me on the beach. I was painting the very beach from my vision.

As I put in the details, the music crept into the painting, syncing with the rhythm of my strokes. And the yearning I'd felt that night so long ago struck me with such force that I almost dropped my brush.

I'd been looking for something. Someplace. I'd needed to *do* something. I painted Dr. Mordoch's shadow stretching huge across the beach. Her hand clamped on mine. Keeping me from it.

Dr. Mordoch scooping me up and carrying me to the beach. *"I don't want to hurt you."*

Then there was another voice speaking from the shadows. *"You should've let her go."*

The memory rushed at me and I filled in the white space. Painting the speaker into the picture. *A hand. An arm. The shape taking form in the darkness.*

"That's quite an imagination you have."

I jumped at the sudden voice behind me, sending a black smear across the emerging figure. The Uncle was leaning over my shoulder, an amused look on his face. "It's obvious that you have talent. Too bad you're spending it on this nonsense."

I looked at my painting, full of shadows and stars, then down at the gaudy real-life beach. Where I'd painted cool blues and silvers, heat waves rippled above tar-covered pebbles.

"Everyone gather around. See what this student's done." I cringed as my Family crowded behind me.

"Nice." Zach sounded impressed.

Maya joined in, in her brusque way. "So much for my tree."

She held up a picture of a brown stick with a green blob on top.

Art Uncle took back control. "Faye . . . It's Faye, right?"

Right. The traditional you-aren't-important-enough-for-me-to-know-your-name maneuver.

"You can see that Faye here has a good sense of color. She sets her mood wonderfully." Smiling, Art Uncle held up the painting so people could see it better. I wished Kel were here. There weren't many things I was good at, but this was one of them. I wanted him to see what I could do.

"And this line here"—Art Uncle pointed to the slope of the cliffs near the beach—"really balances the composition."

Then still smiling, he picked up the cup of water and doused the painting. "But these techniques are wasted if you're too good for the basics. Though I suppose, why bother with realism when you live in a fantasy world?"

The black sky dribbled down the paper, turning the whole painting into an ugly brown. It'd felt so real a second ago—Dr. Mordoch, whatever I was looking for, the third figure—but everything was blurring together now. Within seconds, the beach, the people, the memories were completely swallowed up.

14

I WAS GRATEFUL for one thing. That Kel hadn't witnessed my humiliation. But when I saw he wasn't waiting for us at the lunch table, anxiety buzzed in my stomach, making me feel sick.

Just then it occurred to me that his absence might have something to do with whatever was going on with us all at night. I thought about the flash of memory I'd had when I'd seen the flying bird carved into the column. Hands digging through the mud, covered in blood. I shuddered.

When I sat down at the table, I almost jumped up again. Something sharp and pointy poked at me from my already uncomfortable chair. I forced myself to relax, so I wouldn't draw any attention. While the Takers moved around, rationing out the food, patrolling the room, I eased whatever it was out from under my leg.

It was smooth and metallic. My throat felt too tight to swallow. A knife? But I couldn't feel a blade. My eyes flicked down to it in the weak cafeteria light. Silver gleaming in the shadows.

Then my eyes made sense of it and I almost laughed with relief. It was my Japanese brush pen. Superfine nylon bristles. Refillable ink. A little shorter than most, so I could carry it in my pocket. Mine.

I made a show of spooning tomato soup into my mouth while my mind spun with questions. I'd brought the pen with me to Holbrook, but it'd been taken away from me, along with my sketchbook and clothes and everything else I owned.

What is it doing on my seat? Is this some kind of test? Are they watching to see what I'll do?

A scrap of paper was folded and tucked under the metal clip of the cap. Hands under the table, I slowly teased the paper out from under the clip. There was just one word written on it.

Thanks.

My pulse throbbed in my throat. I didn't know how it'd gotten there, but I knew it was from Kel. It had to be. His handwriting was just like him, dark letters slanting toward the edge of the paper with a kind of contained energy. *But why "Thanks"?*

I slid the pen down into my boot and bit off my smile. Suddenly it felt easier to swallow the salty soup, easier to sit through the silence. Easier to be here. Five minutes ago I'd just been another degenerate in a uniform. But feeling the cool metal of the pen tucked down in my boot, I remembered who I was. Despite my ruined painting. Despite the cryptic pictures. Despite Dr. Mordoch's sanctioned bullying. I was still here.

And, somewhere, so was Kel.

Lunch felt like it went on forever, and of course our table was the last one excused from the cafeteria, making it clear that we were still on Dr. Mordoch's blacklist. It also conveniently made us as conspicuous as possible as we went to our mandatory Free Time. We were officially the "example."

A Taker led us to the corral I'd seen on my way to Solitary that first morning. The five other Families who were also scheduled for Free Time were already inside. Some of the kids were like tigers in a zoo, pacing around and around the dusty yard. Others stood in twos and threes, whispering to each other, heads close together. Of course, this place wasn't for barnyard therapy. No. *We* were the animals Dr. Mordoch kept in this holding pen.

Freddy stood at the gate, sneering down at us.

"No shouting. No fighting. No running. And no touching. I don't think I need to remind any of you what happens if you break the rules. *Zz-zzzz-z-zzz!*" Freddy jolted his body like he was being electrocuted. He roared with laughter at his own performance, then doubled over when it turned into a coughing fit.

He hacked and spit for a bit. Then, still wheezing a little, he unlocked the gate. "Have fun!"

Thirty-five heads swiveled to stare at us as we filed inside. Evidently, no one had forgotten about yesterday's lunch. But I didn't care. Kel was at the other end of the corral, his hoodie, sunglasses, and gloves standing out against the sea of jumpsuits. I took a deep breath.

"Yum-my," Nami whispered over my shoulder. "That's what I call a tall drink of water."

I studied her face, trying to tell if she was making fun of me.

"Come on." She grinned and elbowed me. "You can see those arms even under all those layers. He's not fooling anyone. And all that hair hiding those killer eyes. Melty. Yep, I do love me a rebel without a clue."

Watching him, sitting by himself in the corner of the yard, I tried to look at him through Nami's eyes. I had absolutely no experience with girl talk, but I knew enough to see that she was right. I combed the snarls out of my hair with my fingers and looked down at my jumpsuit, painfully aware that there was nothing I could do to make it less hideous.

"The way he's been looking at you, I don't think he'll notice your outfit." Nami gave me a little push in Kel's direction. Eddies of flies churned around my feet as I made my way across the fenced-in yard to him. Kel glanced up and smiled his slow smile at me.

"Pull up a chair." He patted the ground next to him and I sat down.

I wanted to ask him about the pen, but doubt nibbled at my mind. *What if it's not from him? What if he's got no idea what you're talking about? At least say something!*

"You missed art." *Thank you, master of the obvious.*

"Yeah? Well, I decided to take a vacation day. And I can tell you, Nami's right. This resort does *not* deserve five stars. Did you know there's not even room service?" Kel's voice rose in fake outrage and he grinned at me. My stomach flipped over and wagged its tail.

Kel shifted a little closer and took off his sunglasses. I was shocked by how tired he looked. In Solitary, he'd said something about getting sick, and by the look of things, he still was. The circles under his eyes were darker and sunken in. Red patches streaked his cheeks and across his nose, like he'd been sunburned. Kel hadn't been playing hooky. Not that you'd be able to at Holbrook. Something was genuinely wrong with him.

"Are you okay?" I reached out to touch him. A shadow fell over us and I froze, my arm outstretched awkwardly, inches from Kel's arm. A Taker hovered behind us, daring me to complete my gesture.

I dropped my hand in my lap and the Taker backed off, continuing his patrol of the fence. Here Kel and I were, finally face-to-face, but there might as well still have been a wall.

"I took a lovely stroll around the grounds this morning—" I couldn't tell if Kel was still kidding or if he was being serious. The green in his eyes glinted at me. "Did you get my present?"

My face went red and I smiled, relieved. "But 'thanks' for what?"

Kel shrugged, and winced with the jarring movement.

"Are you okay? Kel, you look sick."

"Way to stomp on a guy's ego." He played it off, but I could tell that he wasn't okay.

What's wrong with him? When I opened my mouth to keep pushing, he cut me off.

"Look. I needed a few extra hours' sleep is all." Kel's voice had an edge to it now that ended my questions. "I felt better, so I took a look around the place."

"How'd you get my pen?" I tried to keep my voice level. Then I regretted asking. If he had some sort of deal with Dr. Mordoch, I didn't want to know about it. So I changed my question before he could answer. "How'd you get out of your room?"

"How'd any of us get out of our rooms?" Damion stood looking down at the two of us. Nami sank down next to me and Zach next to Kel. Seeing the look of hero worship still in Zach's eyes, I guessed no one had ever cared before if Zach got into trouble, let alone kept him out of it.

Maya hesitated for a second before she sat down, like she was trying to decide whether or not to join us. But it was just for show; she wasn't welcome anywhere else.

Damion squatted down, facing Kel and me, and winced. I was glad to see that even mighty Damion was sore from yesterday's sit-in. He eased himself the rest of the way down, finishing off the circle.

He looked around to make sure we were alone, then gave us that appraising look he had. "We've been discussing this whole bloody-hands thing, and it seems like there are two possibilities. Either someone is trying to frame us for something. Or—"

"Or something creepy is going on," Nami finished his thought. She tilted her head, smiling sideways at Damion. Clearly they'd already disagreed about this point. "I vote for creepy."

"I vote creepy too." Nervous energy played across Zach's face, coming out in a rushed string of words. "I mean, who would go through all that trouble to sneak in and pull us out of bed and cover our hands with . . . with whatever that crap is. Not to mention, highly unlikely that someone could pull it off without waking us up. I mean, the drugs are strong, but . . ."

"Maybe Dr. Mordoch has something to do with it. Maybe she's double-dosing us or something." Damion's black eyes looked sharply at Kel. "Maybe one of us is in on it."

"'Cause we're all just dying to get into your bedroom, right?" A smile floated on Nami's lips.

Damion stammered, "No, I-I-I just meant—"

"I know what you meant, and I also vote that we stop that here and now. Whatever's going on, creepy or not, it's happening to all of us." Nami wiggled her stained fingers, reminding us of the thing that tied us together.

"All for one and one for all?" Kel raised an eyebrow.

"Right. 'Cause if something goes down, we're all screwed. Okay?" Nami looked around the group at us.

No one nodded, but no one disagreed either. It was a start.

Maya, who'd been unusually quiet up till now, looked at me and asked, "So anyone got an idea what *is* going on?"

I shook my head to let her know I didn't know anything new.

"Vampires?" Nami guessed.

"Be serious," Damion snapped, trying to regain control of the conversation.

"I am being serious. Think about it. I mean, it's the middle of the night—"

"Ghosts? No, ninjas!" Zach jumped in, his eyes lighting up.

Damion tried to keep the discussion from slipping away. "Don't be stupid . . ."

But it was too late. The conversation descended into banter and it was bizarre, sitting there in the middle of it all. I'd watched this same scene a hundred times in the hallways of my high school. And I'd have given anything for someone, just one person, to let me join in. Now I had five someones. Sure, we'd been thrown together and shunned, but it still felt real. I couldn't risk losing this makeshift Family. The symbols from this morning came back to me. I had to figure out what was going on before someone got in trouble.

Or gets hurt.

Kel shifted and his leg brushed against mine with a soft *shush* of our uniforms touching. It happened so fast that it could've been an accident, but it wasn't. He picked up our conversation again, whispering in my ear, "I found something this morning. Something besides your pen."

I nodded. *Go on.*

"You know that pattern you were looking at yesterday? The one on the column?"

My breath caught in my throat. Had everyone seen that? I nodded again.

"I saw another one, during my 'tour' of the facilities this morning. It's in the sitting room, part of the pattern around the chandelier. You'd seemed kinda fascinated by it."

There was a question implied in Kel's tone, but he didn't push it. I kept my face neutral and turned the questions back on him. "Why were you sneaking around the Compass Rose, anyway?"

"I thought I might be able to find some of my stuff that Dr. Mordoch confiscated."

"Where's she keeping it?"

"It's all in her office. Luckily, it was the first place I looked. I figured she's the kind of person who wants to keep her weapons close to her." Kel reached into his sweatshirt pocket and pulled out a guitar pick. It was mottled brown like a tortoiseshell, and Kel rubbed it gently with his thumb. "It was my mom's. She used to play in a band. I mean, they weren't on a big label or anything, but I have a couple of tapes people made of her shows. You know that song I was singing the other day in Solitary? That was her favorite."

Kel flipped the pick back and forth between his fingers. "She was good. Really good. She quit after she married my dad, but she taught me my first chords. And when she got sick, she gave me this."

He stared at the ground, blinking hard. "I never got to tell you thanks."

"Thanks?" I thought about the single word on Kel's note.

"For talking to me the other day."

Solitary came back to me in a rush. Our whispers drifting back and forth through the wall. How calm I'd felt talking to him.

"I wish—" Kel stopped himself and a crease marked his forehead. I could hear the same feeling in his voice. The same longing to reach through this wall between us. "You know, if we were anywhere else. Anywhere but here, I'd—"

His eyes flicked up and speared mine. Splaying my thoughts wide open. Every buried yearning sizzled to the surface. And as I burned, the world froze around me. The fence, the chatter, the Takers dropped away, and all that was left was an island of us.

Never before, even during my most intense visions, had I felt so alive. Never before had every single muscle and cell and thought sung with power. The words of Kel's song came back to me again.

I would teach my feet to fly. Straight up into the hot sky.

15

THAT NIGHT, Maya and I stayed up talking. Our voices bounced quietly from bed to bed. The volley of words helping us stay awake.

Despite Zach's totally plausible theory of alien abduction, by the end of Free Time our group had come up with a plan. We just wouldn't go to sleep, thus putting an end to this weirdness.

Then there'd been a whole futile discussion about how to deal with the drugs. It didn't surprise me that most of us had tried the hide-it-under-the-tongue maneuver, with equal amounts of failure. Of course, Nami had taken it a step further, throwing up the pill right after lights-out. But evidently a Taker, patrolling the halls, overheard her and Nurse came in with a double dose. Only Zach admitted that he'd willingly let himself be drugged, mumbling something to us about needing to feel calm.

Since we didn't have a solution for the drugs, we weren't sure staying up would work. But we hoped at least one of us would make it through the night.

That was the plan, at least. But I had one of my own.

"So," Maya's voice whispered through the dark. "What'd Kel have to say that was so important?"

"What?" I kept my voice steady. *How much did she hear about Kel's Holbrook "tour"?*

"Come on. I saw you guys during Free Time. Everyone saw you. Whispering to each other and making moony eyes."

I let out my breath. I wasn't sure why I didn't want her to know about Kel's discovery.

No. I did know why. It was the same reason that I didn't want to talk about the drawings on the floor. Or ask Kel about his gloves and sweatshirt. These new friendships were tenuous and fragile. If my Family knew about everything, the music up on the rooftop, the crazy water hallucinations, the symbols I'd drawn on the floor . . . would they still trust me? I couldn't go back to being an outcast.

And there was another reason. One I didn't want to admit to myself. There was this new feeling at the center of my chest. A secret thrill when I thought about Kel. I didn't want to do anything, say anything, that would make that go away.

"Fine. Don't answer me. But don't pretend you're so innocent."

Maya kept up the soft chatter, moving on to analyzing Damion and Nami's flirtation. I tried to make the appropriate responses as I thought back to what Kel had said about his foray to the Compass Rose. He hadn't said how he'd gotten in or how he'd found his stuff— or my stuff, for that matter. But he *had* found what they'd taken from him. He'd gotten in and discovered the symbol. And so could I.

Then Maya's words stopped and I glanced over to see if she was asleep. But instead, she was staring up at the ceiling. She must have felt my eyes on her, because she started talking again in this quiet, tentative voice, so different from her usual aggressive tones.

"I'm scared. I mean, I know it's not really vampires or anything, but . . . Faye, something awful is going on, isn't it? I'm remembering these little bits of things, but it's not like a dream. It's . . . it's like how I remember the first time my stepdad cornered me.

Everything comes back in these ugly flashes. His hand on my arm. The streetlamp making thin strips of light on the carpet. My cat hissing and fluffing himself up as big as he could get. And then nothing. It's like that."

I didn't know what to say. Not about the hell she'd gone through. Or about what was going on now. I grasped at the same pitiful words that hadn't even worked the first night. "I'm sorry."

"No. That's what my stepdad's gonna be." Her voice had its edge back. "But thanks."

I didn't want to, but I had to ask. "Maya, what kind of things *are* you remembering?"

"Like I said, nothing solid . . . more like déjà vu." She propped herself up on her elbow so she could look at me. Moonlight filtered in through the window, and I could just make out her face. "Like today, when I was painting that tree, there was this strong smell. Spruce and salt. And there was this sudden rush. Like there was more there than I was seeing."

I'd felt that way my whole life. Like there was an invisible layer under everything that only I could sense. Maybe I wasn't crazy.

"It was like I knew every tree and bush and weed growing in that forest. Like I belonged to it." Maya's face shone as she told me about the experience. It outshone her too-thin body and her sharp face. Making her beautiful. "No. It was like that place belonged to me."

Maya dropped back on her pillow, looking up at the ceiling. Then, her voice small again, she said, "Then the feeling left and I was just me again."

She fell quiet, but this time, she squeezed her eyes shut. After a few minutes, her soft snores filled the room. Time to get some answers. And not just for me anymore.

I reached down and grabbed my boots out from under the bed. The brush pen slipped out and rolled across the linoleum. Grabbing it, I thought of the big suitcase my parents had packed. Kel could've picked out any of that other stuff to give me. But he hadn't.

He'd brought me my pen. Kel had known exactly what I'd want.

Tears welled in my eyes as I tied my shoes. I was so tired, and Holbrook had taken so much from me. My sketchbook, my clothes, my freedom. I clutched the pen in my fist and pushed open the window. Parts of me might be missing, but I wasn't lost.

I'd find out what was going on in this place. What the drawings were about. And the music. And Maya's déjà vu. I wasn't waiting around anymore.

Leaving my pen on the ledge for safekeeping, I climbed out through the window like I had the first night. From my perch on the ledge, I counted four Takers guarding the dorms. Two of them made constant patrols around the building. Blood sounded in my ears as I counted how long it took them to make their circuit. Eighty-two seconds.

Unfortunately, that still left two of them in the courtyard at all times, sweeping the dark corners with their flashlights. I racked my brain for usable schemes, but all I could come up with were bad movie stunts. Throwing a rock at the other side of the courtyard? Yelling "Fire"? Tackling one of them from above?

Then the solution appeared all on its own. A muffled grunt came from the guys' side of the dorm. The door swung open and Freddy appeared, hauling out a kid in handcuffs.

"I don't care what the bastard said to you and it don't matter, 'cause he's coming too." Freddy's growl drowned out the boy's pleading.

A second boy was hauled out right behind them. I didn't recognize either of them. Suddenly the second boy turned on the Taker and swung, clocking the guard in the jaw. Freddy and the other Takers ran over to help.

I didn't waste any more time. I crossed the ledge and went down the ladder. This time, the bottom part slid easily to the ground. The padlock was warped and twisted, like it'd been melted, but I didn't have time to figure out how. I shoved the bottom section of the ladder back up and hid in the shadow of the building.

Nurse came out and her sharp voice cut across the chaos. "Let's see what they do to each other in Solitary. There's nothing like being locked in the dark together for a little conflict resolution."

One of the kids yelled something. I sprinted around the corner and into the woods. As soon as I was a safe distance away, I made myself throw up in the bushes. Getting rid of whatever bit of medicine wasn't already in my bloodstream. Then I headed down to the Compass Rose to get some answers.

It was dark under the trees. I knew where I was going now, but they still towered over me, their arms blocking out the night sky. I felt them moving around me, great beings creaking and moaning.

Crack.

A twig snapped behind me and I dropped to the ground. I crouched in a layer of pine needles and dirt, watching, listening. The musty scent of decaying leaves and growing things surrounded me. A spider crawled up my leg, tickling me as it ducked under the cuff of my jumpsuit. The low moan of a tanker's horn quivered through me. Crickets sang of heat and sex.

I was ready to get up when I heard it again.

Crack! And then heavy footsteps.

I tried to stay still. As they got closer, my brain screamed for me to run. I leapt out of the bushes and took off down the hill.

The person was right behind me, gaining on me, my breath wheezing in time with their steps. I zigzagged through the trees, trying to lose them, knowing I was running out of space between me and the Compass Rose. My pulse shrieked in my ears. *Faster!* But the trees thinned, and I knew I was out of luck.

I skidded to a stop and spun around. Ready to face whoever was there. But there was no one. The dark woods were silent except for the thud of my heart.

They were gone.

My throat squeezed with fear, but I tried to shake it off. To concentrate on making it into the Compass Rose. Flood lamps created a moat of light around the building. Since there weren't any guards, I guessed there must be motion sensors or something.

The huge tree out front grew halfway in and halfway out of the circle of light. And its branches stretched up to the second-floor windows. If I could manage to climb up the shadowed side, I just might make it. Of course, the windows were probably locked, but I'd already come this far.

I sprinted to the big tree and grabbed a low-hanging limb. Swinging myself up, I monkeyed up the trunk, staying out of the light. Then I felt my way through the branches till I was sitting high in the shadows.

The smooth bark was warm to the touch, as though blood flowed through its limbs. The tree swayed under me, and I wondered if it would pull its roots from the ground and walk off into the darkness.

The flood of energy pumped through my hand, filling my mind. *Whoosh. Whoosh. Whoosh.* Alert and grounded, I moved along the branch toward the windows. There were three of them within reach, but somehow I knew that the farthest one was the right choice.

Keeping my eyes fixed on the window, I balanced easily, putting one hand in front of the other. The hinged window was latched, but as I touched it, I could sense the sagging weakness of the old wood. I tugged and the latch pulled free.

The window swung open and I stepped onto the sill. My other foot pushed off the tree branch and, as I tumbled through the window, exhaustion swept over me. I landed in a heap on the floor, feeling drained and empty. I must not have gotten all the medicine out of my system in time.

I staggered to my feet, feeling even more overwhelmed as I saw where I was. The room was dully lit by little brass lamps hanging over framed diplomas. I was in Dr. Mordoch's office.

Then again, maybe I was lucky. Maybe I could find my sketchbook. Kel said he'd found his guitar pick in here, but he hadn't said where. There was only her oak desk, the wall of filing cabinets, and the leather chairs for visitors. I didn't see anywhere she could keep a hundred students' earthly possessions.

The shadows and dim lights were disorienting. So I just started opening doors, hoping I'd stumble onto something. The first door, leading out into the hallway, was unlocked, but a skeleton key stuck out of the keyhole. *So much for high security.* Dr. Mordoch must be pretty cocky about the quality of her knockout pills and Takers.

Another door led to a tiny closet stocked with office supplies. The third door opened on an enormous coatroom full of suitcases and plastic bins. *Bingo.*

There weren't any windows in here, so I shut the door behind me and turned on the light. Bright yellow tags were stuck to everything. "Martinez, Frederick." "Johnson, Zach." Dr. Mordoch might be bogarting everyone's stuff, but at least she was well organized.

I quickly found my bag. My mom had obviously been the one who'd packed my suitcase. My nice pair of jeans. Shirts I hated and never wore. A Tinkerbell watch. But no sketchbook.

I dumped everything out and checked again. Nothing. I looked around for a bin with my name on it.

Instead, I found Kel's. I peeked inside his bin, but there wasn't much. A broken steel guitar string. Two quarters. Ginger Altoids. And a smooth gray rock. He must've had this stuff in his pocket when they'd dragged him to Holbrook. I opened the Altoids tin and there was just one left. I smiled.

Like he left it for me. I put the chalky yellow candy in my mouth. It was sharp and sweet, making my eyes water.

I couldn't find anything else with my name on it, so I headed back to the main office to keep looking for my sketchbook.

Rummaging through the desk, I pulled out staplers, a hole puncher, a squeezy penlight with "Zoloft" written on the side, a pocket *Tao Te Ching*, an address book, and a few loose keys. No sketchbook.

The filing cabinets were the only other place I could think of. With the help of the penlight, I tried the small keys in the cabinet's lock. The second one fit and all three drawers popped open, revealing rows and rows of alphabetical files. Dr. Mordoch had pulled my file from the bottom drawer, but I didn't look there right away. Because halfway back in the top drawer, my eyes caught on the label "Fujita, Nami."

I hesitated for a second, then pulled out the manila folder. Her application had been filled out by the Nihonjinron Cooperative, her parents signing off at the bottom. Under "Reason for Application" was a list of Nami's offenses. She'd been caught sneaking out at night to play shows with her band in the city. She was also accused of smoking pot and sexual promiscuity. Bad, but not that bad. Then, reading the final deadly sin, I understood why she'd been sent to Holbrook. "Disregards cultural values."

Her family must live in one of the back-to-your-roots Cooperatives. The war and rationing had done more than divide people economically; it had sent people scurrying back to the safety of their pasts. All kinds of people suddenly realized that they were fundamentalists about something. Anything that could keep "Us" together and "Them" out. There were White Power Cooperatives and

Chosen People Cooperatives, and, in Nami's case, Japanese Nationalist Cooperatives. But evidently, Nami was now, officially, a Them.

Something about her in-your-face bravado clicked into place. When you get expelled for being different, then "different" is all you have. It made me feel sorry for her in a way I knew that Nami would hate. I wished I could've unread her file, so she could just be fearless Nami again. I shut the top two drawers without looking for anyone else's files.

In the bottom drawer, the folders were labeled with dates instead of names. The most recent one was this year, and I was surprised that the first thing inside was my confiscated sketchbook. I let myself touch the rough cardboard cover and straighten the spiral binding before I moved on.

Behind the sketchbook were reports from my past few days at Holbrook. In addition to notes like "Confinement to Meditation Center" and "Peer demonstration at lunch," there were details about my eating habits ("consumed a sandwich, six Tater Tots, and a glass of orange drink"), my behavior during Free Time ("appears to be assimilating into Family Unit"), and a hundred other tiny moments during the day. And also, the letter from my parents enrolling me at Holbrook.

There was nothing about anyone else in the file. It was creepy to think I was being watched so closely, but also extremely boring.

The next folder was also about me and was much more interesting. It held pages and pages of correspondence from the past three years. Letters back and forth between Dr. Mordoch and my parents. Copies of articles from psychiatric magazines about teenage suicide from Dr. Mordoch. A few of my "bone" sketches from my parents. Descriptions of the Holbrook facilities.

The deeper I went into the drawer, the further back in time I went. When I was in seventh grade, the files changed. It was bizarre.

Instead of focusing on me, they were centered on the creation of Holbrook Academy. Brochures for the new school. Legal permits. Zoning for solar panels. The Transfer of Property from the monastery to Dr. Mordoch.

This document was heavy in legalese, but it set out the conditions specified in Ms. Holbrook's will. Except for superficial changes, the forest, statues, and buildings were to remain untouched.

Paper-clipped to the deed was another newspaper article from the local Maine paper. "Economic Hardship Forces Monastery to Sell Holbrook Estate."

There was a note scribbled at the bottom. "This will bring Faye back."

What?

The now familiar sensation of heaviness hit me. The medicine was definitely kicking in. And my mind struggled to stay focused. To grasp what I was seeing in front of me. I flipped through the next file. Old report cards of mine from sixth grade. Paperwork for enrollment at the new South Hills Cooperative School in fifth grade. The hospital report from when I'd been pushed down the stairs in fourth. And it kept going. File after file.

Trying to push away the suspicion that was gnawing at me, I skimmed faster. A school psych evaluation from third grade, noting my difficulty in making friends. A drawing of my hand decorated like a Thanksgiving turkey, the crayon pressed hard into the page. Immunization and doctor records, clearing me of autism, learning disabilities, and a dozen other ailments. The entire drawer was about me. My whole dysfunctional life, neatly color-coded and dated.

Chills crept down my back and I realized something. I wasn't like the other kids in the top two drawers, a thin file holding an application and some school records. And I wasn't just one of Dr. Mordoch's patients. I was *the* patient.

All of this, all of Holbrook, was about me.

But why?

My hands shook as I pulled out the final file from ten years ago. The corners of the manila folder were soft and worn, the cardboard stained with an ancient coffee cup ring.

The file started with a form labeled "Patient Evaluation." It was dated March 11 and was filled out in my mother's handwriting: Faye Robson, Age 6, along with a Maine address and Social Security number.

The bottom section was filled out in Dr. Mordoch's handwriting.

Referred by Mr. and Mrs. Robson (parents) for marked personality change and conduct disorder.

Parent interview: Parents report that Faye, previously a well-adjusted child, has recently undergone a marked personality change. They now find that she is difficult to talk to and avoids eye contact. They describe the child as "disobedient" and "sullen," often keeping to her room for long periods and refusing to come out. She frequently succumbs to night terrors, screaming and flailing, from which her parents find it almost impossible to wake her. The child also refers to a "lady" who comes and speaks to her, and Faye's parents assume this is a new imaginary friend. Faye's aberrant behavior has been ongoing for several months, and is becoming more severe. The parents are able to pinpoint the specific day of the personality shift, December 8, after the family took an evening walk down to the beach. They have no hypothesis about what triggered

*the change and insist that they were with Faye the
entire time. Despite their protests, it is obvious that
the child suffered a trauma, and I have agreed to
take her on as a patient.*

Paper-clipped to it was a neatly typed transcript labeled "Interview with Faye Robson." I read it eagerly.

"Faye, I'm Dr. Mordoch, a friend of your parents. Would you like a cookie?"

(Patient doesn't answer.)

"I want to talk to you for a little bit. Can I come play next to you?"

(Patient shrugs.)

"Your parents tell me you like to play in your room. What do you like to play?"

"I color."

"Would you like to color now?"

(Patient nods.) "I like the red crayons."

"I like red too. It's very bright. What else do you do in your room?"

(Patient shrugs.) "Sometimes she tells me stories."

"Your mom?"

"No."

"Who tells you stories, Faye?"

"The lady from the beach."

"Tell me about the lady, Faye."

(Patient shakes head.)

"Can you tell me what she looks like?"

(Patient shakes head again, visibly agitated.)

"It's okay, you don't have to. We can just sit here and color instead."

(Patient breaks the crayon and stomps it into the carpet.)

A dotted line signaled the end of the session. It was weird reading words I must've said but didn't remember. I didn't even know who I'd been talking about. I tried to remember the sessions, the room, the beach, anything. But my mind was blank.

I moved on to the next interview and the next. After the first session, Dr. Mordoch varied her questions. How was I feeling? Had I had any more bad dreams? But they all ended up in the same place—with Dr. Mordoch asking about the woman and me refusing to answer.

Sometimes there were pictures I'd drawn too, normal little-kid stuff with houses and cats. Sometimes the transcripts had scrawled notes along the bottom. "Is this woman a manifestation or the perpetrator of Faye's trauma?"

The last transcript in the file was from June 2. It was labeled differently. "Hypnotism and Overnight Observation of Faye Robson, Age 6. 2 mg of diazepam administered to patient for anxiety."

"I want you to just relax, Faye. Are you comfortable?"

(Patient wriggles around in the chair for a moment, then nods.)

"Good. Now I want you to look at this light. I know it's bright, but I want you to keep looking at it. Now take a deep breath and let it out."

(Patient inhales and exhales.)

"Good. Keep looking at the light, and take another

big breath and let it out. Let your muscles relax and go limp. You are comfortable and safe."

(Patient inhales and exhales again.)

"Now Faye, I'm going to count backward from three, and as I do, I want you to relax and let your eyes close slowly. Just concentrate on the sound of my voice. Three, just relax. Two, let your arms and legs get heavy. One, close your eyes."

(Patient closes her eyes.)

"Very good. Faye, can you hear me?"

"Yes."

"Okay, Faye. I'd like you to remember something for me. A day from a long time ago. From before you and I met. I want you to remember the first time that you met the lady from the beach. Can you do that? Can you make a picture in your mind?"

"Yes."

"It is a Friday night in December. The trees outside your house are decorated with white Christmas lights, and it's snowing for the first time all winter. Your dad made your favorite meal, spaghetti and meatballs. It's after dinner now, and your mom is helping you put on your coat and mittens. And your red hat. Are you picturing this in your mind?"

(Patient nods.)

"Good. Now you and your mom and dad all go outside for a walk. It's dark and there are lots of stars. Your mom is holding your hand. Then you get to the beach and something happens. What happens, Faye?"

"I lose my mitten."

"That's right. You get excited about the waves. You

pull away from your mom's hand and your mitten comes off. Then you run down to the water and stick your hand in. How does it feel?"

"Cold. I want to splash, but it's too cold. My breath looks like big puffs."

"Good, Faye. Good. What happens next?"

"A wave comes. It sounds like music and my head feels funny. Like it's too crowded in there."

"What kind of music do you hear, Faye?"

(Patient pauses.) "Drums. Then the lady comes and talks to me."

"On the beach? Does the lady talk to you on the beach?"

"No. Daddy tells me my story first and tucks me in."

"Then the lady talks to you?"

(Patient nods.)

"What does the lady say?"

"'I've waited a long time for you.' And that I'm special ... that the water made me special."

"What else does she say?"

(Patient shrugs.)

"Can you draw the lady for me, Faye?"

(Patient picks up crayon and draws attached picture.)

I flipped to the next page, holding it up toward the brass lamps above Dr. Mordoch's diplomas so I could see better. And there it was.

A rough outline of a person. The winged-V drawn where there should've been a face. The dark red wax biting deep into the paper.

16

WATER FLOODED ACROSS the rug. It surged in through the window in a thunderous tide. It stormed down from the ceiling, sizzling as it hit the lightbulbs. And the memory surfaced.

Clutching that ten-year-old drawing in my hand, I pushed the soaked hair out of my eyes and braced myself for the oncoming waves. Spray spattered my jumpsuit. The cold weight of the water squeezed my chest. Salt choked me and blood rang out in my ears. *Whoosh. Whoosh. Whoosh.*

My parents had taken me down to the beach. It had been cold and windy that night, and my mom had held my mittened hand tight inside her gloved one. I'd felt safe, warm, loved, a feeling almost as foreign as this hidden memory. My parents had been laughing at something, but I wasn't paying attention. I was listening.

Music played across the beach, unlike anything I'd ever heard. Drums beat in the pebbles under my feet. An eerie chorus played in the shrieks of seagulls. There were words too, rising on the tide. Beckoning me to the water.

And I went. Pulling my hand out of Mom's. Leaving my mitten behind.

I ran down to the water, the music growing with every step. I reached out, and just before I touched the waves, I heard my name echoing through the night.

Faye.

Then my fingers plunged into the icy tide and I was swallowed up. Bees stung. Water keened. Wind tore at me. And the whole world spun into pristine focus, as if I'd been sleeping all that time and had just woken up.

Later that night, a woman came to me when I was sleeping. I had only a shadow of a memory of her now. She'd told me I was special, but I'd already known that. The water, something in the water, had made me more than I was. Had given me a purpose.

All these years, I'd felt that. Known that there was a reason behind the nightmares and visions and seeing into others' thoughts. I'd known they were important. I just hadn't remembered why.

The memory cleared and with it, the water. I was left holding the piece of paper with the red figure and the symbol. Even though it was years later, I recognized it as something I'd drawn, like I had this morning when I'd seen the same design on the dorm room floor.

I still didn't know what the pictures meant, but I could feel myself getting closer. The answers teased at me. Dangerous and exhilarating. Even though I was scared, I needed to understand.

There was one final page in the folder. A newspaper clipping dated the day after Dr. Mordoch had hypnotized me. The day after I'd told her about that night with my parents and made that drawing. The headline read, "Six-Year-Old's Near-Drowning Sends Family Packing."

The article didn't say much, just that six-year-old me had wandered off that night and almost died. But there were two handwritten notes in the margins: "What about the digging?" And then, a little farther down, "Should I have let her go?"

Neither made any sense to me. And I'd reached the end of the files.

I thought about looking over everything again, but I was impatient with cryptic notes. *Enough.* I dropped the final folder back in the drawer and grabbed my sketchbook. But as soon as I had its familiar weight in my hand, I knew I couldn't take it with me. If Dr. Mordoch was keeping track of every Tater Tot, she was sure to notice if my sketchbook went missing. I risked keeping the penlight from her desk, though. It would help me find what I'd come for.

The charged memory and the weight of the drugs had swirled together, leaving me with the kind of clarity that you only get deep in the night. When you're too tired to lie to yourself. Somewhere downstairs more symbols were waiting for me. I could almost feel them. Their lines drawing me closer.

Sucking in air, I steadied myself and headed for the door.

It was pitch dark in the hallway, and I used the tiny penlight to navigate down the stairs and into the sitting room. Windows lined the wall looking out on the back porch. Light filtered in, and I could make out the striped wallpaper, a faux-antique coffee table, and leather couches, all carefully set up to make the place look old-worldly and lived in. This was one of the few rooms parents might see, and Dr. Mordoch had made sure it had the perfect feel.

The chandelier Kel had described was in the center of the room. The brass fixture glinted in the weak beam of my penlight, illuminating four V-shaped flying birds ringing the fixture. A flowery letter was inscribed next to each of the shapes, N, W, S, and E. And in the center, where the chandelier hung down, was an intricate metal rose. Its petals unfurling delicately.

I get it . . . The Compass Rose.

Beneath it, on the floor, bloomed a similar rose. This one was mosaicked in red marble. I shuddered. In the dim light, it looked like blood. The rest of the floor was done in cream tile, arranged in stars and octagons. A reddish ring circled the whole thing, mirroring the compass theme.

The flower pattern was covered up by the coffee table, and I pushed it aside a little, looking for more symbols. The legs of the table shrieked against the floor, echoing in the open room.

A few seconds later, a door slammed somewhere in the direction of the cafeteria. I shoved the table back and rushed to the corner, pulling at the door to the back porch. The porch door didn't budge, and I saw, too late, that it was nailed shut.

Now I heard voices and dove behind the couch. I wasn't going to get caught. Dr. Mordoch was not going to win this one.

Dust itched my nose. From my view of the slice of floor under the couch, I watched two pairs of shoes stride into sight. Then I heard Freddy's gravelly voice.

"Hit the light switch."

The chandelier blazed and I flattened myself even more.

"I told you, I saw a light in here." It was Dragon.

"You said a flicker. A flicker could be anything." Freddy paced around the room, sounding irritated. Getting closer. His shoes stopped right in front of the couch and I thought about shadows and stealthy mice and not breathing.

"Well, we both heard that noise. Like someone screaming." Dragon didn't sound like she was in a good mood either.

My cheek pressed against the cold red tile of the outer ring. The drugs were making it hard to focus again, but I didn't dare close my eyelids. Instead, I stared at the cream tiles, keeping myself alert by following the pattern with my eyes. The four-pointed stars touched, tip to tip. Like they were holding hands all the way across the floor, forming octagons in the space between them. The floor looked old, some of the tiles were cracked, and the mortar was grimy and blackened with age.

No. Only some of the mortar was dark. Only some of the points of some of the stars were outlined by black mortar, whereas most of the points were outlined by dull gray.

I stopped looking at the bigger star pattern and focused on the darker mortar. It was like one of those optical illusions where you have to relax your eyes and suddenly a 3-D image pops out of the seemingly random design. I traced my finger over the rough grout, the stunning realization sinking in. The outline was the same winged-V shape I'd drawn on the floor of my room. The same shape from the column and the chandelier and the picture in the files.

Something between excitement and nausea stirred in my stomach. Each of the black Vs pointed toward the next one. *They're not birds. They're arrows.*

"Listen," Freddy ordered. "You search the top floor and I'll do the bottom and we'll meet in the middle. Just be sure not to set off any of the sensors."

So there are alarms.

One pair of boots thunked up the stairs. The other went down the hallway leading to the cafeteria.

I looked from the receding feet back to where the path of arrows ran under a pleather couch. I wanted to follow the tiles, to shove the furniture out of the way and get to whatever it was they pointed at.

But not with Takers stomping through the house. It'd have to wait. I had to get out of here. *Now.*

I climbed the steps as carefully as I could. I didn't dare use my penlight, so I jammed it down in my sock. At the top of the stairs I listened for Dragon. She was still up on the third floor. I sneaked into the second-floor hallway, immediately pulling back against the wall, confused. Someone was there.

A tall girl was heading away from me, down the hall. A long, blond braid swung behind her. Rita.

I hurried after her, wanting to talk to her again, but afraid to call out. Rita turned the corner and I followed, closing the distance between us. Moonlight streamed through a hall window, and the tail of her braid gleamed as she turned again. Just ahead of me. Gaining on her, I broke into a run. Rounding a third corner, I reached out, ready to stop her, and ran straight into Kel.

"Wh-what are you doing here?" I stumbled against him, the drugs making me dizzy. Pressing my hand into the wall, I steadied myself, looking around the hallway. "Where is she?"

"The Taker? I thought *you* were her." The relief in Kel's voice was obvious. "Or she was you. Or whatever. Last *I* saw, she went upstairs."

He looked up. As if expecting to see Dragon through the ceiling.

"No. Not the Taker. The other student. The girl. She was right here." I shook my head, trying to clear the drug fog that crept back into my brain. Nothing was making sense. "What are you even doing here?"

Kel grinned at me, and his slow smile made me suddenly aware that we were both leaning against the wall, shoulders almost touching. "I knew you wouldn't be able to resist checking out the chandelier, and I thought you might appreciate a tour guide."

I thought about the footsteps chasing me through the woods earlier. "Did you follow me down here?"

Kel looked a little sheepish. "I didn't mean to scare you. I just wanted to catch up to you. It wasn't until you started running that I realized what it must've seemed like. So I waited a bit, then came in to find you. Unfortunately"—Kel gestured around the hallway, grinning at the dangerous game—"I seemed to have gotten a little . . . um . . . trapped."

We were standing at a dead end. Rita must've known another way out, but I couldn't see where. There were no doors. No windows. No place else to go.

As if to demonstrate this point, we heard the ominous *thud, thud, thud* of Dragon coming back down the stairs.

Smile still on his face, Kel's eyes glittered. "Like I said . . . trapped."

"Come on." I grabbed his hand and pulled him back down the hallway. His excitement stung at me. Making my palms sweat. Adrenaline clearing out the drugs.

We raced the encroaching footsteps toward Dr. Mordoch's office. *Please. Please. Please.* Flying into the room, I eased the door shut behind us. Just as a boot smacked the hallway floor.

Dragon's footsteps grew louder. Doors creaked open, then slammed shut again as she worked her way down the hall. I lunged for the skeleton key sticking out of the office door and twisted clockwise. There was a satisfying, soft click. I inched the key out of the lock, and Kel and I backed away from the door.

Our hands were still linked, and I noticed that for the first time since I'd met him, Kel's gloves were gone. His long, bare fingers intertwined with mine. I felt the pulse racing in his wrist. The wild ache buzzing in his chest. Tension crackling across the surface of our skin.

Was this what it was like to be with someone? Aware of every inch of their body? So close that their sensations became your own?

I looked up into Kel's eyes and suddenly, like thunder catching up with lightning, we were in sync. Our breath fell into a single hush of rising and falling. Our hearts slowed and matched each other beat for beat. And standing there in the dark, the house itself holding its breath around us, I could no longer see where Kel's body stopped and mine started.

A soft hum floated into my mind. Kel's song from Solitary. I let it wash over me. Let its refrain soak into my consciousness.

His thought drifted into my head, and even though I should've been surprised, his voice felt like it belonged there. *"I am with you."*

He pulled me closer. Hands enveloping my own. Bodies folding together. Lips inches from mine.

And the humming grew louder. A stinging, delicious, terrible chorus. Drowning out my thoughts. Until everything was Kel.

"You are not alone."

Strong and irresistible, the song rose into a buzzing frenzy. Calling to me. My heart pounding out its beat. *"You don't have to do this alone."*

I wanted our skin to melt away. Our bones to grow into each other. Our veins to twine and merge like vines wrapping tight.

I wanted to taste his lips.

"Nothing on this end." Dragon's voice came from right outside the door, and startled, I pulled away from Kel.

And I was alone again. But now there was no loneliness. The exhilaration of being known, of being seen, was like a drug. Powerful and revelatory. Something new had woken inside me. I felt it stirring, fighting its way up through years of isolation and doubt.

The Takers could not touch us. The footsteps outside the door were nothing now. This was just a game of cat and mouse.

And we were the cats.

The doorknob rattled. I watched it, body taut, ready to bolt or maybe pounce, the second I saw movement. Kel's body was ready too, and a current of energy ricocheted back and forth between us.

But there was no sound of a key in the lock. Only more footsteps. And Dragon moving away again, back down the hall.

I grinned at Kel and moved toward the window. "Not trapped. Just temporarily inconvenienced. Shall we move on?"

"Indeed. Ladies first." The flecks of green within his brown eyes caught the dim light of the office and seemed to shimmer. Teasing and electrifying me simultaneously.

I held his eyes for a second longer, only breaking away to bend down and slip the skeleton key into my sock. Right next to the penlight. Then I sprang to my feet and raced to the window. I was out of it and onto the ledge before Kel even noticed I'd moved.

I leapt from the ledge, easily bridging the distance between it and the tree. Tightrope walking along the branch. Even though he moved more slowly, Kel was right behind me. Playing my game. Swinging down from branch to branch, we both kept to the shadows. Careful and reckless at the same time.

I was balanced on the lowest branch, almost down, when Kel grabbed the sleeve of my jumpsuit. "Faye—"

He was breathing hard, and my name came out louder than he'd meant it to. I put my fingers to my lips, trying for a frowning scold. But his mouth pulled tight, his pupils narrowed. I could read that look now. Confusion. Seriousness. Talking. All the questions I didn't want to deal with right now.

I was tired of questions.

Leaves quivered in the muggy breeze. The wild tang of sea salt teased my tongue. Shadows and moonlight chased each other across the grounds. And under it all, the cadence of the waves called to me.

Kel's hand still on my sleeve, he swung his legs over the branch just above mine so we were facing each other. He pushed the hair out of his eyes, and I was struck by the haunted look I found there. I forced myself to be still. To listen.

Kel started again in a low whisper. "Faye, what happened back there?"

"Maybe it was just the adrenaline." I shrugged, not meeting his eyes.

"Yeah. Maybe." But he didn't believe it either. He reached out, and before he touched me, I knew exactly what his hand would feel like. The whorls of his fingerprints reeling across my skin. Elation edged with pain. His eyes pinning me down. Making me his own.

But I didn't want to be his. I wanted to run through the dark. I wanted the hot breath of night against my skin. I wanted to be touched, but not eclipsed.

I tugged my sleeve out of his grip and pushed off the branch. Leaping the rest of the way to the ground.

"Missed me, missed me," I called in a singsong voice.

Now you gotta kiss me.

Kel looked down and I held his shadowed gaze. I loved being able to read the thoughts flickering across his face. A crease of frustration here, a lifted eyebrow of amusement there. Finally settling into that slow smile that tingled warm, up and down my body. His eyes glimmered with my challenge, then suddenly flared with danger.

I swung around, looking for the threat. And there on the front porch of the Compass Rose was Freddy, with Dragon right on his heels.

I froze in the shadow of the big tree, but Freddy had already spotted me.

"You there. Stay put!"

Before I could move, before Freddy was able to pound down the stairs or bark orders into his radio, Kel jumped down too. But unlike me, he stayed hidden, pulling me back behind the tree with him.

Kel flashed me a smile. "Last one back's a rotten egg."

Then with a battle cry, Kel bolted into the spotlights and across the lawn. Alarms shrieked as he sprinted off into the forest.

Dragon and Freddy were after him before Kel made it to the trees. In the dark, they hadn't realized there were two of us. Stunned, I wasted another second watching them all disappear into the woods.

Then I took off too. Racing up the path to the dorms. *I wish I had a river so long. I would teach my feet to fly.*

The other Takers were already running toward the Compass Rose's wailing siren. I dodged through the trees, avoiding their streaking flashlights and thundering boots. Refusing to think about Kel getting caught. Or the drawer full of files detailing my dysfunctional childhood. Or Dr. Mordoch, itching to send me to Solitary again.

I just pulled spruce-scented air in and out of my lungs. Listened to the drumbeat of my feet against the dirt. My heart singing with the adrenaline coursing through my veins.

When I reached the courtyard, it was abandoned. I used a branch to pull down the bottom part of the ladder and started climbing, pulling the lower section up behind me. Then I hesitated. If Kel was being chased, would he have time to pull it down? Had he used this ladder too?

Then I remembered what I'd seen out the window that morning. A blur of green streaking across the rooftop. It'd been Kel. It made sense that there'd be a ladder on the boys' side too.

Climbing higher, I looked for Kel. There was no sign of him yet, but I swore I felt him getting closer. I shimmied through my window and into bed. Lying there in the dark, I counted the seconds, wondering how much time Kel had to get to his room.

He'll make it. He has to.

One hundred and ninety-three seconds later, the overhead lights snapped on. *Was it enough?*

Maya groaned, "No fucking way it's morning."

I remembered my boots and hurried to pull them off. Shoving them under the bed, I tried to sound sleepy. "Is that an alarm somewhere?"

Footsteps clacked down the hallway, locks clicking one by one as Nurse did a bed check.

"Sit up. I want to see faces and movement," Nurse barked when it was our turn. We obeyed wordlessly and she was gone.

Fifteen minutes later, the lights flicked off again. But I couldn't sleep. His name looped over and over again in my head. *Kel.*

Kel. Kel. Kel.

Yesterday, I'd been overwhelmed by unexplained drawings and secret symbols and crazy visions. But now they were just clues pointing the way. And I didn't have to find the path alone. Together, Kel and I would follow it to the end.

Thrum. Thrum. Thrum. Even now, I could still hear his heartbeat. Somewhere out there in the night. Shunning sleep, I let it sing me through the dark hours of the morning.

17

I WAS STILL AWAKE when the lights came on. The speaker crackled into life. Nurse ordered us out of bed.

And this morning, I was actually *in* bed. And so was Maya.

No waking up on the floor. No red hands. No strange drawings.

"Was it because of the alarm that went off?" Maya asked from the open bathroom. "Or do you think one of us managed to stay awake and stop whatever it was from happening?"

I stayed awake. Me and Kel. It didn't happen because of us.

Last night came back in a rush. Standing in the dark with Kel. And I was on my feet, ready to get through the lines and the showers. Ready to get down to breakfast. Ready to see Kel again. My whole body buzzed with the question.

Did he make it back?

Maya's question had been curious instead of suspicious. Her voice easy and relaxed. After all, I'd promised her the truth. But I had so few things that were private here at Holbrook. So few things that were mine. I didn't know if Kel was in trouble. I had no idea how today would turn out. But what I did have was last night. And I wasn't giving it up.

So I aimed my smile at her and settled on a smaller truth. One that I hoped wouldn't inspire any more questions. "I bet someone made it through the night."

Except for the lack of red hands and strange pictures, the morning was the same as the rest. People ran out of hot water in the showers. A shoving match started over underwear. The Takers insulted us as we marched down the path toward the Compass Rose.

But I was different. Wide awake, like I'd been swigging espresso. The ocean shimmered in the humid morning, the rhythm of the waves calling to me. And today I wanted to answer them. Today I could handle whatever mystery was lurking under their glittering surface.

The path curved, and the Compass Rose waited imperiously for me at the bottom of the hill. The question I hadn't had a chance to ask the night before finally demanded my attention. *Why have a hallway that doesn't go anywhere?*

In my head, I laid out the floor plan of the Compass Rose, drawing the building from the outside in. I mentally sketched the hallways outside of Dr. Mordoch's office and Rita's path through the house. Yes. There should've been more building there. If I was right, and I was pretty sure I was, the turret on the corner was exactly where the hallway had dead-ended.

Kel grinned at me from the breakfast table. A cocky smile that let me know he'd gotten back to his room undetected. I should've had a million questions about how and why and what-was-happening. I should've been freaked out. But my mind was too full of imagining us alone together again. The warmth of his hands brushing against my skin. His lips closing the distance between us. And I just grinned back.

Damion and Zach must have thought we were just happy that our fingers weren't stained red again. They both displayed their clean hands and the same question showed clearly in each of their eyes: "*Is it over?*"

The question echoed in Kel's eyes too. But while Damion's tone was skeptical and Zach's hopeful, Kel was disappointed.

I answered him with a little head shake. After what I'd found in Dr. Mordoch's files the night before, I knew that our red hands were just the tip of the iceberg. Thinking about my red crayon picture and the trail of arrows grouted into the sitting room floor, my heart pounded out an impatient beat.

Kel nodded back to me, the green of his eyes catching my eagerness. As we sat down, Nami and Maya and I silently answered the guys' question. Copying their gesture. Showing them our unstained hands. The tension at the table eased, and despite the bland, gluey texture, everyone ate their oatmeal with gusto.

Dr. Mordoch still presided over us from the main table, but after the late-night disturbance, she and her kingdom looked diminished. Empty chairs were scattered throughout the room, and it was even quieter than usual, if that was possible. As if the students were waiting to see what would happen next. No one else knew who'd set off the alarm, but they knew that *someone* had sneaked out of the dorms. *Someone* had found a way.

Across the table Kel, back in his gloves and hoodie, fiddled with his spoon. His whole body was tense with the same quiet expectation. But the whites of his eyes were tinged with red, his brown cheeks flushed. Exhaustion peeking through.

What did it cost him to make it back before the room check?

Kel rubbed at his spoon, and then, for some reason, stuck it on his nose. He looked up at me with a triumphant smile, totally incongruous in the grim setting, the plastic spoon dangling from his crooked nose. Then it slipped off, and he snatched it dramatically out of midair with his other hand. A muffled snort came from

Maya. She shot a look at Damion, waiting to be reprimanded. But even he managed to smile this morning.

Kel bowed as grandly as he could without drawing attention. I mimed a tiny round of applause.

I'd been alone for so long, isolated and ignored, that it seemed impossible to be sitting here with Kel, playing around. How much could I tell him? How much would he accept before he turned away too?

Can I tell him about the pictures on the floor? About my vision of Dr. Mordoch? The bonfire on the first night?

I didn't know. My eyes drifted around the table, taking in this new Family of mine.

It all depends what you're willing to risk, Faye.

But even if I'd wanted to tell him, there was no time. We were shuttled straight to Socialization with dear, sadistic Auntie.

"You are unbelievably lucky to be at Holbrook." Aunt smiled condescendingly. "In the news this morning, every story was about this heat wave that's hit the country. In New York City, the solar arrays have overheated, and without power, hundreds of people are dying from heatstroke. In California, fires have already wiped out twelve Cooperatives and one wind farm. In Indiana, millions of acres of crops have been lost. And you're here, fed, clothed, and sheltered, given the time to concentrate on getting well. It's more than you deserve, so let's not waste another class."

I could think of a couple things *she* deserved, but I kept my mouth shut.

Aunt tapped a manila envelope against her hand. "In the outside world, each of you wears a specially tailored costume. At Holbrook, we've stripped you of this crutch. But even in your uniforms, you're still presenting a facade to the world, by the way you sit"—Aunt looked at Damion, who was stick-straight, chin up, eyes ahead—"the way you wear your hair"—she nodded at Nami's narrow strip of blue hair sadly flopped to one side and Kel's falling across his eyes—"or even by your lack of engagement with the world." Aunt looked at me without ever meeting my eyes.

"Today we'll be verbally acknowledging these disguises. For this exercise, we'll be working in pairs."

My eyes darted over to Kel. He was already looking at me and I was back in the office again. His hand in mine. *You don't have to do it alone.*

But Aunt cleared her throat and went on with a conniving smile. "I've already chosen your partners, so no need to worry about that. Simply concern yourself with making today's lesson better than the last one. For your own sakes."

Kel and Damion were paired together. Nami was with Maya. And I was partnered with Zach. Aunt was smarter than she looked.

"Take a look at these pictures." Aunt pulled xeroxed pages out of the envelope. Each one had a badly printed black-and-white photograph on it. Like a Wanted poster.

Aunt handed me a picture of Zach. He was wearing his backward-Superman shirt and frowning in the general direction of the camera.

Zach's paper had a picture of me. My face was expressionless and I was in the brown T-shirt I'd worn to Holbrook. I had a fork in my hand.

Spiders creepy-crawled up my back. These were pictures from dinner the first night. Someone had been taking pictures of us.

"Now," Aunt instructed, "think about the person you see in this photograph. Do they look hostile? Closed off?"

Aunt pulled out a copy of Nami's picture. "Take this one, for instance." Nami was standing in the courtyard. She had smears of mascara around her eyes from the pepper-spray incident and her Mohawk stood up at an awkward angle. But still she gave the camera an in-your-face grin. Her right hand was a blur in front of her chest, as if she'd flipped off the camera at the last second. I loved it.

Aunt was not so fond. "This girl is clearly trying hard to look different. Special. She has to dye her hair, act sassy, flaunt her curves, because in the deepest pit of her stomach, she's afraid that she's forgettable. That no one will ever truly love her. That she will never do anything great."

Nami's face went blank and I saw the fear mirrored in her eyes. Next to her, Maya must have seen it too. She shifted positions, her foot "accidentally" kicking Nami in the shin. Surprised, Nami looked up and Maya gave her the slightest smile. Nami blinked and shook herself, like a dog after a bath.

All of this happened in seconds, and Aunt was too busy acting superior to notice. By the time she looked back, Nami's screw-you smile was back in place. "Now you try it. Remember, you aren't talking about your partner. You're merely unraveling their costume."

Zach and I sat in silence, waiting for one of us to start. Aunt eyed us from across the room, and I broke the stalemate.

"Well . . ." I studied the photo, trying to concentrate. Zach looked small and off-balance in the picture, like he was about to collapse in on himself. ". . . the person here seems—"

I stopped. Zach didn't deserve to be talked about in the third person. I tried again, dropping the game. "You look quiet here. Reserved. Like you're holding yourself back."

He looked at me, surprised.

I tapped the picture, pointing at Zach's T-shirt. "And I'm guessing you like comic books."

Zach's anxiety transformed into a sheepish grin, and his eyes came alive. It made him look like a totally different person from the guy in the photo.

"It's geeky, right?" Zach nodded to himself, still uncertain. "But I really wanna draw them someday. And write them."

Evidently, we were more alike than I thought. "Me too. I mean, not comic books. But art stuff."

The last trace of terror slipped off Zach's face. "I liked your painting yesterday. Sorry he was such a dick about it. How . . ."

Zach hesitated, checking that Aunt was out of earshot. "How did you do that? Without sketching it out first? Mine was an exercise in chaos."

I couldn't think of anything to say that wouldn't make me sound crazy or stuck-up. But it didn't matter, because Zach rushed on.

"Your picture, the way you painted those stars, they made me think of these dreams I've been having. They're crazy intense, like the ones I get when I sneak my mom's OxyContin. I'm walking outside and there's this music playing in the background . . . and it's pulling me toward it, like I'm a zombie or something.

"But I don't try and fight it, instead I keep looking up at those stars. And I can feel them, you know? It sounds crazy, but I can actually feel their radiation from all those light-years away and it makes me—" Zach's voice cut off and he looked up and away, like he was hunting for just the right words. Then, in a hushed voice, he said, "Well, when I look up at them, I don't feel too awake like I normally do. Or anesthetized like with the drugs. The only way I can describe it is, they make me feel solid."

I could see a new confidence in his face as he talked, and I wanted to ask him more about the strange music he'd mentioned. *Maybe we're all hearing it. Maybe I'm really* not *alone in this.*

As Zach waited for me to respond, his confidence slid away. He seemed unsure again, wanting my approval. "She doesn't really need them, you know. My mom, I mean. She doesn't need the OxyContin and all that other crap. And sometimes the world just gets too noisy for me and I can't filter it all out. But I wouldn't take them if she was actually in pain. Nah . . . She's just on another planet entirely."

Zach's face twisted into a grimace as he blurted out the next part. "She just let them take me, you know . . . She just let the Cooperative send me off to Holbrook for 'rehab.' My druggie-of-a-mother signed the papers without even reading them. How fucked up is that?"

An awkward pause sat between us while I tried to think of anything that might sound supportive. I was relieved when Aunt interrupted.

"Time to switch!"

Zach also looked happy to change the subject. He studied my picture, then looked up at me. Then at the paper again, looking a little unnerved. I braced myself for whatever was coming. "You kinda seem—"

A loud siren cut Zach off. I clapped my hands to my ears. Aunt's mouth moved but I couldn't hear anything over the shrieking wail. She motioned toward the door and we all rushed for it, glad for any excuse to get out of there.

I smelled smoke as soon as I hit the hallway, but I didn't see any fire. Kids were streaming past, holding their sleeves over their mouths. I tried to keep an eye on Kel, but lost sight of him and the rest of the Family as I got sucked into the crush. The panicked mass funneled down the stairs and out onto the lawn.

Chaos ensued. Takers shouted into earpieces and argued with the Aunts and Uncles about how to regain order. Kids were everywhere. Lounging on the grass. Heading off in pairs. Starting fights. It was like my high school parking lot.

I spotted Maya standing by herself, her thin body looking stiff and breakable. Her reddish hair bright against her washed-out skin.

Then I caught a glimpse of Nami leading Damion around the far corner of the building. I guess hormones trumped rules every time.

I didn't see Zach or Kel anywhere. But no one seemed to be hurt, so I wasn't worried. Plus, I had a good guess where Kel was.

Ducking into the woods, I headed toward the Compass Rose. Every once in a while, someone came hurrying toward the fire alarms and I crouched behind a tree. When I got inside the Compass Rose, there wasn't a Taker in sight. But I wasn't alone either.

Kel stood in the middle of the main room, craning his neck up at the chandelier. Then he looked down at the floor.

He always seemed to be one step ahead of me. Knowing where I was going before I did. After last night, it was strange watching him like this. Being separate from him. I knew why I was trying to solve this puzzle—it wouldn't seem to leave me alone—but why was he?

Only one way to find out.

I walked into the room, my boots scuffing across the marble floor. Hearing my footsteps, he dove for the nearest couch. I tried to keep a straight face as a second later he peeked back out, scowling.

He stood up, managing to get some words out. "You scared me."

"Well, you scared me first."

"I'm rubber. You're glue . . . ," Kel started, and we smiled. "I never asked you if you'd found anything. I didn't have time with . . . everything going on last night."

Our eyes locked and I could feel him pulling me into him. I wanted to walk over to him. To make things like they were last night. But I stayed where I was, letting the charged air build up between us.

How much can I tell him?

It wasn't easy to let go of years of doubt and isolation, but I let the memory of last night push all that out of my mind. *You are not alone.*

"I found this." I forced my feet to walk across the room to him as I pointed to the outlined tiles.

Kel's forehead creased as he studied the marble, pushing the long hair out of his face as he tried to see what I was talking about. Then his expression cleared up into a surprised "Aha."

He crouched down and touched the grouted pattern. "How did you even notice this?"

"Well, last night, while you were safe upstairs, I was participating in what Dr. Mordoch might refer to as an 'avoidance exercise.'"

Kel grinned at me, understanding perfectly. "Do they lead somewhere?"

"Well, if you weren't here distracting me, I'd know already, wouldn't I?"

Kel caught my eye sharply and stepped toward me. The heat from his body, centimeters away, seared into mine.

But when Kel spoke, his voice was soft. "I'm lucky I beat you here or I would've missed out."

We were only a breath away from each other. There was hunger in his eyes and I answered it, leaning in. Only atoms separating us.

Police sirens wailed down the driveway, shocking us both back to reality.

"We should probably hurry." Kel stepped back and I remembered to breathe.

Together, we pushed the couch out of the way so we could follow the trail of arrows. But they led straight into the wall.

Frustration bit at me. "Another dead end."

"Like last night. I've been wondering about that . . ." Then Kel asked the same question I had. "Why have a hallway going nowhere?"

"Right. I took a look at the Compass Rose on my way down to breakfast this morning, and that hallway *should* lead to one of the turrets. But if it does, then where's the door?"

"Maybe"—Kel looked down at the path of arrows—"the door is somewhere else."

We both looked at the wall again. The thing was, this wall wasn't anywhere near the dead end we'd found the night before. That hallway was upstairs and on the front side of the house. Still.

The upper wall was covered with thick, striped wallpaper. Two-thirds of the way down, decorative oak panels were built into the wall in wide, beveled squares. Heart pounding in excitement, I knelt down and took a closer look. There was a dark smudge on the wood panel closest to the arrows. So, we weren't the first students to decipher the pattern.

We were close. I could feel something on the other side of this wall. Answers.

I pushed on the smudged wood and the square gave a little. Shoving my shoulder into it, the square swung open, like the tiny door in *Alice in Wonderland*.

And I was already crawling through. Ready for the rabbit hole.

On the other side, there were arrows everywhere. Thousands of them, carved into the black stone walls of the dim passageway. Not ornate like the ones on the column. There was a crudeness to these marks, a violence. Like someone had gouged them into the soft stone with a knife. Over and over.

The gashes whispered to me.

It's time. My mind filled with their chanting song. Drums pounded in my chest.

It's time for you.

18

WHOOSH. WHOOSH. WHOOSH. Their raw power rushed through me.

I stretched out my hand, touching one of the arrows. A howling filled my head, the rasping of steel against stone. A gray mountain of water rising up to meet me. Screams shattering the air. I ripped my hand away.

With a splintering *pop,* a tiny crack formed where my thumb had been and shot up the wall.

"What's wrong?" Kel crawled in behind me and closed the small door.

"Nothing." My voice shook in the sudden dark. Torn between terror and exhilaration, I reached out and felt for the crack in the wall of arrows. Checking if it was real. Goose bumps shivered across my skin as my fingers found the fracture in the cold stone.

Fear is an illusion. I'm in control of my own reality.

I fumbled with the penlight I'd stuck in my sock. Making a circle of light in the darkness. The solid rhythm of drums steadying me.

"Sneaky girl." Kel's voice was relaxed, teasing. But he looked genuinely impressed that I had a secret flashlight.

"You don't know the half of it."

"I wouldn't mind finding out." The secret passage suddenly went from horror movie to James Bond flick.

My tiny light ran across the gouged symbols. The insistent drumming trembling through me.

Does Kel hear them too? How could he not?

They shook my every thought now. Thrilling through every molecule of my body. And, there in the dark, I gave myself to them.

"Race you!" I yelled over my shoulder, already running. My feet already matching the pounding in my skull.

I careened around the corner. Left. Then right. Then left again.

Everything was so clear. The maze of hallways twisting through the rest of the Compass Rose was genius. They hid this passageway perfectly. I ran through the cool darkness, the crazed arrows pointing the way. Kel's footsteps right behind me, egging me on.

The passage narrowed into a spiral staircase at the end of the labyrinth. The pulsing beat surged through me and I sprinted up the steps. Toward the door at the top. Toward the final arrow carved into the wood.

I grabbed the doorknob and twisted, throwing my weight against it. My shoulder slammed into the unmoving door. Kel crashed into me a second later.

"Locked." My body ached with the blow and the drums and closeness of Kel.

Kel let out a huff of breath, his body still tangled up with mine.

"Perfect." He didn't sound that sorry about it.

I'd dropped the penlight in the collision, but even in the dark I knew where every inch of him was. One hand pressed against my leg. The other braced against the wall. I even knew the smile he was wearing on his face. My throat was dry and I forced the words out of my mouth. "I still have the key. In my boot."

"What?"

"I still have the—"

"I heard you. Do you have wire cutters stuck somewhere? Maybe a getaway car?"

"Just help me find the flashlight." We fumbled on the stairway. Hands grazing each other. Arms crisscrossing in the dark. Finally, a circle of light appeared by Kel's face.

The green in his eyes glinted in the weak light. The familiar smile hovering on his lips. I tried not to think about how close he was to me. Or the warm scent of him.

I reached into my boot, smiling. There was something exhilarating about having a partner in crime. The skeleton key fit in the lock, and with a twist and a click, we were in. The sunny room was blinding after the dark stairway. My eyes ached as I stepped in, blinking.

The place was covered in books. Stacks and piles and shelves of them, smelling like dust and leather and years of warm fires and closed windows. Sunlight streamed through the windows of the octagon-shaped library, turning it into an oven.

I was right. We were in the turret. Keeping low, I peeked out a window and down at the driveway. Firefighters and Takers hurried here and there.

"The crisis still crisis-ing?" Kel spoke in a quiet voice, close to my ear. His breath hot on my neck.

"Wonder what happened."

"The rumor I heard, on my way out, was that some pyro got hold of matches and set the toilet paper on fire."

"Really?" I couldn't tell if he was kidding.

"Yeah, I know. I mean, sure it's scratchy, but it's not *that* bad."

I turned away, not letting Kel see my smirk.

He gazed around the room. "I guess they *really* don't want us to study at Holbrook. All these books locked away . . . but where's the fun toy surprise?"

Suddenly, I was anxious. *Something* was here in this room, I could feel it. Something that would explain what was happening to us at night, my visions, Dr. Mordoch's files. Kel was here with me now, but would he really be able to handle whatever we found? Would I? Ominous blood-red symbols weren't likely to lead to unicorns and rainbows.

"I mean, why would you make a secret room unless you wanted to hide something in it? Right?" Kel opened a rolltop desk with an old photo of the Compass Rose hanging over it. Inside the desk, there were more books, a lamp, and a mostly empty bottle of Jim Beam.

Maybe we wouldn't find anything. Maybe I could come back here later. Alone.

"Let's check the bookshelves. You go that way and I'll go this way." Kel pointed for me to go counterclockwise.

I ran my fingers along the frayed bindings as I looked for more arrows on the bookshelves. Then my throat tightened, and a strangled yelp escaped my mouth. There, carved into the fifth shelf up, was the outline of a person. Stubby arms and legs. Arrow instead of a face.

Just like the ones I'd drawn. *How is that possible?* Fear returned hard and fast, blotting out my excitement.

"You found something?" Kel was right behind me and it was already too late to hide it. I kicked myself for making that stupid noise. What if Kel somehow made the connection between me and the symbols? What if Maya told them all what I'd been drawing on the floor? *Will Kel blame me for what's happening at night? Will he think I'm crazy?*

He ran his finger over the little man etched into the wood. "That's not the same marking. How do you know this is it?"

I just know. The real question is, What does it mean?

Kel pulled out the book that was sitting directly above the carved figure. "Maybe it has a secret compartment."

Maybe what's inside is worse than not knowing at all.

I squeezed my hands into fists, forcing myself not to knock the book out of his hand. Instead, I concentrated on breathing as Kel opened up *Tides and Waters of New England.*

The binding creaked like it hadn't been read in years, and the book gave off a damp, musty odor. But there was no secret compartment. There were no coded messages. There were just maps. Lots and lots of maps. Maps of the shore at high tide and low tide. Maps of the moon endlessly looping and spinning around the Earth. Maps of the coastline thousands of years ago and maps of what it would look like in another thousand years.

I took it from Kel, flipping through the pages, sure there must be more. Relief and disappointment battled inside me.

"It could take hours to look through that whole thing. And what if the books got rearranged? It could be any of these. *Geological Movements* or *Avians of Maine.*" He pulled books off the shelves, shaking each one out, checking for secret compartments.

Then I saw something in the open space where the books had been. Something in the shadows. "Keep pulling them!"

Electricity shot through me. This was it. At the back of the bookshelf, the arrow and the rough figure were carved into the wood, one below the other. Making it look like a man standing on the peak of a mountain. Wary, I touched the marking and a panel sprang open.

Kel and I peered into the hole. Kel laughed. "Surprise. Another book."

Before he could move, I thrust my arm into the hole. My hand closed around soft leather and I pulled out the worn book.

"There's something else . . ." Reaching over me, Kel grabbed what looked like a tiny statue. "Look at this! It's the same as that carving on the bookshelf."

Same as my drawing in Dr. Mordoch's files. Same as the picture I made on the dorm floor. The figurine fit in the palm of Kel's hand. A metal person with crude arms and legs, but no eyes or mouth. Only that strange arrow staring out of its face.

He held out the statue for me to look at, and I shuddered.

"Faye, what's wrong?"

I don't know. All I knew was that I didn't want to touch it. "Let's start with the book. Okay?"

"Sure." Kel's voice was gentle and I was grateful he didn't push for answers I didn't even have.

Wiping off a thick layer of dust, I uncovered the initials "M. H." burned into the suede cover. I traced the letters with my fingers, wondering who had gone to so much trouble to hide these things here.

Sitting down on the floor, I opened it up, reading aloud the black, cursive handwriting.

July 29, 1911

Cousin Bea is here. Again. I've been hiding up in my room all afternoon. But they'll have to haul me off to the asylum if I go back down there. Bea will want to take another "constitutional," as she says in that pretentious, grating voice of hers. Then when she has me in her clutches, her arm stuck onto mine like a leech from Hodge's Pond, she'll drone on about her admirers.

"Weren't his eyes divine?" she'll squeal as she drags me around the gardens. Or "Did I tell you what so-and-so said to me at the Dumonts' party?"

I scanned the rest of the page and the next. It was more of the same. Phrases like *infernal petticoats* were interrupted, here and there, by a sketch of a snail or an island.

I shut the book. "This M. H., whoever she is, just led us on a wild-goose chase . . . It just keeps going like that."

I eyed the figurine and a shadowy terror rose up in my mind. I'd wanted answers, but I was in over my head here. I couldn't bear to drag Kel down with me. Or let him watch me drown.

Maybe I could still convince him that this was all nothing and I could come back later. On my own.

"We should keep going. I bet it says something about this thing." Kel sat down next to me, laying the figurine on the floor between us. I edged away. I didn't want that thing anywhere near me.

He opened the book back up, flipping through pages of neat, even penmanship. "Hey, how 'bout this one? It's got a bookmark."

I pulled out the oversized playing card that marked the page. It had a picture on it of a winged woman pouring wine from one goblet to another. She stood at the edge of the ocean, one foot on land, one on water. Above her, planets spun in their orbits. At the bottom the word "Temperance" had been marked out and "The Circle" had been written in. On the back of the card, nonsensical words were scattered across the blue flowery pattern. I studied the gibberish while Kel read the entry.

October 14, 1911

We picnicked on the beach today. It was one of those tremendous autumn days when the wind whips through you, sweeping out all the dust and doubt. It would've been perfect if not for Bea's insistence on telling our "fortunes." She's obsessed with the tarot fad, which might be entertaining if she weren't such a spiteful shrew. But she always winces as she deals out my cards, fabricating the most tedious futures for me. At least she could have me die in a tragic

*ballooning accident, but no. I'm forever bound to be
a spinster with a bad complexion and a penchant
for cats.*

Kel stopped reading and took the card out of my hand. "So, not a bookmark, then. A tarot card." He studied it for a second, then went on reading.

*Luckily, nature has a wicked sense of humor.
Halfway through my "reading" the wind gusted
down on us, sending the tarot cards flying. I'm
afraid that my shriek of alarm may have sounded
a bit like a hoot of joy as I chased the rogue cards
across the beach and out of sight of my dour mother
and cousin.*

*I followed the narrow beach trail up the hill,
collecting cards as I climbed up the cliff. At the
top, the view was breathtaking. Deer Island was
bursting with reds and oranges, looking like a great
bonfire floating on the waves. More cards bobbed
cheerfully on the water below me, just as happy as I
was to be free.*

*Looking down at them, something else caught
my eye. On a small ledge a couple of feet away,
something winked in the sunlight, bright against the
gray cliff.*

*Curious, I climbed down, ripping my dress in the
process, and perched on the little ledge. I brushed
the pine needles and lichen away from the spot.
A chunk of metal was wedged in a small crevice
in the rock, and as I touched it, my head felt*

strange—like it was full of music. My heart drummed in my chest as I carefully cleared the debris away and worked the metal object out of the crack.

When I finally got it out, my arms were sore and there was rust mottling the surface of the metal. But I could still tell that it was a lumpy iron doll, small enough to fit in my palm. I took it down to the beach and washed my prize, scrubbing it with sand until the surface gleamed dully in the sun.

An iron doll.

It was just like M. H. had described. The tarnished metal of the figurine still had a hint of shine to it, even though it was pitted with rust. Almost against my will, I reached out and touched it. Even though the doll was small, it was heavy. I closed my fist around it, but somehow the metal felt all wrong in my hand. The diary talked of music, but there was nothing. The iron was cold and dead.

There had to be more here. There had to be answers. I flipped through the diary looking, and the entries started to change. They were written in the same loopy handwriting, but now the letters careened across the page at an angle. Rushing to fill the space.

Then twenty pages later, I found another tarot card. "Death."

My breath stuck in my windpipe, and I reread the bold printed word at the bottom of the card. A grim reaper walked through a graveyard, wielding a scythe.

"Not so boring now." Kel raised an eyebrow at me and read the diary entry out loud.

November 29, 1911

This morning in church, Preacher Matthew spoke of the end of the world. Fire and Brimstone. Locusts and Plague . . . But that is not how it ends.

The world will end. In swollen waves. In crimson-stained hands. In the dark of the pregnant moon.

I see it over and over, in my dreams at night . . . The visions will not abate, the drums throbbing through my body. I tell myself they are merely nightmares, preying on my weak mind. But even in the daylight . . . I know the truth.

This is The Path.

The same arrow marked the bottom of the page. But that wasn't what made the entry unsettling. And it wasn't just creepy descriptions either. It was that every word, every line, had been written in blood.

19

"OKAY." Kel's eyes were wide as he looked down at the diary. "Is this what I think it is?"

M. H.'s words echoed in my ears. *The world will end.* "If you're thinking it's a century-old prophecy scrawled in blood, then yes."

"Pretty much, yeah." Kel swallowed and looked me full on in the face. "Did she say crimson-stained hands? Do you think she was talking about us?"

"How could she be?" They were just delusional ramblings, right? But then what about the arrows? My drawings? The metal doll? My brain buzzed with impossible questions and I wanted to bolt.

"What is it, Faye? What aren't you telling me?" Kel's eyes still pinned me down.

I clutched the metal figurine, the chill from it biting my fingers. I was trying hard to keep it together. Forcing myself to stay very still, I searched for something to say. "Well . . . that arrow thing's every-where, right? What do you think it means?"

"Don't avoid the question." Kel's eyes flashed a warning at me. "Why were you so fascinated when you saw that mark on the porch yesterday? Why does this book talk about stained hands? Faye, do you *know* what's going on with us?"

Fear, feral and snarling, rose up inside of me. *He'll never believe you! The second you tell him what's been happening, he'll abandon you like everybody else!*

"I don't know!" I screamed at him, angry that he was here, that he'd made me so vulnerable. "I read the same thing you did! Whoever this M. H. is, she thinks we're headed for an apocalypse."

Snatching the diary, I jumped up, reading from it as I paced the room. "'The world will end. In swollen waves. In crimson-stained hands. In the dark of the pregnant moon.' What does that even mean?"

I dropped the book with a thud on the floor, wanting to get away from those words written in blood. Away from all the hateful arrows. Then I slid down the wall and rested my head against the door frame, covering my face.

Maybe it's better when no one looks at me. Maybe I could go back to being invisible. It would be easier for everyone. "I don't want to drag you into this. You should leave. They probably haven't even noticed you're gone."

"Drag me into it? Faye, I'm already here!" Kel crawled over to me, his glove touching my arm gently. But I refused to look at him. "I get it. Crazy stuff's happening and you think it's got something to do with you. But it's got something to do with me too. With all of us. And we can handle it. *You* can handle it, because you're . . . I knew it when I first looked at you. No, when I first heard you on the other side of that wall . . . You're different. *More* than everyone else somehow. Just let me in and I promise, I'll do whatever it takes. Please, Faye."

I lowered my hands. *More than everyone else.* I met Kel's eyes and tried to recognize myself there. The me that was strong and smart and likable. The me that he saw.

It felt dangerous. No one had ever looked at me so . . . so absolutely. I longed to be that person Kel envisioned.

But what if I lost whatever dazzling connection I had with Kel? What if I told him about *everything* that's happened since I came to Holbrook. Since before Holbrook. *And what if he turns away from me?*

Then I had an even more dangerous thought. *What if he doesn't?*

Alarm bells wailed in my head. *Keep your secrets, Faye.* But I wasn't sure I could trust my instincts anymore.

His forehead creased and I longed to smooth it away. I longed to let him all the way in.

"Please, Faye, this is too big to figure out on your own. Let me help."

So I told him. About going up to the dorm roof and hearing the music. About the drawings on the floor. About the vision of Dr. Mordoch and the picture I'd made when I was little and remembering that night with my parents. About everything.

And as we talked, sitting next to each other on the floor of the library, the closeness of the night before came back to us. Breath for breath. Beat for beat. The noises from the outside, the heat of the room, disappeared. There wasn't space for anything else.

The words poured out of me and I felt strong again. Free from the weight of it all.

"And these visions, you said you've had them since you were a kid? With the water and stuff?" Kel's face was open, engaged.

"Well, they used to just be nightmares. But over the last year they've become"—I hesitated—"more real."

It was strange to finally tell someone. I'd expected Kel to pull away, to blame me for whatever's been going on with us at night. But he'd come alive, almost excited.

Sometimes he stopped me to ask questions, then nodded thoughtfully at the answers. Like he was scrambling to put the puzzle pieces together in his mind. "What about seeing the bonfire from the dorm roof? Was that the same kinda thing?"

I don't know. I tried to answer him anyway. He'd earned that much. "Well, part of it was real, I mean, I saw the Screamers and they're real, right? But I checked the next day and there wasn't any sign of a fire."

Or the seventh person.

"What about the song? What did it sound like?" Kel's face was intent, his gloved hand squeezing my arm.

"It was kinda like a chant. With drums and a flute thing. Why?"

He dropped his hand and looked down at the floor. "That day in Solitary, when they first put me in . . . I think you were singing it."

I remembered the waves crushing down on me and the drums thrumming through my feet.

Then Kel's dark eyes were back on mine. "Up on the roof was that the first time you heard that song?"

"I thought so, but even then it sounded familiar. Then I got sucked into that nightmare with Dr. Mordoch—" This all sounded so insane. I had to push myself to finish my thought. "And I heard it again. I must've learned it when I was a kid, 'cause I was singing it in the vision."

Kel nodded and I could tell he believed me. My heart squeezed. It hurt almost too much to hope that Kel wasn't afraid of me or didn't think I was crazy. The idea seemed fragile and stunning.

"There's a reason for all of this." Kel shifted closer to me and I breathed him in. "We have the diary now. Maybe it'll give us answers. I promise you, we'll figure this all out."

Kel pulled off his gloves and reached up, touching my cheek. His face was so close to mine that I could see the sandpaper of stubble on his chin. My skin blazed where he touched me, and I leaned into him.

We can handle this. We'll figure this all out.

Then he pressed his lips against mine. He tasted like ginger and honey and . . . and something so familiar. Like something I knew inside and out, but couldn't name.

"Faye." He said my name like . . . like he was saying something sacred.

His hand cradled the back of my neck, fingers tangling in my hair. It was electrifying and delicious and dangerous. And we came together again. My hand melted into his. I was flying, and I let myself fall into the green sea of his eyes.

I closed my eyes and kissed him back. But I was falling too fast. I couldn't stop. Images swarmed past me. Dizziness tried to pull me under and suddenly the world went dark. I tried to pull away from Kel's grip, but he wasn't there anymore. It was like what'd happened with Dr. Mordoch. Blurry shadows morphed until they finally solidified into a scene in front of me.

I was running. Dodging past branches and tree trunks. Up ahead, a girl fled through the dark forest.

I can't lose her.

The thought wasn't mine. I knew it was Kel's, the same way I'd known his smell and his taste. His thrill of adrenaline surged into me.

My big Converses closed the distance between me and the girl. And now I could make out her long hair streaming behind her.

I was eager, chasing her in the dark, matching her pace up the steep hill. The trees thinned and I put on speed.

Almost. I almost have her. I reached out for her—

Then pain shot through my knees. My lungs seized up. My shoulders burned. And I was down.

But it didn't matter. She'd stopped. The girl had reached the Screamers, and breathing hard, she knelt at the center of the tortured statues. Her knees planted in the grass.

The girl's hair fell in front of her face as she threw herself forward, clawing wildly at the ground. Digging in the dark earth. Then, as if in pain, she threw back her head toward the night sky, letting out a wailing chant.

The familiar drumbeat filled my mind and my heart beat in time. Eager. Impatient. Moonlight flooded the girl's face, her skin blazing white, and I flinched.

It was my face. It was me.

Stunned, I forced myself backward through the crackling, dizzying link and managed to rip away from Kel's kiss.

Falling back on my hands and knees, I stared at Kel. Questions battered at my mind, trying to get out. But they were overwhelmed by my intense, heart-rending fear.

"How did you . . ." Kel's voice trailed off.

So he saw it too.

I scrambled backward toward the doorway, away from Kel. I could still feel his eagerness. His feet pounding through the woods.

"What do you want? What did you do to me?" I didn't even know the right question to ask. Then, in a tiny voice I didn't even recognize, "I trusted you."

"I was trying to keep you safe." Kel's stunned eyes pleaded with me. "Please, Faye, I didn't do anything. You have to believe me!"

"Why?" I looked up, terror and confusion and betrayal all battling it out inside me. Tears rushed into my eyes followed by a wild, animal rage. "Why on earth would I believe you?"

I stumbled down the spiral stairs. Fumbling through the dark hallway.

"Wait! Faye!" Kel's voice echoed in the empty passageway. My hands smacked against the stone walls, barely keeping myself from careening into them. I slammed into the secret door, trying to get it open.

Behind me, Kel felt his way along the hallway, groping in the dark. Suddenly, I remembered the night before, his footsteps chasing me down to the Compass Rose. Kel had claimed he was just trying to catch up with me. But it hadn't been the only time he'd followed me in the dark.

"Faye. Stop!"

My hands hit a latch and I yanked on it, jerking the door open.

I sprinted across the main room, heading for the front door. Kel was right on my heels. The front door swung open and I screeched to a stop.

Dragon loomed over me. She grabbed her pepper spray and gave me a cruel smile, even while avoiding my eyes.

I did a 180. Kel was gone. I ducked down the maze of hallways. Left turn. Then a right. Another left.

"I found her!" Dragon shouted, not far behind me.

I took a right and slammed straight into Freddy, a grin spreading across his meaty face. His eyes focused behind me as I heard Dragon rounding the corner.

His fat fingers dug into my shoulders. "So nice of you to—"

Then we both heard the *pssssss* of Dragon's pepper spray. Freddy managed to yell, "Jesus Christ! You stupid f—" before it hit us.

Fumes from the pepper spray smacked me in the nose. Snot and tears streamed down my face. I fought to get my arms free from Freddy's grip, desperate to get out of the tiny hallway. To rub my eyes. My throat ratcheted shut.

Freddy growled, letting go of one of my arms. He pulled his heavy shirt up over his nose and mouth. My jumpsuit was too tight to cover my face, so I just swiped at my eyes.

"Why don't you just spray it right in my face, you jackass!" Freddy yelled muffled curses at Dragon, who was down on her knees, choking.

I couldn't breathe. Everything burned from the inside out. Even so, it hurt less than Kel's betrayal.

Kel'd gotten me to tell him everything, playing dumb, while he'd been sitting there keeping secrets of his own. It hadn't taken much, had it? Whispered words. A couple of heated glances. And poor Faye was spilling her guts.

All the while he'd been— What? Stalking me? What else had he done to me? How had I ended up digging in the mud? Or sprawled on the floor of my room?

What about the others? Did they know more than they were telling too? A few minutes ago, I'd felt so certain. So confident. Now I wasn't sure what to believe.

All I knew was that Kel had gotten me to confide in him from day one. Confessions in Solitary. Secrets at Free Time. "Accidental" meetings. *But why? What does he want with me?*

Freddy yanked me to the floor and started crawling down the hallway, pulling me behind him. I tried to use my free hand to crawl, but my body was just a spasm of coughing. Finally, I let Freddy drag me out of the noxious fumes, grating my hands and face against the marble floor. Behind me, Dragon was left abandoned, gagging on the ground.

20

I WAS STILL CRYING and wheezing when Freddy hauled me to Dr. Mordoch's office. She sat perched behind her desk as if nothing was wrong, though a few strands had come loose from her usually perfect ponytail. The filing cabinet loomed behind her, and all I could think of was the drawer full of notes and the drawing I'd made under hypnosis. Somehow Dr. Mordoch was involved with all of this, and I almost begged Freddy not to leave me with her. This wasn't the way I wanted to face her.

I don't want to face her at all.

"Many students are learning the Consequences of their actions today." Dr. Mordoch shook her head plaintively, a sad smile poised on her lips. She looked at the papers on her desk. At her diplomas on the wall. Anywhere but my eyes. "As much as I'd like to, you know I can't make exceptions for you, Faye, simply because I knew you as a child."

She was gearing up for a lecture, but even though I was sniveling and bruised, I refused to let her run this meeting. "I don't want special treatment."

If I surprised her, she didn't show it. "Of course you do, Faye. We all expect the world to treat us special. We are, after all, us. That's what causes us such pain and makes us hurt those around us."

Dr. Mordoch stood up and came around her desk, really enjoying her own speech.

"That's why we wear uniforms here and use the titles of our positions, like Uncle or Caretaker, instead of names. The sooner we lose our illusions that we are special and stop expecting the world to treat us that way, the sooner we can be happy. Don't you want to be happy?"

Happy? Happy's an option?

Would I be happy if I stopped waking up on the floor? If I could kiss Kel without plunging into a nightmare? If I let Dr. Mordoch numb me into normality? Maybe I'd be better off.

"Faye, as a child, you were too caught up in your fantasy world. But now things are different." Dr. Mordoch's eyes were shining as she spread her hands wide, as if she was trying to get them around all of Holbrook Academy. "With this school, these resources, I have . . . we have a chance to change things. To remedy the past."

Yes. I could start over. I could be someone else. I rubbed at my eyes, aching from pepper spray and exhaustion, and thought about the frenzy of arrows calling to me in the passageway. About red-stained hands and apocalyptic diary entries. About watching myself claw at the ground like a madwoman. And about Kel.

I would do anything to unsee that vision. To go back to that moment when I wasn't alone anymore. Dr. Mordoch sat down in the chair next to me and I scooted closer. Maybe she could take it all away.

"Don't you understand that I'm trying to make it up to you? Can't you see the opportunity we've created for you?"

I thought about the deed to Holbrook mixed in with my files. I was right, then: this was all about me. Dr. Mordoch kept her eyes fixed on my hand. As she reached for it, I could hear the waves coming to drown me. Feel the salt stinging my swollen tongue. *No.*

I yanked my hand away. *Whatever she's offering, it's not happiness.*

Dr. Mordoch looked hurt for a second, like I'd slapped her. Confusion flitted through her eyes and something else—fear, maybe? Then her eyes dimmed and her usual cloying smile found its way back onto her face.

"Fine, Faye. We can play it your way. Tomorrow morning, while your Family is at Art and Life, you will be cleaning every shower stall, sink, and toilet on campus."

A punishment crafted especially for not-special me. My mouth tasted bitter as I was escorted out of Dr. Mordoch's office and down to the cafeteria. As demeaning as art class had been, I longed to have something solid to hold on to. A paintbrush in my fist. The grain of the paper under my fingertips. Ever since I'd come to Holbrook, I'd been slipping. Slipping where? Away? I didn't know and I didn't want to find out.

Dinner only made things worse. Kel kept trying to catch my eye from across the table. I felt his hand in my hair, his lips against mine. And then I was racing through the woods again. Chasing myself down.

I shut my eyes, trying to block it all out.

Nami squeezed my arm under the table. Had Kel told the Family what had happened? Was Nami keeping secrets too? My face flushed in embarrassment and terror, but I made myself meet her eyes. They were clear and concerned. She'd dropped the usual bravado and all that I saw was Nami. A girl who was trying hard to be herself. *That's what we're all doing.*

I took a deep breath, letting the pressure of her hand steady me.

Fear is an illusion. I'm in control of my own reality. I tried to give her a smile. But it wouldn't come.

What had happened to Nami, to the rest of the Family, the rest of the school, today? From the way Damion was staring at Nami, with a surprised, open look, they'd gotten their moment alone and made it back without being caught.

Most tables had at least one person missing, and in the middle of the room, a whole family was gone, their table bare. Everyone's eyes were glued to their food, not daring to look around.

And Kel? Had he made it back to the group without being noticed? I simultaneously wished that he'd gotten caught and that he'd gotten away. My eyes met his and he stared at me, pleading.

Maybe there was a reason for what I saw. Maybe he can explain it all away.

But how could he explain knowing where I'd gone at night, what I'd done, and never telling me? And even if he did explain, how could I believe him? I'd been inside his thoughts. My heart had raced with the same anticipation.

Almost. I almost have her.

Nothing Kel could say would change what I'd seen for myself. I glared at him and he dropped his eyes.

After dinner, as the Taker led us back through the twisting halls of the Compass Rose, I remembered M. H.'s diary and the tarot cards. Were they still up in the turret? I stared at the secret door as we passed by the sitting room. I was sure it held the answers, if I could just get back up there.

I felt eyes on me. From three people behind me, Kel was watching. From the anxious way he followed my gaze, I knew he hadn't had time to go back for the diary. I just hoped I could find a way to get there first.

21

I SHOULDN'T HAVE WORRIED. When I woke up the next morning, I was hugging the diary to my chest.

I had no idea how it got there. Or why I had a tarot card clutched in my other hand. I crawled over to the window to see it better in the gray dawn light. In the center of the card was a person wearing a blindfold and a robe. His arms were crossed over his chest, gripping a sword in each hand. The ocean spread out behind him, islands scattered across the waves. And above it all hung a full moon.

But something wasn't right. The vermilion color of the moon stood out against the rest of the card. I scratched at it and paint flaked away, uncovering a yellow fingernail moon beneath. Why had M. H. changed it? She'd also titled the card, her slanted letters marching across the bottom: "The Harbinger."

The word rang out in my head but without meaning. I turned the card over, reading the same sort of ramblings I'd seen on the back of the other cards.

fully for the ded from the glare ill know them ill carry onely places will smother the sick wash this world.

Was it written in some archaic form of English, like Shakespeare, with *ded* instead of *dead* and *onely* instead of *only*? Even if it was, it still didn't make sense.

Maybe it was a code and there was a key written in the diary. Reaching for the book, I noticed another picture had been painted on the floor. And the design was even more complicated this time. The drawing spread halfway across the room now. Two days ago, there had been one crudely drawn person, with an arrow symbol instead of a face. Today there were six of them. Arranged with their heads pointing inward, so they made a circle.

Music pounded in my head and I saw a flash of hands, clawing through the dirt, looking for something. Then I saw myself through Kel's eyes again, kneeling in the middle of the Screamers, digging. *But for what? What was I looking for? And what about the others?*

Where was Maya? Chest tight, I jumped up and hurried across the room, blurring the red strokes of the picture as I went.

There she was, sleeping in the corner, behind the bed. As if the painting had pushed her off to the side.

She was shivering, despite the stuffiness of our room, and I wondered what all this was doing to her. And the others. Suddenly, the weight of so many questions collapsed in on me. I was just so tired.

Tired of worrying. Tired of these vague hints. Tired of never getting answers.

Not anymore. Walking back to the window, I picked up the diary and paged through it, looking for the next marked entry. It didn't take me long to hit another tarot card. This one showed a person startled out of sleep. Like he was waking from a nightmare. He'd flung out his arms, shielding himself from a barrage of swords piercing the air above his bed. M. H. had labeled this one too: "The Vision."

February 4, 1912
I can't have any more of those nightmares. Ever since I found that metal doll, I've been plagued

with hallucinations, memories of things that never happened.

A stone knife dripping with blood. The stink of wet bonfires. The unbearable thump of bodies hitting the ground.

Last week, when Father came home from surveying his newest paper mill, I overheard Mother speaking to him about me.

"She's waking up the whole household with her screaming. Two maids quit last week, jibbering about demons."

I stood very still, at the top of the stairs, listening for his reply.

Father was quiet for a long time, and then he said, "Perhaps it's time? I hoped she would get better while I was gone, but she's more sullen than ever. Simply staring out the window with those morose eyes . . . like she's waiting for something. If she doesn't improve soon, I'll take her to the Augusta Asylum myself."

So, I've taken to reading at night. It doesn't matter what. The solid, square letters calm my nerves and keep the dreams from coming. I started with Mother's romances, simply because they were easier to lay my hands on. But they were so full of weeping countesses and mustachioed villains that I moved on to Father's scientific texts. Anything to keep me awake.

They will never lock me away. I will die first. Or kill.

I haven't had the dream in weeks, but I've

barely slept either. And now, these phantasms have begun to haunt me by day. I'll be eating supper or tediously embroidering with Mother or doing any number of mundane tasks throughout the day and I'll hear them. In the distance, the thump-thump-thump of drumbeats and the hungry roar of waves.

My hands tremored with the familiarity of her words. The childhood nightmares. Then the hallucinations flooding over me even when I was awake. Sitting here, holding the diary, I heard that same rumble in the air. What had happened to M. H.? What was happening to me?

I hurried through the pages, finding another card. This one had a picture of an ominous crowned figure with a sword in one hand and a set of scales in the other. He stood, towering in front of the Earth, the sun and moon hovering in the background. It was a disturbing picture, this omnipotent figure hidden beneath robes and an inhuman mask. At the bottom the word "Justice" had been marked out and replaced with "The Path."

August 21, 1913

I received Professor Warren's reply today. I perused it twice to make sure I'd read it correctly, then flung it into the sea.

How dare he.

Despite the fact I'd told him about the iron person I found. Despite the fact I'd informed him that the marking precisely matched his photograph in Father's book, he dismissed my theory.

"I do not expect a young girl such as yourself, with little book learning, to comprehend the subtleties of

archaeology. *No, my dear, you have not found an ancient talisman. Your enclosed sketch looks like nothing more than a rusty toy."*

Pompous idiot! He wouldn't know a talisman if it materialized out of the ether and hit him on the head.

It is very well I didn't add my wilder theories. The ones that scare me. How I am linked to this thing. How it holds some greater truth. There is something I am meant to do, some purpose to these mad hallucinations and dreams.

Damn Professor Warren's hubris. I'd hoped he might hold the answer. Now I must make my own.

And there are obstacles I must clear away before I give in to this insanity that is creeping upon me. I must carve the mark upon this world. So much to do before I can follow The Path.

I turned to the next page, but it was blank. So was the page after that. And the one after that.

Tarot cards were stuck here and there, but there were no more entries. No more answers.

A lump formed in my throat, making it hard to swallow. *What did you expect, Faye?*

M. H. was obviously crazy. Even her parents, even she, thought so. Though, using that logic, what did that make me? Maybe M. H. deserved the benefit of the doubt. I flipped through the blank pages again, sure I was missing something, until the fluorescent light buzzed to life.

Maya groaned from the corner. Instinctively, I wrapped my arms around the book. Hiding it.

Two nights ago, I'd hidden my brush pen on the ledge running under the window. Peering outside, I watched Takers crowd into the courtyard, waiting to escort us to breakfast. The window was already open a crack, and I stuck my hand out, feeling around. My pen was still there.

I imagined throwing the worthless diary out the window. But the last lines echoed in my head, and I grudgingly shoved it out onto the ledge. *And there are obstacles I must clear away before I give in to this insanity that is creeping upon me. I must carve the mark upon this world.*

I thought about the arrows gouged into the secret hallway. Had M. H. made those? What else had her nightmares and visions made her do? I looked at my red-stained hands and the diary that'd somehow ended up in my room. *What are my visions making me do?*

"Another masterpiece." Maya crawled out from behind the bed.

We stood together looking down at the six outlines on the floor. The roughly shaped people reminded me of the metal figurine Kel and I had found with the diary. What had M. H. called it? A talisman?

"It's not over, is it? It's getting worse. I mean, even the crap on the floor is getting bigger."

My throat was raw and I had no idea what to say. So I nodded.

"I know you've been trying to figure out what these pictures mean, but maybe one of the others knows something." Maya's voice was gentle, but I wondered if she suspected I was the one drawing them. She shrugged. "We should ask. It's worth a shot."

This time, it was me who couldn't look her in the eye. Her whole life, she'd been betrayed and manipulated. *Didn't I promise to tell her if I knew anything?*

My eyes flicked to the window. I could show her the diary. Tell her what I'd found.

'Cause that worked out so well with Kel.

I made myself meet Maya's worried eyes. "It'll be okay. Trust me."

Then I turned my back on her and walked out of the room.

The same anxious tension pulled tight across the breakfast table. The whole Family had dark rings around their eyes, and their fingernails were ragged and tinged with red. They all looked stretched thin, and soon, something or someone was going to snap. I just hoped I'd have something real to tell them before that happened.

I refused to look at Kel, afraid of what I'd see in his eyes. Or what he'd see in mine.

Does he know I have the book and the cards? Has he told any of the others about them?

My chest squeezed as I watched the rest of the Family head off to art class. I should've told Maya about the diary and Kel stalking me. Now he had all morning to feed the others whatever kind of story he wanted. And then why would they believe me, a person hiding secret diaries and drawing cryptic pictures, instead of him? Sweat broke out on my palms, the only place on my body that wasn't already sweating.

Dragon escorted me back to the dorms. She handed me a mop, a bucket, steel wool, and rubber gloves. Oatmeal sat like a bowling ball in my stomach as I looked around the first-floor shower room in the boys' wing. All I could see was the blindfolded picture of the Harbinger, burned on my retinas.

"Get scrubbing." The Taker's bark echoed off the ceramic tiles, and she pointed to a jug of industrial cleaner. Red letters shouted their warning from the top of the label. USE ONLY IN WELL-VENTILATED AREAS.

The humid air of the shower room pressed against my skin. I

wondered if one tiny window near the ceiling and a mildewy drain in the middle of the floor counted as ventilation.

I filled my bucket and started mopping. The stained tiles didn't look any better once I'd cleaned them. The astringent fumes of the cleaner made my head spin a little, but at least it drove Dragon out of the room.

For a while she lingered at the door, watching me scrub the walls with steel wool. "I expect that grout to sparkle!" she warned. "Put your back into it."

She'd obviously seen one too many army movies. I continued with my pointless scrubbing, sweat dripping down my nose and mixing with the bubbles. The heady pine-stink stung my eyes, and I thought about the rest of my Family. Were they outside right now, painting another realistic landscape? I imagined a paintbrush in my hand. With the finger of my rubber glove, I sketched the arrow symbol in the soapy film. The lines dripped into each other as I drew the outline of M. H.'s iron talisman around it. *What the hell did it mean?*

Using the mop, I obliterated the design. My thoughts tired of running in circles.

The smell must have gotten to Dragon. When we got to the second-floor boys' shower room, she guarded me from out in the hall, occasionally peering in. And by the time we got to the girls' showers, she was pacing. On my hands and knees, I listened to the Taker's shoes clunking up and down the hallway as I tried to make a dent in years and years of mildew.

Making giant soapy circles on the tile, I tried again to put it all together. The stained hands. Pictures on the floor. Dr. Mordoch's files. The music. Kel chasing me through the forest. The diary. The tarot cards—

Maybe I did miss something.

By the time I'd cleaned the last shower in my section of the dorm, Dragon had disappeared completely. I dumped the filthy water out of the bucket and carried it to the high window. Standing on top of the overturned bucket, I peeked out into the courtyard. Down below, Dragon puffed on a cigarette on the other side of the lawn.

Yanking off my gloves, I hurried to my room. This time, I was grateful that the bolts were on the outside of the door. I grabbed the diary from the windowsill. With one eye on Dragon in the courtyard and the other on the diary, I turned it upside down and shook it out. A shower of tarot cards tumbled to the ground.

22

THERE WERE NINE CARDS IN ALL.

Some had names printed down at the bottom: Death, The Lovers, The Sun, and The Moon. On other cards, the names had been crossed out and changed, like The Path and The Circle. Still others hadn't originally had any names at all, but M. H. had added them anyway. The Vision. The Ritual. The Harbinger.

But all of them had words scribbled on the back. I read and reread them, but I couldn't get "ill carry pain" or "an of blood" to mean anything to me. Then one card tugged at my memory. It read:

nant moon with
Autumn will be born
Death will be Autumn's
ill cradle the Earth

I flipped over all the cards, my eyes flitting across their backs. Searching for what had to be there. *Yes! There it is.*

Another card had the words "ark of the preg." I lined that card next to the first one and was struck by how simple it'd been.

Putting the cards together had lined up other phrases too. And now I had

ark of the pregnant moon with
as midwife Autumn will be born
an of blood Death will be Autumn's
its mercy will cradle the Earth

Remembering those words from the diary, I found the card that had "In the d," which seemed to complete the phrase. It was hard to tell, since there was no punctuation, and I tried out a few of the other cards just to make sure. None of them worked.

But these three cards, put together, made sense. Well, not sense, but at least I could read what they said.

In the dark of the pregnant moon with
the sun as midwife Autumn will be born
in an ocean of blood Death will be Autumn's
twin and its mercy will cradle the Earth

I didn't understand and read it again, out loud this time. The words had weight, each one falling heavy on my ears. Like the beating of a drum. Now, instead of ramblings, they sounded like a prophecy.

Hand shaking, I turned over the cards.

The Moon. Walking a path across the Earth. Its yellow face frowning.

The Sun. Glowering at the city below it.

Death. The grim reaper pausing by an open grave.

Not good.

I grabbed the pen off the ledge, checking that Dragon was still smoking across the yard. Then I scribbled the words down on a blank diary page.

My heart was thudding. There had to be more. Now that I knew what I was looking for, the words fell into place as I rearranged the other cards. The next message was another set of three cards. I spoke the words cautiously, fearing and yearning for them at the same time.

Stronger than the others the Harbinger
peers far into the Future There men
will feast off of the Earth like maggots There The
Circle will fail the Family Two quarrel and the
Harbinger alone slaughters
the lambs Forging a new Path and journeying
the sea of time To finish what has begun

Dread knotted in my belly, and far away, at the edge of my hearing, music thrummed. Drums joined my pounding heart. I flipped the cards over.

The Vision. A sleeper waking from a nightmare, warding off swords.

The Lovers. This card was upside down. Two masked lovers reaching out for each other. A sword slicing the air between them.

The Ritual. A figure hidden behind a mask and a robe, rowing a boat away from shore. Six swords glittering, just under the water.

A voice cut across my thoughts. "That's the Past."

My heart stopped and the music with it as two bare feet appeared in front of me. I blinked up, seeing the white sundress and the blond braid.

Rita.

"Shit. You scared me!" It'd been stupid to let myself forget where I was. I fumbled with the cards, stacking them together as I got up and checked out the window for Dragon.

Through the hazy waves of heat rippling off the sidewalk, Dragon gestured violently at another guard with her cigarette. Her voice drifted in through the window. ". . . No. I told you, not locusts. Crickets. Practically covered the whole damn state of Utah. The crops, rations, even the grass . . ."

"You're doing it wrong." Rita crossed the room and stood next to me at the window. Her words were soft and her eyes vague as she peered outside. "We used to do this all the time when I was little. You have to lay them out the right way if you want to tell your fortune. Three rows of three."

"I don't want to tell my fortune," I snapped, my pulse still hammering in my head from her surprise appearance. I'd been lucky it'd just been Rita. Dragon would come back inside soon, and I still didn't know the last message.

"But you laid out the cards." Rita sounded dazed. "Three for the Past. Three for the Future. You only need three more to bridge the gap between them."

To bridge the gap?

"To know how the Future will come to pass." She beamed at me. A little girl's smile.

I don't want that Death card anywhere near my future.

Then Rita's eyes went wide and she skewered me with them. "Only one person can stop Death's approach."

I backed away from her. She'd just answered my thought. And what about her disappearing the other night? Were there other secret doors in the Compass Rose? Or was it something else? *Maybe she's just another of your hallucinations.*

No. Whoever Rita was, what she'd said about the Past and the

Future had gotten my attention. I took a deep breath. "Can you show me what you mean about the cards?"

She nodded, giving me a simple smile that wasn't all there. "Deal out those cards you were looking at when I came in. One, two, three . . . the Past you'll see." She pointed at the floor, showing me where to lay them down.

The smell of cigarette smoke drifted in through the window, and Dragon was still safe on the other side of the courtyard. So I sat back down on the floor and laid out the top three cards again. The nightmare Vision. The upside-down Lovers. The Ritual, with its shrouded boatman and swords.

Rita knelt next to me, reaching out toward The Lovers. Her voice was sad. "The Past is unfinished . . ." Then she pointed to another spot on the floor, just to the right. "Time moves forward. Lay down the next three, right here. Four, five, six . . . the Future it predicts."

She sang the rhyme in a little child's voice, sending shivers up my arms as I dealt out the next three cards, arranging them in a row. The frowning Moon. The glowering Sun. Death's sharp scythe.

She shook her head. "No! Not so close to the others! Those cards are the Future."

Tears welled up in her eyes, and I hurried to put space between the Past and the Future cards. I didn't want to be the one who sent Rita off the deep end. I scooted the foreboding Future cards a little farther to the right, so now there was a bigger gap between the two lines of cards.

She rewarded me with a smile. "Yes. Seven, eight, nine . . . a bridge across time."

Rita pointed to the blank space between the Past cards and the Future cards, showing me where to put the final three.

Not sure of the order, I put the blindfolded Harbinger, with its crossed swords, in the middle of the open space.

"Higher. You're building a bridge." Then she sang to herself, "Over the river and through the woods . . ."

Trying to finish this before she completely stopped making sense, I shoved The Harbinger card farther up, so it sat a little higher than the other cards.

This time, Rita nodded her approval. "This is the one who brings destruction."

She waited for the next card and I showed her The Circle, with the winged woman with the goblets. Rita pointed to a spot to the left of The Harbinger.

"One foot in the water and one on land. Time flows through the goblets, back and forth, back and forth." Rita's soft voice wavered, getting lost in her own words. "Time balances strong with weak. Weak with strong. The planets spin round and round. And her— she's part of The Circle. Connected to all. She'll teach you the pattern, but she won't change it."

Her words prickled at my mind, agitating my thoughts. I wanted to finish this. To be done with these eerie pictures and secret messages.

The last card in my hands was the most disturbing. Some of the people in the other cards were wearing masks, but this crowned figure was completely hidden from the world. Only the hands hinted at its humanity. And above the palms floated a set of scales and a sword. The card had originally been labeled Justice, but M. H. had renamed it The Path. I laid The Path down on the right side of The Harbinger.

This final card completed the literal bridge between the line of Past cards and the line of Future cards. Now that Rita had begun to explain the cards, I recognized some of the symbolism. "The Path means balance too, doesn't it?"

"Yes." Rita pointed to the picture. "A king rules alone, one fierce leader controlling the fate of the world. Weighing weak against strong. Not just observing the balance, but keeping it . . . with the might of the sword.

"The Circle goes nowhere . . . round and round, round and round, round and round. But The Path . . . The Path forges into the Future, leaving terrible retribution in its wake." Rita shuddered, her eyes cloudy. "These three cards, The Circle, The Harbinger, The Path, they are the bridge between the Past and the Future. Only one person can stop this."

Suddenly, the vagueness went out of Rita's face. Her eyes turned wild, like a caged animal. "You must be careful, Faye. He is here. You are both crossing over the bridge now."

Then the fog returned to her eyes and she looked down at the cards with a puzzled frown. In her wispy voice, she finished off her eerie rhyme. "Nine cards portend . . . the day this world shall end."

Hand shaking, I turned the three bridge cards over, the words lining up perfectly. This final prophecy was the longest of the three, the slanted letters crammed onto the cards.

Look carefully for the Harbinger
is shielded from the glare of day
But the moon will know them Peer into strangers' eyes
for the Harbinger will carry pain with them
through the lonely places of the Earth When the hour
arrives the Harbinger will smother the sickness that is humanity
Only the Harbinger can wash this world clean

The words were sour in my mouth. *Only the Harbinger can wash this world clean.* I didn't think M. H. was talking about some kind of angelic cosmic baptism.

No. The words sounded more like someone ready to drown a litter of unwanted puppies. Now I was the one who shuddered.

"Does this mean what I think it does?" I looked up at Rita, but she was gone.

The words on the tarot cards rang in my ears the rest of the morning as I finished cleaning the bathrooms. I hadn't finished copying down the prophecies before Dragon came back from her smoke break. But I *had* managed to rip my scribbled notes out of the diary and stick them into my sock. The folded paper jabbed into my ankle while I scrubbed sinks and breathed in chemical fumes. While I choked down cold tuna fish casserole. While I wondered about the Harbinger.

Was any of this real? Rita seemed insane, totally out of touch with reality. And yet I couldn't deny that something real was going on with the diary and Holbrook and my Family. When Dragon escorted me to Free Time, I was relieved to have something else to think about.

Ever since the arson attempt the day before, the tension had been crackling at Holbrook. An undercurrent of agitation bristled through me as Dragon locked the gate. Forty disaffected kids fenced in together. Add blinding heat and no shade, and it was a recipe for anarchy.

My Family was sitting back in the same corner as the other day. There was a gap between them and everyone else. A no-fly zone.

I thought about following suit and avoiding Kel altogether, but Nami had already spotted me. She was waving and doing some sort of air guitar riff. I wanted to stop her before our Family attracted unwanted attention from the Takers. I hurried through the hostile forces to get to them.

Kel pulled off his sunglasses and looked up at me. The adrenaline of the chase pounded through my body again, and I wanted to run. Had Kel told any of them about yesterday's exploits? Had Maya told them about the symbols on our floor? My body tensed, not sure what to do.

But everyone acted normal. In fact, they'd lost the exhaustion I'd seen this morning. Nami scooted closer to Damion, making room for me to sit.

"Miss us?" Nami's eyes not-so-subtly darted toward Kel. The real question showed plainly on her face. Trying to figure out what was going on between him and me.

Her guess was as good as mine. It didn't look like Kel had said anything to turn the Family against me, but after yesterday, I didn't know what to believe.

"Back from the front lines, I see." Damion's face was still serious, but relaxed now. Like his proximity to Nami had melted some of his ice.

Zach cut off his explanation of Gray Hulk versus Green Hulk and saluted me. Maya scowled in my direction, but I guessed this was more an expression of her disgust with the conversation topic than her feelings about my arrival.

I sat down, wishing I could feel more comfortable, more a part of the group. The rest of them seemed like they were taking a vacation from reality. From red hands and Tasers and the other students. But I was too acutely aware of Kel, sitting just a few feet away, to be able to relax.

Kel pulled off his hoodie. I'd never seen him without it. He looked like a different person, smaller, more vulnerable. Unlike everyone else, he looked more tired than he had that morning. Whatever he was sick with, it was getting worse. His cheeks were tinged red and he sat stiffly, like he was in pain. He peeled off his gloves, exposing a rash speckling his long, brown fingers. No one else noticed, their attention on me.

"What'd they do to you? Lock you in Solitary?" Maya asked.

Kel's eyes met mine. I tried to look away, but they held on to me. I thought about his low voice drifting through the wall, wrapping me. About his body so close to mine.

"No." I shook my head, clearing it all away. "Bathrooms."

Groans of sympathy came from them, and I felt a little more stable.

"Latrine duty." Damion's usual bark was quiet now, softer around the edges. "That's what they called it at the cadet training I went through last year. Fifty guys. One bathroom. Enough said."

"Anything would've been better than being exposed to what Zach calls art." Nami rolled her eyes over-dramatically. "You should've seen the busty ninja chick he drew as his 'self-portrait' in art class. The Uncle flipped."

Zach turned red as both Nami and Maya struck a karate pose, but I could tell he was enjoying the attention.

"Now that you're here, Faye—" Damion cleared his throat then and everyone's face fell. Like Dad telling the kids to get out of the swimming pool. Not that there were many pools anymore. "We've gotta talk about what's going on. I can't afford to get in any more trouble. This is my last chance . . ."

We were silent while Damion struggled with his words. This was the first time he'd revealed anything personal to the group, though I could tell by the tears in Nami's eyes that she'd already heard this story. She reached out as if to hold his hand, but Damion pulled into himself as he talked, physically distancing himself from all of us.

"Last year, my parents were deployed." Damion's voice was terse. As if sticking to the facts would make it less painful. "They both got killed in the Peak War. I freaked out and did some pretty stupid shit. Two months later, I got kicked out of the Air Force Academy. But I worked my ass off this summer, and the dean finally gave me one more chance to prove I can keep it together. If I toe the line at Holbrook, I can graduate from the Academy next year. I can make my parents proud and help win this war. I can't screw this up."

I ached for Damion. And his pain was not only echoed in my eyes, but in everyone's around the circle. Suddenly, despite what had happened with Kel the day before, I wanted to tell them everything. To open up the way Damion had.

But Kel's dark eyes locked on mine again. Was it a threat? A dare? A plea? I had no idea.

And what if I do tell them what's going on? They'll think I'm crazy.

What good would it do anyway? I didn't have any answers to give them. Only hallucinations, a symbol drawn in crayon, and a fistful of tarot cards.

I looked down at my hands, thinking of what Rita had said about the future the tarot cards foretold.

Only one person can stop Death's approach.

The bathroom cleaner had finally gotten rid of the red stain on my palms, but I could still feel it marking me.

Maybe I'm the person. Maybe I can stop it. The words perched precariously in my mind. If I was supposed to stop the Harbinger, then everything made sense. My nightmares and visions. Whatever happened when I was a kid. The arrow markings in the Compass Rose. The tarot cards. They were all signs. For me.

That powerful thought tremored through my body. *For me.* I wouldn't have to hide anymore.

A shout sounded from the other side of the yard. Two guys were shoving each other, yelling something I couldn't hear. A mass of kids circled them, drawn into the fight's gravity. Takers rushed to get inside the fence.

But a few of the students beat them to it. They barricaded the gate, keeping it from swinging open.

The fight was exploding into a riot. By now most of the kids were punching someone, half fighting each other, the other half fighting off the invading Takers. One of the revolutionaries screamed and flew back from the fence.

It's all fun and games until someone gets a Taser in the crotch.

Under all the chaos, I heard my name.

"Faye?" The voice was weak and low. "Faye?"

I turned reluctantly. Kel's face was pink. The rash on his hands had grown into scaly blotches. Sweat beaded up on his forehead, and invisible lines pulled his skin tight across his face.

"Kel?"

This time when I looked in his eyes, all I could see was pain.

"Kel?" I tried again, crawling over to him. His cheeks had darkened into a red rash that spread across the bridge of his nose. "What's wrong?"

His voice wheezed, dry and faint.

"Help."

23

THE WHOLE FAMILY was on their feet now.

"Is he okay?" Nami's voice rose in panic.

"I don't know." I racked my brain, trying to remember exactly what Kel had told me in Solitary about what he was sick with. Nothing. He'd told me exactly nothing. "I'm getting help."

Freddy and the other Takers had rammed open the gate by now, and there was a guerilla war going on. Screams and pepper spray filled the air.

"Help!" My voice got lost in the mutiny. I tried again, and this time my shout was louder, stronger. Zach was right behind me, his voice joining mine.

We nodded at each other, then jumped into the fray. Freddy manned the gate now, shouting into his earpiece. Takers streamed in from all over Holbrook. We fought our way through the mob.

"Kel's sick. I think—"

"Sure, princess." Freddy was a professional bastard, remembering to patronize me even in the middle of a crisis. He kept his eyes on the crowd while he talked to me. "I'll be right over to deal with his tummy ache. Right after I deal with this little riot we're having."

"No. Something's wrong. He looks like—"

"Just in time to distract me, huh?" He swung the gate open to let out a Taker who was dragging a girl by her hair. "How long do ya think I've worked with you monsters? I know every pathetic thought that goes through your head before you do."

Zach stepped up, right in Freddy's face. Zach's body trembled, but rage lit up his eyes, driving him forward. "Listen, you fucker . . ."

Freddy laughed down at him, spit flecking Zach's face.

"Remember who you're talking to." Freddy fingered the canister of pepper spray in his fist. "Your little friend here already knows what a bitch this is to inhale. Think of what it'll feel like directly in your eyes."

Maya ran up behind me. "Damion says Kel's getting worse. He's having some sort of fit or something. All spasmy and his skin's burning up."

Through the chaos, I spotted Damion and Nami huddled over Kel. Damion was propping Kel up against him, adjusting the tilt of his head, while Nami felt his forehead.

Doubt flickered across Freddy's face. I had to find some way to convince him I was serious. Some way to reach him through all that Taker bullshit.

"Kel told me he's been sick for a while. As in hospitals and doctors. Please! Just call it in to Nurse."

Freddy turned away. Desperate, I grabbed his hand to stop him. "Please, it might be too late—"

He looked back and met my eyes, alarm spreading across his face. We were no longer standing in the battle zone. A cacophony of sounds and images buzzed around me. Fractured sensations stung at my mind. Then they distilled into individual moments. It was like what had happened with Kel, but this time it wasn't just a single memory. Vivid scenes whipped past me with alarming clarity.

A drunk man, leather belt gripped in his white knuckles.

Three suitcases surrounded by glittering glass.

A whiff of pot smoke, angry voices coming from the other side of a closed door.

Then there was the car crash.

Even though I could barely see, the memory came into cutting focus. Slumped in the driver's seat of the car, I wiped at my eyes. Pain flared, obliterating all thought, and my hand came away with bright blood on it.

Whimpering came from the seat next to me. The girl in the passenger's seat was only a few years older than me, and she would've been beautiful if her body hadn't been twisted into an unnatural angle. Her eyes were closed, and blood seeped from her dark auburn hair, streaking her face. A cell phone lay on the floor. I reached for it, a gravelly grunt coming from my mouth as fresh pain cut into me. The whimpering grew louder, and struggling, I reached for the phone again. But it was too far away and the pain was too sharp.

Then the girl went quiet.

Fear drenched my body in the silence and I surged forward, grabbing the phone off the floor of the car. I tried to focus on the light of the cell phone glimmering in front of my face and—

The phone, the car, the pain vanished as Freddy pulled his hand out of mine. His eyes bulged, and his face turned redder than usual. The old scars turned white with tension, and I knew. The girl had died. Because he'd smashed the car. Because he hadn't gotten to the phone in time.

Freddy ordered into his earpiece, "Send Nurse. We got a sick kid down here."

It took me a second to realize he was actually calling it in. Freddy had experienced that memory along with me.

Zach looked at me with awe. Maya's expression was stuck somewhere between confusion and disbelief.

"I don't care if she's dealing with kids from the fight. We need her here now!"

Pause.

"I don't care about effing protocol either. I'll bring him in myself." Freddy tore out his earpiece and turned to me. "Crap! Let's get him to Nurse."

We raced over to Kel. His whole face was red, with a fuchsia band across his cheeks and nose. His hands looked swollen, and he was curled in a ball.

I knelt next to him. "Kel, can you stand? We're gonna—"

But Freddy pushed past me and, with a cry of pain from Kel, picked him up.

Kel reached out and grabbed my arm. "Don't leave me," he croaked.

"I won't, Kel. I'm right here."

Freddy just growled, "Keep up."

I followed in Freddy's wake as he charged through the warring factions, out the gate, and straight into the woods. Shielding Kel, Freddy barreled through branches that whipped back to smack me in the face. He zigzagged through the forest, clearly knowing the fastest way through the trees. We were making good time when Kel started flailing.

"Damn. Damn. Damn." Freddy's scarred face puffed red. He fumbled in his pocket, trying to hold Kel and get out his earpiece. He finally laid the bucking Kel on the ground and jammed the device back into his ear. "Kid's having some kind of seizure."

Pause.

"Okay, we'll stay put." Freddy stared down at Kel's jerking body. "We're out in the woods, close to the . . . the . . . Damn it. I'll have to come get you."

Freddy'd had the same look of horror on his face since he'd jerked his hand out of mine. Like he was reliving a nightmare. "They said to be careful he doesn't hurt himself. And turn his head to the side so he doesn't choke."

Then Freddy was off. No warnings or threats about me staying put. Just a final look backward.

Kel's eyes were closed, and his body seemed to be settling down. Was that a good sign or a bad one?

Panic exploded in my chest. I wasn't one for praying, but I looked up into the green canopy of pine needles. Searching for guidance. Through the trees, the sea shimmered in constant motion. Its rhythm steadying me.

"Don't do this, Kel, come on. Wake up. I'm sorry." No matter what secrets he'd kept, no matter what I'd seen in his mind, I didn't want this. I knelt next to him in the soft pine needles, in case he started flailing again.

But he was so still, it was eerie. Kel's whole body burned. I pulled him onto my lap, reassuring myself he was still breathing, putting my ear to his heart. I tried to remember the ABC mnemonic from Health class. Something, Breathing, Circulation?

"Please don't die."

Kel shifted slightly, opened one eye, and asked, "Is he gone?"

24

I STARED AT KEL in shock. *He's not dying*. I was elated and relieved and confused all at the same time.

"Is he gone?" he asked again. "Faye?"

Wait. He's not dying.

Kel reached up to touch the tears streaming down my cheek and I shoved him off my lap.

"Don't touch me."

Kel groaned as he hit the ground. I almost felt bad for him.

"I'm done playing games." I backed away, listening for any sound of Freddy coming back. But there was only the cicadas' incessant shrilling.

Kel showed me his hands, covered with splotches. "It's not a game. I swear. I have lupus. The rash, the fever, they're real. My body doesn't like the sun. But Faye, we have to talk about yesterday. You have to let me explain about—"

But I'd stopped listening.

"You don't like the sun," I repeated. I heard the words whispering in my mind. *The Harbinger is shielded from the glare of day*. The pieces were starting to fit together. "Your hoodie and sunglasses. Your gloves."

"Look, we don't have time for this. That Taker will be back any second." Kel sounded desperate and small, huddled there on the ground. He didn't look like he could end the world.

"Faye, I didn't mean to follow you. I mean, at first, I didn't mean to. It's just that I'm used to doing stuff at night, when I can pretend like I'm normal and I don't have to walk around wearing twenty layers of clothes." He took a shallow breath and rushed on. "And they don't give me those knockout pills, 'cause they'd interfere with my other meds. That's how I caught up with you in the Compass Rose the other night."

I'm so stupid. I thought he'd just found a way around the pills. Or thrown up like I did.

"But that first night I just stared out the window, wondering if I was ever gonna fall asleep. And I saw you climbing down that ladder and . . . I followed you."

The moon will know them. I inched backward, ready to take off if I needed to. That little voice still echoed in my head. *For me.* The prophecies were a warning *for me.* So I could stop what was coming. So I could stop the Harbinger. But the thought that it was Kel was too epically ironic. I groped for another explanation while the words of the tarot cards screamed in my head. Kel had hidden things from me. Betrayed my trust. But I didn't want him to be the Harbinger. "Then why did you take off your gloves and stuff during Free Time?"

"I know, it was stupid. But I had to find a way to talk to you, and causing a flare-up of my lupus seemed like the only option. I couldn't stand you looking at me like . . . like you are now. I did play it up a little, faking that seizure." Kel winced as he tried to sit up. "But trust me, my joints feel like fire every time I bend them."

For the Harbinger will carry pain with them through the lonely places of the Earth.

"Trust you? How could I trust you?" But there'd been a moment, in the library, when I *had* trusted him. When the two of us had been a we. I could still hear the way he'd whispered my name. Our bodies melting into each other.

"Please, Faye. I'm so sorry." His hands stretched out to me, opened palmed, plaintive. I relaxed my runner's stance a little. Green sparks shimmered in his deep hazel eyes, and looking into them, I wanted to believe him. I wanted to do more than that.

He reached out for me and I let him take my hand. Then the threatening buzz swarmed in my ears and I was thrust into another of Kel's memories.

He was up by the Screamers again, but I could tell by the moon that it was a different night. And that wasn't all that was different. The grass in the middle of the statues, the place I'd been kneeling in the first vision, was gone. In its place was a wide, deep pit. Kel stood at the edge of the hole, and through his eyes, I stared down into the frightening scene.

I watched myself crawling blindly through the mud, my fingernails scraping at the red dirt. Digging. And the others were there too. Nami, Damion, Zach, and Maya. All of us. Our eyes staring and empty.

"Nothing," Kel whispered to himself. "Every night they dig and still they find nothing."

I jerked away and I was back in the bright sunlight. I fought to clear the horrible image of us scrabbling in the mud like animals. "What— What's going on?"

"I followed you. All I wanted was to catch up with you so I could talk to you again. But . . . but, you were sleepwalking or something. You all were."

"Why are you doing this to us?" I tried to keep my voice steady, but I could hear it verging on hysteria.

"No." Kel sounded desperate for me to believe him. "No, Faye, I'm not doing anything. Please! I don't know why this is happening. I was trying to find out, like you. I wanted to keep you safe."

"How? By stalking me through the woods? By watching me and the rest of our drugged-out Family thrash in the mud? Why didn't you just tell us? Why didn't you tell me?"

Through the trees, I could hear distant voices, calling out for us.

"I was scared. I was afraid they wouldn't believe me. That they'd think I was crazy." Regret mingled with the pain on his face. "You're right, I should have told you yesterday up in the library. That's why I left the diary and tarot cards for you last night. So you could see them for yourself. So we could trust each other."

Why would he do that if he's the Harbinger?

"No more secrets. Please, Faye." Kel reached out for me, and more than anything, I wanted to take his hand. Tiny red lines veined through the creases of his palm. Red stains showed under his broken fingernails. But Kel said he hadn't been sleepwalking. And he hadn't been digging in the vision either.

Ice inched up my spine as I asked the real question. "Why are your hands red too?"

Kel looked down at his hands and I understood. He'd gotten his hands muddy so he'd blend in with the rest of us. He'd faked it. Just like he'd faked the seizure.

"Poor, sick Kel. You're still putting on a show for us all."

When he finally looked up at me, there was no denial in Kel's eyes. He hadn't wanted any of us to know.

Freddy ran through the woods toward us, Nurse right behind him. Kel slumped to the ground, playing sick again.

I took a step back, bracing myself against a tree. *Why Kel?* He'd been the only thing at Holbrook I'd dared to trust. My arms and legs trembled, barely holding me up.

Together Freddy and Nurse threw a blanket around Kel and maneuvered him onto a stretcher. Nurse slid a needle into his arm, and I saw him flinch.

If I was right— If I was the only one who could stop this—

Kel's eyelids drooped, his eyes pleading with me as they took him away.

Then I had to stop Kel and whatever he was going to do.

No, not Kel. The Harbinger.

Kel wasn't the only student missing from dinner that night. The cafeteria was only about half full. Where was Dr. Mordoch keeping them all? Under house arrest?

The whole room seemed to be holding its breath. Dr. Mordoch didn't say anything about the fight, but she no longer wore her patronizing smile either. With so many students to punish, I thought she might be celebrating, but her face looked pinched and gray.

My Family kept glancing at Kel's empty seat and then at me. Tears pounded at my eyelids, but I refused to let them out. I just concentrated on keeping my face impassive as I forked burnt baked beans into my mouth.

Once I was drugged and back in my stuffy room, I couldn't hold it together anymore. The day was still raw, like a bruise on the surface of my mind.

"God, I'm hungry. I couldn't eat any of that tuna crap at lunch . . . Do you know how many other animals die in those fishing nets? Dolphin-safe, my ass. And if you're a shark or a turtle, you're really screwed. Seems like if you're not cute and cuddly, no one even gives a shit about you." Maya rambled, almost on automatic, as she picked at a hangnail. She glanced at me out of the corner of her eye, as if judging what kind of mood I was in. "Not that I really wanted to eat it. I mean, it was bad enough having to sit there and breathe in that awful fish stink. And then baked beans for dinner? That's not a meal. Aren't you still hungry?"

Not even a little. I could still taste the panic in the back of my throat when I thought Kel was dying. And the nightmare flashes of Freddy's life. And the vision of us all digging in the dirt.

Nausea flooded my body and I ran to the bathroom, puking up the little dinner I'd eaten and whatever was left of my sleeping pill. My hands shook as I rinsed my mouth out at the sink, but at least I felt a little more in control. I couldn't risk another nighttime sleepwalk. Or meeting Kel out there in the darkness. I'd deal with the Holbrook Consequences when they caught up to me.

"Sorry." Maya looked a little shocked as I came out of the bathroom. She pulled her knees up, hugging them to her chest. Curiosity and concern both showed on her face. "You all right?"

Concern had won out, but not by much. Before I could answer, she rushed into her next question. "What happened to Kel?"

I sat down on my bed, aching head in my hands. I should tell her about Kel. About the tarot cards and the Harbinger.

"Nami was pretty worried about you guys." Maya actually came over and sat on the end of my bed. "I guess she's had some first aid training, but she said she had no idea what was going on with Kel. And then one minute you were arguing with Freddy, and the next you were both just standing there with these weird looks on your faces. I didn't know what was going on."

Sitting on my bed without any of her rhetoric or posturing, I was struck by how breakable she looked. I could see the shadow of veins just under her almost translucent skin. She sat there looking at me, knees tucked, arms wrapping her slight frame. How could I tell her any of this? She wouldn't have any better idea what to do with it than I did.

All I said was, "Kel's okay."

Maya looked like she wanted to ask more, but she shrugged and accepted my half answer. "Faye, I don't wanna go to sleep. Something's happening to me . . . messing with my head. I don't want any more nightmares or whatever they are. I don't want to hear that music. And I really don't want to wake up on the floor again."

This was the first time she'd mentioned the music, and now it was me that wanted to ask more questions. But she was scared enough as it was. And I was scared too.

"It's gonna be okay." I wanted to hug her, but I wasn't brave enough.

"You go to bed and I'll stay up. You won't have any more nightmares." I couldn't bear to tell her what I'd seen through Kel's eyes. About us digging in the red dirt. But I could make sure it didn't happen again tonight. "It's too hot for me to sleep anyway."

A half hour later, Maya's little snores filled the dark room. My feet hit the floor. I pulled the folded page out of my sock and slid the window open a crack. Grabbing the diary and the pen, I finished copying down the messages from the tarot cards, rereading them in order this time. Trying to put together the pieces of the story.

First the Past. The dreamer waking from a nightmare. The divided lovers. The boat and the six swords beneath the waves.

Stronger than the others the Harbinger
peers far into the Future There men
will feast off of the Earth like maggots There The
Circle will fail the Family Two quarrel and the
Harbinger alone slaughters
the lambs Forging a new Path and journeying
the sea of time To finish what has begun

I reread the middle section. *There The Circle will fail the Family.* I shivered. *Is it talking about my Holbrook Family?*

Then there were the three middle cards that connected the Past and the Future. What had Rita said about The Circle card? Something about it going nowhere. Round and round. Round and round. But looking at the card, the woman seemed powerful as she stood there at the edge of the water.

Next to The Circle card sat the blindfolded Harbinger, swords crossed, sitting in front of the sea. Last was the crowned figure of The Path, wielding a sword and balancing the scales. How did these cards make a bridge across time? I flipped them over.

Look carefully for the Harbinger is shielded from the glare of day
But the moon will know them Peer into strangers' eyes
for the Harbinger will carry pain

with them through the lonely places of the Earth
When the hour arrives the Harbinger

will smother the sickness that is humanity
Only the Harbinger can wash this world clean

And finally the Future. The disapproving moon. The glaring sun. The grim reaper in front of an open grave.

In the dark of the pregnant moon with
the sun as midwife Autumn will be born
in an ocean of blood Death will be Autumn's
twin and its mercy will cradle the Earth

After today, I understood only the tiniest part of the prophecy.

Kel was the Harbinger, and the Harbinger was bringing Death. But how? As unnerving as the prophecies were, they didn't change the fact that Kel was just a sixteen-year-old boy. Unless—

I thought about the last vision I'd had, Kel watching us dig through the dirt. What had he said?

Nothing. Every night they dig and still they find nothing.

What did Kel expect us to find? Was he using us to uncover some sort of device? And the iron talisman we found with the diary . . . Maybe it was some sort of key?

Why not? It made about as much sense as Nami's vampires or Zach's ninjas. The only thing I knew for certain was that something bad was happening and I had to stop it. I sighed and gathered up the diary, pen, and cards. Hoping things would be clearer tomorrow.

The Vision. The Lovers. The Ritual.

The Circle. The Harbinger. The Path.

The Moon. The Sun. Death.

Turning to replace them on the window ledge, I studied the only card that was upside down. The Lovers. A movement on the ground caught my eye. From the shadows of the courtyard, Kel watched my window.

Two quarrel.

I dropped to the floor, crouching out of sight. If Kel was the Harbinger, then I was . . . My face flared red as I remembered Kel's eyes singeing into mine. The feel of his lips and the taste of something so familiar.

I crushed the card in my fist. But sitting there tucked under the window, my back against the wall, I could still feel the Harbinger out there. Pulling me to him. Waiting to stalk me through the night.

Abandoning the diary and cards, I crawled across the floor, climbed into bed, and pulled the covers over my head. I couldn't deal with this. I understood M. H.'s words in her diary, when she described the madness creeping up on her. Then I thought about her chasing cards across the beach, laughing as she escaped the boring picnic. Before she'd found the talisman, before she'd seen any visions.

What was my "before" like?

My fingers drew the invisible scene against the rough sheets. M. H. standing on the cliff that October day. She looked out over the sea toward the beautiful island, and the trees shone with the same reds and oranges that I must have seen during my childhood.

Then I drew myself, standing next to her, watching the waves lap against the shore. And I waited for the long night to be over.

25

MY HANDS DUG DEEP into the soil. Above me, the bright moon was being devoured by shadow.

Hurry. Hurry.

Drums throbbed, accompanying the rising tide's chorus. A flute wove its voice into the song.

The tide is high. The moon is full. It is time. Hurry.

I dragged a body, a girl about my age, through the dirt. As I rolled her into the deep hole I'd made, her head lolled horribly. Not fully connected to her body. Then I climbed down into the pit after her.

Something cold and hard weighed down my hand. I opened my fist to reveal a polished metal figurine, an arrow engraved on its face. Lifting my head, I joined the song. A stranger's voice keened through the night air, chanting strange words.

Then I bent over the girl and placed the tiny statue on her unmoving chest. The girl's pale face was empty, drained of life, but the talisman was heavy with it. In the fading light of the moon, the metal gleamed with power.

Someone's thought floated through my head.

It had to be done.

I rested the girl's hand on the iron talisman. The skin on my fingers tingled and crackled, every cell alert to the memories and vitality dormant there. A whole life trapped inside that metal. Just waiting for a new body.

Another thought swam into my mind. *Waiting for the Harbinger.*

I pulled a long stone dagger from my belt. The blade was already stained with blood, and the same arrow mark was carved into the shaft. With a swift striking motion, I sliced a red gash across my palm. I made a fist and blood gushed, mixing with the dirt.

Then I picked up a heavy leather bag and flung a cloud of red powder over the body. A sharp, metallic smell filled the air as the red dust settled over the skin of the dead girl, masking her perfect face, her hands, the talisman.

I pulled another body into the hole and another. And another. All of them teenagers. All with their throats slashed open.

Making a circle of corpses, I repeated the ritual. Placing the glittering talisman. Reopening the cut on my hand. Pouring the powder over each corpse.

Finally, I reached the sixth and final body. A boy. A look of surprise on his handsome face.

I knelt next to him in the red earth of the pit, glad to be at the end of this gruesome task. Reaching out, I placed the last gleaming talisman on his chest and closed his hand around it.

The boy's eyes flew open. Dark eyes, crystallized with green. Kel's eyes. Kel's face.

Then the green was snuffed out and it was the dead boy again. Then Kel. He grabbed my hand and pulled me to him. His face flickering between the stranger's and his own. His voice coming out in a low rasp. "It's too late."

Caught somewhere between nightmare and reality, I screamed. Fighting to get free.

And the world flickered around me too. The talisman in Kel's hand was gleaming one second and rusty the next. His eyes black, then green, then black again. The clouds appeared and disappeared in the sky. Two images overlapping, fighting with each other.

It's a dream. Dizzy, I closed my eyes. Trying to catch my breath as the night air moved heavily in and out of my lungs, saturated with humidity.

Thunder growled in the distance and there was that smell. Ginger and musk.

My eyes snapped open again. The world had stabilized and Kel was there in front of me. But different. Something of the dead boy was still in Kel's face, still there in the dark of Kel's eyes. And clutched in his hand was a rusty talisman.

I didn't know what this was, but it was no dream.

"Faye, you are fulfilling the prophecy." His voice was different too, infused with bitterness.

"Get away from me!" I scrambled back, trying to put distance between him and me. Lightning struck, illuminating a girl splayed in the dirt inches from me. Despite the red smudges on her face I recognized the stubborn chin, the sharp nose, the hennaed hair. Maya.

"No!" A sob squeezed my throat and I rushed to her, sprawling next to her in the dirt. I grabbed Maya's limp hand, sending another rusty talisman skittering into the mud. A red smear sliced across her throat.

The sky exploded again and I saw them all there. Arranged in a grotesque circle like the figures drawn on my floor. Maya, Damion, Zach, Nami. And Rita.

"What have you done?" I could barely force out the words as I glared up at Kel.

"Me? Look at yourself." His voice was dazed. His eyes suddenly green again. "Look in your hand."

I clutched a stone dagger, stained with red. I remembered the tug of its blade across my palm. And the truth of the unmoving bodies soaked into my consciousness.

A tremor shook my body and it was echoed by another low groan of thunder. "What did you make me do?"

"Isn't this what you wanted?" His now black eyes looked up, out of the mass grave, and I followed his gaze to the Screamers. They looked down at us with unseeing eyes. Their faces twisted in horror.

Dropping the dagger, I tried to get away, but he was already on me. Grabbing my arm. Backing me against the side of the hole. Sending crimson earth cascading down on us.

I tried not to think of Kel's body pressing against mine. I concentrated on the feeling of the high dirt wall, solid behind my back. Letting the cool earth steady me.

Kel's hands gripped mine, so much stronger than before. In his eyes, through his skin, I felt only power. His sickness had been obliterated.

"Please, Kel . . . why are you doing this?"

"I'm not! I didn't do this!" Kel screamed at me. Lightning flashed again and I saw the green flickering in and out of his eyes. Doubt sketching itself across his face. Then, as if begging for it to be true, he said, "I couldn't have."

"Then let me go." My voice rose, thunder rolling across my words.

"I can't." Confusion trembled through Kel's voice. He looked down at his own hand, locked around my arm, like he didn't even recognize it.

Sweat trickled down my forehead, and through my fear, I tried to think. Hadn't Kel told me that we'd been sleepwalking? Hadn't he told me that he hadn't been taking Holbrook's knockout pills? Hadn't I even seen him in that vision, standing at the edge of this pit, watching us dig?

"'Every night they dig and still they find nothing.' Isn't that what you said?" I was trying to buy time. To find a way to escape from him. "But we found something tonight, didn't we? We found the talismans?"

Kel nodded slowly, like he was trying to remember. But he still gripped my arm.

"Then you made me kill them." My voice cracked, but I had to hold it together. I had to make it out of this alive.

"No!"

"Then talk to me, Kel. Make me understand—"

A weak groan interrupted me. Maya blinked up at us and her eyes were different too. Her face a mask of confusion.

Kel turned toward her, loosening his grip. And I sprang away from him, clawing up the side of the pit. Kicking foot holes in the loose dirt, I flung one arm over the top of the hole.

"Wait!" Kel grabbed my foot. "We have to help them. Please, Faye. I need you!"

I looked back, drawn in by the hint of green barely guttering in his eyes. By the groans of my friends, emerging from their trance. Then I thought about how Maya's eyes had looked strange. Just like Kel's.

I clung to the grass and roots at the top for leverage, kicking back hard. Kel shouted with pain, my muddy foot slipping out of his grasp. The momentum carried me the rest of the way up and out of the grave.

I was on my feet again, getting my bearings. Thunder crashed, and a cool drop of water hit my face. Then another and another. This time the water was real, and I welcomed it. Lightning lit up the world, and I tried to orient myself in the midst of the hideous, agonized faces of the Screamers.

Only now did I see the gashes cut in the statues' throats. The coppery water stains shining through the black patina like tears.

The pedestals decorated with the incessant arrow marking.

And in the same instant, I remembered M. H.'s final diary entry. *And there are obstacles I must clear away before I give in to this insanity that is creeping upon me. I must carve the mark upon this world. So much to do before I can follow The Path.*

M. H. had left these six statues for me, one more sign of what was to come. One more warning.

Only one person can stop Death's approach.

I looked behind me as lightning forked through the sky and saw Kel climbing out after me.

Behind him, another hand thrust itself out of the hole. Then a head. Maya.

Then there were more arms. Reaching. More smeared faces emerging from the deep pit. Crawling, dazed, out of the earth.

I took off running.

The sky opened up, and I could barely see. But that meant Kel and the others couldn't either. I flew down the hill, weaving in and out of trees, my bare feet sliding across the wet leaves. Air tore in and out of my lungs, tasting like wet earth and green things.

My feet took me toward the dorms without consulting my brain. I was too stunned to think of anywhere else.

Checking over my shoulder, I saw Kel in the light of the storm, just twenty feet away. Thunder rumbled, and I remembered the drums in my vision. *Hurry. Hurry.*

I burst through the woods and out onto the long, dark driveway that led to the road. The open sky pelted me with hail, stinging my wet skin. I sprinted across the gravel and back into the cover of the forest.

Kel's voice carried over the noise of the storm. "Faye! Wait!"

The lights of the dorms were just up ahead. Putting on a burst of speed, my legs strained to reach the protection of its walls. I threw myself through the beam of floodlights and crouched, gasping, into the shadows.

The vague outlines of two Takers stood huddled by the front door. The floodlights barely made a dent in the downpour, so I hoped my dash would go unnoticed. I raced through the shadows, finally reaching the safety of the ladder. The sliding part was already down, the padlock hooked over one of the rungs. I launched myself up the steps just as Kel hurtled through the spotlights toward me.

Hurry. Hurry.

Hail pelting my back, I climbed. Fighting to get a firm grip on the rungs. I dried my palms on my jumpsuit, but it was soaked too. Kel reached the ladder at the same time I reached the main section. I grabbed the bottom part and hauled it up.

But Kel jumped after it. My arm was nearly ripped out of its socket when his weight hit the ladder, dragging it back down a couple of feet. But I held on.

In a flash of lightning our eyes met. The storm. The nightmare. It all disappeared, and it was just Kel. I wanted to reach down to him. Kiss him again.

Then he lunged for me, snatching at my hand. Jerking back, I yanked up hard on the ladder and Kel, eyes wide, slipped off the wet rungs and dropped down into the darkness. The bottom part of the ladder flew up, slamming my fingers in the locking mechanism.

I shoved my fingers into my mouth to stop the scream. With my good hand, I grabbed the padlock. I'd forgotten it was broken, the metal warped and melted. I just hoped Kel couldn't reach it. One-armed, I climbed through the blackness. Finally, my hand touched the lip of the ledge. Relief rushed through me as I pulled myself onto the little shelf. But it was short lived.

The next streak of lightning illuminated Kel's contorted face, still watching me from the ground. I pushed the window up, tumbled inside, and for the first time since I'd gotten here wished for more locks.

The adrenaline seeped away, leaving me shaking and exhausted. I stripped off the wet jumpsuit and wrapped a thin blanket around myself. Before my body collapsed under me, I checked the door, making sure it was still locked. The knob didn't budge, but then again, it was locked from the outside. My blood pounded in time with the rain. *Hurry. Hurry.* I slid down the door, pressing my weight against it. Hoping that would be enough.

On the other side of the room, Maya's bed was empty. The covers shoved back. I sat shivering in a puddle on the floor, trying to understand what'd happened out there in the storm. It was just like what had happened in dreams M. H. had described. The same kind of talisman she'd found.

The diary, the pen, and the tarot cards were spread across the floor where I'd left them. I risked leaving my post at the door, scrambling to gather them up and carrying them back with me. Bracing my back against the door again.

I put the Past cards together one more time. The Vision. The upside-down Lovers. The Ritual with its six swords. And the scene came back to me. The dagger in my hand. The six bodies. Shuddering, I turned the cards over, rereading their words. Searching for answers.

Stronger than the others the Harbinger
peers far into the Future There men
will feast off of the Earth like maggots There The
Circle will fail the Family Two quarrel and the
Harbinger alone slaughters the
lambs Forging a new Path and journeying
the sea of time To finish what has begun

Is that what Kel's doing? Completing some horrific ritual that'd been started ages ago? Hadn't Rita said something about the Past being unfinished? She had been there tonight, lying in that circle of bodies. I didn't know who she was, but I doubted that she was just one of Holbrook's finest.

Footsteps tiptoed down the hall, growing louder. Closer. The door shook behind my back as the lock clicked and the knob twisted. I braced myself against the linoleum, thinking of dense, immovable things. Boulders. Trees. Mountains.

Terror sounded in my ears as the door pushed against my back. *Whoosh. Whoosh. Whoosh.* I gripped the metal door frame, concentrating on anchoring myself to the floor. My legs grew heavy and my back strong as I managed to hold the door shut.

"Faye." Maya's voice whispered through the wood. "Please."

So she really was alive. I looked at one of my stained hands. There was a red line of mud smeared across my palm, but I wasn't cut. Maybe I'd seen the same red mud slashed across her throat, instead of blood. My chest loosened a notch, but should I really have felt relieved? *Should I let her in?*

She sounded scared and lost. Exactly like I felt. At least we could figure it out together. I eased away from the door.

Then I heard a low voice whispering out in the hall. Was Maya helping Kel get to me? I pushed my body back against the door. I didn't dare trust any of them.

My teeth chattered and I cinched the blanket tight around my shoulders. The temperature had dropped fast with the raging storm, and my skin was damp and clammy. I stayed there until I heard the footsteps receding down the hall. Until dawn eased itself through the window. Until the lights in the dorm switched on.

I tried to sleep, but I kept seeing it. The gray faces. The talisman. My Family crawling out of the grave.

And Kel. The green fading out of his eyes. The rusty talisman in his hand.

Kel is the Harbinger.

The refrain repeated over and over in my head. And I was supposed to stop him. Before he really did kill us all.

26

I WAITED AS LONG as I could before I went out to the showers. I stalled, double-checking myself in the mirror. I looked like hell, but at least my jumpsuit had dried. Scraping a fleck of mud off my face, I headed out. Before the Takers came in after me.

Nami and Maya were already there at the front of the line. Both of their heads swiveled toward me when I walked down the hallway, as if they could sense me coming.

As I looked closer at Maya, it was as if a stranger stared out of her eyes. No, not a stranger. But not the Maya I was used to. All the distrust had been swallowed up by a growing surge of power. A storm of memories churned inside her, new ones mixing with old. But I couldn't read any of them clearly. One phrase emerged from the chaos: *The Circle.*

It was the same with Nami. Her eyes were filled with the same turbulent force, one thought reverberating in the clamor: *The Circle.*

The Circle will fail the Family. That's what the prophecy said. But what did that even mean? It was frustrating to think that I'd have to figure it out by myself. Just when I'd gotten used to the idea that I might have help, I was alone again. They might have been my friends, but I didn't even recognize them anymore. *What did Kel do to them? To us?*

I remembered them rising out of the graves the night before, like people possessed. Even this morning, a faint pink line still sliced across their necks, stained the same color as my fingers. My hand involuntarily went to my throat.

They echoed my gesture and something flared in their eyes. Like they were remembering something. Their bodies sagged a little, looking smaller. Their eyes cleared and the Maya and Nami I knew were back. But Nami didn't even try for her brash smile, and Maya barely gave me a shrug.

The moment I stepped outside the dorms, I gagged. The air was foul. Like rotting fish and death. I breathed through my mouth as the Takers corralled us down the path to the Compass Rose.

As we came out of the woods, there was a shout from the front of the line. The rest of us pushed forward to see what was wrong.

The ocean was red. And not pretty sunset red. The brown red of dried blood.

Across the crowd of girls, Maya and Nami turned and looked at me. As one, they mouthed, "An ocean of blood."

Did Kel tell them about the tarot cards?

Maybe. The only thing I knew for certain was that whatever was going to happen here, it was starting now. We were walking across the bridge that led from the Past to the Future. I wanted to run away, but I had no place to go.

The rest of the Family looked different too, especially Kel. He no longer had his hoodie or gloves on, and the red patches on his cheeks had disappeared. His angular face glowed bronze even in the weak cafeteria light.

I did the only thing I could think of: I faced them all across the breakfast table. Kel, Maya, Nami, Damion, and Zach. The only person missing was Rita. I still wasn't sure who she was or how she fit into this nightmare. Only that she did.

They all looked back at me and I held their strange, fierce eyes. Not flinching away. Then Maya dropped her gaze. Then Zach. One by one, they broke away, refusing to look at me. Till only Kel was left.

His eyes weren't black anymore, but a gray so dark that it blotted out all the green. And when he looked at me, there was a hardness there that I'd never seen before. I searched in them, but I couldn't find the Kel who'd talked me through the darkness. Who'd gallantly set off the alarms and run into the woods to save me. Who'd kissed me.

Only the Harbinger was left.

Kel's gaze was hot against my skin, and I wondered if I was in danger even now, sitting here eating. The spoon pressed into my bruised fingers as I scooped the tasteless oatmeal into my mouth. Scrape, chew, swallow.

Dr. Mordoch's voice cut across my thoughts. "Today is the last day of summer. A day of change. Marking the end of one cycle and the beginning of another. Just like you, over the next months, the trees will be shedding their leaves, exposing their very skeletons. How lucky you all are to be here at Holbrook, where we can observe these changes step by step."

Dr. Mordoch stared right at me during her little speech, and again I wondered how she was involved in all of this. It was like being inside a painting done in pointillism. I was surrounded by bewildering pinpricks of color. I knew there was a picture there. I knew if I could find a way to step outside of the painting, to back away from the mass of dots, I'd see a perfect scene laid out on the canvas.

Whatever Dr. Mordoch's role was in all this, she was back in full form today. Her face was animated with a manic energy, and her singsong voice resonated in the cafeteria. Her words slowly sank into my brain. *The last day of summer.* Then tomorrow must be the first day of fall. The words from the tarot cards echoed in my head.

With the sun as midwife, Autumn will be born in an ocean of blood.

But what was the part about the sun? *And how am I supposed to stop it?*

"Let us take a moment to think over our first week here at Holbrook Academy. You all are settling into our routine, learning what to expect, but as Buddha says, 'As soon as we think we are safe, something unexpected happens.' As you all saw on the way to breakfast, our campus was transformed during the night. I'm hoping our students have been as well. I talked with many of you after yesterday's events, and I think we understand each other now."

I bet she did more than talk. The cafeteria was full of students again, but most of them looked shell-shocked and drained. I didn't want to know what she'd done to them.

"At Holbrook Academy, we're always eager to use the unexpected as a learning tool. On Saturdays we usually have a less rigorous schedule. But it's clear to me that this group isn't ready for more freedom or privileges at the moment. Thankfully, life, in its lovely synchronicity, has provided us with the perfect opportunity."

She beamed at us. "I know you'll find it fascinating."

Whenever a teacher used the word *fascinating,* alarm bells went off in my head. But this time, Dr. Mordoch was absolutely right.

The ocean swirled with murky clouds of deep red. *An ocean of blood.* There was no other way to describe it.

I tried to stay away from my Family as our Aunt led us and two other groups through the woods behind the dorms. As she unlocked the fence that separated the beach from the Holbrook campus, my throat squeezed shut. This was the beach where I'd almost drowned as a child. The beach I'd painted in class.

The scene came back to me. Shivering on the wet beach. The moon casting an eerie red light. Dr. Mordoch clutching me.

And the voice coming from the shadows, *"You should have let her go."*

Ignoring my instinct to run, I forced myself to follow the other students out onto the beach.

The putrid stink that had been awful up at the Compass Rose was eye-watering down here on the beach. The tide was low now, but last night the waves must have almost reached the fence. Dead fish were washed high up on the rocky beach, their scales gleaming silver. Their fogged eyes staring at nothing.

Out in the water, corpses of seagulls and turtles bobbed in the red waves. Some of them were wreathed in seaweed. Others were tangled up in the lines of the generator buoys.

I hesitated on the fringes, not wanting to go any closer to the water. Or my Family. Nami, Damion, Maya, Zach, and Kel stood in a tight cluster, whispering to one another. Occasionally, one of them would glance over, staring at me with their unfamiliar eyes.

What is Kel telling them? Were they on his side in this—fight? Was it a fight?

Nami whispered something and pointed toward me, and I was right back in the hallways of my high school, wishing I could melt into the endless rows of lockers. In that moment, I didn't care about prophecies or saving the world. I would've given anything for it to be yesterday again, when I was still a part of the Family. But more than the color of the ocean had changed overnight.

Dragon and the other Takers fanned out behind us, herding the three families of students forward. We crunched across the beach, strewn with glittering glass and tar-covered rocks.

"What is this crap?" The skinny guy who'd berated us at lunch the other day jabbed at one of the fish with a stick.

"It's sometimes called a red tide," our Aunt informed him in her patronizing tone. Her snub nose wrinkled at the smell and she looked at a little cue card in her hand. Like always, we had to go through the charade of Holbrook being a real school. "But that's not a fitting name, since it has nothing to do with the tide or the moon. Scientists call it a harmful algal bloom, or HAB. Of course, the bloom of the red algae isn't as pretty as flowers"—she laughed at her little joke—"but it does glow bright blue in the dark. Runoff from last night's storm and the sudden temperature change must've given the phosphorescent algae the perfect conditions in which to grow."

"Runoff?" Maya's voice was quiet, as if she were speaking from somewhere very far away. Then she shook her head, and the rebellion came back into her eyes and with it, her old self. She stepped forward, and I saw that this still wasn't the Maya I knew. A new sense of authority inhabited her body, a sense of ownership over herself and the world around her. "Do you mean all the dirt that's washing away because they clear-cut the forests? Or are you talking about the crap from those oil tankers? Or maybe the shit that's overflowing from the sewers?"

Aunt turned on Maya, but then Aunt noticed the change too. Saw the fire in Maya's eyes. Aunt's voice was cautious as she reprimanded Maya. "You know not to speak out of turn. Keep your mouth closed and maybe you'll learn something."

"No." Maya's answer was mutinous, but it also had a certainty I'd never heard before. Like she was merely stating a fact. "I won't keep quiet anymore."

Aunt looked uncomfortable and motioned the Takers to move in. Dragon came and stood right behind Maya, and Aunt scanned her notes, looking for where she'd left off. "As I was saying, scientists don't know exactly what causes algal blooms like this. The unusual heat, ocean currents, or any number of other natural causes could have contributed."

Maya opened her mouth, but Nami stepped forward and started talking before Maya could get in any more trouble. "Yeah, I'm sure that global warming had nothing to do with it."

Then, in one ominous movement, the rest of the Family closed ranks around Maya and Nami. Seeing them there like that, I shuddered. And I saw another group of people, superimposed on them. Seven people, standing on a mountaintop looking down at the sea. We were connected to the ground as if our feet reached deep into the earth. The wind whispered stories to us. People sought us out for council. We were servants of The Circle. Speakers for those who had no voice. For our voices were mighty.

The image vanished, and we were just students again. Standing on the beach. But something of that power lingered in all of us.

Aunt must've sensed that she was losing control, because she stuck her note cards in her pocket and started handing out big black trash bags. "Don't worry, the algae's only toxic if you swallow it. So don't go sticking your fingers in your mouth."

I grabbed a trash bag, keeping an eye on Maya. Her eyes shifted between a steely reserve and a vague confusion. Her face mimicked the changes, as if she were shifting back and forth between two personas.

Aunt stood with her hands on her hips, looking at us expectantly. "The beach isn't going to clean itself. Get moving."

Students spread out, making retching noises and shrieks as they picked up dead animals and slimy clumps of seaweed. I looked down at the trash bag and then at a seal sprawled on the beach. A rotting, fishy smell wafted over to me, and bile rose in my throat, but I forced it back down. The seal's milky blue eyes stared up at nothing. Flies crawled across its matted fur.

Men will feast off of the Earth like maggots.

Reaching down, my hand covered with the trash bag, I gripped the cold animal through the plastic. I nudged it with my foot and my other hand, trying to get it into the bag. But the seal was too big, and my fingers slipped. As I touched the wet fur, absolute silence descended over me. I couldn't hear or feel anything. I couldn't breathe, but I wasn't gasping for air. I couldn't see, but it wasn't dark. There was simply the absence of all things. No smell, no desire, no cold or heat. No connection to anything.

I pulled my hand away. And the world came rushing back.

What I'd felt wasn't just death. Growing up when I'd collected bones, I'd felt a calm quietness in them. But never this terrible blankness. Like all traces of life inside the animal had been eradicated. I leaned back, steadying myself. My fingers sank into the pebbly sand, and the same overwhelming void swallowed me up.

Alarm rang out inside me as I touched a nearby coil of seaweed. Nothing. A stone. Nothing. A crab shell. Nothing. Nothing. This wasn't death. This was obliteration.

Nausea swept over me. The whole beach was barren. Kel was already destroying this place. Maybe what he'd said last night was true. *Maybe it is too late.*

No. I stood up, my fingers tingling with electricity. Now I was certain why I'd seen the visions. Why I'd been drawn to this place again. Why I was separate from other people. I was the one who would stop the Harbinger.

I'm going to save them all.

If only I knew how.

Kel's voice buzzed in my ear and there was no sardonic edge to it. No trace of humor. "'With the sun as midwife, Autumn will be born in an ocean of blood.'"

I hadn't heard him come up behind me. I shook my head, not looking at him, and moved away, submerging myself in the mass of squeamish students.

But he was right there, following me, whispering again. "'Death will be Autumn's twin, and its mercy will cradle the Earth.' This is The Path. Faye, it's happening right now. Isn't it?"

I couldn't bear to be close to him. This Kel who was not Kel. I walked away, toward the arcing high-tide line marked by seaweed and rotting fish. Using the edge of the trash bag as a glove, I picked up a dead fish, shuddering as its slimy, rigid body slid into the bag. Kel's steady footsteps crunched toward me again, but I was tired of playing cat and mouse.

I spun around to face him. "What did you do?"

"What?" His solemn gray eyes bored into me.

"To our Family? To this beach. Is this just the beginning?"

"Faye, last night is a blur to me. One minute you were all singing and digging up the talismans. Then suddenly I was lying in the dirt, holding one of them in my hand. And the whole world looked different. Brighter. Richer. It was like I'd been asleep for years and finally woke up."

I remembered that feeling. From when I was six. I'd pulled away from my parents and plunged my hand into the waves and suddenly, everything was new. Everything around me was lit up from inside, rumbling with the drumbeat of that song. But it'd also been confusing. I had thoughts I didn't understand. Nightmares of things I never could have imagined.

Then I understood what Kel was saying, even if he didn't. *He woke up. Last night, the Harbinger woke up.* And we'd helped. He'd literally gotten us to do his dirty work.

"Sometimes I almost understand what's happening to me. Then it slips away again, like a word just on the tip of my tongue. Please help me remember." He tried to put his hand on my arm, but I stepped back.

After last night, I would never let him touch me again. But.

But, maybe *I* could touch *him*.

I thought about clutching Kel's hand in Dr. Mordoch's office. About seeing not just shadows of his thoughts, but a whole memory when we'd kissed. Yesterday, when I'd grabbed Freddy's hand, my entire mind had been filled with the fear of Kel dying. And somehow, I'd triggered Freddy's memory of the car crash. Maybe I could do it on purpose this time.

Snatching Kel's hand, I flooded my mind with the image of the arrow. The one thing that seemed to tie all this together.

This time, everything was more violent. What I'd thought of as a swarm of bees was now a tornado. A torrent of thoughts and images screamed past me. A sad-looking woman wearing a protective mask. A staticky snatch of music. An abandoned subway tunnel. Kel's gloved hand reaching out.

The images pushed and pulled at me, playing tug-of-war with my mind. I braced myself, trying not to be ripped apart by the maelstrom. Then, in my physical self back on the beach, I felt Kel struggling to pull his hand out from mine.

No. It's my game this time.

I focused every fiber of my being on resisting the chaos. *I am Faye. Fear is an illusion. I'm in control of my own reality.*

Somehow, I managed to shove myself through the turmoil, into the eye of the tornado. It wasn't that the storm of images had calmed down as much as they veered around me now, leaving me untouched. Inside this bubble, I felt an excruciating intimacy with Kel. His entire life swirled around me.

Euphoric islands of time with his guitar. Brutal arguments with his dad. And an intoxicating electricity that crackled in between. It was like being inside that kiss again, and I longed to throw myself into the phantasmagoria.

Hurrying, I concentrated on trying to find the arrow. I reached in and snatched an image out of the flow. Kel and a man stood facing each other.

Everything shifted and I was standing, looking at the man. Anxiety swept through my body.

"Dad, I'm sorry I ran away. I didn't handle things well and I screwed up." Kel's voice came from me. A mix of fear, anger, and hope jangled through me as I forced myself to take a deep breath.

"You sure did. And crawling back here isn't going to change that. You made your choice. You don't want to be part of this family? Well, you're not." The man spit the words at me.

His words stung and I let their rage fuel mine. "Family? This hasn't been a family since Mom died."

"Don't use your mother as an excuse for running away from your problems. She'd be ashamed to see what a coward you've become."

Anger screamed in my mind. It was so powerful I could taste it. I don't know who threw the first punch, but suddenly my body was moving, my fists finding their target, and it felt good.

Kel's voice thundered in my head. "Get out!"

Shocked, I lost my footing and was slammed backward into the cyclone of emotions and memories. Then Kel was inside my mind. Raking through my memories.

Tumbling down the stairway in fourth grade. The laughter and bruises stinging.

Sitting down at lunch. Everyone around me getting up and moving to another table.

My parents asking me again and again, "Why do you want to kill yourself?" Not even meeting my eyes. As if they didn't blame me for trying.

Every horrible, lonely moment of my life, flashing through my brain. I cried out, struggling to get back in control. To get back into Kel's mind.

I am Faye. Fear is an illusion. I make my own reality.

I gripped his hand and concentrated on the arrow. The symbol pointing me toward where I needed to go. And I was back at the edge of Kel's memories. Then, from outside the whirlwind, a chilly darkness pressed in. It wasn't like the rest of Kel's mind. It crept into my bones and tore at me.

"Leave!" Kel shoved at me, trying to push me out of his mind.

Not until I get what I came for. I focused on the arrow again as the pressure from Kel's mind grew almost unbearable. The strange blackness pulling me toward it.

I dug in my heels, thinking of the arrow, refusing to be sucked into the dark.

But maybe that's the only way. So instead, I let go, letting myself be drawn in. And there, in the darkness, I found myself face-to-face with Kel.

We stood at the top of the hill. Hand in hand. I looked into Kel's black eyes and realized it wasn't him. It was the dead boy I'd seen in the grave the night before. Only now he was alive.

His face was different and he was taller. His golden-brown skin radiated power. But the way he looked at me was the same. As if he were seeing all of me and liked what he saw.

"You can't do this." His voice was different too, more serious, but it held the same tender confidence. "You don't have it in you."

Anger flared inside my chest: he was always underestimating me. Ever since we were kids. "You have no idea what I'm willing to do."

"Even if it means losing me?" His eyes pulled at me, and my heart shredded.

I looked up and there was the full moon again. It hung low in the sky, being consumed by a blood-red shadow. Afraid, I looked down at the polished talisman in my hand, glinting in the red light. *This is The Path.*

I dropped his hand. "Even if it means losing everything."

"No!" Kel's voice blasted through my brain. It was like someone grabbed me by the throat and whipped me into the air. All the breath was squeezed out of my lungs as I was thrown back into the hurricane of memories and spit out onto the beach.

Kel growled down at me, sunlight glowering behind his head. "I don't want you to get hurt."

A little late for that. I clutched my tender ribs and gulped for air.

His face was a snarled mix of the face I'd just seen in the vision and Kel's own exposed one. I was stunned by what had happened. The Kel that was not Kel. The me that was not me. The feelings I'd had for him were the very skeleton that'd held me up. But I'd known that, to make things right, I'd have to destroy him and that it would shatter me. The upside-down Lovers.

Looking at him now, I wanted to hide from him and hold him at the same time. And I wanted to cry for both of us. Instead, I pushed myself off the ground, using the motion to disguise my pain.

My Family moved into a protective half ring around Kel, as if they were daring me to try something. Pushing the panic down, I reassured myself. At least that last vision had finally made something come into focus. The moon.

A lunar eclipse. I understood now. Maybe this was the key. I just needed to get to the library to check, and I knew exactly how I was going to get there.

Carefully stepping around Kel and the others, I strode over to Dragon.

"What do you want?" With a sneer she flipped open the snap on her holster, hand hovering above her Taser. I guess the pepper spray was still fresh in her mind.

It was in mine.

"Just this." In a single movement, I grabbed the Taser and zapped her with it. As she dropped, I turned and ran.

"Dah-daaah-daah-dah dum-dum." I sang the *Chariots of Fire* theme song as I ran down the beach, arms raised and shouting, "Faye Robson triumphs again!"

Seagulls scattered under my flying feet. The wind rushed at my face. I heard the Takers right behind me, but I reached up into the piercing blue sky, trying to pull myself into it.

"Dah-daaah-daah-dah—"

The jolt hit me. In all-too-familiar slow motion, the sky slipped out of my grasp. And I smashed back to Earth.

27

THIS TIME, I found out what the metal ring was for. Nurse sat me against the wall in Solitary and ordered me to pull my knees to my chest, pretzeling my arms through my legs so that my hands were holding the inside of my ankles. I'd never seen her smile before, and the expression looked unnatural on her narrow face. She whistled as she cinched cloth cuffs around my ankles and wrists, securing both sets to the ring bolted to the wall near the floor.

"This is what happens when you bite the hand that feeds you. It bites back. I'm sure Dr. Mordoch will want to talk to you, but I might wait a little while before I mention that I already . . . collected you." Then she spit in my face and slammed the door behind her.

This wasn't going according to plan. I rolled my shoulder, trying to wipe the saliva off my cheek. But with the restraints, it hurt to move my arm even that much. My whole body screamed against my cramped position on the cold floor.

Last time I was in Solitary, the water had come for me, but this time it was worse. I felt the waves hovering, like a great shadow in my mind, waiting to crash over me. And this time when they came, I was afraid I'd be washed away.

The words of the tarot cards reverberated off the walls of the tiny room. I closed my eyes and saw the faces. Always the dead faces of my Family staring up at me through the dark.

I wasn't supposed to be in Solitary. I'd been so sure they'd take me to Dr. Mordoch's office in the Compass Rose. Just one floor away from the entrance to the secret library. Now I was trapped, while Kel was out *there* doing whatever he'd been planning.

Only one small line of light filtered through a crack in the door. A crack I'd made last time Dr. Mordoch had locked me in here. My heart slammed against my chest. *Hurry. Hurry.* But there was nothing I could do.

Time passed, measured only by breaths. It could've been ten minutes or two hours. The dark was still dark.

Then the door rattled, and the sun blinded me. Dr. Mordoch came in, bringing a whole new nightmare.

"Why are you doing this to me, Faye?" She knelt down next to me and took my chin in her hand, daring to look in my eyes. I searched hers for clues to what she knew, but they were too muddled. Her breath stank of alcohol, and I tried to pull away.

"You made them hurt you," Dr. Mordoch slurred, fumbling with her key ring. By the time she managed to unlock my hands and feet, it was very clear that this was a face of Dr. Mordoch I hadn't seen before. I didn't dare move. I just sat there feeling the blood pulsing back into my limbs.

"It was my fault . . . all those years ago. I only had one little drink that night, just a nightcap, I swear, but I must have fallen asleep. I don't even know what happened, I only remember waking up by those hideous statues, clawing at the ground. And your parents too. And others I didn't even recognize . . . I tried to wake them all up. But they just kept digging, like animals."

They were trying to reach the talismans.

"Then I saw you walking down to the beach and I went after you. Faye, you were so little and you walked straight into those waves. All I thought about was saving you." The terror was still alive on Dr. Mordoch's face.

"All these years . . . It's all we've ever done. Tried to save you." She looked infinitely sad for a moment. Then her eyes froze over, and she slapped me. "But all you do is throw it in my face."

Tears sprang into my eyes. The slap was more noise than pain, but my face still stung. More disturbing was Dr. Mordoch's manic look. She seemed out of control. Desperate.

"She told me to bring you here and I did. There was more for you to do, she said, and I knew we could work through your child-hood trauma if I brought you back . . . teach you to function in the world." Dr. Mordoch panted like an animal caught in a snare.

She?

"But it wasn't enough for her, was it? So I gave you extra chances. Looked the other way when you sneaked into my office. But now you've crossed the line."

What else does she know? What else is she hiding?

I tried to back away from Dr. Mordoch, but I was already against the wall. Her voice rose to a shrill howl. "I'm done listening to her and you are done resisting. I will save you, Faye, even if I have to break you first. Do you understand?"

Then she closed her eyes, as if she were in pain. She reached up and straightened her tight ponytail. She nodded to herself.

When Dr. Mordoch opened her eyes again, they were focused, back under control. "Starting tomorrow, you'll be escorted by a Caretaker everywhere you go. Someone will be watching while you scrub out the showers, while you sleep, while you pee."

She smiled at me then, tears glistening in her eyes. "I won't let you destroy this opportunity we've made for you, Faye. All of our plans. We've come too far."

I didn't understand what Dr. Mordoch was talking about. Maybe *she* didn't even understand. She was looking right at me, but I wasn't sure she really saw me.

I nodded, not wanting to set off the crazy again.

"You will stay here in the dark and think about what you've brought down upon yourself. Tomorrow morning, I'll send a Caretaker to collect you."

Then she was gone. I brought my hand up to my cheek and winced, not because of the slap, but because of my stiff fingers. I flexed them slowly. I straightened my legs. It hurt, but I kept going until I could move again.

I was safe now. Safe from Kel. Safe from Dr. Mordoch. But I couldn't stay here for long. I needed a plan and it had to be good.

By the time the afternoon light coming through the crack in the door turned amber, I knew what to do. Find the book. Find the answer. Find Kel. I went over and over it in my mind as the sunlight slid across the floor and faded away.

It's time.

I got up, dusting off my hands, and faced the door. I'd made one chink in the wood, I could do it again. Laying my palms on either side of the narrow crack, I closed my eyes. The boards were rough and splintery under my fingers.

What now?

I thought about touching Kel and Freddy, how I'd relived their memories. I thought about that first day in Solitary, how Kel had said his door was solid, but somehow mine had cracked. And no one else had been able to open their windows, but I had. Even after they'd nailed it shut. How had I done it?

That first morning in Solitary, I'd pounded my fists on the door in sheer panic. But the moment the door cracked had been different. Blood had whooshed through my head. Drums had pounded with my heart. And a strength had shot through me.

I didn't understand how or why, but for that fleeting instant, I'd felt invincible. Now I imagined that feeling of power flowing down my arms. I pressed my hands against the wood.

I am Faye. I create my own reality.

My fingertips tingled. Surprised, I pulled them away from the door.

Steady.

I tried again, focusing on the exact spot where my skin stopped and the planks of wood began. Heat spread across my palm, and I envisioned power pouring out through my hands and into the wood. The door seemed to vibrate under my fingers. But nothing happened.

I pushed the boards, bracing myself physically and mentally, trying to force my way through the barrier between my skin and the wood grain. My pulse throbbed its insistent beat. *Whoosh. Whoosh. Whoosh.* My whole body trembled, but I was still me and the door was still a door. Exhausted, I collapsed against it.

Then the wood pushed back.

I gave in a little, opening up my mind, relaxing my clenched hands. And the wood pushed a little more.

It was different from what I'd thought. The power wasn't going from me into the wood, it was the other way around. The power was coming from the door.

The wood grew hot, almost burning, and I tried to pull my hands away, but I couldn't. It *was* a little like what'd happened with Kel and Freddy, but this wasn't so much a swarm or a hurricane of images as it was a surging river of sensation.

I waited on the bank of the strange river, feeling it all rushing by me. The noise was deafening, like standing inside a plane engine. Trembling, I bent down and stuck my hand into the current, trying to understand it. My fingers grew stiff and rough. A vein of energy flowed just under my skin. Then my hand seemed to burst open from the inside. Stretching, reaching out with a desperate longing. The river swelled up around me, swallowing my arm. Enveloping my body. Tugging at my feet. I struggled to stay standing, to remember who I was.

I am Faye.

But the flood of sounds and feelings and textures didn't care who I was. They pulled me under anyway. I flailed at the surface of the stream, trying to separate myself from it. Trying to pull my hand away from the wooden door. But I was drowning. I gave into it as my head went under the raging current.

Then everything was quiet.

I was standing in warm, green light. I couldn't see the sky above me, but I knew it was there. Clear and radiant. Wind rippled across my skin, making my entire body shiver. I'd never felt a sense of wholeness like this.

I wiggled my toes deeper into the solid ground and found a cool trickle of water, making me feel bright and awake. And secure.

A small vine wrapped itself around my legs, tickling me. A squirrel chittered and scampered across my shoulders. Cold inched its way into my core and then was gone. Soft rain caressed me, and I fell in love with each prismed droplet.

Then a loud buzzing filled my ears. Jagged, metal teeth ate me alive. This was not the ache of growth, but the searing pain of death. I was falling, crashing through the world, until I thudded on the unforgiving ground.

Now there was nothing beneath my feet, no water flowing through me, no connection.

Then I was here. This door. A lifeless parody of what I'd been. But the wind still brushed my skin. Drops of rain still flung themselves against me. I was still strong.

Until the crack.

Weakness emanated from that spot. The first of the dreaded decay that would eat away at me.

I honed in on that aching gap. Imagining wet winters soaking into the wood. Freezing nights and sunny days, expanding and contracting.

The hole grew bigger.

I envisioned termites munching, slicing me apart in minuscule mouthfuls. Unrelenting storms sheeting down. Wind rushed through the widening hole, making me wail.

The two boards buckled away from each other. The nails rusted and loosened.

Years passed in a blink and my strength disintegrated. I cried out as birds peeled away my splintered flesh with their needle-sharp beaks. Microbes feasted. Time agonizingly sandblasted its way through.

The pair of boards fell away. They were only sawdust and splinters now, littering the ground in front of the Meditation Center. Only air beneath my palms.

I slumped down onto the floor, drained. My head resting against what was left of the door. I closed my eyes, shutting out the unbearable agony of loss.

"I'm sorry."

28

WHEN I CAME TO, it was still night. I wasn't sure how long I'd been out, but through the gap in the door I could see low lights bordering the path back to the Compass Rose. Wind swirled around in mini-cyclones. I felt its agitation.

My hands shook as I touched the door. It'd been split in two. One half was held up by the hinges, the other by the lock. I tested the remaining wood. It was solid. The door was exactly as it'd been before, except for the two missing slats in the middle. I squeezed through and smiled.

Flexing my hands, a prickle of power shivered through my fingers. *This is what my life has been leading to. Tonight.*

I needed to find Kel. To stop whatever he was going to do. But first, I had to go back to the library.

I knew the cryptic warnings from the tarot cards were coming true. My stained hands. The red tide. The autumn equinox. And something about an eclipse. Maybe if I completely understood what was going on, I could find a way to stop it.

The campus was deserted, with everyone locked away in their rooms. A gust sent the trees shivering against the black sky. *Hurry. Hurry.*

But so far, there was no "pregnant" full moon peeking through the branches. I still had time.

Rushing through the woods, I paralleled the path to the Compass Rose. I clung close to the trees, pine boughs hiding me in their shadows. Their roots intertwined beneath my feet, and I could feel the water and sap pulsing through them all. Like one giant, magnificent creature.

The same pulse flowed through me, and I felt strong. I wouldn't let Kel kill my world. I would stop him.

More Takers were on patrol tonight outside the Compass Rose, but the shadows seemed to cling to me. Hiding me from sight. I waited for the right moment, slipped past the Takers, and shimmied up the tree. The branches under my hands spoke, sending memories whispering through me.

A sapling, weak and skinny, taken from the forest and planted in the ground outside a half-built Compass Rose.

A girl, my age, patting down the dirt around young roots.

An eerie silence around the Compass Rose, broken by the steady chanting of monks.

Then spotlights and harsh voices, the constant presence of people and fear and rage.

There was something else there too. Just a trace of the void that swallowed me when I'd touched the dead seal on the beach. A poison deep within the tree that left me queasy and weak. It was a relief to climb through Dr. Mordoch's office window and leave it behind.

My senses were magnified. Even the quiet of the Compass Rose sounded loud. A Taker paced the wooden porch outside the front door. Another patrolled the forest outside. But the house itself was empty.

By the weak light illuminating Dr. Mordoch's diplomas, I unlocked the filing cabinet and rifled through the folders. On a hunch, I grabbed the last file of psychiatric evaluations and took them with me. Then I crept out of Dr. Mordoch's office, down the stairs, and through the secret door in the sitting room. The arrows on the walls screamed at me now.

Hurry! Hurry!

I ran down the twisting passageway, careful not to touch the tortured walls. Up the spiral stairs. Banging my shins against the steps. Bursting into the library. I closed the door behind me, finally shutting out the screeching voices.

Like Dr. Mordoch's office, the library was already dimly lit by a little brass light hanging over the old black-and-white photograph of the Compass Rose. Dark swaths of books covered the walls. But in the half-light, I saw that some of them were leaning, crooked on their shelves. *Has Kel been here? Or did they just fall over on their own?*

Then I saw the book spread open on the desk near the window. *Tides and Waters of New England.* Kel had beat me to it, and he didn't care if I knew. And lying on top, weighing down the page, was a talisman. Touching the cold iron, I knew it wasn't one of the ones we'd dug up the other night. Those had been dirty and coated with rust. But they'd also been saturated with power. Practically alive.

No. This talisman was the one Kel and I had found in the secret compartment. The one M. H. had found. Even though her talisman still gleamed softly in the low light, it was used up and empty. A metal shell.

I moved the talisman, checking the page Kel had marked. He'd left it blatantly open to a map filled with overlapping ovals and shadowed spheres. The one I'd come here looking for.

"Lunar Cycles and Tides" showed a diagram of the orbits of the moon, the Earth, and the sun.

"The highest tides occur when the moon and sun are both in

line with the Earth, increasing the gravitational pull on the oceans." There was a diagram of the three spheres, lined up in a row. The moon was on one side of the Earth and the sun on the other, each pulling at the blue planet.

With the sun as midwife.

A small note was scrawled beneath the picture in M. H.'s now familiar handwriting. "This alignment can occur during a lunar eclipse."

I went back to the text, trying to put it all together. "If the moon is at its proxigee, its closest point to the Earth, during this alignment, then the tide may be particularly high and can cause flooding. The moon's orbit is a fixed cycle, spinning close to the Earth and then away from it. Because of this, high tides technically can be predicted with accuracy."

There was a table of dates, starting in 1905, listing when the moon would be closest to the Earth. I scanned down the list, my finger stopping at an unnervingly familiar date. Tomorrow—or, since it was probably after midnight already—today. Right now, the moon was as close to the Earth as it would ever be.

Flipping to the index, I found another table listed, titled "Lunar Eclipses." I turned to it, already knowing what I'd find. Today, the autumnal equinox, was listed on this table as well. September 21 at 6:09 a.m.—total lunar eclipse.

I pulled Dr. Mordoch's interview papers out of the folder, playing my hunch. The interview with my parents said that I'd changed after they took me to the beach on the evening of April 3. My finger slid down the chart eleven years, looking for the date. That year there was a total lunar eclipse on April 4, just after midnight. Meaning it had started on the night of April 3. My parents must have taken me out to the beach to see the beginning of it.

There was a second total lunar eclipse that year early in the morning of September 27. I checked the transcript of Dr. Mordoch's hypnotism session, September 26. The night I'd almost drowned on the beach.

More clues. More crumbs leading me to *what*? Kel was just taunting me. He had auspicious prophecies written about him, and what did I have? A lunar calendar, a rusty doll, and an affinity for trees? I chucked the talisman against the wall, slammed the book shut, and shoved it back onto the shelf.

The book next to it caught my eye. *Ancient Maine Burial Sites*, by Professor B. Warren. That's who M. H. had written to about the talisman.

I grabbed the tattered book off the shelf, paging through it with shaky hands. Searching for anything that looked like the talisman. There were photographs of a carved bird. A spearhead. A stone dagger like I'd found the other night. But none of them had the arrow marking.

The Compass Rose creaked and strained. I froze, barely daring to breathe. Had Kel come back for the book? For me? A gust of air smacked against the window and the house trembled.

Just wind. I forced my shoulders to relax and went back to the book.

I found it at the start of the third chapter. M. H. was right. It was the same symbol, carved into a long stone pendant. Beneath the photo was a section called "Ancient Burial Practices of Maine."

The State of Maine was once home to a forgotten and mystifying race. Thousands and thousands of years ago, these highly skilled people lived along this coast, hunting swordfish from the ocean, creating intricate carvings, and trading goods up and down the Gulf of Maine. Our knowledge of them is extremely limited. But the glimpse we've had into their culture has been stunning and not a little perplexing. These are the few facts science has uncovered.

That they were an ancient people.

That their artisanship illustrates a sophistication far beyond any other Stone Age peoples.

That they buried their dead with red ochre, a metallic powder made from oxidized iron, as well as with ritualized talismans and tools.

That they had a profound belief in life beyond death.

That they vanished from this earth, without a trace of what had befallen them.

Things fit into place. Hands pouring red powder into a fresh grave. Placing the talismans on each still corpse. This was what Professor Warren was describing.

I rushed on, looking for answers in the archaic text.

Archaeological digs have excavated grave sites dating from as far back as 3000 BC. But by 1800 BC, not even a remnant of this distinctive culture remains. Compounding this disappearance is the fact that over time, this coast has slowly sunk into the sea. Their villages, their shell middens, all the little signs of day-to-day life have been submerged. Lost forever. This is a profound loss to the archaeological community. The meager information we do have about these people's day-to-day lives has left us with unanswerable questions. Who were they? How did their art and culture transcend the limitations of their primitive time? Why did they perform such elaborate burials? And most important, what happened to them?

They did not migrate north or south. They did not slowly

fade into another people to the east or west. They simply vanished, leaving archaeologists with a fierce debate. What destroyed this lost civilization?

"Do they live happily ever after?" A voice spoke from the shadows.

I suddenly had déjà vu. That voice had spoken to me from the darkness before.

I'd been six years old, wet and shaking in the grip of Dr. Mordoch. *"You should've let her go,"* the voice had said.

Then, and now, the speaker stepped out of the darkness and the face was the same.

Rita. I remembered now. She was dressed in the same white dress. Her braid hanging down her back. Looking exactly the same.

"How?" It was the only question I could force out of my dry mouth.

"Once upon a time . . ." Rita's soft voice drifted eerily through the room. In the dim light, shadows settled on her face, making it look caved-in and old. "That's how it starts, right? Because we really should start at the beginning. My mother used to read me stories . . . I'd almost forgotten. That's how it starts, right?"

She tilted her head toward me, like a kid waiting for encouragement. I gave her the tiniest of nods, barely daring to move.

Rita smiled. "Okay. Once upon a time, there was a girl who lived by the sea. Life was dull, but most of the time, it was good. Then one day she found a small metal doll. A talisman.

"But you already know all this, don't you?" Confusion clouded her face and she stared around the room, as if trying to remember how she'd gotten there. She seemed to be struggling to keep her mind clear. "You read the diary?"

"Yes."

"Yes," Rita repeated, her voice more forceful now, and she moved closer. "After she touched the talisman, everything changed for the girl. She saw things that weren't there, heard music where there was only silence, remembered things that'd never happened. And her parents, who already thought she was strong-headed and stubborn, now thought she was insane."

As Rita spoke, the change was shocking. Her eyes became brighter, like her words were scraping away the grime that had muddied them. She stood taller and her vagueness was replaced by a sharp-edged bitterness.

Scared, I stepped away from her, but Rita followed. Getting between me and the rolltop desk. The lights from the photograph on the wall backlit her with an eerie glow.

"And maybe she was insane. Once she found the talisman, it was like she had another person in her mind. Because she did. She had another set of memories and desires from long, long ago. And power. She had power too."

With her head skewed to the side, staring with wide-awake eyes, Rita echoed the sepia-toned photograph behind her. The grainy print showed a tall girl, about my age, posed in front of the Compass Rose, the building still under construction. The turrets were only skeletons of wood, and the front porch hadn't been built yet.

"They wanted to lock her away as the new memories, the new life, overtook the old one. But the girl realized she couldn't let them. She was here for a purpose."

The girl in the photograph gripped the trunk of a sapling at the side of the house, as if sharing its strength. The old-fashioned dress made her look different, but the face was the same. Same haunted look. Same long braid. Same disdainful tilt to her head. It was Rita.

"The girl was waiting for the Harbinger. Faye, she was waiting for you."

29

NO. I AM NOT THE HARBINGER.

My head was dizzy with what Rita was saying. But this was not the whispering, vague-eyed girl I'd met that first morning by the Screamers. I compared the photograph with Rita again and saw the undercurrent of power that now ran through the lines of both faces. *Rita is M. H.*

"Margaret Holbrook. My dad gave me the nickname Rita. The only decent thing he ever gave me. Nice to make your acquaintance." Rita curtsied, and I noticed the puddle near her feet. Blue-gray water seeped under the door from the secret passageway.

"How?" I was starting to sound like a broken record. *How are you here? How is this happening? How can I get away?*

"You haven't let me get to the Happily Ever After. That photograph was taken a year after my parents died. When I was seventeen."

Water inched up the soles of my boots, soaking into the leather. I ignored it and tried to focus on what Rita was saying. I made my face into a sympathetic frown. But that was the wrong thing to do.

Rita's eyes glinted with anger. "Save your pity. They were nothing but an obstacle. My real Family was already long dead."

Yes. My Family. Her words triggered a memory, and I thought

of my double vision down on the beach this morning. Seven of us standing on a mountain. Connected to all things. Like the tarot card showed. Keeping true to The Circle.

Round and round. Round and round. Round and round.

Water trickled down the walls, leaving little glittering tracks in its wake.

Rita paced around the room as she went on. "But after my parents were gone, I was truly alone. I didn't belong in this world, and there was nothing I could do to change that. I wasn't strong enough. No. I still needed the Harbinger." She spit the word at me. "You."

No. I am Faye.

It was Kel who'd made us dig up the talismans. It was Kel in the prophecy. Kel was the Harbinger, not me.

Fear is an illusion.

The waves were biting at my ankles now. The sharp chill making them ache.

Not me.

"Yes, Faye. You were the one with the vision. You were the strongest of the Family. The one who felt most constrained by The Circle."

I thought of the prophecy on Rita's tarot cards. *Stronger than the others, the Harbinger peers far into the Future. There men will feast off of the Earth like maggots. There The Circle will fail the Family.*

A door downstairs opened and closed, sending a shudder through the house. Making the rising water quiver. *Is it Kel? A Taker?* Anyone would be better than being alone with Rita. Watching her eyes growing wild.

Through the ripples, I saw the talisman lying on the floor. Rita's talisman. It reminded me that this was all real, even if it seemed crazy. And impossible. The cold waves had made my muscles freeze up, but I forced myself to slosh over to the metal figurine. I reached down into the pooling water and grabbed it. I needed to wrap my hand around something solid.

"Oh yes. Now you've come to the crux of the problem. My talisman was found too early, more than a hundred years before your little group uncovered theirs. You didn't see that in your vision, did you?" Her voice bubbled up in a high-pitched shriek that might have been a laugh. "I became the enchanting Rita Holbrook. Sharing her mind, we were bound together. To her decaying world. Stuck here waiting while your apocalyptic vision revealed itself. Factories spewing smoke. Airplanes and cars and submarines infesting every crevice of the Earth. Armies, outfitted with bombs and chlorine gas, marching across its face. The great triumphs of the modern age."

More noises came from downstairs, and I begged whoever it was to hurry. I wanted someone between me and Rita. Rain drizzled from the ceiling, splashing onto the yellowed pages of the open books. Making the notes on my psychiatric evaluation run into blurry purple lines. Plastering my hair to my face.

"And even though the talisman gave me power, I wasn't strong enough to rid the world of the maggots that feasted on its flesh. Not to mention, I was in the wrong time. Separated from my Family. From the Harbinger. But even in this body, I knew I still had *some* power. So I cleared the obstacles from my path." Rita's voice softened, her face almost looking tender. "Then I built this house. I commissioned the statues. I locked away the diary and the tarot cards and my talisman. All of it safely hidden so that only you would find it.

"So that when you finally came back, you would know that things had gone wrong and I'd already been here and gone." Rita's voice cracked. "Then one night, I turned my back on this crumbling world and walked into the sea."

The room fell silent, except for the frothing waves. I imagined confused, insane Rita, dressed in only her white nightgown, taking one final desperate action. The image chilled me deeper than the icy flood.

Her bitter laugh cut through my thoughts. "That was the final insult. I should've known that one of the Family wouldn't die so easily. The ocean claimed my living body and sent back this frail facsimile. I was doomed to stay here, watching the world rot. Until the time of the vision was near and the Harbinger chose a new body."

The door flew open then, letting in a fresh gush of dark water. I'd never been so relieved to see another person.

"What are you doing here?" Dr. Mordoch stood in the doorway, wrapped in a robe. In the light from her flashlight, Dr. Mordoch's pale hair looked more gray than blond and hung in thin wisps around her lined face.

I tried to think of an answer that would make sense. Then I realized she was looking at Rita.

Dr. Mordoch stumbled toward us, staring at Rita, the whites of her eyes showing. "You're not even real. You're a manifestation of my guilt. You were supposed to disappear when I brought Faye back."

Rita looked from Dr. Mordoch to me, grinning maliciously. "I may have found a way to keep busy over the years . . ."

Dr. Mordoch cringed as she moved past Rita, wobbling a little as she made her way over to the rolltop desk. Hands shaking, she fumbled around behind the stack of books. She traded her flashlight for the bottle of whiskey, draining the dregs.

She pressed her hand to her forehead and then, her face composed, Dr. Mordoch turned back to me. "Faye, I'm sorry I didn't watch you more closely. I'm sorry you were out on the beach that night. I'm sorry I ever brought you back here. But I couldn't get rid of her any other way. All these years . . . she murmured in my ear . . .

insisting . . . swearing that by rescuing you that night, I'd damned you. That we still had work to do. That I'd driven you away."

Rita walked around Dr. Mordoch, circling her. "A hundred years I waited for you, Faye. Impotent. Powerless to leave. And when you finally arrive to enact the ritual, she ruins it."

"No!" Dr. Mordoch covered her ears and I could see the terror Rita instilled in her. Dr. Mordoch reached out to me. "I tried to help you. I kept you from drowning!"

I didn't know what to believe. Who to listen to. High silvery waves rushed in through the open door now. Tugging at my legs. It poured down the walls in great savage waterfalls.

Dr. Mordoch reached for the whiskey bottle again, forgetting it was empty. "I thought she was some kind of angel, showing me how to help you. If I could get you back, I could cure you of your hallucinations. Socialize you. Show you your place in the world. Later, I thought she was the devil. Now I don't care. I just want her to leave me alone."

The water crept up my chest. Its cold hands pressing in on my body. Cinching tight around my lungs.

Rita stepped in front of Dr. Mordoch, blocking her from my view. "You know I was right to make her bring you back here. You've felt the power of this place from the moment you arrived. Felt the dead places inside you stirring with life. The sea calling to you."

"Yes." It called to me now. Down the stairs, through the hallway full of arrows, I could hear the wave coming for me. It'd been building for almost ten years, since that night on the beach with Dr. Mordoch. I couldn't hold it back any longer. "But I'm supposed to be the one who saves the world."

"That's right, Faye." Rita's voice was filled with a terrible certainty.

The roaring wave was getting closer now. The water rose up my neck. Leaving salty kisses on my lips.

Rita smiled as she repeated the words of the tarot cards. "'Only the Harbinger can wash this world clean.'"

I couldn't get enough air. Frigid fingers squeezed my throat. My breath came in little gasps.

The frothing wave surged up the stairs. The roar shaking my bones. I didn't try to run. It was too late. It'd been too late since my dad had abandoned me here. Since I'd almost drowned ten years ago. Since I'd first touched that wave.

The water closed over me. Its icy arms holding me under. Its howl blotting out everything else. Until the whole world went quiet.

And I remembered who I was.

30

I STAND ON THE BEACH, staring out at the slate-colored water. The sky mirrors the stormy color, clouds overwhelming the horizon. It's dry and calm here, but rain slashes the faraway sky, and lightning erupts without any thunder. My feet ache. I've been standing here for an hour, ever since I smelled the rain, watching for their canoe.

"Come eat something, little one." A soft voice calls out behind me, but I ignore it until they go away.

I swear I can hear my parents out there. My father's scream is tangled up with the seagulls'. I taste their fear on my tongue. The only time I take my eyes off the horizon is to look up at the mountain. Dark figures gather around the great boulder on the peak. The Family . . . who promised that the skies would be clear today. That the sea would be calm.

"Come inside. It's almost dark."

No.

"At least eat some soup."

No.

My father told me he would teach me a new song when he came

home. My mother promised that I could have the jaw from the swordfish she speared.

I stand there, waiting. As the storm clears. As night comes. As stars fling themselves across the sky, like debris on the water.

I'm at the top of the tallest pine in the valley. I hug the trunk, my feet braced on the branches, my cheek pressed into the rough bark. A year has passed since I lost my parents, and it's summer again. Everything smells wild and green, and I can feel the sap running through the trunk. Like blood in my veins. From up here the wind murmurs secrets to me as it pushes me back and forth. Back and forth. I close my eyes. I feel like I'm flying.

Down below, my friend is about halfway up the tree. The boy turns his golden face toward me, his black eyes squinting. "I don't want to go any higher."

I shout down at him. "Scared like a field mouse. *Squee, squee, squee.*"

His face screws up in determination and he keeps climbing. I close my eyes again and fly.

It's low tide, and the boy and I are collecting mussels. He's older now. Maybe even a little older than me.

I reach for the basket, but suddenly, the boy takes my hand. His fingers are gritty, but they still feel nice wrapped around mine.

A crease folds his forehead. "They told me that I belong with the Family. That I'm needed to serve The Circle."

"But my connection is stronger than yours! I can see farther." I sound petulant, even to myself.

"Maybe." He'd never actually admit it. "But you're not thirteen yet."

"You'll be bored. Listening to the breeze all day. Endlessly advising strangers. You'll hate it."

But we both know that's not true. The Family is powerful, the gifted ones. They see deeper and farther than everyone else. So we do what they say . . . even when they're wrong.

The silence sits between us like a third person, eavesdropping. Then I say it. "You can't leave me. You're all I have."

He leans close and kisses me. I feel the cool pebbles under his feet. The sun shining on his dark hair. His heart thudding in his chest.

Then he looks at me, and I see myself in his black eyes. Bright and fearless. "And you're all I have."

I stalk away from the village and walk down into the valley. I can't bear to listen to the Family jabber on about the way of The Circle. Don't they see how thin the people are? Don't they hear the babies howling with empty bellies? But all the Family says is that there are times of plenty and times of scarcity. Balance in all things.

I can't stand to watch the boy up there with them. Nodding his head. Looking solemn.

They offer to help track the deer, but it's almost winter, and most of the herds have moved on. They say they can reach into the earth and help find more roots and nuts. Or watch for good weather for fishing. Since they're *so* good at that.

Why don't they *do* something? They can change things! I know they can . . . because I did it. Even if it was just an accident. I pull a handful of dried cranberries out of my bag and see if I can make it happen a second time.

Winter is coming, bringing the hungry cold, but I still feel summer in the cranberries. All those bright hot days glowing just under the wrinkled, maroon skin. I think of warm rains and the sun warming up the bogs. Of children splashing through the muddy water, popping ripe fruit into their mouths. Then I open my hand. The cranberries are plump and red, as if they've just been picked. I bite down on one and let the bittersweet juice burst on my tongue.

All year, since the boy's been gone, I've felt my power growing. Now I understand what the Family can do. Now I'm ready to be one of them.

The boy and I climb up the mountain. I look over at him, walking next to me, and I realize that he's not a boy anymore. Even if I still call him that. He's grown taller than me and his shoulders stretch wide. The shadow of a beard darkens his cheeks and I shiver, thinking of the scratch of it against my skin. It's one of those scarce, perfect days away from the rest of our Family. Just the two of us.

I hum and hold the boy's hand, tight in mine. This makes us slower when we come to logs or rocks in the path. We have to work as a single, awkward creature, each of us with one free hand to steady ourselves as we climb over. But I won't let go.

When we're almost at the top, he gives me one of his rare grins. "Race you!"

And he breaks away, running up the path.

"Cheater!" I take off after him. Even though he has a lead . . . even though I fall and skin my knee, I still win. But just barely.

At the top of the mountain, we cling to each other, trying to breathe through our laughter. Collapsing near the immense, black boulder. Then it's my turn to smile.

"Race you?" I say, putting my hand against the pockmarked boulder, speckled with rust. Inviting him into our own private game. Even though I've touched it a hundred times, the shock of its age stuns me. It's so old. Older than The Circle. Older than humans. Older than this world.

Touching the iron rock, I see it falling through space. It shoots past planets and comets and suns, until it finally slams into Earth. In an instant I see mountains crumble. Great sheets of ice bully their way across the land. Seas rise and fall.

When my people found the boulder, it changed everything. They'd already had a connection with the world around them. They could read the first shifts of summer into fall or the signs that showed water was close by. And some could see more than others.

But with the metal stone, the strong seers became stronger. Through it they saw the orbits of the planets. Understood the pull of the moon against the ocean. Learned to track the cycles of days and years. And they grew to worship the perpetual ebb and flow they saw there and called it The Circle.

Then some of my people found they didn't need the boulder. Even without the stone, some of us could look inside a person and see their secrets. Some of us could touch a drop of water and feel the cold grip of the ocean. Some of us were born listening to the stars.

We became the Family.

This rock came from the beginning of time, and my people used it to unlock the mysteries of the universe. But that was an old story. And I want a new one.

A restless energy jitters through my body as I think of what we could see through this stone. Not just what has happened. Or is happening. But all that is to come. The Family is capable of so many things. But the rules of The Circle hold us back. Make us turn away from our people.

"Race you?" I repeat my challenge to him, cringing at the eagerness that betrays how badly I want this.

His forehead creases. It's not the first time we've had this conversation. "You know we can't look into the future. It's forbidden."

I fold my arms across my chest. "Why? Why is it forbidden? We hold so much power. But still, we're shackled by the narrow ways of The Circle. What good is seeing the pattern beneath the universe if we can only use it to point the way? Why can't we change it? Why can't we look ahead and see what shape the future will take? Think about all the good we could do. Think about the tragedies we could prevent. Think about my parents!" I'm yelling now, and the wind rips the words out of my mouth, carrying them out across the water.

He puts his hand to my cheek, sharing my pain. He looks down at the beach glittering wet below us. Finally he nods. "You go first."

And I do. I put both hands on the boulder, on the iron stone forged when time began, and make the tiniest push into the future. An ant zooms across the rock. It's almost funny. Then the boy goes, pushing deeper. He watches the moss grow as the sun and moon chase each other through the sky. Then me. Frost shimmers on the boulder and ice rims the bay. Then him. Back and forth. Back and forth.

It's a rush, seeing what no one else has ever seen. And we get caught up in the game. Pushing deeper through the years. Huge boats ride the waves. Strange people and creatures rush across the land. We shove forward in time. Testing our limits.

Then comes the vision. Black-slicked oceans. Rotting carcasses. The obliteration of everything.

I pull my hand away and grab the boy's. I can't describe it to him, but he sees the image burned into my mind. Looking out over the water, all I can see is destruction.

"I have to stop it." And with those words, I become the Harbinger.

31

SCREAMS REVERBERATED in my mind, ripping me from the memories. There was something more. Something that I couldn't—that I didn't want to—remember.

I opened my eyes, and I was no longer on the mountaintop. Or in that ancient valley. I was back in the dimly lit library. Rita still looked at me expectantly, waiting for me to say something. Dr. Mordoch still clutched the empty whiskey bottle in her hand. But the water was gone, leaving flotsam from a different time in its wake.

It'd only taken seconds. All those memories exploding in my brain. Another lifetime of experiences that'd been buried for ten years, ever since my parents had taken me to see the lunar eclipse. Ever since I'd touched that first wave. Dead parents. The boy whose talisman I'd given to Kel. A vision of the future that was now the present. And the screaming . . .

"You've seen it, haven't you? You remember being the Harbinger." Rita's voice was triumphant. "After your vision on the mountain, you said that The Circle was failing us. You told us that we couldn't leave the future in the hands of the mindless masses. Your vision of a dying Earth proved that, right?"

It was like looking at old photos of myself when I was a kid. I didn't always remember the moment the flash went off, but I knew I'd been there. Once Rita described the scene, I knew I had said all those things. When the others in the Family heard of my vision, they were devastated. They'd trusted in the ways of The Circle for so long, but now they agreed that we needed to do something. Well, all of them but the boy. As usual he was full of caution and warning.

In truth, I think the rest of them liked the idea of a more powerful Family. One that would change the course of the world. So I forged the talismans from the great boulder on the mountain, marking them not with The Circle, but with the new symbol of The Path. We agreed that as a Family we would be stronger. It might take all of us to prevent the vision from becoming reality. We would use our power and the power of our people to fix this world. And I would lead the way.

"You told us it would work. We sacrificed everything. Our power. Our lives. The Circle. All because of your vision. Your Path." Rita's voice was hard, her face twisted with her torment. "And he tried to stop you then, like he'll try to stop you now. He fought against you all those years ago, and now you've given him the power to do it again."

Yes. The boy had taken some persuading. I tried not to think about what I'd done to him. Or what he, as Kel, might do to me. But I'd done what I had to do. And we'd begun the ritual, a phenomenon that would take thousands of years to complete. First, the Family had locked their power deep within the iron. Then, I'd cut their throats, so each of them would stay safe inside the talismans. We couldn't go forward in time, but we could wait it out.

But someone needed to be able to know when the time of the vision was drawing near. Someone needed to be first, to dig up the talismans and choose new bodies for the Family to inhabit. So I became part of the ocean. Passing the millennia on the rise and fall of the tide.

"The night we started this, when our people gathered to sing about our bravery and sacrifice, I thought I'd be an avenging angel and right the world. But, it wasn't like that . . ." Rita's face was possessed, and I saw what all those years out of time had done to her. "Now you must finish this so I can be free. So we all can."

What went wrong? How did Rita's talisman get separated from the others? The screaming of that still-forgotten memory tore at my mind again, and I put my hands on my head, trying to make it stop.

"You're the only one who can end this, Faye. After all those years as part of the sea, the Harbinger chose *you* to finish the ritual. Even as a little girl you had an uncanny sense of the world around you. But you were so young . . . just a child. All those new memories, all that power. You didn't even know what to do with it. So I showed you The Path, told you where the talismans were buried, how to rid the world of this blight. Then I brought you to the ocean on the night of power. It should've worked. I should've been freed from this decaying world. But she interfered." Rita spun on Dr. Mordoch, who still cowered near the desk.

"I'm sorry." Dr. Mordoch hugged the whiskey bottle to her chest as she sank to the floor. Her eyes pleaded with me. "I just wanted to help you."

I still didn't like her, but I knew what it was like to be trapped in your own private hell. Sidestepping Rita, I reached down to help Dr. Mordoch.

"Faye, your hands—" Dr. Mordoch's strangled voice rang out in alarm.

A faint silver glow radiated from them as we touched. An ugly blur of malice and arrogance and fear poured through Dr. Mordoch's fingers into my thoughts. Seeing how the years of obsession had warped her, I pulled my hand away as soon as Dr. Mordoch was standing. Trying to hide my repulsion.

Rita's face twisted with disgust. "She's served her purpose, Faye. She got you back here. You might as well get rid of her."

I looked at Dr. Mordoch again—her frayed robe, her crumpled face framed by limp scraps of hair. The efficient headmistress had been stripped away, leaving nothing but weakness. The contempt must've shown on my face, because her hand struck out, slapping me. Hard across the jaw.

"You ungrateful bitch." Dr. Mordoch swayed uneasily, backing away toward the far wall. Then she lost all composure. "I sacrificed my entire life for you. I saved you. Don't you remember? I saved you from the ocean."

"That's what happens when you show them pity." Rita's words were warm in my ear. "It was the same way with my parents. They turn on you. Now that you understand what you are, Faye, you have a choice to make. This world is teetering on the brink. You can join the maggots and allow Dr. M. to numb you into one of them. They'll consume the Earth, but at least then you won't have any more pesky visions. Or—"

She stepped between me and Dr. Mordoch again, her eyes burning. "Or you can do exactly what you dreamed of doing. You can save the world. You can wash it clean. This is *your* Path, Faye. Take it."

A warm pulse of power fed off Rita's words. I thought about the heady intimacy of being inside Kel's memories. The strength I'd felt as I'd merged with the wooden door in Solitary. Even now, I could feel the forest surrounding Holbrook, the wooden beams holding up the Compass Rose. I trembled with their energy. Finally part of something bigger than myself.

"Faye, you're not stable. I *know* you, maybe even better than your parents. Maybe even better than yourself." Dr. Mordoch's voice cracked as she tried to regain control of the situation. "You've never been well. Why don't you go back to your room and get some sleep. We'll pretend this never happened."

Dr. Mordoch, my parents, the Cooperative, they all wanted me to be normal. Wanted me to hide my strangeness, to keep quiet and make nice. But I was so much better than that.

Rage flowed through me, and the wind rose, buffeting the trees outside. The silver glow around my hands grew into a bright flare, and power coursed just beneath my skin.

"Know me? You think you know me?" I yelled at the woman who had taken me away from my purpose. "You don't know me. I am the Harbinger."

When I said the words out loud, I knew how right they were. Maybe I'd always known. *I am the Harbinger.* I grabbed the lamp from the desk. Electricity snaked through it, hissing like a wild animal. I coaxed the power out of the socket, letting it build up around me like a storm cloud. It was delicious, and I wondered how I'd ever survived without this charged euphoria.

Reaching out into the air, I wrenched aside electrons and ions, forcing a path between me and Dr. Mordoch. A silvery bolt shot across the room, slamming into her chest.

Dr. Mordoch screamed as she was blasted against the wall, smashing into the shelves in a hailstorm of books. The smell of burnt hair filled the room. The shock jolted through me as well, and Dr. Mordoch's cries joined the screaming in my head. That one last, terrible memory fighting to surface.

Dr. Mordoch tried to sit up. I could smell her from here, the sour stink of alcohol and panic. Looking at her slumped against the bookshelf, I felt sorry for her. The screaming memory receded and, with it, the heady sense of power. The glow around my hands dimmed and I was just Faye again. Weak and insignificant. A freak.

But I'm supposed to be the hero.

Then I understood. I'd thought the Harbinger needed to be stopped. But I'd been looking at it all wrong. I was *still* the hero, but when I was finished, there wouldn't be a ticker-tape parade. There wouldn't even be anyone left to cheer.

Not Dr. Mordoch. Not Kel. Not even me.

But at least there would be *something* left.

Power surfaced inside of me, like a shipwreck hidden for years under the waves. And now I could feel the sickness too, strangling the Earth.

"Show her who you are." Rita was excited. "She hurt you. Locked you in the dark. Even now, she wants to take you away from your Path."

I growled, still feeling the sting of Dr. Mordoch's hand on my cheek. *How dare Dr. Mordoch touch me. Me, the strongest of the Family.*

I would show Dr. Mordoch what real authority was. This was what I was meant for. I was here to wash the world clean.

"You are nothing." I thought about being chained up in Solitary. I could almost feel the cuffs still cutting into my wrists and ankles.

The marble floor under my feet started to vibrate, and I braced myself in the doorway.

Dr. Mordoch huddled on the shaking floor. "Listen to me, Faye . . . Buddha says—"

"You're just a bug, trying to find smaller bugs to eat." The taunts from the cafeteria rang in my ears. *Whoosh. Whoosh. Whoosh.* Deep in the stone, I felt all those years of pressure beneath the ground. Limestone bullied into becoming marble.

"Please, Faye. I never wanted to hurt you," Dr. Mordoch whispered.

Distant drums pounded in my ears and the fire of transformation rushed into me.

"Do it!" Rita's cry sounded like the baying of wolves.

A thick crack shot across the floor between me and Dr. Mordoch, shattering and scorching the stone under her. I screamed as the heat burned through me. The wooden joists warped and the floor buckled.

Nails melted. Long millennia seeped from the marble into the wood, and it disintegrated into sawdust. With an earsplitting crash, the floor caved in under Dr. Mordoch. She grabbed at the empty air, her eyes pleading with me before she plummeted through the gaping hole.

"Yes!" Rita grinned. "This is how we shall answer their arrogance."

I stared at Rita, standing on the other side of the rift. After a hundred years, she was weak, used up. No more substantial than a shadow. "There is no we. You may be one of the Family. But *I* am the Harbinger. I say what will be done."

Rage crossed Rita's face and her mouth opened. Without a word, I struck her with the full strength of my newfound power. Rita blinked at me in disbelief, our eyes locking. Then in a blaze of light, she flew apart, vanishing in a million little pieces. Dots on a canvas.

The house let out a fatal groan, sending the library ceiling crashing down. Rita's legacy swallowed up in an explosion of shingles and splinters.

I buckled to the floor. Tremors of pain ran through me as the room collapsed in on itself. I threw myself into the hallway and ran down the spiral steps.

The stairs moaned, boards smashing as my feet pounded out the beat. *Hurry, Hurry. It's time.*

The arrows carved into the dark passageway sang a song of

power. Cracks split across my skin, mirroring the ones spiderwebbing across the black stone walls. I cried out as the passage caved in behind me.

The secret doorway fell away in a shower of sawdust and plaster. And there in front of me, tiled into the floor, was the compass. Still pristine.

Rita had been clever. Leaving this house for me to find, the trail of arrows, the diary, the tarot cards. But I was glad she was gone. She was a reminder that something in my plan had gone very wrong. Her and this off-center house. Even now, the corner of the back porch stuck irritatingly over the cliff.

The Compass Rose. As the walls crumbled into dust and gypsum around me, I suddenly understood how truly genius Rita had been. The name didn't just refer to the design in the floor. Or the arrows carved into the walls. This whole house was a compass.

Shouts were coming from outside now, barely audible over the destruction. Running to the back door, I twisted the knob, forgetting the door was nailed shut. I reached out to the trees all around me, felled and butchered. To the roots creeping beneath the house. With the lightest touch, the door splintered away.

The same splintering pain shot through my bones. But it was lost in the aching chaos.

Stepping out onto the porch, I blocked out the yelling and running footsteps. Wind blew off the sea, carrying its stench with it. I clutched the railing and peered straight down into a transformed ocean. In the dark, the toxic tide shimmered blue, lighting up as the waves crashed against the night beach.

I remembered Aunt saying that the algae glowed in the dark, but I hadn't imagined it would be so beautiful. The phosphorescent water swirled and spun with turquoise light. As if dancing to the same terrible power that was inside me. I focused on it, trying to find the final clue Rita had left.

Behind me, windows exploded and the back wall of the Compass Rose crumpled, glass shards and slate shingles raining past me. I was untouched, the cliffs beneath the porch holding it steady. Then the house roared, the entire back half sliding past me and plunging into the sea.

I looked back. Flashlight beams raked across the rubble. It felt right that the house was gone. Like Dr. Mordoch, like Rita, it'd served its purpose.

A dull pain still throbbed through me, and that felt right too. The ache of metamorphosis.

Standing on the porch, I heard the boulder and the mountain calling to me from across the years. Waiting for me to take vengeance for the Earth. This rectangular frame was the only piece left of Rita's compass. It angled out over the edge of a cliff, pointing out across the dazzling, putrid sea. Pointing the way.

I walked to the very corner of the porch and there it was. The criss-crossed iron railings made a perfect window. Framed in the middle of barren islands and bright oil rigs was my destination. The biggest island. And I finally understood what I was looking at.

Slinging my legs over the railing, I set my feet on the edge of the cliff. Behind me, Takers clambered through the wreckage of the Compass Rose. I didn't have time to deal with them. I needed to gather my Family. One last time.

Running through the forest, following the path, my heart pounded out a drumbeat as I climbed the hill. *Hurry, Hurry.* Wind howled through the trees. They knew the Harbinger had come.

As the woods opened up, I looked out across the water. The night flickered like an old filmstrip playing across the dark sea. I could see an ancient mountain, superimposed across the island. A green valley dipping down where the ocean was now, connecting Holbrook's cliffs with the mountainside.

I remembered climbing that mountain hundreds of times. To collect visions from storms out at sea. To listen to the rocks rumbling beneath the earth. To create the talismans.

Professor Warren had written that the coast had been slowly sinking into the ocean, destroying all traces of the mysterious people. Years of shifting land, of melting ice caps and storms swamping the coast, had flooded the valley that'd once connected the mountain to Holbrook. Where there was once a tall peak, now there was only an island.

I'd seen the end of the world from that mountain. The sea had been thick with blood and oil. There had been nothing but bloated bodies and thick smoke billowing across the horizon. In the vision, I'd reached down and thrust my hand into the waves. There'd been no fish. No seaweed. Even the rocks hundreds of feet below the icy water had been silenced.

Nothing, nothing, nothing. My world had become a graveyard. I'd wept then, understanding what I would have to do.

Now, I banished the same tears from my eyes. There was no time for mourning. No time for hesitation. The full moon was already making its way across the sky.

Tonight, I had this one chance to keep my vision from coming true. If I failed, nothing would survive. Humans would annihilate everything. Billions of hands stripping the bones bare until there was nothing left. They'd already started.

"Murderers!"

With the luminous, deadly sea as my witness, I renewed my vow to safeguard this world.

And to save what I loved, I had to destroy them all.

32

LEGS PUMPING, pulse hammering, I ran along the cliff toward the Screamers. *Hurry, Hurry.* Adrenaline streamed through my veins as I played chicken with the drop-off. For years I'd been afraid of the strangeness inside me, but not anymore.

It was like a new part of my brain was awake, and now the ground was familiar under my feet. Night after night, I'd been following this path. Singing, calling to the rest of the Holbrook Family as I climbed the hill. And night after night, they had followed me as the song awakened the power in the buried talismans. Pulling in Maya, Nami, Damion, Zach, and even Kel. Gradually transforming them into the Family that I needed.

I'd begun this ritual four thousand years ago, but I didn't do it alone. The Harbinger could crush stone and see visions, but the Family could reach beyond the impossible. Tonight we would walk The Path together and change the future.

I came over the rise of the hill, and it was as if I could see across the millennia. Back to the night when this had begun. A vast bonfire leapt at the star-studded sky. People crowded onto the bluff, flocking to the fire. Chanting and singing. My people.

All those years ago, thousands of my people had converged here.

Their rich voices had throbbed with power, lending it to me, to The Path, as they'd danced around six fresh graves carved out of the earth.

I will save you, I promised them. *I will save this world for you.*

I sprinted toward them, the rhythm of their chant urging me on. They looked so solid. So real. I would be with them again. I would be home.

It wasn't until I reached them that I noticed the blur of orange and green jumpsuits, bright in the firelight. These were not my people. Everywhere around me were the faces of students who had ridiculed and rejected me.

The Holbrook students swarmed around the Screamers, pulled into the spell of this night. Stand-ins for those who had helped me during the first half of this ritual. Their possessed faces turned up to the stars. Their feet stomped in rhythm to the Song of Balance. A parody of power.

The throng of students parted as I walked through them. I knew some of them from the cafeteria incident—a girl with a long nose, a geeky-looking guy—but there was no spark of the people they'd been. They didn't even look at me as they shuffled backward to form a great ring around the Screamers, their unfocused eyes in some sort of trance.

Then I stood alone in the circle of statues. A bonfire blazed in the center of the deep pit, casting its flickering light into the night. And for the first time, I recognized each one of the terrified metal faces. They were the people I'd buried last night in my vision. My Family from the past. I lifted my face to the sky. Letting my voice soar up into the night. Calling the others to me one more time.

"Faye." Kel's voice cut through my song and he stepped into the circle of light. He stood straighter, no longer stiff with lupus. The rusted talisman gripped in his hand. One of the Family.

I ran to him, my heart thudding. Of course he was already here. Now that he actually saw this damaged world, he'd come to help. A fierce joy leapt inside me, knowing he'd be with me tonight.

Kel's eyes were not the cold black of last night, or the hazel green of before. Instead it was like being underwater, hints of deepest emerald lingering in the fathomless dark. I let myself get lost in them. Our fingers weaving together. His lips pressing against mine.

I was enveloped by waves of heat, like stepping into a fire. Kel's new power surged through me, calling out my own. Tongues of flame shivered over me, and I wanted to stay there forever in this delicious agony. But Kel's mind shifted, showing me something else. Hesitation. Fear. Anger.

I pulled away. "What is it?"

"I can't be a part of this." He laid his talisman in my palm and gently folded my fingers over it. His hand covering mine. "You have to stop."

I'd thought the heart of the Harbinger was hard. Hard enough to purge the Earth. But now it shuddered and cracked. *How did I forget about the tarot cards?*

The upside-down Lovers. *Two quarrel.* Kel was still my enemy.

"Or what? You'll stop me?" Sparks spit from the tips of my fingers and sizzled across my skin. The wind pulled its fingers through my hair, egging me on. "I'm the Harbinger."

"I have to try." Kel's words were tinged with regret, longing filling his eyes. Then I saw the stone dagger gripped in his other hand. "We have to find another way."

"No!" The wind blasted my angry words at him, throwing him up into the air and slamming him down into the pit below me. Knocking the dagger out of his hand. "You don't get it. Either *I* flood the world, save the Earth, and everybody dies. Or"—I laughed, my voice sounding crazy, even to myself—"we stand around doing nothing, people destroy the world for us, and everybody *and every-thing* dies. Which would you choose?"

I leapt down after him, landing inches from where Kel lay, sprawled in the mud. "Never mind. It doesn't matter. You don't get to choose."

I kicked the stone dagger into the fire. "You remember that night, don't you, Kel? It was exactly like tonight. It was the equinox. The moon full and as close to the Earth as it would ever get. The sun was in perfect symmetry. Everything was the same. Except last time *I* had the dagger."

Kel pulled himself to his hands and knees. Firelight flickered across his face and he held my eyes, not flinching. The air between us crackled, and memories from a lifetime ago poured into my mind. That first consuming kiss. Racing him up the mountain. The power that joined us both. I gasped, struggling for breath, as four thousand years of yearning tore into me.

And tangled up in the storm of memories was Kel. The spicy scent of him intoxicating me. The burn of his lips against mine. Everything that'd happened between us at Holbrook was still sharp and strong in his thoughts.

Fighting not to be overwhelmed by his memories, I cleared my mind with words. "You certainly had me fooled. 'The Harbinger is shielded from the glare of day.' And you with your hoodie and gloves and sunglasses. You were the one with lupus."

"'But the moon will know them.'" Kel stood up, his voice a low growl as he finished the prophecy. "You were fooling yourself, Faye. You spent your days hiding who you were, but you can't do that anymore. Look at yourself."

He grabbed my hand and held it up against the sky. My fingers glowed with the same silver shimmer as the moon.

I ripped my hand out of his grip. "What about the last part? The tarot cards said that the Harbinger would 'carry pain with them through the lonely places of the Earth.'"

"There's more than one kind of pain." His eyes paralyzed me, his face inches from mine. "You didn't know it, but you radiated power. Even before. Didn't you see the way people looked at you? They couldn't even meet your eyes."

"But I thought—"

"No, Faye." His voice was sharp, commanding me to listen to what he was saying. And I gravitated toward his words. "I know what you thought . . . but there was never anything wrong with you. Nothing missing. You are the Harbinger, and I'm the one who is supposed to stop you. But it doesn't have to be this way."

"Oh, it doesn't? Then why did you have the dagger?" I backed away from him, adrenaline surging through me. *How did I let him draw me in?* "You are nothing next to me."

"You're right, Faye. You are stronger than me. That's why I couldn't keep you from burying the talismans or starting down this Path. But are you stronger than all of us?"

The statues ringing the hole seem to come alive as Zach, Maya, Damion, and Nami stepped out from behind them. Each of them gripped their talisman. They jumped down into the wide pit, forming a circle around me and Kel and the fire.

Fear stabbed my belly as they closed in on me. *Am I stronger than all of them together?* I didn't know. My mind spun out into my surroundings, searching for a new advantage. In the distance, I heard a shift in the ocean roar. The tide was changing. Rising. *Hurry. Hurry.*

Knowing what I had to do, I yanked a burning branch out of the flames. The end I held was hot, but unburnt. I focused my mind, picturing mossy, damp logs and green wood. I shivered and the bonfire guttered and went out, plunging us all into the dark. In the sudden blackness, I crouched down and grabbed the dagger out of the ashes. Hiding it in my sleeve.

"We're not your puppets, Faye." Nami's voice rang out in the darkness, and as my eyes adjusted to the paler light of the full moon, I saw that the Family had used the moment to close in on me and Kel.

Nami's face was fearless. Her cockiness had metamorphosed into true power. "We're not about to let you play Noah-without-the-ark."

"We made this plan together." The sharp stone of the dagger pressed into my palm, and I saw how badly things had gone. Yes, my Family had survived the long years inside the talismans. But, when the time had come, when I'd chosen new bodies for them to inhabit, the Family was supposed to have reemerged unchanged. *Ready to rid the world of humanity.*

"That was a different time," Damion said, and they all stepped closer. Tightening their circle. Damion radiated the same strength he always had, only more so. But his face was alive with emotion now as he took Nami's hand. "And a different us."

Like Kel, touching the talismans had changed the rest of the Family. Made them stronger. Given them new memories. But they were still the same people who'd arrived at Holbrook a week ago. They were still rooted in this modern world. By giving them the talismans, I'd created my own enemy. Now I would have to get rid of them.

I gripped the dagger hidden in my sleeve, covering my intentions with words. "Can't you smell death on the water? Can't you see the wrongness of Holbrook? A forest wrapped in razor wire trying to pretend like nothing is wrong. Maya was right from the beginning: people just close their eyes and keep gobbling."

"No. I wasn't." An aggressive tension still ran the length of Maya's narrow body, but there was no bitterness in her words now. "We have friends here. Some of us have family. And, Faye, so many are still voiceless."

"Someone has to care, right?" I threw Maya's words back at her. "You think, like I did, that the Harbinger wants to destroy the world. But I don't. I care more than you could ever know. Enough to do what must be done."

"We can't just slaughter them like lambs," Zach said as they took another step closer. The change in Zach was shocking. His shoulders were thrust back and compassion tinted his voice instead of doubt.

I steeled myself for what was coming, hiding my thoughts from them. "You have to believe me, there is no other choice."

"Faye, you *chose* to give me that talisman. You wanted someone to stop you." Kel touched my cheek again, sending a shiver through me. I rested my head against his hand, shifting my balance. Then, with a swift sweep of my arm, I brought the dagger up to his throat.

Kel froze, his body rigid as the sharp stone blade touched his bare skin. *This was how it happened the first time.* This is how I killed him. All of them.

"Now, get out of my way." I held Kel in front of me, edging backward, toward the wall of the pit.

But the Family stood rooted where they were. Their circle trapping Kel and me.

"Can't you see?" I tightened my hold on Kel, the dagger poised at his throat. "This is where The Circle has brought us."

"No," Kel whispered. "No, this is where *you* brought us."

So be it. I didn't know if I was powerful enough to finish the ritual alone. But I had to try. I would walk The Path. Even if it meant going against them all.

Even if it means losing Kel.

I readied the dagger, and images flooded into my mind. Slashing the blade across their necks. Warm blood spilling over my hands and soaking into the ground. The rest of them had gone willingly, but the boy who was now Kel . . . who I'd loved more than life, but not more than the world . . . he hadn't agreed with The Path. He'd fought me, professing that I wasn't a killer. But I'd proved him wrong.

And now I had to do it again. But I couldn't bear to have more of his blood on my hands. So my thoughts stretched out into the air, pulling in the energy and power I needed.

Maya reached out to me. "Don't do this."

A bolt of electricity shot out of my other hand, striking her in the stomach. Maya's eyes went wide with surprise as the current held her.

Then the bolt fanned out on either side of Maya. A lethal thread connecting me to Maya to Damion to Nami to Zach. The eerie silver gleam lit up the night.

"I'm sorry," I said, dropping the dagger from Kel's throat.

Kel and I faced each other from inside the crackling circle. Electricity coursed through me as I held the others suspended in its current. Burning me from the inside out. Tears spilled over, sizzling and steaming as they hit my skin. "I don't want to hurt you."

Kel's eyes softened; I could see myself in his eyes perfectly now. There was nothing missing. No void. No Harbinger. There was just Faye.

"You can't do this, Faye. You don't have it in you."

All I could think of was laying my head against his chest and breathing him in. "You're right. I can't."

But the Harbinger can.

I leaned in as the electricity surged through the others. I tasted

Kel's lips just as the current reached him, completing the circuit. The fire consuming us both.

I clutched him closer, kissing him hard. Grateful for the tears that made it impossible to watch the last bit of green burn out of his eyes.

Then I let go.

33

KEL DROPPED TO THE GROUND. Like puppets with their strings cut, they all collapsed.

This had all happened before. The five bodies lay in a circle. Only Rita was missing.

I swallowed hard, forcing myself to step over his body. To climb out of the hole. To walk away.

From Kel. From my Family. From Faye.

I was only the Harbinger now. I needed to get to the mountain. I'd been waiting four thousand years. There was no more time to mourn.

The mob of students gathered at the edge of the cliff, staring mesmerized across the glowing bay to the island. The tide was coming in fast now, and they shuffled restlessly in the dark. *Hurry, Hurry. It's time.* Hanging low in the sky, over all of it, the moon crept into shadow. The eclipse had begun.

I rushed back down the path, to the beach. The lights from the dormitory gleamed through the trees. But when I reached the shore, it was empty and dark. The gate still locked tight.

I threaded my fingers through the chain-link fence and closed my eyes. I felt the pure metals hidden in there, before they'd been ripped from the ground and diluted. Chunks of iron ore formed in the Earth's core when humans were no more than a glimmer in a microorganism's eye. *If they had eyes.*

Veins of zinc wandered deep underground. The elements separated from each other and my body felt like it was being torn apart. Then a rich metallic flavor resonated in my mouth, and I knew what it was like to be old. So much older than the trees, older than this hillside I was standing on. Ancient and primal. A force unto myself.

My eyes opened. The fence around my hands had melted, leaving a hole big enough to climb through. Drops of molten steel glowed and then solidified into harmless lumps on the ground. I pushed aside what was left of the wire and squeezed through.

I ran across the pebbles, tar sticking to my shoes. Waves glistened blue as they broke on the shore. The island, less than half a mile away, was surrounded by the same dim glow. A shimmering line cut across the black water, connecting the two places.

I squinted at it. Out of all the strange things that had happened tonight, an incandescent, magical path leading to my destiny seemed the least likely of them all. Then I laughed, a short bark jabbing the darkness, as I realized what it was.

Not magic, but toxic algae. It lit up as the waves crashed against a narrow sandbar. A ridge that had once run the length of the valley.

Can I make it across before the tide closes over it? I pulled my shoes off and, one foot in front of the other, I hurried out onto the thin slice of land surrounded by glittering waves. Water sprayed against my legs, and I winced.

Aunt had told us that touching the algae wasn't supposed to hurt you, but I guess there was no "supposed to" anymore. Toxins seeped out of the murky water and into my skin, poisoning me. I could feel the tide's hunger as I ran, wanting to drag me down and suck the life from me.

"I am the Harbinger!" I shouted. But the lethal waves simply crested higher.

The current tore into the sandbar. The path was only a foot wide now, and I was only a third of the way across.

I ran faster and the blood pumped through my skull. *Whoosh. Whoosh. Whoosh.* My feet slammed down, pounding out the rhythm. I had to get there before the land bridge was swept under.

I heard the drums again. Chanting their chorus. *Hurry, Hurry.* Halfway there.

The strip of sand was now hardly big enough for my bare feet side by side. Seagulls shrieked and dove around me, fighting to get the last mussel shells before the tide stole them away.

I burst through the flock. Flashing wings batted against my face. Angry squawks trailed me.

Foam filled my footprints and my feet splashed through the seeping water. It burned like acid against my soles.

The tide is high. The moon is full.

My foot slipped and I fell down hard. My jaw smashed into the wet sand, my face on fire with the stuff. The salt of blood and spiked seawater mixed in my mouth. I felt the poison dragging at me, making my limbs heavy. Waves clawed my hands and I gagged on the stench.

I forced myself back up and raced the glowing waves. I had to do this. Everything depended on me making it to the island. I sucked in great lungfuls of stink. I was closing the distance. Twenty-five feet. Twenty. Ten.

But the tide wouldn't let me go so easily. Its eagerness trembled through my feet as a huge swell began to build. Icy fingers strained forward in the moonlight, ready to rip into me. I wasn't going to make it.

I hummed, calming myself down, like Kel had that first day in Solitary. *I wish I had a river so long.*

I focused on the water flooding agonizingly around my ankles. It rose and curled. *I wish I had a river so long.*

The huge wave crested the sandbar and came at me, threatening to capsize me. Instead, I let its savage energy fill me. Turning my song into a chant of power.

I would teach my feet to fly!

My hands blazed silver as I pictured the seagulls, soaring out of the water. The waves pushing them up into the air. Wings catching the wind.

And I leapt.

The ocean leapt with me, carrying me high into the dark air as it swallowed the last of the sandbar. The wind gathered behind me, thrusting me forward those last few feet, to the safety of the beach.

Shells scoured my body and gravel filled my mouth. But I was across. Even as I lay on the beach, scraped up and spitting sand, the blunt violence of the tide thrilled through me. I shouted wildly up at the sinking, disappearing moon.

"I am the Harbinger!"

But the sea was still rising. I crawled across the beach until my legs were strong enough to hold me. Then I started climbing. Even though it was dark, even though most of the mountain had been swallowed by the sea, I still knew my way to the peak.

The large pockmarked boulder was waiting for me when I reached the top. Stars still dusted the sky, but the iron meteorite was purpley gray in the first hint of morning. And, there, illuminated by the blood-red moon and the emerging dawn, was the mark of The Path.

It was a bird balancing on the wind. It was a mountain rising out of the water. It was a compass arrow pointing the way.

I reached out to touch the symbol I'd engraved here, so long ago. A shock stung me and I snatched my hand away. Blood pounded in my ears. *Whoosh. Whoosh. Whoosh.*

Remember, you are the Harbinger.

I touched the boulder again and my feet reached deep into the bedrock, into the beating heart of the planet. The connection that'd been reawakened over the past few days was nothing compared with this. The vitality of the universe poured through my arteries. *Whoosh. Whoosh. Whoosh.* Uncontrollable tides. Molten lava surging through the Earth's core. Wind that galloped across the land. It lived inside of me.

The Earth spun and, standing on this island, I spun with it. Planets wheeled in cosmic circles around me, and I danced with them, through tawny rings of ice and faithful asteroids. A blaze of stars hit me, and I basked in their heat.

There, seeing into the shadow of space, I watched the sun and Earth and moon spin into alignment. Sitting in the middle of the perfect row, the Earth blotted out the sun's light. Drenching the moon in darkness.

In the dark of the pregnant moon. With the sun as midwife, Autumn will be born in an ocean of blood.

From both sides of this smog-shrouded planet, the sun and moon called to the ocean in unison.

My voice called with them, "Rise!"

The ocean boomed its answer. Rearing up, the tide climbed the island's slope. Coming to me, so I could join with the waves. The wind gusted to spur it on.

As the bay drained, seagulls teemed across the exposed seabed, feasting on fish and scurrying crabs. I summoned the ocean from its chasms and depths. A towering swell rose up before me, and my voice soared above the eager waves. Telling them the next chapter of the story.

"Together we will wash the beaches clean. We will reach into the greedy heart of man and squeeze till it stops beating. We will make a new Path, and all that survives shall follow it and grow strong."

My instructions were drowned out by the harsh screams of gulls. Suddenly, hundreds of birds descended on me. Beaks jabbed at my face. Claws scrabbled at my scalp, tangling in my hair.

This isn't right. The birds shouldn't be fighting me. Straining to hold the waves with my mind, I snatched a seagull. Ripping it from my hair.

Clutching it in my fist, I felt its heart quivering. Its madness driven by panic and fear. And power.

Kel. I felt his feet walking across the earth again.

I tasted him on the air.

34

I TURNED INTO the fury of feathers and wings. Reaching out into the wind, I felt for the spaces between molecules. I gritted my teeth as I dragged the atoms together, compressing the air. The diving birds slowed, their muscles straining against the dense atmosphere. Their lungs struggling to breathe. One by one, they plunged from the sky.

Now I had a clear view of Kel down below. He strode toward me across the empty stretch of sand that used to be the bay. Wind pulled his hair back from his face, and I swore I saw sparks, blazing green, in his eyes.

"Harbinger!" Kel's voice boomed across the dawn. Flanking him on either side were Nami and Damion, Maya, and Zach. Evidently it would take more than a shock to stop them.

Calling to the wind, I pushed the heavy air down on them. The dense cloud dropped, trapping them in a bubble of unbreathable air. Zach fell to his knees in the damp sand, hands clutching at his chest.

Then they were all down. Tears welled up in my eyes, but the wind dried them before they could hit my cheeks. I turned my concentration back to the great waves. Anxious to join them and be done with this.

But my ears popped, the pressure changing. Down on the sand, the air around Zach rippled. Excited molecules hurtled around him, bouncing off each other like bumper cars. The hair on my neck prickled in the charged atmosphere. Standing, Zach raised his arms, warming the air. Allowing the Family to breathe again.

"Faye!" Kel, Maya, and Nami were back on their feet.

Only Damion was still kneeling, stone-faced, his hands flat against the ground. The sand underneath him seethed and roiled. And a noise keened in my ears. A billion grains of sand rasping against each other.

Kel and the others struggled to keep their balance as sand filled in under their feet, lifting them into the air. The ground swelled up beneath the Family as a giant sand dune rose out of the middle of the drained bay. Bringing them to meet me.

Now the five of them faced me from a tall bluff, just two hundred feet away. Kel stretched out his hand, heat shimmering in the air between us. "Stop this before we all get killed."

"Why do you make me hurt you?" My words drifted across the gap to Kel. My legs trembled. I knew how this was going to end.

But they wouldn't stop. Nami grabbed a handful of sand. She swirled it with her finger, whispering to it in her cupped palm.

Sweat dripped down my face. "Don't you get it? Whether I do this or not, we're all dead. Let me salvage what I can."

The gathered waves began frothing like an attack dog as they absorbed my growing anxiety. They crested higher and higher, rising far above my peak. But I kept a grip on them. I hadn't completed the final step of the ritual.

I'd waited four millennia. I could be patient. Pressing my hands deep into the iron meteorite, I braced myself just as Nami opened her fist.

The sand around her took flight, sparkling on the hot air.

Infinitesimal grains of rock, glass, and plastic whirlwinded into a glittering sandstorm. A beauty brutal enough to blind me and shred my skin.

Self-preservation took over and I threw a tiny fistful of waves into the air. I concentrated on the memory of wet, winter mornings. Snow days and icicles. Breath turned brittle in my lungs as frost crystallized around the roaring sandstorm.

As the water condensed on the hot dust, it froze and plummeted from the sky. Huge chunks of hail pelted the Family, but they stood their ground. Cradling their arms over their heads.

Too late, I saw what I'd done. My cold air slammed into their searing dust cloud and churned into a dense fog. Mist poured in around us, hiding Kel and the Family's sand dune from sight.

"Faye, I love you. But I will not let you destroy us all." I heard Kel's voice, but all I could see was five dark shapes in the fog. They'd just been waiting for me to make a mistake like this.

Above me, purple storm clouds materialized out of nowhere. Wind tore at my hair and tried to chop the massive swell into puny whitecaps. I clutched at the water, holding it together.

Thunder snarled. Lightning lit up the sky behind the Family. As one, Kel, Damion, Nami, Maya, and Zach all threw their arms into the air. A white-hot spear of lightning flew out of the clouds toward me. I threw myself out of the way and the bolt smashed into the boulder. The great chunk of iron cracked in two. Molten metal raining down around me.

The force of the blow rumbled through the peak beneath me, opening a jagged rift across the mountaintop. Gravel spewed as part of the steep slope crumbled away. Trying to keep my balance, I lost my grip on the wave. Vast sluices flooded back into the bay. Kel's eyes went wild as an oil tanker careened toward the shore. Then his sand dune folded in on itself, sinking into the water. The Family clawed at the mound as it sucked them under.

I dug my feet into the seesawing ground and reined the sea back in. "Wait for me. We must do this together."

I managed to stop the charging tide before a rock slide sent me tumbling. My fingernails tore at the ground as I slid, and I caught an exposed root. Just before I went over the edge of the peak.

Clinging to the root, I fought to regain control over the world. I froze underground springs. Melted and re-formed the fractured bedrock. But the island was too unstable, and it shattered again.

Then my root snapped and I plummeted through the air. The whole island coming with me.

"No! Faye!" Kel's scream cut across my terror and something grabbed my ankle, yanking me to a painful stop.

I hung, dangling upside down, from what was left of the sheared-off slope. A tree root squeezed tight around my ankle, holding me there. More roots shot through the crumbling island. Weaving the rock back together.

The root cinched around me, hauling me up the cliff face by my ankle. Pulling me back up onto the peak. Then the root released me and I looked around in awe. My island was whole again, a living mass of knobbly roots and branches. And that wasn't all.

Kel and the others still stood on a ridge in the middle of the empty bay. Their mountain of sand was now an enormous knot of roots. In the center of it Maya sat, looking alarmed at what she'd done, at the top of a single, tall tree. Embraced in a throne of branches.

Bruised and exhausted, we all faced one another across the now-clear dawn. Kel, who I loved. The people who were my Family twice over, through two lifetimes.

At that moment, the sun peeked over the far horizon and the moon hung low over the land, glowing the deep red of a total lunar eclipse. This was my moment.

But I ached to stand with them. To call off the sea and begin my life again. To be just Faye this time.

"Thank you," I whispered to my Family. I would love them the only way I knew how.

Kel stepped forward, his eyes full of grief as he stared across the gap still yawning between us. He said my name, just once, in his low, quiet voice.

"Faye."

I turned my back on him and bellowed my command again. "Rise!"

Waves charged back up the side of the island. A wall of water surged up from the sea, blotting out the rising sun. Vaulting into the air. Plucking gulls from the sky.

The water stretched from horizon to horizon. Leaping, rising, creating a force as unstoppable as the orbit of the moon. Roaring with the waves, I stepped into the oncoming flood. Exchanging my fragile body for its silvery armor.

Hurry. Hurry. It's time.

I was part of the sea now. Lunging at my prey. Jaws wide and dripping, I stormed the beach.

35

THE THUNDERING WAVES should have drowned out the Family's screams. But I could still hear the shrieking. The noise reverberated in my skull, overpowering all thought, as the monstrous tidal wave raced toward Kel and the Family and Holbrook.

With the screams, the final, buried memory from so long ago came rushing at me. I tried to stop it, but it came anyway.

I stand at the crest of the mountain. Across the valley, the light of the massive bonfire is almost blotted out by the masses of people crowded onto the cliff. They raise their voices and thunder on drums, and the power of my people trembles in my very core. They believe I can become part of the ocean. That I can ride the waves into the future, and save this world we love. And I believe it too.

Hands pressing into the cool boulder, I wait. Knowing my moment is coming. The sun peers above the horizon, just as the moon is eclipsed. Both calling to the ocean. My voice joins their song.

It is a potent fusion. The moon and sun pulling at once. The eclipse. The voices of my people pulsing in the night. My hands still tinged with my Family's blood. One silvery tendril of water stretches up into the sky. Climbing the mountain.

A cloak of dazzling waves swirls around my shoulders. I let the power of the ancient meteorite flow through me into the sea. And we are fused together by the fire of great suns and long-lost stars.

But even as the first half of the ritual succeeds, I sense my horrible mistake. The sea keeps coming. Rising up the mountain. Drawn to the great boulder. I cannot control it.

I'm dragged along with the sea as it tears across the valley, ripping up trees and salting the earth. But my people stand their ground, chanting as the sea rushes at them, believing I will keep them safe. Believing I can.

As the wave reaches them, it is *my* fist that crushes the village elders. *My* claws that rip apart the children. *My* grip that squeezes the last breath from the very people who sang my name moments before.

When the carnage is over, there aren't even bodies left behind. The Family's graves are flooded, one of the talismans is lost. Nothing is left but gray stones and the empty valley. I've murdered everyone I ever loved.

"No!" I yanked my soul out of the sea and fled back to my body on the island.

But the tsunami rushed on without me, heading for my Family and the throng of students still watching from the Screamers' cliff.

The repercussions of the memory convulsed through my mind. There was no more mystery. My entire culture had disappeared because I had *killed* them. That wave had been small compared with this one, but it had exterminated my people.

They hadn't wounded the Earth. They were innocents. I'd never meant to hurt them.

Thousands of years later, I understood the depth of my mistake. Without them, without anyone to become the new Family, there'd been no one left to be a conduit for the Earth. No one had even known enough to try. That night, so long ago, I had made my own vision come true.

Now the giant wave was only a hundred feet away from Kel and the others. And like my people before them, they stood their ground. Reliving my nightmare, I threw ice at the colossal wave, but nothing happened. I ripped apart hydrogen and oxygen, barely slowing it.

Kel and the others huddled in the shadow of the towering flood. The wave was only forty feet away from them now and closing the distance.

Pleading with the water to listen, I whispered of deserts and droughts. Twenty feet and still cresting.

I commanded the moon to pull against it. The sand to dam it. The wind to drive it back.

Heart pounding, I screamed over the howling sea. "I am the Harbinger!"

Five feet from Kel, his eyes open to greet it, the tsunami stopped. Suspended by my voice.

"You must do it now, or all those deaths will have been for nothing." Rita suddenly appeared next to me on the peak. I'd forgotten that she was bound into this ritual. She would never truly be gone until I stopped the vision from coming true. "Crush them and be done with it."

I looked up at the deadly wave, shrouding the Family in its murky pall. Tears streamed down my cheeks. "I can't. I can't go through that again. I won't kill everything I love. I'd rather die."

"And you will. If you're too weak, then everything is doomed. Not just the humans." Her eyes gleamed with malice. "And you and I and all of the Family will have to watch the entire Earth wilt and die before we are released. Knowing you could have saved it."

"There must be another way," I begged her. I wasn't sure how long I could hold the tidal wave.

"I've had a hundred years to think about the choice we made. There is no other way! Do you think I *wanted* this?" Her voice shook with anger, but she wasn't the same mad girl I'd mistaken for a student. Rita's shoulders sagged and her next words came out in a hoarse whisper. "I'm so tired, Faye. None of us will be free until you reach the end of The Path."

It was horrible to see her like this. Rita's braid was limp and bone white. Her eyes haunted by dark shadows. She looked pale, almost translucent.

I never meant for this to happen. I never meant for her to end up abandoned and tied to this time.

Her eyes glittered with my betrayal. "You're supposed to be the Harbinger. You're the only one who can end the suffering."

Rita was right. The tide was at its zenith. The great wave shimmered crimson. The moon was still dark. I had to end this now. But no one else was going to die today.

No one but me.

From my mountain peak, I chanted the Song of Balance. That ancient cadence from my first life that had followed me to this one. The looming wave stopped straining forward and listened.

My voice soared out over the exposed sand and barren islands. I sang of pelicans skimming across the water. Of sea turtles gliding on dark, ancient currents. Of oysters slowly, slowly, shaping pearls in their bellies. The wall of water pulled back toward me, lowering itself by inches, then by feet, as it remembered where it belonged.

I cajoled the tidal wave, reminding it of deep ocean trenches and icy, dark caves. Calling it home. The waves swirled gently around Kel's island of roots and eased themselves back down onto Holbrook's empty shores.

Slowly. Slowly. The time has passed.

Then I added a dissonant harmony. One thread of water spilled up the island to me. I bathed my hands in it, summoning the blood-red algae to me. Letting it stain my fingers.

Oil came with it, and the poison soaked into my skin, making me nauseous. As the toxins spilled into me, the bay below deepened into a rich ultramarine hue.

"Faye!" Kel's voice tugged at my mind. "What are you doing?"

I didn't answer. I couldn't listen to Kel. He'd only make me want to stay.

I grasped at the nuclear sludge that'd settled in the fathomless ocean canyons. The poison didn't want to let go of its prize, but I sang of movement and new places to claim, luring it to me.

The radiation scalded my fingers, blistering my throat, my lungs.

"Don't do this!" Kel's voice seemed to be closer now, demanding my attention. Trying to tether me to this world.

But I shut out Kel's pleas, letting the taste of chemicals quench my grief. Death clung to my tongue and I embraced it, swaying on weak legs. *This is my fault and I will make it right.*

I rooted my feet down into the island. Thinking of thick trees and timeless mountain ridges. Borrowing their strength, I sucked in the smoke and smog, watching the horizon clear. A delicate, early-morning blue filled one corner of the sky.

It isn't enough. I was powerful, but even so, I could feel my lungs clogging. My mind seemed to be playing tricks on me too. I swore that Kel was walking across the air toward me. His mouth opened and closed, but his words were drowned out by the ringing in my ears.

My rasping voice rumbled through the Earth. Decay and venom siphoned through my fingers, draining like acid into my muscles and organs and bones.

My heart slowed. *Whooooosh. Whoooooosh. Whoooooooosh.*

My eyelids drooped and I sank to my knees, pressing my hands into the Earth. *I never wanted to hurt you.*

Then I imagined that Kel was cradling me in his arms, tears swelling in his eyes. I reached up to wipe them away, but my hand wouldn't obey.

I'm sorry. I only wanted to save you.

The pain softened as I faded. I closed my eyes, finally ready to enter the void one last time.

But instead, heat flooded back into my numb hands. The world bucked and shook around me. I forced my eyes open.

Kel was really there, looking down at me, worry creasing the middle of his forehead.

"What happened?" The words leaked out in a harsh whisper. *Did he stop me before I was able to fix my mistake?*

A smile crept onto Kel's face. Not the wry half smile I was used to seeing. But a giant grin. "You're still here. You scared me."

"You scared me first."

Kel's arms tightened around me, and he pulled me to him, kissing me hard. I closed my eyes and savored the peppery taste of Kel, salted with tears. I could barely breathe, but I didn't care as I relaxed into his body, letting him hold me up.

When he finally let me go, I asked the question that frightened me most. "Did it work?"

"See for yourself." Kel took my hand, helping me up.

We stood under a canopy of silvery leaves. The lattice of roots holding the island together had somehow burst into a full-fledged forest. The ground still shifted beneath my feet, and every few seconds a new tree would erupt somewhere nearby.

Still weak, I rested against one of the trunks. Through the twisting veins of sap and resin, I felt the Family. Somewhere in the great network of branches and roots, they were working to siphon the poisons through this living filter. The trees were absorbing the pollution, breaking it down into harmless molecules. Binding the worst of it deep within their cells.

Doing what I could not.

"You are still more than everyone around you, Faye." The green in Kel's eyes sparked as he led me through the trees to the edge of the cliff. "But that doesn't mean you have to do it alone."

The Family still stood on the mass of roots out in the bay, but it was a forest now too. And the thick roots had intertwined, looped, and doubled back, knitting together the space between their new island and mine, creating a walkway so that Kel had been able to reach me. One giant tree stretched out of the center of their island, rising hundreds of feet into the still-smoggy air. The Family circled its enormous trunk, each pressing their hands into the bark.

Maya, Damion, Nami, Zach, Rita. Kel. And me.

Yes. We were all part of this now. Even Rita. In the end, she didn't have a choice. All her clues and prophecies were gone, the eternal years spent scheming and waiting for this moment. If we didn't fix our mistake, we'd all be trapped in this dying world.

But as Rita stared at me from across the gap, the anger faded from her eyes. This is what we'd sacrificed ourselves for a lifetime ago. Her hair shone yellow again in the sunlight, and her shoulders were strong as she pushed her hands into the great tree, channeling its power.

The anger left me too. I reached up and kissed Kel again, and this time it was like stepping onto hot coals. All the violence and doubt burned away, leaving me bare. I couldn't hide behind my past. Or my visions. Everything was gone but this instant. This self. Kel looked at what was left of me and smiled.

I answered his smile, knowing what to do. Knowing how to undo The Path we'd all set in motion so long ago.

Reluctantly, I let go of Kel. I knelt down and pressed my hand into the vast chain of roots. Together, Kel and I sang.

We sang of fruit bats flying from their forests, ready to feast. Of lemurs welcoming the sun in faraway lands. Of people who didn't understand this connection but could learn the song.

Rita, Maya, Zach, Damion, and Nami sang with us. They pulled the pollution up through the maze of roots. They soaked it in through the leaves. Helping the tree to contain and transform it.

I thrust my hands into the air, singing of hawks spiraling through the skies. Of seedpods floating on the wisps of breeze. Our words wove nets of wind. Drawing the smog and gases in toward the great tree. In toward the Family.

I stomped my feet, sending soft tremors through the Earth, and the Earth answered. Shaking free of its illness. Letting go of the poison weighing it down.

The moon escaped the shadow of the Earth, dipping below the horizon. The sun dazzled its way into the sky. The last refrain faded into silence.

And then it was done.

36

I SMILED AT KEL, exhausted and elated at the same time. The sea unfurled around us, cradling the new forest. Colors I'd never seen outside of my visions streamed across the landscape. Cerulean blue. Viridian. Cadmium yellow.

I sank down to the ground, touching my hands to the Earth gratefully. Sending it my thanks. But there was only grit and sharp rocks under my fingers. I felt for the underground streams, the deep layers of granite, but there was nothing.

"No!" Panicked, I called to the wind, but there was only a suffocating silence. The power was gone. Used up. I shivered, feeling naked on the island bluff. Alone.

Then Kel was next to me, kneeling on the ground. "Faye, it's okay. It's over."

I shook my head, refusing to look at him as I absorbed what I'd lost. "I don't think I can survive being cut off again. I can't go back to that. To being just Faye."

"You will never be just Faye. Listen." He took my hand in his and we sat there in the new morning.

A small breeze drifted across the peak. It carried the clean tang of the sea. The shriek of gulls calling back and forth. The rhythm of the waves.

I rested my head on Kel's shoulder as the earth beneath us grew warm in the sun. *Whoosh. Whoosh. Whoosh.* Its pulse drummed in time with ours.

I wasn't alone.

Maya strode across the bridge of roots, looking mesmerized by the world around us. Hand in hand, Nami and Damion followed close behind her. And Zach brought up the rear, whistling as he picked his way over the uneven roots. The Family finally coming together.

Except, I realized, for Rita. I looked toward the immense tree, but she wasn't there either. Two dark handprints were seared into the trunk, proof that she'd been here and gone.

Then it really worked.

As they got closer, I could hear their excited voices. Going over what had happened. How beautiful it all was. What was going to happen now.

The same babbling came from the shore. The students, released from their trance, crowded down onto the beach. Now that the water was calm, boats were cautiously making their way toward us.

Kel turned to me expectantly, asking the very question that was in my mind. "So, what's next?"

"I don't know. But whatever it is, I'm not sure I'm ready for it yet."

Kel's eyes smiled his understanding, the flecks of green shining. He kissed the palm of my hand and let it go. Then he stepped onto the path of roots and went to join our Family.

I turned and walked into the forest. Through the trees, I watched the waves rippling out to the horizon. The sea mirrored the intense blue of the sky, the sun gleaming in both.

It wasn't perfect. What was left of the oil rigs still marred the horizon. The cliffs bordering Holbrook were still stripped bare. The world wasn't done changing.

But it would change. We'd make sure of that.

I hummed the Song of Balance to myself. My feet stomped out the beat. My hands reached into the sky. The wind picked up the chant, and the ocean murmured. High up on the mountain, I danced.

Me, Faye. I danced.

AUTHOR'S NOTE

When I first imagined this story, the character of Faye and the landscape of coastal Maine came to me hand in hand. They are both isolated and stark, and both a bit outside of time. But when I went poking around in the prehistory of Maine, looking for an ancient culture that Faye could be connected to, I was stunned by what I found.

The Red Paint People (named for the red ochre they used in their burial rituals) are a people outside of time as well. They lived around five thousand years ago, but their culture was much more developed than that of anyone else around them. They carved elaborate symbols into their daggers, built seaworthy boats for hunting swordfish, and created sophisticated tools for hunting. But the most extraordinary thing is the way they buried their dead. In ritualized, ordered cemeteries. Excavated graves have held intricate bone daggers, decorated pendants, and carved stone animals. To me these artifacts hint at a fierce people who treasured beauty and held a deep belief in the mystical.

I became obsessed. What had happened to make *these* people so different from anyone who came before them or anyone who came after? And the *after* is the strangest part. Because a little less than four thousand years ago, the Red Paint People suddenly vanished. No more graves. Or carvings. Or tools.

The title of a paper written in 1930 wryly sums up the situation. "The Lost Red Paint People of Maine: A few things we think we know about them and more that we know we don't." With very few clues about what happened to these incredible people, all kinds of theories have popped up. Were they really Celts visiting from across the ocean? (They weren't.) Did a great tidal wave wipe them out? (It probably didn't.) But the point is, no one knows. So my mind started spinning a story and *Harbinger* was born.

And though my interpretation of the Red Paint People is fantastical and takes obvious liberties, it is rooted in a place of fact. Amidst the debates of archaeologists, wild theories, and tantalizing evidence, *Harbinger* seeks to give answers where there are no others to be found.

ACKNOWLEDGMENTS

A story is a scary endeavor. For a long time it's just you and your dogs and your computer. And no one has to know if your characters aren't likeable or you don't know the ending. But the tricky part is . . . for your story to really live, you have to show it to people. If you're lucky, there'll be people in your life who'll tell you which parts are good and help make them stronger. And there'll be other people who'll be ready to listen and applaud when you get to "The End." And that helps make you stronger. Until finally, one incredible day, your story is strong enough to live on bookshelves, and you're strong enough to let it. For me, that day would've never come without these extraordinary people . . .

My fearless agent, Michael Bourret, who saw the heart of my story even when it was half the length and double the mess. You're a Wonder.

My editor, Stacey Barney, who knew exactly where I was trying to go and drew me a map of how to get there. You pushed me to color in the edges of my world and saved me from a deep lake of dark deepness. Thank you for making this process better than I dreamed it could be.

My talented critique groups, who read so many drafts and incarnations. Lee Wind, Rita Crayon Huang, and Maya Creedman. The New Directions: Gail Israel, Talisen Winder, Jean O'Neill, and Suzanne Casamento. And my HH cohorts, Edith Cohn and Jennifer Bosworth. All of you have inspired me, pushed me forward, and kept the faith with me. And the humor.

The fantastic SCBWI community. When I started this book, I was alone. Now I look around and see a crowd of incredibly talented friends. And especially Kim Turrisi, who was looking out for me and this story before we even met.

All the people who took time to answer strangely specific and seemingly random questions. Bruce Bourque, Susan Wennrich, Ken Logan, Colin Bell, Caren Mahar, to name a few.

Bear McCreary, whose brilliant music, unbeknownst to him, beckoned me back into my world every morning.

Joni Mitchell, whose haunting songs inspired me and my characters.

My parents, who always sent me to bed with a story and would interrupt dinner to look up an interesting word. Thank you for always asking to see what I'm working on. My sister, Megan, who fought with me over the best books, sent me skull chocolates, and got excited for me every step of the way. To Dan, who first dreamed the dream and made me believe a mere mortal could even be a writer. You are filled with wonderful stories and wicked humor, even if you suck at Monopoly. And all of the Etiennes, I love being part of your family and the tenacity with which you all pursue life, your dreams, your happiness, and your egg rolls.

And, of course, Tony, for always believing, always wishing, and, without fail, always reading. You declared me a writer from day one and never, ever asked what was taking so long. Thank you for bringing my world to life with your amazing illustrations. May this be the first of a thousand projects we do together.

Sculpture Garden

Free Time Area

Knowledge Annex

Meditation Center

HOLBROOK

Welcome G

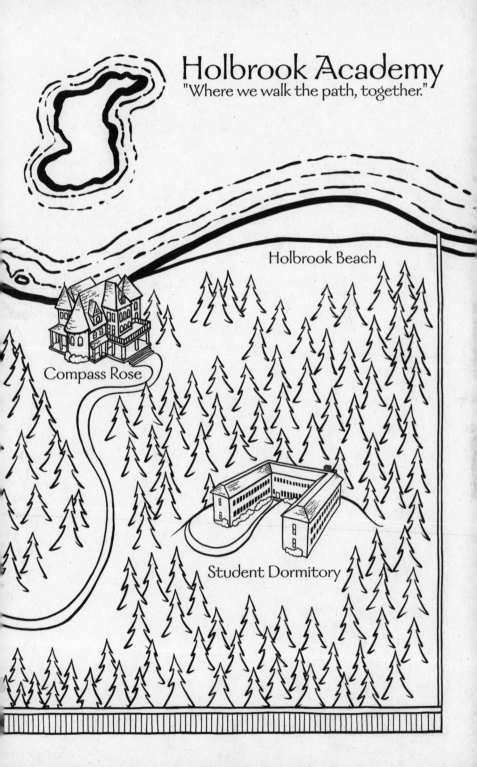